THE WEST PASSAGE

THE
WEST
PASSAGE

JARED PECHAČEK

TOR PUBLISHING GROUP

NEW YORK

THE WEST PASSAGE

Copyright © 2024 by Jared Pechaček

Interior illustrations copyright © 2024 by Jared Pechaček

A Tordotcom Book
Published by Tom Doherty Associates / Tor Publishing Group
120 Broadway
New York, NY 10271

www.torpublishinggroup.com

Tor® is a registered trademark of Macmillan Publishing Group, LLC.

The Library of Congress Cataloging-in-Publication Data
is available upon request.

ISBN 978-1-250-88483-1 (hardcover)
ISBN 978-1-250-88484-8 (ebook)

Our books may be purchased in bulk for promotional,
educational, or business use. Please contact your local bookseller
or the Macmillan Corporate and Premium Sales Department
at 1-800-221-7945, extension 5442, or by email at
MacmillanSpecialMarkets@macmillan.com.

First Edition: 2024

Printed in the United States of America

0 9 8 7 6 5 4 3 2 1

To JE

TABLE OF CONTENTS

BOOK ONE THE PALE KEY

1. The Mask Is Broken and the Women in Grey Say Very Little About It

With the guardian dead, the question remained: *Who would do it?* There was talk among the women of sending to Black Tower for someone, or of the old woman's apprentice taking over, but he, a pale youth who looked more used to handling books than beasts, turned paler when it was mentioned to him, and they would not shame him, nor distress themselves, by speaking of it further. But in the meantime, the West Passage remained unguarded.

The women in grey took the body for washing and wrapping. Due to the importance of the deceased, Pell, who was *their* apprentice, was not permitted to touch, only to look, and as she looked she saw the pale youth slip something off the old woman's corpse just as everyone entered the small dark room. A trinket of some sort, on a string, perhaps a keepsake promised to him by the old woman. Pell said nothing.

A strong smell of death had settled on the room. It had not been a dignified death, and the old woman was very dirty. There was a song to be sung during washing, but the women in grey could only hum it through closed mouths. They filled basket after basket with soiled linen before she was clean. Yarrow, the taller woman, directed Pell to take the baskets out to the burnyard reverently but quickly and set them afire as soon as possible.

"And for North's sake," said Yarrow, "don't touch them, and wash your hands directly—seven times, remember, with some lavender oil to finish."

Pell did not need to be told, but it suited Yarrow to order and be obeyed, and it suited Pell to please Yarrow. The Mother of Grey House was a tall, stern woman, and the backs of her strong hands were covered in spines; you didn't want *her* boxing your ears. Pell did as she was told—burnt the baskets too, since they seemed fouled beyond repair—and as the linens and wicker settled into charred shreds in the furnace, she went to wash. Smelling of lavender, she returned to the old woman's room, where the apprentice sat in the corridor next to Arnica's wheelbarrow, his knees drawn up to his chest.

"Out of my way," said Pell, an important person with important tasks. Someday she might take Yarrow's place. Then people would stay out of her way and not just sit in it, staring.

The apprentice only moved a fingerwidth, as if his misery held his body full and taut and he couldn't compress it anymore. He did not look at her.

"I'm needed inside," said Pell, which was not strictly true. Yarrow and Arnica had only told her to keep out of the way and watch.

"What's to become of me?" said the apprentice.

She could not remember his name, and did not have the patience to try. "I can't speak for the future, but in the present, if you don't let me past, I'll box your ears."

They were the same age, or nearly, but Pell could talk like Yarrow when needed. He moved.

"Thank you," said Pell. To make up for her manner, she took a stick of candied angelica from her sleeve and offered it to him. He stared at it as if it were some unknown beast. "Take it," she said. Then again, more loudly, and added, "It's a gift."

He obeyed. Pell left him and entered the room, which smelled much fresher now, in time to pick up the winding sheet and hand it to Arnica. Fitting so immediately into their rhythm kindled a spark of pleasure in her heart, and in its warmth she forgot the apprentice.

The women in grey wound up the old woman in the white cloth. Over her shrouded face they strapped a green stone mask with closed eyes. They could sing now, and Yarrow's fine clear voice filled the room with the winding-song, while Arnica's huskier one rumbled in the flagstones. Pell was not allowed to sing the songs yet, but she memorized the tune and the way Yarrow and Arnica would clap in unison at certain beats and words. In her mind, she built a room for the winding-song and hung each line as a picture on the walls.

The women in grey hoisted the corpse onto a stretcher—Pell could help *here,* as the women in grey were really not much younger than the old dead woman—and carried her out. Pell was left to clean up.

Any unused linens and herbs must be repacked in their chipped urns. The floor must be swept and mopped, and the sweepings put in a basket to burn.

The room was not much bigger than any others in the palace. It held a bed, a stool, a chamber pot, a large wooden table, and a wardrobe. One wall had three small windows, latticed with stone like the others in this old part of the palace. Nothing was very remarkable, except an open wooden chest at the bed's foot, where three or four books lay.

Books. Women in grey were not supposed to meddle with personal property, but Pell was not one of them yet. She could still do some of the forbidden things, like eat meat or handle bread. So when the floor was swept, and she'd pulled herbs out of her sleeves to steep in the mopping water, she knelt by the chest and picked up the smallest book. To her disappointment, it was all words. None of the lovely pictures that she'd seen over in the Archives, with patterns winding over pages like vines. What use was a book that only had *words*?

"Put it back," said a timid voice. The apprentice had entered the room.

"Out! Get out!" said Pell. "We aren't done yet!" She scrambled to her feet, slamming the chest shut as she rose.

"But the books—" he said.

"Are safe here!" she said. "Women in grey don't take. Get out! It's not clean here!" She snatched up the broom and shoved it at his feet.

Even though he was two heads taller, he obeyed. Either she had absorbed some of Yarrow's immense personal authority, or he was incapable of confronting anyone. Though Pell would like to believe the former, she knew it was probably the latter.

She slammed the door shut after him and set about mopping. The water was fragrant with lavender, thyme, and lemon, and it chased the last of the death-smells away. She stripped the bed and put the soiled clothes in the basket. Someone else would take the old woman's belongings—probably the apprentice, but it wasn't Pell's concern either way. The women in grey only handled death and birth.

When she came out of the room, he was gone. Pell took the burn-basket to the furnace and tossed it in, then went back for the urns. She loaded them into the wheelbarrow and trundled back to Grey Tower. Its atrium was still dripping with the morning's rain, and Yarrow and Arnica were struggling up the spiral ramp with the stretcher.

Pell took the things into the storeroom and put them on the

shelves. When she emerged into the atrium again, the women in grey had not made much progress. Before she reached them, Arnica stumbled and the stretcher twisted, tumbling the old woman's body off. Yarrow stopped it falling from the ramp, but the mask slipped and plummeted.

"Catch it, girl!" said Yarrow, unnecessarily and too late. The mask evaded Pell's outstretched hand and hit the mossy flagstones with an ominous *chnk*. "Is it whole?" Yarrow added as she and Arnica maneuvered the corpse back into place.

Pell gathered up the mask. It was in two halves, and badly chipped and scratched. She took it up the ramp anyway.

"Ah, well," said Yarrow.

"Some glue," said Arnica vaguely.

Yarrow sighed. Arnica sighed.

Pell, remembering some of the long, long rhymes, asked, "Isn't that a bad omen?"

"Oh, that's what we always say," said Arnica. "Truth is nobody knows."

"The truth is," said Yarrow, "that the masks are our responsibility. Shame it happened, but someone might fix it in time." *Someone* was usually one of the girls. "Take Arnica's place, girl; was her old foot that slipped and got us here. If you mayn't sing, you may at least carry."

Arnica took the mask and stood aside to let Pell pick up the end of the stretcher. This was a great honor, and Pell flushed with pride as she stepped forward. She found it difficult to maintain her pride, however: the ramp was slippery with moss and rainwater. Old age or not, anyone would be hard-pressed to walk it. And as it coiled around the atrium wall it seemed to grow steeper and steeper, so that the risk of falling made Pell's head swim. You'd splatter on the uneven floor like an old peach.

"By rights someone should've been singing this whole time," said Yarrow as they wrestled the corpse up and up. "But neither of us had the breath. Arnica, you might, now you're unburdened."

Arnica immediately began. Her deep voice echoed and re-echoed off the stone walls until the whole of Grey Tower seemed to be one droning throat. Pell's very bones vibrated.

Pell had never been more than halfway up the ramp. It was forbidden for apprentices, but Yarrow, uncharacteristically, did not mention to Pell the immense distinction conferred on her. Maybe Pell had been chosen as her apprentice. The years of learning and training might finally go somewhere. A warm glow spread up her neck and across her face at the thought. To be the next Yarrow . . .

They passed many doors, some whole, others decayed so Pell could glimpse the rooms beyond. Full of urns some of them were, others of moldering chests or furniture or miracles. One seemed full of people, until she looked again and saw it was only dozens of statues with veiled eyes. Grey Tower had always been for the dead, but it seemed in earlier years it had been for other things, too.

They reached a landing and Yarrow stopped, pressing her spiny hand to her side.

"A moment," she gasped. "North above, a moment."

Pell took the opportunity to look around. There were only three levels more of Grey Tower, each lined with twelve great yawning arches. The arches rested on pillars carved like people with flowering heads, no two alike. Each arch opened onto a dark space, like a huge niche, but with the sun now shining straight down into the atrium, Pell could not see what lay beyond. The ramp led up past the arches to the top of the tower, where a wide parapet lay open to the sky.

"Give us a share," said Yarrow. Arnica had taken some nuts out of her pocket and was cracking and eating them with quiet pleasure. Pell's face must have registered her shock, for Yarrow rolled her eyes. "We have an awesome duty in an awesome space, but a body does like something to crunch now and then."

"*She* certainly did," said Arnica, nudging the corpse with the tip of one dirty shoe. "All them offerings of ortolan and almond. Proper thing would've been to share it out again, but time after time you'd try to talk to her and hear naught but the crunch of little bird bones. She didn't even share her name with that apprentice. Didn't swear him in before the end. Couldn't stand the thought of another Hawthorn while she lived, I suppose. And here we are."

Yarrow chuckled, a sound like a pestle in a stone mortar. "All them West Passage guardians were always of a sort. Whoever's next'll eat a songbird banquet right down to the feathers and save you out just a talon or a half-gnawed beak."

"Best get a new guardian soon," said Arnica through a mouthful of half-chewed walnut. "Or Grey Tower'll have more work than it wants, if the stories hold true."

Both Yarrow and Arnica made a curious gesture of the left hand, common to the elders of the palace, that always accompanied mentions of the West Passage. Pell did not.

"Who'll do it, I wonder," said Yarrow. She tossed a shell out into the air. A moment later a distant click echoed from the floor of the atrium. "That boy of hers? I'll give him the name of guardian if he asks, but we'd have as much luck with a statue of a Lady."

"He might do," said Arnica. "Not 'sif there's other choices. If he knows his duty . . ."

The women sighed in unison. Duty. Everyone in Grey House knew theirs. The guardians, though, in their little court—who could say what *they* knew?

"What do the guardians do?" said Pell.

"Protect," said Arnica, who was generally more disposed to answer that sort of question. "Ain't you paid attention in lessons?"

Stung, Pell said, "But protect from what?"

"The evil."

"What evil?"

Arnica spoke around a mouthful. "The one that comes through the Passage now and again. Ain't no matter for us, though. It's guardian business."

"Then let *them* gossip about it," said a bored Yarrow, standing and brushing nutshells off her grey gown. "Let's be off."

A nut fell from Arnica's hand unnoticed. Out of habit, Pell scooped it up and stuffed it into her sleeve for later. You could hide a lot of things there, if the women came upon you suddenly.

The tower was now quite hot, and Pell and Yarrow were both dripping with sweat when they reached the top. The wide rampart shimmered under the sun, and the three took shelter in the shade of a turret to catch their breath again.

The five turrets of Grey Tower each had their own name and song, and each was meant for a different section of the palace's people. The old woman needed to be taken to Tamarisk, whose floral moldings were worn away to nubs. Pell's body, when her time came, would go to the Hand, in whose shade they nestled, with its tumbled parapet and meticulously maintained yellow chevrons.

Pell recovered faster than the women. Being so high up was a rare treat, and being atop Grey Tower had never happened to her before, so she would take advantage of it. She went over to the rough granite parapet and got up on her toes to peer over it. All the ruinous grandeur of the palace was at her feet.

The sun glinted on the South Passage hundreds of yards away and below, where water gurgled through the chasm beneath the palace.

Bridges crisscrossed it, bulging with houses. A pigeon launched itself from a courtyard, drawing her eye up to faraway Red Tower, purpled with distance, its beacon dull in the light of day. If a wind came from there, you could get a whiff of the sea. In the windless noon, white smoke from that eternal fire drifted over all the southeastern district of the palace. Much closer was lapis-domed Blue Tower, rising from a field of white plaster walls, swirling with pigeons and the bright flecks of hummingbirds who came to drink from the flowering vines that spilled down its sides. A woman in a near window was hanging laundry. She waved at Pell, who ducked beneath the parapet.

Yarrow and Arnica permitted her to look from here, close to the corpse that was their *duty,* but if she went around to the other side of the rampart to see Black and Yellow Towers, that would be *leisure.* Suddenly Pell would be shirking. Anyway, Yellow Tower was plainly visible, slashing into the sky like a knife into flesh. That way lay the West Passage. Black Tower was more to the north, hidden behind the turret where its people went after death: Varlan's Love.

Grey was the living heart of the palace, built of the grey bedrock under everything; Grey was the oldest; Grey was the center. Grey was death.

Yarrow's whistle startled Pell. Five notes, starting high, and descending down minor thirds: a call Pell had heard from the foot of the tower many times, but never so close. It pierced the eardrums and reverberated through the hollow center of the tower as if it were a resonating chamber.

"All right, girl," said Yarrow. "Let's get her over to Tamarisk quick, before they arrive."

Arnica resumed her song as Yarrow and Pell trotted the stretcher along the parapet. In the heat, the old woman was beginning to smell. She'd had a horrible death to begin with, but how much more horrible to die in high summer and make every bit of your passing a burden to others.

Tamarisk, like all the turrets, was open and hollow on its inner face. A spiral staircase wound up through three platforms to the open roof; you could watch anyone climbing it as if looking at the open side of a dollhouse. The stretcher stopped at its foot, jarring Pell's stomach.

"No, girl," said Yarrow. "Arnica helps for the last bit. You're not yet a woman."

Not *yet.* Pell handed the stretcher off to Arnica, and the two women started up the stairs. She watched their laborious progress, and wondered whether Arnica would make it. Twenty steps to the top, nineteen, eighteen, seventeen, and then Arnica stumbled on the fifteenth. They nearly lost the body, and the mask almost fell once more. But Yarrow was determined, and they pushed on.

A murmur filled the air. It rose in volume, came nearer, turned into a rustling and a cawing. Pell looked over her shoulder.

Streaming past the bright face of Yellow were hundreds of crows. They knew the whistle and what it meant, and by ancient treaty they had arrived. Yarrow and Arnica set down the body and reached the safety of the stairs just in time. In a moment, Tamarisk was covered in a shivering blanket of black. Scratching, rasping, tearing, squelching: the noise was horrible.

The old woman did not take them long. The crows even carried away the bones, and for a moment their neatness was exhilarating, until Pell saw the bones dropped into the Passage, and she remembered: to get at the marrow, the crows had learned to break bones on the canyon rocks, and there were red-daubed vultures who fed on them as well. Everyone who had ever died in the palace lay splintered along the banks of the river.

All that remained atop Tamarisk was a bloody shroud and the damaged mask. Yarrow and Arnica stood watching it, as if something might move. Pell stood with them. As the afternoon wore on, Pell's headscarf soaked up the heat. A trickle of sweat ran down her back. The two women must have been miserable in their wimples, long gowns, and leather aprons.

"Oughtn't we clean up, Mothers?" said Pell.

"A moment," said Arnica. "A bleedin' moment."

"Hush, girl," said Yarrow.

An iridescent butterfly fluttered past Pell's nose. Its wings flickered like flame. She put out her hand to tempt it into landing there, but Yarrow slapped her.

"Don't interfere," said Yarrow, as Pell rubbed the back of her hand.

The butterfly made its way to the top of Tamarisk and landed on the shroud. Another followed. Then another. Soon the shroud shimmered with their wings.

"They like to sip us up," Arnica whispered. "Anyway it's less to mop."

When the last of the old woman had been drunk down hundreds of tiny throats, Yarrow solemnly mounted the stairs once more. She wrapped the mask in the shroud and carried it back down.

"To the glory of the Lady," she said.

Pell followed her and Arnica onto the ramp. The sun had moved and the atrium was beautifully cool. Down they went, singing another song, to place the mask on its plinth, where it would wait for the next guardian to die.

The two green halves looked balefully at Pell. While Yarrow and Arnica took care of some other business, she ran some rough twine through the eyeholes and tied it together. *Would* there be consequences? It was only a mask, after all. And the women didn't seem worried.

Pell put the issue out of her mind. It should not concern her in the slightest. The palace took care of such matters, and she had a tale to tell the other girls.

2. The Mask Is Taken and the Women in Grey Know Nothing About It

The apprentice shouldered his pack. The taste of angelica was still in his mouth, and the smell of his master's death still in his nose. He took a last look around the tiny room, now clean and empty, and set off through the corridors of the Court of Guardians, with his feet turned toward the West Passage. His name, which we have not had occasion to learn, for Pell herself never bothered, was Kew.

He did not precisely *want* to leave Grey Tower. A titheling from the southern cloisters, Kew had only ever known Grey. Its granite walls, its slate roofs, and the five-pointed crown of the tower itself, were all part of his blood in a way he could only define by going away. However, that self-knowledge was not why he had dressed in traveling robes and tied on his master's soft boots. Hawthorn's last words to him had been *Tell Black it's coming.* Her last words, when she should have been swearing him in to the office of Guardian. Kew was obedient to her wishes, when he would rather have stayed.

Nobody in Grey thought much of the Guardians. Like every other position, the office was respected for its age if nothing else, but since the Guardians had not been needed in generations, hardly anyone remembered what they were for or why they were for it. Unlike the women in grey, the Guardians served no function in ordinary life, except to take a tithe of the cloisters' produce and stand at the mother's side for certain antiquated ceremonies. And so everyone believed that a Guardian could be anyone and come from anywhere. They ignored the long, careful apprenticeship. They knew nothing of the Bestiaries, the rites, the rhymes. With Kew gone, the stern old mother would either appoint a Guardian from among the citizens of Grey or she would let the office lapse, as so much else in the heart of the palace had lapsed into dust and cobwebs over the long, long eras.

Kew should have replaced the old woman. He should have become the next Hawthorn, seventy-fourth holder of that title. His name should have changed; he should not still have his child's nonsense name, but the flower-name that was the right of a Grey official. He *should*, he *could*, he *must*. Why hadn't Hawthorn confirmed him? Why had she trained him his whole life, only to turn him into a South-damned *messenger*? They had birds for messengers, or people in the outer districts to send, or the rampart horns to blow. Guardians had something better to do. *A Guardian is sworn to protect*, she'd said at least once a day all the time he'd known her.

In her case, that meant eating a lot of ortolan, belching ferociously, and drilling Kew on fighting forms and pushing him page by page through dusty archives, but she'd been ready to leap into battle if necessary. When some children from Madrona's cloisters had bullied him, she sent them home with bruises the size of dinner plates. He had loved her. Under his tunic he had the amulet he had made her ten years ago, a simple circle of copper etched with an eye "to watch over her," crusted now with verdigris. She had never taken it off. She had loved him. Then she had denied him his name.

He passed cell after cell dug into the walls of massive stone: the living places of the Hawthorns. They had been numerous, once. Now he was the only one. The roofs here had partly fallen, and the watery early-summer sun threw puddles of light on the rough floor. There was a faint drone: the women singing as they went up-tower. Mice scattered at his approach, their mandibles clicking in alarm. It was cool in these damp halls.

When the prickly one, Yarrow, had asked him if he was ready to be the next Guardian on her way to handle Hawthorn's body, he had quivered with rage and been unable to speak. He *was* ready. Why hadn't the old woman known that? Before the rage passed, it transmuted into fear: of the journey he must now undertake from the palace's cold heart to its distant center.

There was no time to lose. Not because he knew how much time there was: precisely because he did *not* know. It could be now, it could be later. But Hawthorn had made him promise. *Before anything else, tell Black it's coming.* And a Guardian, or a Guardian's apprentice, who could not keep their word—? Such a person did not deserve their name. He would not deserve even the no-name of *Kew* if he broke this promise. He would not deserve it if he delayed even one day.

The Court of the Guardians came to an end where the cells turned into a hall. To go to Black, he would simply head north, and there would be the West Passage. Easy. *But.* Black Tower would not believe him, surely. Hawthorn had been there once or twice, but that was in her youth, long before Kew was even born. The Ladies of Black would have no idea who he was. He needed proof. The steel of the Guardians would have done, but that holy weapon was forbidden to an unnamed apprentice. But there was something else.

Kew turned south. The halls disgorged him into the courtyard at the foot of the tower. Grey House loomed to his right, all steep roofs and warty turrets and broken windows. To the left was the broad, high gate of the West Passage. Ahead, the dry grass and trees were interrupted where Grey Tower thrust upward from the worn flagstones. Unlike the cloisters and the huge gloomy house, the tower seemed to have grown where it stood. The courses of large, unpolished stones were uneven and random, shifted out of place here and there as if the tower had been shaken. The few windows were small and dark: they looked on storerooms, each holding items of unknown age and obscure purpose. The tower narrowed suddenly about two-thirds of the way up, and this slim neck rose seventy or eighty feet before widening into the turreted top. At night, Grey Tower looked very much like a half-buried person wearing a five-pointed crown. According to Hawthorn, there was an ancient, sacred reason for this. For reasons of her own, she never told Kew what it was, and she rarely took him inside when she attended to the strange ceremonies Guardians held in the mossy atrium. But, like everyone else, Kew had heard of the Room of Masks, and he knew that was where the Guardian's mask would be, and besides the steel, it was the only thing a Lady of Black Tower would recognize as belonging to the Guardian of the West Passage.

The last butterflies of Hawthorn's funeral were still streaming away from the tower when Kew entered it. He saw the women and the girl coming down the ramp and ducked into a storeroom to watch them go past. There was the tall mother, the spines on her head and back poking through her ragged wimple and robe. There was the short woman of simple flesh, her face lined with laughter. And there was the tiny girl with the twiggy hair who had given him angelica in the corridor. Pell, he thought she was called. They'd met now and then, but apprentices had little time to speak, and they were not friends. She probably didn't even know his name.

Kew moved away from the door and his foot hit something hard. The room was full of waist-high effigies. Each of them was veiled with grey linen; the oldest could be told from the decayed shreds that clung to them. At the base of each was written the name YARROW. There were perhaps sixty or seventy of them. Though their eyes were all hidden, Kew felt them staring.

Pell left the tower, while the women went on to the Room of Masks, singing. After the funeral, the mask had to be cleaned and returned with proper ceremonies. Would they *ever* stop that dirge? The Yarrow statues were making his neck prickle. It would be so satisfying to smash one.

At last their song ended. From his vantage point, Kew could see the tower entrance. The two women trudged out, one eating nuts, the other scratching under her wimple. He slipped across the atrium to the Room. The stones of its corbel-arched door were carved into grieving faces; the keystone had the form of a veiled head. Through the moss and mud of the atrium, a path had been worn by the passing of the women year after year. All other chambers of the tower were disused.

The Room was long and fan-shaped: small at its entrance, but widening toward the outer wall, so that the whole place felt like a trick of perspective, like a stage in one of the mystery dramas that entertainers from Blue occasionally put on in the house. From floor to shadowy ceiling, shelves lined the room. Blank stone cylinders filled them, and onto each cylinder was tied a mask. There were several hundred of them, one for each named office in the cloisters of Grey, from the Yarrows, Arnicas, and Foxgloves of the house to the Madronas and Jasmines of the outermost districts. An irregular lattice pierced the far wall, pouring in cold sunlight over the ranks of masks. Under the lattice, an uneven dais held four granite plinths, and upon each plinth was a marble head. One held the jasper mask of the tutors, who taught the law. One held the slate mask of the mothers, who upheld the law. One held the oaken mask of the doctors, who cared for followers of the law. And the last held the serpentine mask of the Guardians, who protected followers of the law.

It was broken. The women had lashed it together with twine passed through the two eyeholes, then left it at the head's base. Tears stung Kew's eyes. How could they break it? How dare they take so little care? Their whole *purpose* was to care!

Hawthorn had always said the women in grey wouldn't piss on you if they saw you on fire, but Kew had believed it was professional jealousy speaking. Grey Tower's crumbling administration still squabbled over favor and privilege as if a Lady remained to grant them, and there were deep, ancient feuds between many of the offices. Most of them were petty at best. Hawthorn's had seemed petty, too, but never in all his apprenticeship had Kew encountered such sacrilegious incompetence. Whatever the women in grey deserved for this, he'd give it to them.

He wrapped the mask in a handkerchief and put it in his pack. The halves scraped past each other with a sickening noise and a sensation that made his hands cramp. Once it was safe, he took a last look around the room. Most of the masks were coated in decades of dust: Hawthorn had once told him that Grey currently housed at most a couple hundred people, and many of those were no-names like Kew. Unless they were apprenticed, they would never achieve a name, and if they were not named, they went to their deaths unmasked.

Kew had expected to go to his funeral with the mask he now carried. But now he never would, unless he could get to Black Tower and deliver Hawthorn's message. They would use their authority to name him, and he would become Hawthorn and defend the palace against the Beast, and die with honor after all.

He went back into the corridors, keeping his face to the north, and soon came through a low oaken door into the side of the West Passage. Easy, he'd thought, but his foot hesitated on the cracked threshold. In the quiet, his heartbeat almost shook the stones.

This postern was called Hawthorn's Sally: on its lintel were three scratches from a battle in the Apple Era, eroded but still deep. This was the last entrance to the Passage on the Blackward side of things. If he hadn't taken this path, the tricky nature of Grey would have shunted him here and there until he ended up at the Passage's beginning, and that would have meant a long journey through Yellow and into North knew what before looping back to Black.

Above him were battlements and ivy. Across a paved chasm, he faced the far wall of the Passage, high and solid, battlemented and ramparted and towered. Along the lower courses of stone were parallel striations: more scratches, increasing in size as they got farther from Grey, until they stopped abruptly at the edge of sight, and there the paving stones were stained, even after so many centuries. It was exactly as Hawthorn's book *Campanula* depicted it, except the catapults atop the towers had rotted into spikes of crumbly wood and rusted iron rings, and where smoke had blackened the walls, it had faded. There was not a stone, not a bit of mortar, not a window, not a beam that was not named, that had no history.

A songbird flitted overhead, and the vast silence of the Passage swallowed it up. This place was too somber for song. There were bones in the walls and blood in the floor. Kew swallowed. No ink, no tempera, no gesso or gold leaf had prepared him for this.

A warm wind stirred the ivy. Its dry leaves rattled. A mason bee burrowed into some mortar. In one direction lay Yellow Tower, peering over the top of Grey like a hawk, and in the other lay Black Tower's misty head. It was approximately one day's journey, if the books were correct.

If he kept moving, with Grey always at his back, he should have no trouble at all. He *would* have no trouble. This was his place. Hawthorns had fought and died here for as long as *here* had been. He was not a Hawthorn yet, but this was the way to that name. Kew stepped into the Passage and started walking.

3. The Women in Grey Eat Dinner and Pell Has Something up Her Sleeve

The women in grey and Pell took their dinner in the refectory of Grey House. The other two apprentices, Grith and Ban, joined them at the long oak table. Meant for dozens, if not hundreds more, the table's age-worn length stretched away into the dim corners of the refectory, while the five residents of the house huddled around three candles at one end and ate their barley gruel in silence. Yarrow and Arnica sat at the head; the apprentices, according to custom, were several places down. They were served, if service it was, by the nameless ancient retainer who had always cooked and cleaned for the women. Each woman had her proper chair, carved with their names and as old as anything, having contained the buttocks of generations of Yarrows and Arnicas since time immemorial. Other chairs bore other names, but were now dusty and disused, as one by one the lines had died out: Goldenseal, Lavender, Agrimony, Comfrey, and so many others.

Pell had always liked the refectory, with the quiet, half-conscious liking one feels for something one has known since childhood. A clerestory of tiny square windows ran along the eastern wall, letting in morning sunlight and evening breezes. Vast old tapestries covered the stone walls. Their rich colors had dimmed, many were moth-eaten, and some had fallen, but the stories and strange figures they held made her feel as if she were a creature of legend herself. Bats roosted in the south rafters, pigeons flew in and out, and ivy curled in at the windows, but even in its state of decay the refectory held some clear beauty quite separate from the ancient chaos of the rest of the palace.

Yarrow and Arnica kept the tradition of silence while eating, but they did not enforce it for their apprentices unless the conversation grew too loud or annoying (or if Yarrow simply didn't want to hear anyone talk when she couldn't), so Pell, Grith, and Ban were able to whisper gossip to each other all through the meal. Grith had news from Blue Tower, where a harvest accident had injured one of the laborers, and Ban had heard from a cousin near Red Tower that the beacon had nearly gone out when an apprentice forgot to bring in more wood. Pell had no people elsewhere: she was no titheling, just a baby left on the doorstep in secret. She never had any news to share, but now both girls went silent as Pell, with an agreeable feeling of superiority, detailed the funeral rites of the old woman.

"The mask *broke*?" said Grith. Her whiskers twitched.

"And Yarrow didn't have a fit?" said Ban.

All three glanced at Yarrow, but she didn't seem to have heard and went on spooning gruel.

"No," said Pell. She reached for the ladle to take a little more gruel and something in her sleeve thudded against the tabletop. Pell froze. All that should have been in her sleeves were washing herbs, a handkerchief, and some little stalks of candied angelica—certainly nothing that would thud. A glance at Yarrow and Arnica told her that they had not noticed, or maybe didn't care. Pell resumed eating. "Yarrow didn't say a thing," she added, in as normal a tone as she could manage.

The women in grey always said the laws and customs were sacrosanct and unbreakable, but this was not the first time one of them had reacted calmly to a breach. Arnica frequently went so far as to crack and eat nuts in the schoolroom, something she expressly forbade even as she did it. But a broken mask seemed to warrant stronger feeling.

"Well, thank North for that, at least," said Ban. Her voice cracked a bit at the end, as it often did these days. She clicked her talons against her bowl.

"And you got to see the funeral," said Grith. "It must have been beautiful."

Pell thought of the butterflies' yellow shimmer, the crows' sable, the dark blood. "It was," she said, forgetting to whisper.

"Sshh," said Yarrow.

The apprentices hushed and lowered their heads. With her hands under the table, Pell rooted around in her sleeve until her fingers touched a small, flat object. She pulled it out halfway. It was the book from the old woman's room.

Pell jammed it back into her sleeve and looked at the women. Yarrow was scraping the last bits of gruel from her bowl. Arnica was doing the same with a finger. If they knew Pell had taken something, even accidentally—well, it would be worse than the time she spilled the breakfast curds all over the kitchen floor. Her palms still ached from that feruling.

Servant cleared away the bowls and brought out some dried fruit for the girls and two tiny glasses of honey wine for the women. A bottle of it came once a month from the cellars of Black Tower, and was one of several house privileges so old that nobody remembered its origin. Yarrow and Arnica raised their glasses cursorily to the North, then each let a little golden drop fall to be drunk up by the dusty floor. When the women finished their wine, it would be bedtime, so the apprentices hastened to eat their fruit, which they could not take from the table. Even just a few years ago there had been more women—Foxglove, Willow, Marigold—and they had all taken long enough to drink that the girls could linger as well. But Yarrow and Arnica were quick.

Then each woman took a candle from the table, and Yarrow handed the third to Pell, the eldest girl. Pell quaked as she put out her hand for the light. What if the heavy swing of her sleeve alerted the woman to the book? But Yarrow only muttered the proper words for passing a candle to a girl and opened the door.

Everyone proceeded out of the refectory and up the damp stairs into the dormitory. The women had their own room, where they slept end to end in a huge curtained bed, while the girls slept in little cots lined up against the vast central chimney of Grey House. They parted, and the two other apprentices followed Pell into the dormitory, where their three beds sat white and clean amidst dozens of empty, dusty, mildewy ones.

Each girl kept one pair of shoes under her bed and wore the second, and each kept one brown dress under her pillow and wore the second. But they only had one pale surcoat apiece, which they had to keep quite clean, or Yarrow would be angry. Grith was very bad at cleanliness, Ban was very good at it, and Pell was somewhere in the middle. They unbuttoned each other's surcoats, but the dresses were easy enough to remove. Pell tried to take hers off as quietly as possible, but when she hung it on her peg, the book thumped against the stone wall. She stilled its swinging, but the others had noticed.

"What's that?" said Grith, shrugging into her nightgown.

"A book," said Pell.

Grith shrugged, not much interested: sleep was more important than getting details. Pell was always in the Archives looking at the pictures in those moldy volumes.

Pell traced the writing on the first page with her finger. Perhaps she could sneak it back in the morning. If there had been pictures she might have wanted to keep it, but girls and women in grey could not read. Even with pictures, it wouldn't be worth the risk: Arnica occasionally inspected the dormitory.

"Blow out that candle," said Grith, snuggling into her bed.

Pell put the book back in her sleeve. She wrapped a soft cloth around her twiggy scalp, slipped into her nightgown, and extinguished the candle.

In her clammy bed, Pell closed her eyes. All she could see was the blanket of crows, shining black in the sun, and the broken mask with its sightless eyes. She rolled over. Her hair crinkled inside the cloth; Servant would need to steam and rebind it soon. On her side, she closed her eyes again. Butterflies, bright gold and blue against darkening red. Sighing, she rolled onto her back and looked at the dark, raftered ceiling. The latticed windows let in filaments of moonlight, illuminating only dust. Ban and Grith were already asleep, it seemed, or at least had no interest in talking.

Yes, she could return the book. It would not take long, and nobody need ever know she'd left. She slid back her covers and swung her legs out of bed. The cot creaked and she paused. Neither Ban nor Grith said a word. She put her shoes and headscarf back on. Taking the book and candle, she tiptoed out of the dormitory and down the stairs.

The fire in the refectory had not been banked yet. She relighted the candle with a spill and left Grey House. The great front portico opened onto a courtyard of grass and twisted trees, and before that a fountain. The grass and trees and fountain had all been dry for centuries. Above them rose the shadowed shoulders and crown of Grey Tower, with the moon snagged on Tamarisk like a bit of lint on a thorn. Nothing moved, not even the wind.

Pell started down the wide, deep steps. Something flickered in the corner of her eye. She stopped dead. When nothing else happened, she kept on. Once under the trees, she felt a little freer. Even if the women in grey had been looking, it would've been harder for them to see the candlelight through the branches.

There was another slight motion. She turned.

A lone fleck of white was fluttering down through the trees. It vanished on the flagstones. Another came down. Then another. A cold wind rose. Pell's breath became a white vapor.

Snow? But winter was supposed to be over Yellow, at least by Arnica's reckoning. Grey was scheduled to have summer for at least another month. A season out of step—they had always said that was a punishment. Red Tower's rebellion had been quelled by imposing winter on it for a year and a day: its harbor frozen solid, Red's supplies were cut off, and it was starved into submission. Did breaking curfew disturb the ancient mechanisms of palace seasons?

The snow was coming faster now, and it was sticking. Shivering, Pell returned to Grey House, though the guardians' side of the courtyard was nearer. Would Yarrow and Arnica blame her? She determined to confess in the morning. It might bring back summer. And it would certainly be better than Yarrow finding out on her own and summoning Pell in for a punitive audience. This way, at least, Pell would only get penance.

She pulled the huge ratty curtains over the windows and blew out the candle. Her bed was still clammy, and now it was chilly, too. She gritted her teeth and bore it. She'd taken a book; she'd broken curfew. She deserved the cold.

4. Kew Makes a Friend

The road was cracked marble. Once it had been highly polished, but the years had nibbled at it, and the corners of the paving stones were all broken, and grass grew between their edges. It ran straight and level between high walls, with no windows, doors, or decorations to be seen. Even the little postern by which he'd entered the Passage seemed to have been swallowed up in the distance. Some doves mourned along the wall tops, but aside from them, there was hardly anything moving except Kew and a few beetles.

After some time, the road crested a hill. Directly ahead were the roofs of Black, then the pinnacles and spires of the tower jutting up against the setting sun. He was level with the court rooftops, so the base of the tower itself must lie a little lower down. That was all right, but going up and down hills would add time to his journey. He needed to find somewhere to spend the night, and fast. Hawthorn had mentioned things that lived in the Passage. From the sound of them, they were not the sort of creature one would wish to meet in the dark.

There were still no doors or windows. As he went down into Black, the walls grew taller and taller, so their tops ran still at the same level. If he'd known how to get up to the parapet, he would have taken that route and not needed to worry about the road's ups and downs. Soon the crenellations were so far above him that they nearly closed over his head, turning the sky into a ribbon of velvety blue, and still the road went down.

How low did Black sit compared to the rest of the palace? Yellow, he knew, lay in a valley. Blue was on a hilltop. Red was on a hillside.

But Black—according to all the lore of Hawthorn—was not hard to reach. *Follow the lanterns,* said one book. Well, the lanterns were in the tower, and the tower was still straight ahead, but the road was getting harder. Was it possible the lore was out of date? That, in this changeless place, something had shifted?

The granite of Grey seemed to have been replaced with a darker stone, but it was hard to tell in the dimming light. There were still no means of egress. His heartbeat quickened. There seemed to be footsteps other than his own in the Passage, but when he stopped, they stopped. Either something was following him, or there was an echo.

No—there was something. Jackals? The *Grand Bestiary* had a lot to say about jackals. Vicious progeny of the Beast, shed during one of its appearances in the distant past, breeding unchecked in the waste areas of the palace. As a boy, Kew had been badly frightened by a drawing in the book, wherein a person was pulled apart by a pack of them. Terror warped their face into something inhuman. They were sometimes seen in the Passage.

Kew pressed himself against the cold wall. It felt odd. His fingertips slid over it, searching for the source of his new unease. They encountered no resistance.

That was it. The walls in Black were slick and seamless, either perfectly joined or somehow built of one great stone. Given what he knew of the old Ladies, it could easily be the latter. Perhaps in daylight that would not bother him, but at night, it felt like standing in an artery of some great dead thing. His hand, going out still farther, encountered an edge. There was a deep groove etched into the wall, going higher up than he could reach. Since that was all there was to feel without walking, Kew resumed his flattened position. And still he heard the faint noise, resolving from a mere disturbance of the air into a mechanical clanking.

Far away in the Passage toward Grey, a faint greasy-yellow light glimmered. The rising road and the converging walltops played havoc with his sense of perspective, but the light seemed very high up, hanging above the road as if from the parapet. It grew larger and the noise increased in volume. The echoes were sharp and horrible. Kew waited in silence. Surely it would pass him by. The moving light was too dim for anyone to notice him.

Soon the source drew close enough to see. A great lantern of dull metal was gliding along the wall. Among the clanking was a high-pitched whistling, like birdsong, with a familiar tune. Nothing came to mind, though, except that it perhaps sounded like one of the women's songs, to which he never paid attention.

The lantern reached a position directly above his head. He could see now that a large two-armed mechanism on its back held a horizontal wheel upon which the lantern ran. The wheel itself slotted into a groove under the parapet.

As Kew watched, the tune changed. Gleaming in the sickly light, the wheel turned onto a new axis, ratcheting itself into the vertical groove next to him. Time to move. But as he did, the lantern's gear shrieked, skidded, caught, skidded again, and almost before he could jump out of the way the lantern smashed into the ground and toppled over, spilling light. Its door fell open, and a dark shape leapt out.

"My goodness!" said the newcomer. They rested on their knees for a moment, panting. Armor of some dull metal covered their body. "Dear me!"

The light, which was apparently more of a liquid than a ray, was flowing downhill. The newcomer uttered a short, piercing shriek of horror and, catching sight of Kew as they jumped up, said, "Help! Help me catch it!"

They paused only to snatch a mop from inside the lantern before running after the stream of light. After a moment, Kew tossed his pack on the ground and went to help. The lantern-person was mopping up the light, so Kew whipped off his green overgown and used it to dam the stream. The thick fabric absorbed it eagerly. Where the light smeared his fingers, they went all chilly and prickly.

"Don't let it touch your face or eyes," said the stranger, industriously mopping.

When the light was all soaked up, the newcomer instructed him to follow them back to the lantern, then gave him the mop to hold while they got the lantern back on a vertical axis. Inside was a large basin. They wrung the mop out over it, splashing light practically everywhere but in, then they helped Kew do the same with his robe. Panting after the panic and exertion, they sat down and leaned against the wall. Kew wiped his sweaty forehead with one hand, remembered the warning, and switched to his sleeve. They had not noticed.

"I'm Fourteen Sparrow," they said, extending an armored hand. "One of Her Ladyship's Lanterns of the West Passage."

"I'm Kew, apprentice to the Guardian of the West Passage." The armor on Sparrow's hand shifted a little when grasped; it was not fastened on, but attached directly to their flesh.

"So we are neighbors, of a sort," said Sparrow. "One Sparrow talks about Hawthorn all the time. I think they met several years ago. Are you on a mission for her?"

"Yes," said Kew, hoping his tone conveyed that Sparrow should not ask about it.

"Oh! An urgent one?" said Sparrow.

"Fairly."

"*Oh.* Then as soon as I get the lantern hooked back in I can give you a ride. I'm heading back to the tower. It'll save you a bit of walking, and I owe you for helping with the light. There's precious little of it left these days, and I get in trouble if I lose any."

Sparrow chattered away as they and Kew pushed the lantern back into the groove and got the wheel engaged. If Kew had been paying better attention, he would have learned all of Sparrow's history by the time they were done, from growing up in "the aviary" to their promotion from Fifteen to Fourteen a year ago, but all his mind could focus on was *Soon I will be at Black Tower.* The anxiety of it dampened his mind until it could absorb nothing else. At last the lantern was in place, and Kew and Sparrow climbed in.

"Just sit anywhere there's room," said Sparrow, who was much smaller than Kew and did not seem to notice that he would only fit comfortably if he chopped his legs off. Three of the lantern's sides were translucent yellowish glass. The last quarter was blank metal, behind which the thick iron arms were visible through a small slit. Kew settled cross-legged against that wall with the basin pushing into his folded ankles. Sparrow sat across from him and began whistling a series of four notes over and over.

In response to the sound the lantern shuddered, grated, and the wheel began turning. The lantern rose. Each note moved the wheel a quarter turn, and thus the two of them were ratcheted up and up the side of the Passage. When the lantern had reached Sparrow's desired altitude, they changed their tune, and the wheel rotated to a horizontal position. They began the four notes again. Whenever they paused for breath, the wheel slowed; when they resumed whistling, the lantern resumed its motion.

As the lantern rolled along the wall, Kew tried to remember everything he knew of the Sparrows. They were unimportant to Grey Tower—or perhaps simply not understood well enough to be part of the Guardians' lore—so it did not take him long. Like the Guardians and the mothers, the Sparrows served the Ladies directly, but they were a relatively minor office of the palace. He at first thought they were messengers only, but after a while he remembered an obscure paragraph associating them with bringing light to dark places. That must be where the lanterns themselves came in. *Follow the lanterns* indeed; if the lore had said *Hitch a ride on one,* he could have just waited for it to come along.

Kew's body jerked to one side, pulling him back to the present, and he looked up at Sparrow. They had whistled two harsh notes, and the lantern had jolted to a stop.

"We've reached a waypoint," they said. "It's usually not a good idea to travel too late at night here."

Kew agreed, and Sparrow opened the lantern door and stepped out. Whatever Kew had pictured upon hearing the word *waypoint,* it was not this: a mere niche delved into the wall, with a platform extending out a few feet for the lantern to rest against. There were cupboards all around, and Sparrow produced dry biscuits and water from one, and musty bluish blankets from another.

"So what are you off to the tower for?" said Sparrow as they munched.

"I don't think I can talk about it," said Kew.

Sparrow shrugged. "That's all right. I'm sure I'll hear eventually. Nobody can keep anything secret in the tower, not even the Ladies. Better not say anything inside the walls that you don't want passed on. And certainly don't say it to a Sparrow. We can't keep a secret for love or honey. It's our job to tell, you know, and it's so hard for us to stop."

Kew had definitely gotten that impression. Sparrow continued to talk, mostly about parties they had seen in the ballrooms of Black or who'd been caught canoodling in the aviary, until at last they were both done eating. Kew rolled himself up in a blanket and watched Sparrow, wondering if they would take their armor off to sleep, but they pulled their arms and legs in and folded themselves up under their own blanket, armor and all, like a dying but cozy spider. He was just about to sleep when Sparrow's little piping voice broke the silence.

"If we're back in time, we might see the dance," they said. He could hear the smile in their voice.

"The what?" said Kew, keeping his eyes closed.

"When we Sparrows join together in the tower, from cellar to throne, to dance the Luminous Name."

"Sounds beautiful."

"It is. We've done it every year as a memorial, for as long as there have been Sparrows. You know, as long as the name is remembered, the person is never really gone."

"Who died?"

"I don't know. Some Lady or other, maybe."

Kew only grunted. Sparrow went quiet again, and after some shifting about, seemed to go to sleep. Kew was nearly there himself when Sparrow spoke again.

"Don't leave the waypoint without me," they said. "There are creatures afoot in the Passage at this hour. It's not a good idea to attract their attention."

"I won't," said Kew.

"Good."

Kew was about to sleep when Sparrow spoke again.

"Kew?" they said.

"Yes?"

"You've been good company. I'm glad you're here."

Kew thought about the dusty abandoned cloisters of Grey, the women with their uninterested faces and lackadaisical songs, and the terrible sight of Hawthorn expiring amid filth and pain. His hand closed on the amulet beneath his tunic.

"I am too," he said.

5. The Lantern Moves On and Kew Sees His First Banquet

In the morning, they ate some more biscuits and drank some more water and climbed back into the lantern. Sparrow took the empty bottles along, saying that they would refill them at the aviary, there being no sources of fresh water between the waypoint and the tower. To keep them out of the way, Kew put the bottles in his pack, where they nestled amid the books and food he had salvaged from Hawthorn's room. He and Sparrow did not speak, for Sparrow needed to whistle to keep the lantern going.

The roofs and walls of Black's mansions rolled by, clouded by the scratched, dirty panes of the lantern. While the walls of Grey were built of simple dry ashlar, unadorned and practical, Black's were elaborate and finely worked, with cornices and spires and buttresses everywhere. Gargoyles and grotesques sprouted from every roof; flowers and thorns wrapped every window, all of the same shining black stone. The summer sun gleamed along every polished curve and flashed on every spine and flagpole. It was the most beautiful thing Kew had ever seen.

Dreading this journey had been foolish. Black Tower was awe-inspiring, even terrifying, but the West Passage was *Kew's* territory. He had needed to fear it no more than a cat fears a rat.

The lantern came to a juddering halt. Sparrow whistled, frowned, and whistled again. The lantern twitched but could not move. Sparrow sighed.

"Might need to oil the gear," they said, and sighed again. From a compartment in the lantern floor, they took an oilcan. They opened the door and leaned out to the left to see the gear.

Over their shoulder, Black Tower was stark against the blue sky. The West Passage walls ran straight toward it, limned with sunlight though the road itself was lost in shadow. Across the court rooftops to the east, Red Tower glowed. Through the haze from its beacon, a little thread of bright silver shone.

A train! Kew had never seen one, but he had read of them. Judging by its position relative to him, the train was running along an elevated track or perhaps another wall top. They did not come near Grey; there were stories about why this might be, but probably it was due to the mothers' damnable stubbornness. To take a train—to race along the roofs, almost flying—to arrive at Black Tower like a proper courtier—*that* would have made an impression on the Ladies!

Sparrow finished oiling the gear and closed the lantern. "Damn thing won't *stay* oiled," they said, stowing the can. "I hope we can get back to the aviary before it sticks again. No love nor loyalty will keep me out another night, not with things the way they are."

"What do you mean?" said Kew.

"Oh, troubles in the cellars, like always," said the Sparrow. "Only worse now than before. They say there was a hollowman taken down three nights ago—no, four—and that's a deed generations'll remember you for."

"Brigands?"

"That's the least of it," said Sparrow. They took a long sip of water. "The most of it is that something's astir."

"What?"

Sparrow shrugged. "I'm only a Sparrow. There's a lot that's none of my business, and still more that I won't *make* my business. So I'll only say that when I looked out just now, and I looked back down the Passage just now, do you know what I saw? Clouds. Clouds over Grey Tower. Seemed to me as if they carried a lot of snow."

"But it's summer there," said Kew.

"Summer there and spring in Yellow, I know. But the wheel has a hitch, it seems, and that's a bad sign, and though *I've* never seen a winter out of season, they say it's always a punishment or an omen."

Sparrow didn't know the whole truth, it seemed. A wrong winter could be an omen of the Beast, which, the records said, sucked vitality out of the earth as it approached. It didn't have to be that, though. The women in grey had clearly shirked their duty in the matter of the masks, and the great Lady of Black could be angry over the mistreatment of such important artifacts.

"Could be a punishment," Kew said bitterly.

Sparrow laughed. "What has Grey Tower ever done, right or wrong, to get itself noticed by those that turn the wheel? Nothing, not since Rose."

"Well, there was the Long Winter in Thistle," said Kew. "And the Interdictions all throughout Bellflower."

"Sure, but that's long, long ago. Song-times, not story-times. Again, it's not my business, and when it comes to the wheel, I won't make it my business. I'll only say this: If it's *meant* to be an omen, it's not on the approved lists. Which has me a bit rattled."

Sparrow started whistling again. The gear shrieked and shuddered in protest, but it turned, and soon the lantern was skimming along at a fast clip. After a few minutes of boredom, Kew decided to look at Hawthorn's books. He had to brush up on his court etiquette, for one thing, and for another, if there were a list of omens known to Black Tower, he was unaware of it. There were signs of its approach known in Grey. Hawthorn herself had never seen them in her life, but they were written down somewhere, and winter was one of them. But was it *early* winter, or delayed winter? The latter was preferable, for Grey was not prepared—*Kew* was not prepared—for the other possibility.

Atop everything in the pack was a cloth-wrapped children's rhyme Hawthorn had received from Blue the day she was taken ill. He had brought it as a memento, though what she'd wanted with it he could only imagine. At the bottom was *Times & Changes,* the oldest and largest book. It might have what he needed, but there was so much to sort through that if he could find it in another volume, he'd rather do that. Perhaps in *The Downfall of the Thistles,* which described the Beast and its defeat at the hands of the last Thistle Lady. They had killed each other, but while the Beast could always rise again, latter-era Ladies could not. Past Hawthorns had made helpful notes in the margin, which might clear up some mysteries of the book. *Downfall* was not immediately at hand, but there were the *Grand Bestiary of Blue Tower* and *Campanula,* both of which were promising. Where was *Downfall*? He had grabbed all the books in Hawthorn's chest, even the little paperbound almanacs that she got from Blue and never read. It was the smallest of the volumes; perhaps it was under the mask.

No, not even there. *The Downfall of the Thistles* was simply missing. Kew had not opened his pack the day before, and in the empty, quiet

Passage, he would have noticed anything falling out. *Downfall* had been removed before he ever left Grey Tower. But nobody had been in Hawthorn's room but him, and the women in grey . . . and their little apprentice.

It was her. It must have been. She said the women did not take, and he'd believed her. Why had she stolen it? The book was no use to her. They didn't read or write in Grey House. Was it to spite him for startling her? Hawthorn had filled the margins with notes. It was not an ordinary book; it was practically her *diary*. It was part of her.

"Something wrong?" said Sparrow. The lantern had come to a halt and they were looking at Kew curiously.

Kew shook his head. "It's fine. I just need to head back to Grey as soon as possible. Once I complete my mission, that is."

"Homesick?" said Sparrow, and started whistling without waiting for an answer.

"Not exactly," Kew muttered.

If one couldn't trust even the women, then one thing was plain now, a thing he had suspected for some time. The Guardians did not belong in Grey. Hawthorn had occasionally wondered aloud why they were housed there, in the oldest part of the palace. Black made more sense. It was at one end of the West Passage, and it was the seat of power. The women in grey stayed in their house because their role was small, and because they were stubborn, but the Guardians were entrusted with the defense of the entire palace. They belonged where they could do some good, where their voice would not be lost in the dust and ruin of Grey. They belonged in the court of the Ladies of Black Tower.

When Kew became the Guardian, he would petition to move. Surely nobody meddled with other people's belongings in Black. It was a place of order, not chaos.

Something bumped against the lantern, and Sparrow stopped their music. Their body went very still.

"What—" said Kew, but Sparrow flung their hand out to cover his mouth.

The two of them waited. Sparrow's head swiveled, looking through each of the three panes in turn. The sunlight turned the scratched glass nearly opaque. Where the glass was shadowed and clear, it faced the opposite wall. A few kestrels perched on the top. Perhaps one of them had—

Thud. The lantern trembled. It came from the metal side, where the gear attached. Sparrow let out a long exhalation that sounded like despair. Kew quickly—but with scrupulous silence—put everything back in his pack. He had nearly finished buckling it closed when the lantern shook again. This time, he caught a glimpse of a dark shape flashing past the window.

"Jackals," whispered Sparrow. "If we move, they'll chase us."

"And if we stay still?" said Kew, even more quietly.

"They may ignore us."

"*May?*"

Thud went the metal wall again, right next to Kew. Sparrow motioned furiously for quiet just as the wall beside them shuddered under an impact. Two jackals, then. Possibly more.

Silence fell. Kew's heart was pounding so loudly, it would almost be better to speak just to drown it out. He held his breath and listened. Totally unconcerned, one of the kestrels took flight, diving into the depths of the Passage after some prey.

Bang! went the top of the lantern, and answering bangs came from the sides and bottom. They were surrounded, and the jackals were not going away.

"Hold on," said Sparrow. "And cover your eyes."

They let out an earsplitting whistle. The basin of light flared like the sun. Kew flung his arm across his face, but the light that had soaked into his robe shone just as brightly. He slammed his palms over his eyes. They flashed black and red as the light dimmed and brightened, dimmed and brightened. Meanwhile, Sparrow whistled their old arpeggio so fast that the notes nearly stacked into a chord. The lantern jerked forward, pushing Kew against the glass with the force of its speed.

As it rocketed away, there were barks and howls behind them. Kew could not open his eyes, and could barely hear over Sparrow's noise, but it seemed the jackals were falling away. He tried to take deep, regular breaths, but his heart was thumping more quickly than Sparrow could whistle.

Sparrow paused to breathe, but the lantern's momentum propelled it along. Kew began to relax slightly. They could do this. Jackals would give up the chase if it took long enough. Sparrow's lungs just needed to hold out.

The barking had gone silent. They had outpaced the jackals. As the light dimmed, Kew smiled in relief and took his hands away from his face.

Thud went the glass beside him. A huge yellow eye stared into his own. The light brightened again. Yelping, the jackal veered away.

With the next note, the gear caught. The lantern shrieked, stopped. Kew's body rattled against Sparrow's armor. Sparrow rattled against the door. The ancient latch sheared off, and the door flew open.

Sparrow's upper body fell out of the lantern. The light dimmed. Their hands scrabbled for the sides of the door and caught it by a few fingertips. Green jaws closed around their wrist. Their eyes met Kew's.

"They hate light!" said Sparrow. "They hate—"

A green head clamped onto their shoulder and yanked them from the lantern. Lithe bodies streamed past, running down the face of the wall as easily as if it were a road. A long scream rose from the dark depths of the Passage.

A Guardian's first duty is to protect. Kew scrambled to the open door and looked out. If he could just get to Sparrow—A landing platform stuck out from the wall a few yards below. Sparrow lay there, facing up, surrounded by green and brown bodies. Clever long-fingered paws had wrenched their cuirass away, tearing their torso open. Their eyes were wide and glassy. As jackals' teeth unspooled their guts, they saw Kew.

They whistled a new note, and the door started to close. Kew tried to keep it open. He had to get out. He had to help. This was the West Passage; Guardians protected it. And Kew was practically a Guardian. But the door continued, inexorably, to close. The last thing he saw before it shut was Sparrow's eyes going dim.

The lantern's light kept flaring and dying. Kew put his head between his knees and tried to breathe. He needed to get out of there. He needed to move the lantern. Sparrow's tune was engraved in his memory, but his trembling lips would not let him whistle at first. Again and again he tried. All the while he tried not to hear the jackals feasting. At last he formed the first note.

The wheel twitched. It had stuck again, of course. Even if he could somehow open the door to escape, the jackals were still there. Kew whistled again, more loudly. The wheel grated, but it turned. He whistled the next note. The wheel protested, but turned once more. He whistled the third note. It moved a little more easily.

Below him, the jackals barked again. He had caught their attention. But as long as he heeded Sparrow's last words, he might be all right.

He whistled the fourth note, and the wheel stuck. He tried again. It wouldn't budge. On the third try, something snapped. Kew held his breath and sat very still. Nothing happened. Maybe that snap had just been the rust breaking. If that was even how lanterns worked, and Kew was far from informed on this point. But he knew he could not stay there, so he whistled the fourth note again.

The gear's housing tore free and the lantern plummeted into the depths.

6. The Tombs Have Rats and Pell Confesses to Breaking the Weather

In the morning the snow lay thick on the effigies that lined the north side of Grey. They faced outward toward Black Tower, their stone faces worn away to soft lumps. One or two of them had deeply carved eyes that were now dark holes, staring eternally at the palace center.

Each effigy stood atop a pedestal, and each pedestal had once borne a name, though like the faces, these names had been erased by time and wind and water. These were the Tombs of the Ladies. There had been no Lady in Grey for centuries, and the bones of them had been bones so long that they were now dust, but the tombs were maintained nonetheless.

Old Monkshood LXXIV felt as if he had been dust that long as well. It was his task to keep up the tombs, but nowadays, what with arthritis and long naps, his version of maintenance was sprinkling them with water to wash off the dust and running a rake around the brown grass at their feet, whether it needed it or not. Nothing lived on that side of Grey, so usually it didn't need it. But when Monkshood got up in the cold dawn of unexpected winter, there were tracks all over the light snow. They seemed to come from the tombs themselves, and though the Ladies would not have had feet that small, for a moment he worried something had come back to life.

The statues were named for their Ladies. Away to the north were crumbling effigies of Ladies of Black, Red, and Blue, now all white under the snow, and having no names Monkshood had ever learned, but the one nearest the south wall was Deer, for the antlers that still showed through her hood. Tallest of the Ladies was Madam Carrion;

smallest of the Ladies was Yew. Monkshood was standing near her when he discovered the tracks, and when he straightened (painfully, as everything was those days), something seemed amiss about her hollow, leftmost eye.

It looked full. Perhaps with dirty snow, he thought, but then he looked more closely, and found two eyes staring back from a socket made for one. The eyes were little, beady, and black, nestled in soft grey. With a hoarse bark, he jumped away, and his arthritis protested. Groaning, he straightened, clutching his back, and looked at Yew's unaccustomed number of eyes.

It was a rat. As he watched, it wriggled out of the socket and plopped onto the snow. The rat scampered away, leaving a fresh line of tracks, as a noise rustled from Yew. Another grey rat poked its head out of the grey stone and leapt down. Then another, then another, until Yew seemed to be weeping rodents.

Monkshood turned and, moving both quickly and carefully on account of his back, headed for Grey House to tell the women.

In the huge, drafty kitchen, Yarrow and Arnica were tossing logs into the fire while the apprentices came downstairs in the cold dawn. At the worn oak table, Servant was measuring out barleymeal for the gruel. The apprentices lined themselves up against the wall—Ban's head knocked against a ladle—and waited for Yarrow to speak. Pell was twisting her linen apron in her fingers. Would Yarrow ask about the weather?

"We will eat in the kitchen this morning, girls," said Yarrow. "Grith, fetch the bowls and spoons. Ban, the honey and curds. Pell—"

"If I may," said Pell. "I have something to confess, Mother Yarrow."

Grith and Ban went about their tasks while Yarrow threw one more log in the fire, then set the kettle on its iron arm to boil. Pell waited in silence. She did not meet the other girls' eyes, though their curious gazes prickled her neck. It was rare for Pell to make a real mistake, let alone have anything to confess. Ban and Grith probably savored the idea of Pell's punishment, for, friendly as they were, all three competed for the women's favor. Arnica gave it freely and took it back just as freely; her approval and her punishments weighed as heavy as the wind. But Yarrow's good opinion was the prize at the end of a race you had to run every day, and Pell was an excellent runner.

"Come over here then, girl," said Yarrow with a sigh. She straightened her wimple as she led Pell to a quieter corner of the kitchen. "Now, what's this you've done?"

Pell inhaled slowly, hoping the extra time would grant confidence. It didn't. "I brought winter."

Yarrow's heavy eyebrows lifted themselves a fraction. "You brought winter?"

"Yes. I accidentally took something from the old woman's room, and I—I broke curfew last night to return it."

One corner of Yarrow's small, wrinkled mouth twisted up. "The weather pays attention to the tricks of a girl in grey, does it?"

"It was a book. It seemed important. The apprentice told me not to touch it."

"Of course he would, girl. All apprentices think their own trade is the most important."

"But if it's an heirloom of the name—"

"The guardians' work doesn't rely on books, girl, only on strength and steel. I say keep it to amuse yourself, if you like, or take it to the Archives, if that's more to your taste, but either way, the seasons move at the word of the Ladies, and they're silent. This is just some jog of the wheel, I'm sure. Now, I was about to tell you to stir the gruel so Servant can go about bringing in the laundry. After, if you find your conscience still pricks, speak again and I'll give you penance."

This was not satisfying. Pell had a keen sense of justice, and decided to return the book when she had a spare hour. But at least she would not be punished. The gruel was stirred with an avid care to which it was unaccustomed, and came out of the pot smooth and unscorched. They were just sitting down, and Pell was scooping curds into her bowl, when a cold wind swirled around them and Monkshood coughed from the outer door.

"Shut that, man, or this goes up your nose!" said Arnica, brandishing the ladle.

"Come in, Monkshood," said Yarrow.

Men were unusual in Grey House. Monkshood had left the tombs only once that Pell knew of, when something pained him and he wanted Arnica to doctor him. In the two or three years since, tasks and age had withered and bent him till he looked like the trunks of ivy on the house's south wall.

"Sit," said Arnica. "Grith, some tea."

"None, thanks," said Monkshood. "It's news I'm here to give."

"And?" said Yarrow, sipping her own tea.

"Rats," said Monkshood. When this single word did not convey the depths of his confusion and horror, he went on. "It's rats in the tombs."

Yarrow and Arnica were silent, clearly expecting more. Monkshood spread his fingers as far as they went, which was not far, and shrugged, having come to the limits of his verbal ability.

"There are always rats in the tombs, Monkshood," said Yarrow. "What is so unusual now?"

"It's that they're out of the tombs." The warmth of the fire seemed to unbind an ancient skein of courtesy in his mind, for he added, as if it were a question, "Mother?"

"Not so unusual, I think," said Yarrow, but her composure had soured into confusion.

"Lots of 'em," said Monkshood. "Crawling—crawling out of Yew's head, and as I passed, out of Madrona's and Hawthorn's too. Wherever a hole was. And fleeing, the rats were fleeing." Then, after a moment, "Mother?"

Arnica gulped her tea, which scorched her mouth. She swore volubly at the tea, the cup, and her own tongue. Yarrow took a tiny sip.

"It's just rats, after all," she said.

"It's—it's odd, Mother," said Monkshood. "I think . . . it's very odd."

"Oh, what's the harm in looking," said Arnica. "Be good for you to take a little walk."

Yarrow groaned and stood. "I think, Monkshood, you and I will go look at the tombs. Ban, my cloak is upstairs. Be back quick and you'll have the rest of my honey. Grith, my pattens are also upstairs. Be back quick and you'll have the rest of my curds. Pell, come along with me."

"Better you than me," Arnica whispered to Pell as she hurried into her cloak.

Outside, winter had settled over Grey like a crow claiming a carcass. A flurry had snowed over Monkshood's footprints, but the sky was now a clear white, with only a few flakes to be seen in the air. The gables and dormers of the house were heavy and sullen against that cold purity, and the tower seemed to hunch into itself for warmth.

Yarrow charged ahead through the kitchen courtyard, followed more slowly by Monkshood, and lastly by a scrambling Pell, who had no pattens and tried to step in the trail left by the other two. That courtyard opened onto a series of others, all lined with crumbling colonnades or long-abandoned stables, hemmed in by peaked roofs like knives lying on their backs. At last Grey House's tattered fringes gave way to the Tombs of the Ladies. Monkshood lived there in a little ramshackle hut with a trickle of warm smoke in its chimney, and he looked longingly at it as they passed.

There were no rats to be seen, but tracks showed they had been moving even after the newest snowfall. Yarrow poked around the effigies, glancing here and there, trampling the delicate rat tracks, her mouth held firm and irritated. Monkshood dared not go home without her dismissal, and only stood in the snow like yet another statue: if he sat down in that cold, his joints would freeze up and he'd never be shifted. A jewellike dragonfly, shining darkly against the snow, landed on an effigy and twitched its wings.

"Hm" was all Yarrow said. She touched the face of Yew with a gentler hand than she used on the living. The statue's gaping eyes were little rounds of midnight in the winter light. Why some effigies were hollow and others weren't, Pell had no idea. She had learned the litany of their names and deeds, but the circumstances of their burial were known only to women in grey, not to girls.

"All well?" said Monkshood. "Mother?"

"I see no sign of things amiss," said Yarrow. "Only that the lichen sprouts between their toes. See that each is cleaned by morning. Come, Pell." They turned to go.

Perhaps being on his own ground made Monkshood bold. Perhaps he only wanted to warm his freezing toes by his little fire. But he stood as straight as he could and said, "It's a bad sign."

Yarrow grunted. "Nothing in the litanies about it."

"It smells of guardian business," said Monkshood. "It's something the women don't know: it's guardians. But there isn't one."

"There's that apprentice," said Pell. Yarrow looked down on her, stone-faced, and she shrank into her itchy cloak. "I only mean," Pell said, because sometimes it helped to explain oneself, "it might be time to—"

"The boy should have been to see me at once," said Yarrow. "If he hasn't, he doesn't want the name of guardian. And that's that."

"No guardian?" said Monkshood. "No guardian in Grey?"

"There are a lot of things we don't have here anymore," said Yarrow. "And we survive. It's what we do. Come, Pell." She turned. The sudden flick of her cloak startled the dragonfly away.

Monkshood seemed about to argue, but closed his mouth and waited for the woman and girl in grey to leave. It *was* a bad sign—but the women knew many things. One had to trust them. With a sigh he went to get his own toothbrush and some warm water. It took him far into the night, working by the light of a weak lantern, but in the morning every effigy was clean of lichen, and Monkshood's hands were coiled up into painful shapes. But Yarrow did not come to see whether he had done it.

"What do you think happened?" said Pell as they went back to the kitchen.

"Could be flooding in the tombs," said Yarrow. The *clink-clink-clink* of her pattens nearly drowned out her voice. "Bet that apprentice would also say it's a sign."

"A sign of what?"

"A sign that old women are tired of questions," said Yarrow.

"Yes, Mother," said Pell.

Snow was falling again as they reached the kitchen. Servant was cleaning up the breakfast bowls.

"Help her, girl," said Yarrow, shrugging out of her cloak. "Then find me in the slabroom. It's time you learned a bit."

No breakfast, then. *That* was for talking back.

"Yes, Mother," said Pell.

7. Pell Learns a Bit and the Beast Rises

The slabroom was as long as the refectory, and as high. Narrow windows lined two of its walls, which were of unadorned grey stone. Dark rafters crisscrossed the ceiling, which was white plaster, except where it was black mildew. The flagstones sloped a little toward the center, where a drain went who-knows-where. And all down the length of the room were three rows of granite slabs, each carved with simple channels to drain onto the floor.

When Pell finally arrived, hands dry and rough from washing, Yarrow was already there. She had donned an enormous dingy leather apron and stood near one of the slabs. There was a body on the smooth surface.

Pell's feet nearly drew her up short, but she mastered them and approached with stiff calm. Yarrow waited for her coolly. Who had died?

Nobody, it turned out. The body was of chipped and crackled porcelain. Its abdomen opened on brass hinges to reveal porcelain organs, their paint worn away. Some of them seemed to have been broken and glued back together, and the gallbladder was entirely gone, replaced with a little green sack of beans.

"You are here to learn the ways of the women in grey," said Yarrow. "You are the eldest of the girls, and it will soon be time for you to take on real duties."

"I am ready for a real body," said Pell stoutly. After all the anatomy lessons, after the diagrams in the Archives, what *didn't* she know?

Yarrow laughed sharply. "No you're not. You'll learn with this, as we all did. Besides, nobody's dead yet. And if they were, a corpse is terrible easy to mess. Say you're asked to see the hurt in a kidney, see why someone died of it, and when you're done you put everything back in wrong and it spills out on the way up-tower? Shame and disgrace on the house, it would be. So we start here, with something you cannot harm."

Pell's cheeks burned, but she swallowed her pride as Yarrow showed her the way everything nestled together, the close-packed strangeness of one's insides. When Pell had learned it to Yarrow's satisfaction, the woman began to tell her the rites for Ladies.

"But there are no Ladies anymore," said Pell, once Yarrow had made her repeat the rules thrice.

"Not in Grey," said Yarrow, stuffing an intestine back into the false corpse. "In Black, there are several: great Willow at the top, Lady of us all, and a dozen nattering upstarts at the bottom. In Blue there's the old one and her daughters; in Red the young one and her sisters; and in Yellow they say there's the ancient one. A *true* ancient one. Wouldn't want to go there. But it's no matter, as I won't, and anyway the Ladies haven't sent their own dead here for a long, long time."

"It's said *everyone* dead goes up-tower."

"Yes."

"But I've never seen any dead at all come in from the other towers."

"Yes."

"Does nobody else die?"

Yarrow shut the lid of the corpse and began to pour water from a jug over her hands. "Always wash before leaving the slabroom. Death wants to spread."

Pell washed. "Does nobody else die, Mother Yarrow?"

"Everyone dies except the Lady in Yellow, the songs and stories say. But not everyone keeps the customs of birth and death. By rights we should be the busiest tower, and there are a lot of stories about why we aren't." Yarrow dried her hands on a linen towel and passed it to Pell. "And no, I don't know which stories are true."

She took off her apron and hung it on a peg in the wall, next to several others that had rotted with time. "You'll be fitted for a woman's apron soon," said Yarrow. "And once you know everything about how people die in the palace, you'll learn about how people are born."

She stalked out of the slabroom, and Pell hurried after her. The crumbling halls echoed to her footsteps. Dust rose in her wake. The echoes faded. Dust fell from cold light into colder shadows. All was still.

Under the earth, where nothing had bothered it for a long time, something shifted. Let us, for the sake of knowing it better, pretend three things. First, that there is light beneath the earth for us to see it by. Second, that its motion occurs on a scale comprehensible to people. Third, that something outside nature can be described using words arising from nature.

The earth packed in all around it, for it was so large that there was, indeed, no other way for earth to behave in its presence. There were several limbs, but no obvious head. There were more than several eyes, which it kept damp with several tongues. Despite the tongues, it had no mouth. It was somewhat longer than it was tall, and all down its length were colors and slimes and smells. Any part of it could swivel in any direction, or suddenly move, so that an eye might open where no eye had been, or a limb spiral out where before there had been only smooth slime.

Occasionally it woke. More often it would sleep, dreaming such dreams as such beasts do: dreams of crunching, of gushing, of warm fluids down the gullet. If this beast measured time, it was not in heart-beats but in dreams. The rhythmic slosh of the subconscious was all the calendar it needed, and all the company it kept. But now and then it heard something from up above.

When it did wake, it was always hungry. What did it eat? Oh, all kinds of things: the ends of turnips, cartwheels, babies, sunlight, crumbs. Once it quite enjoyed a potato. If it could conceive of the palace as anything, it was as a buffet. It rarely conceived of the palace, because that gave it a headache—or would, if the Beast had possessed a head. The guardians of the West Passage had often tried to derive some comfort from the knowledge that they were as terrifying and inconceivable to the Beast as it was to them, but that never helped.

Part of its inconceivability was that it could only take one approach to the palace: the West Passage itself. That had been its road time out of mind, and it knew no other way. Indeed, it could not come close to knowing that another way might exist, just as your lungs know no other thing to breathe but air. Just then, the Beast found itself thinking (if it thought) of food, and its limbs and body and eyes and tongues began to uncoil, as slowly as continents drifting, and it aimed its will (if it had a will) toward the surface and the start of the West Passage.

Meanwhile, Pell learned. Winter did not lift. She and the women in grey and the girls in grey did not know it, but this was an infallible sign of the Beast's approach. The rats had been another. The guardian knew, but the guardian was dead, and the apprentice gone who knows where, and so the Beast moved inch by inch through rock and soil, unnoticed by anything except vermin.

8. The Beekeepers Come to Kew's Rescue and He Makes a Second Friend

If Kew shifted the panel just an inch, his foot would be free. But his hands were bloody and torn from sweeping broken glass off himself, so when he grabbed the bent metal panel, he yelped in pain. The darkness absorbed his cry, and he sat very still, listening for jackals.

The fall should have killed him, and nearly had, but no doubt the creatures would finish the job. In the silence he could still hear the wet crunching of their jaws on Sparrow's flesh. All around him was a spill of light, no longer flashing. Venturing beyond it might bring them down. Then his eyes would go dim like Sparrow's. The pain of being eaten was not frightening. He was in pain *now*. It was the fading that terrified him.

Kew, it must be remembered, was the same age as Pell: not much more than a child, just barely brushing adulthood. Sparrow's death affected him more than Hawthorn's because he could not grasp the enormity of her absence yet. He could encompass Sparrow's. Nothing in him could hold Hawthorn's.

Biting his sleeve against another cry, he shoved the panel away and drew his foot toward himself. Pins and needles made him gasp, but he stood. His pack lay nearby. Later he would see if anything was broken, but now he needed to get moving. Apprentices were not supposed to carry weapons outside the training ground, but Kew wrapped his hand in a handkerchief and picked up a long shard of glass, sharp as teeth, to ward off anything that might come. In his hand, it had the weight of the Guardian's steel: he could wield it. Though now it wasn't against straw dummies or an old woman who always pulled back before killing him. This was real.

As he left the luminous wreckage of the lantern, his overgown brightened, or perhaps became visible. Kew almost cried with relief. It was still soaked with light. Though it was dim, it might keep the jackals away. The sky above was a thin tongue of purplish blue between the crenellated jaws of the walls. The road he walked was smooth and level. Behind him, it dwindled and vanished. Ahead of him, it descended farther and farther until it ended some distance away in the tall dark length of Black Tower, where lights had been kindled against the advancing night. He had lost nearly a day to the jackals, but if he kept going and stopped for nothing, he might make it to the tower's base before night fully fell.

Every inch of him ached. Nothing had broken, but he was all over bruises and cuts, and his head had been banged up like a boiled egg someone intended to peel. A metallic taste rang in his mouth—blood? Or light from his sleeve? His water bottle had smashed during the fall, and he wanted nothing more than a drink. Well, nothing more than a drink *and* rest. Well, nothing more than a drink *and* rest *and* food.

The closer he came to Black Tower, the rougher the road grew. Things crunched underfoot or jabbed his soles. At first, they seemed like bits of pavement or rubble from crumbling walls—all the ways in Grey were like that; there was nothing odd about it, except that the Passage had been so clean before—but then something sparkled in the light from his robe. He stopped to look.

All around Kew were what looked like the remains of a gigantic feast. Porcelain and glassware lay scattered about, along with knives and spoons of extreme delicacy and beauty. Here and there were bones, ragged with scraps of desiccated flesh, and odds and ends of other food, all lumpen and brown from exposure. Soon the road was covered in them, and he walked even more slowly, and quite a lot more painfully, with his ankles nearly snapping as empty bottles rolled out from under him. Bent spoons snagged at his shoes, and once he narrowly escaped a carving knife stabbing right into his heel.

The trash had filled up the floor of the West Passage. Though the road seemed to keep going down, he had left it behind and was walking *up* a garbage heap. It was as if the residents of Black Tower had been throwing out banquets for year upon year. Odors of rot and decay wafted up from the depths. He passed an entire cake, once tiered and marvelously decorated with sugar-paste architecture, now melted and sad, with holes eaten into the molding sponges. A rat peered out of the cake at him, its palps coated in crumbs, then whisked away. There were flies all about, but also bees, who investigated old wine-glasses and buzzed companionably around his head.

A glass shattered in the darkness behind him. Kew looked over his shoulder. Two yellow eyes gleamed. Then two more beside them, and two more beside *them*. Lifting his arm, he saw that the light was dying from his robe. Not much, but enough—and it had already been dim.

He quickened his pace. It wasn't easy—the trash heap was hazardous even if you moved slowly and carefully. Soon he was crawling up it, one hand holding out the shard of lantern glass. Insects scattered before him. The walltops grew nearer, and the sky wider.

There were at least ten jackals now. Their footing was surer than his, and as the light faded from him even more, they came close enough that he could count their teeth. The sky had darkened further. Maybe Red would let the little moon up tonight, and maybe it would be full and shine right down the Passage. And maybe a Lady would reach down and scoop him up, since it was the time to wish for improbable things.

The jackals did not growl. Their legs rustled like stalks of grass. Two broke from the pack and got ahead of him. Fetid breath warmed the air. He brandished the glass in their faces, and they stepped back, but did not retreat.

Sparrow had whistled something to make the light flash—what was it? He was on the verge of trying it when he remembered: the light would dim even more between flashes, and it was already too dark for comfort. No, that would make everything worse.

Black Tower rose high above him and kept rising, its necklaces of lamps shimmering in the summer night, its buttressed spires outstretched like welcoming arms. From some window came a voice singing a jaunty melody, accompanied by a sound he did not know. (Kew had never heard a harp, instruments being forbidden in Grey.) The top of the trash heap was very near, and the song gave him enough courage to dash for it. Yelping and growling, the jackals sprang back at his advance, and he crested the heap to find—

—that he stood on a ridge of trash, looking down into a valley of trash, glittering with knives and broken glass, and the base of Black Tower was far, far away, shrouded in the night and its own refuse.

The jackals surrounded him.

The sea of garbage came up close to the walltops, but not nearly close enough. Though ranks of arched windows lined them, he could never climb that high and break in before the jackals got him. If he could dig down into the garbage, he might be able to get away from their jaws and hide long enough for them to lose interest. Kew knelt, one hand keeping the glass aloft, and began to burrow. He threw plates and glass at the jackals and hurled butter knives. They hissed and danced in rage but did not leave. The racket echoed in the narrow Passage. Perhaps someone would hear it and come.

A light detached itself from the side of the tower and raced along the wall. Kew recognized the telltale sound of a lantern in motion. It was coming for him. The tower had heard. The tower was taking care of him. But the lantern blazed past and vanished into the dark like a shooting star. Kew was left alone with the jackals, a pit hardly big enough for a child, and a robe hardly brighter than a patch of moonlight. There was no more time. Better to face them head on than submit. He sighed and straightened up. A bee flew past him and landed briefly on his hand.

"Tell them I tried," he said, for the sake of having spoken.

The bee took off and was lost in the night. After his climb, and with his heart racing, Kew was uncomfortably warm. He wiped his forehead on his sleeve, leaving a faint track of light along his eyebrows. The nearest jackal, a brownish-green one with enormous eyes, stepped even nearer, its large three-fingered paw snapping the stem off a glass. Kew raised his weapon higher.

"Oi," said a husky voice above him.

A small person with a trout's face had opened one of the windows and was looking down at him.

"Yes?" said Kew. The jackal moved and he pointed the shard at it.

"Tried what?" said the person.

"Huh?" said Kew.

"The bee says you tried. Tried what? If you're talking about surviving, that sure as South ain't working, far as I can tell."

"Help?" said Kew. "Help me?"

"Spose I could," said the person. "If only to stop that racket you're making. Thought for sure it was another lizard out and about. Say, you've not happened to see one of those, have you?"

"Help *now*?" said Kew.

"You'd know a lizard if you saw one," said the person. "Big suckers. Teeth like boats."

"Well, I've got jackals now," said Kew.

"I can see that. How good are you at climbing rope?"

"I've never tried."

The person sighed. "Fine, I'll saddle up a hive. Sit tight." They started to close the window, then swung it open again. "If they get you, do you still want to come inside?"

"Do I—?" The jackal inched forward and Kew waved the glass again. "Do I *still* want to come inside?"

"As bones or whatever. Some care about that kind of thing."

"Yes, all right, take me inside if they get me."

"All I wanted to know."

The window closed and Kew was left with the jackals. His robe was almost completely dark. The foremost jackal leapt toward him. He swung the glass. Greenish blood spurted from its shoulder and it twisted, landing next to him, and bounded away with a rattling cry like a dry peapod. At the same time, one jackal got his free hand, and as he made to stab it another clamped its teeth onto the back of his robe. As he struggled, the others raced forward.

A dark shape blotted out part of the sky, then landed in the trash with a vitreous clatter and slipped beneath its surface like a huge fish. Kew and the jackals froze. The trash heap below them rumbled and shifted. A tall, narrow, buzzing pyramid broke the surface. It went up and up and up, leaking bees like a cloud leaking rain, then after it came a shaggy neck and a huge back. Seated there was someone with long rabbit's ears, holding a lantern in one hand.

"Get on quick," they said to Kew. "I don't much feel like hanging around the Passage after dark."

"But I," said Kew.

"Oh," they said. "Of course." They put two fingers in their mouth and whistled. The cloud of bees dove for the jackals.

As the jackals were driven into the dark, the elk-like creature knelt on long, graceful legs. The trout helped Kew onto its back, and the creature got to its feet. It ran for the wall and leapt, clearing it in a single bound and landing on the other side in a quiet dusky court full of trees and the smell of flowers. The trout person stood there with another light.

Rabbit-ears got down from the creature's back in a sort of controlled fall. Not a jump: they simply slid off the creature's back and rolled when they hit the ground, somehow keeping the lantern upright. They looked up at Kew, their eyes gleaming in the twilight. "Now you."

"It's got to be at least ten feet," said Kew. "I'll hurt myself."

The trout sighed and made a buzzing noise with their gills. The creature lowered itself to its knees so Kew could get off. It stood and shook its furry flanks, then glided away under the trees. Now that he had a better look at it, Kew thought its tall head was almost exactly like one of Black Tower's thorny spires.

"I don't like asking them for too many favors," said the trout, taking rabbit-ears' lantern. "Bad enough we take their honey, but riding them and making them kneel? Child, don't you know there's a queen in there?"

Kew watched the hive bend its neck so the pyramidal head was closer to a bed of flowers. "I suppose I didn't," he said.

"You're lucky the bees took a shine to you," said the trout. "They didn't give me your handle, though."

"Kew, apprentice to the Guardian of Grey Tower."

The trout blinked. "They still do that there? Huh." They extended a hand. "I'm Thirty Robin, Keeper of Her Obsidian Ladyship's Hives. This is Frin, my apprentice."

Robin, Robin, Robin. That did not sound familiar as a beekeeper name, but there were clearly gaps in Hawthorn's histories.

"I am pleased to meet you both," said Kew, swallowing his doubt. "And I'm grateful to you and your bees for saving my life."

"Not *my* bees," said Robin. Her scaly brow furrowed and she crossed her arms. "*Her* bees."

"Grateful to her bees, then."

"I'd heard there wasn't a Lady in Grey no more but, North's sake, you could at least learn the ways of the rest of us."

"I will," said Kew. "I'm sorry." He swayed a little. With a gentle hand, Frin kept him from falling over.

"Come inside," said Robin, rolling her eyes. "You may have no manners, but I've got to see to you anyway. And you can tell me how in South's name you banged yourself up like this."

A Treatise of the Doctors of Grey House
(But as the Doctors Are Dead, It Is Forgotten)
Concerning Honey

*I*n the courts of Black Tower are many beehives, and 'tis wondrous
to behold their variety. On divers flowers are their bees fed, and
the Lady in Black Tower hath granted them the privilege of endleſs
ſpring, the which is for the better feeding of the bees. It is ſaid that,
from the end of the Roſe Era to the end of the Thiſtle Era, this honey
was of marvellous virtue, and each era produced its own proper virtue.
Howſoever that may be, none hath ſurvived the great downfall of the
Bellflowers; except, mayhap, in ſome loſt corner of the palace.

It is a maxim of the beekeepers that: The Thiſtle Ladies were Ladies
who fed on Thiſtle honey. This is a matter beyond our knowledge.
What honey can have been in that era but Thiſtle honey? Dr. Comfrey
LV hath written, that the Thiſtle Ladies produced a nectar of their own
ſubſtance, and from this the bees fed, and from it in turn made their
honey; and this honey, being fed to any perſon, produced such changes
in their fleſh as to render them of the ſame kind as any Lady born of
Black Tower. Dr. Comfrey LV likewiſe hath ſaid, that as all Thiſtle Ladies have vaniſhed from the palace, this is a matter of conjecture, and
cannot be taken as a true and uſeful ſaying.

Marvels have been reported ſcatterſhot by travelers through the Weſt
Paſſage, but never of the ſame kind, and by ſuch unreliable folk, that we
muſt believe none of them. In the mean time, aſide from its pleaſance
in the mouth, honey is of great uſe in curing wounds and burns, and
ſoothing ſore throats, and looſening ſtoppages of the bowel.

9. The Beekeepers and Kew Come to an Understanding

Before Kew slept, Frin took him to an apothecary who looked more like a set of ears than a person, and the apothecary gave Kew a small lump of honeyed meat.

"Mellified ape," he had told Kew. "It'll do in a pinch, but North bless me, we live in a world seeming made of pinches."

"What would you rather have?" said Kew, chewing.

"Mellified man, of course," said the apothecary. "Fixes all wounds of violence or accident. A powerful great thing to have around, but it's long since any man went into the casket for another."

"I see," said Kew. Medicine was a matter for apothecaries and doctors, not Guardians, and Hawthorn had taught him very little about it. If he had not been so achy and sleepy, he would have asked a great deal of questions, but he was *so* achy and sleepy, and questions would have to wait until the morning.

Thirty Robin led him to the mess hall where she and the other bee-keepers, all various numbers of Robin, ate their evening meal. It was chiefly bread and vegetables. Then she put him to bed in a half-empty dormitory, where a lot of no-name apprentices like himself also slept, and told him and them he needed to sleep and there was to be no nonsense about that. Obedient to Robin's orders, none of them tried to speak to him, and he slept the whole night through.

If he expected the meat to heal his hurts overnight, he was disappointed, but he was still much better in the morning. The mellified ape had fixed his hands and feet, but his bruises persisted, so when he awoke he was quite stiff. Frin had to help him into his breeches, doublet, and sleeveless overgown. It was much more clothing than the beekeepers wore: they all had beige tunics and hose and black hoods, simple and practical. Next to them, Kew looked like a courtier from some old manuscript.

"What's that on your forehead?" said Frin.

"Probably a bruise or something," said Kew. "I feel *made* of bruises today." He flexed his hands and fingers to loosen up the joints.

Frin did not disagree, only looked at him strangely. In the mess hall, the apprentices and the beekeepers broke their fast on more bread, this time with fruit and small beer.

"I would have thought you'd eat honey," said Kew.

Frin looked at him even more strangely. "It's *her* honey," he said. With his rabbity ears and large, round, orange eyes, when he made that face at Kew, it was more amusing than anything else.

Kew packed up his things by noon and went to take his leave of Thirty Robin. At his farewell, her face became very blank.

"Didn't Frin tell you?" she said. "One says you're staying here."

"I *can't* stay here," said Kew. "I have to deliver a message to the tower."

Thirty Robin shrugged. "My boy, you're to stay here until Her Ladyship arrives."

Kew sighed and leaned against the wall. "When will that be?"

Thirty Robin shrugged again. "She's on progress. Left here a bit ago, will be back—oh, One will know. Might as well go ask her, if she's not busy."

One Robin had a little office up in a turret overlooking the huge central garden of the beekeepers' district. She was sorting through handwritten schedules and making notes on a wax tablet when they entered.

"He can't go," she said without looking up.

"I told him," said Thirty.

One Robin appeared to be made of bluish membranes, and it lent her frowns a grotesque, fearsome aura. "Boy, remind me of your handle?"

"Kew."

"A no-name delivering messages from Grey to Black? Now I've seen it all." One sighed and rubbed her forehead with near-translucent hands. "Kew. The Obsidian Lady, whose fief this is, don't take kindly to strangers. All the Ladies round about the tower's foot hate each other. Always fighting, and when they're not fighting, planning to fight. So there's spies everywhere. Does any of this make sense to you? I hear Grey's a bit out of things."

"I understand," said Kew stiffly. As if he wouldn't. The very idea!

"Good. Now Her Ladyship would *not* forgive us, not *ever*, if we let a stranger come and go. We are the beekeepers for all of Black Tower, and that's a powerful big responsibility, but she'd squash us without a second thought if we went against her. As I hear it, Grey has no Lady. Correct?"

"The last Grey Lady died at the end of the Bellflower Era," said Kew even more stiffly.

One Robin waved her hand. "Sure. Been a while, is my point. The mothers of our mothers' mothers would have died and gone knowing the Grey Lady as a distant legend, so for a squirt like you, any sort of Lady must be incomprehensible."

"All Ladies are," said Kew. If he spoke any more stiffly, his voice would snap in half.

One Robin chuckled. "In the old days, maybe. The Lady in Yellow, who they say is an original, brings it forward to the present. But around the Great Tower we've got Ladies who are pretty shitting understandable. They all dream of taking the tower for themselves, and nothing gets in the way of that dream. Not love, not honey, not their own sisters. And I'm sorry for whatever your message is, and I hope it's not urgent, but I won't risk my women for you."

"Hawthorn always told me they were all petty upstarts," said Kew. "Bits of broken lineages that just haven't been swept away."

"Begging the pardon of the Guardian's apprentice," said One Robin, "but talk like that is the quickest way to get yourself killed, and more'n likely half of us into the bargain. Obsidian may be nothing more than a piece of fallen Apple, and she may need our honey to keep her trim, but she's still a Lady. And her word is law. Grey or no Grey, you'd best be obedient."

Kew met her eyes but said nothing.

"Anyone from Grey'd have to be stubborn to survive this long," said Thirty. "Must be bred into 'em."

Kew still said nothing.

One Robin chuckled again and shrugged. "I spose that's how it'll be then."

She went to a little niche in the wall, where a padlocked wooden chest hunkered. She took a key from around her neck and put it in the lock.

"Are you sure?" said Thirty. "He's just a no-name boy. He don't know what he's doing."

"I know what I'm doing," said Kew with a frown.

"Good," said One Robin. "So do I."

She turned the key and the chest sprang open. Her soft hand snatched at the air and she cooed and trilled to whatever her fingers had closed on.

"Hold him, Thirty."

"Sorry," said Thirty Robin, and caught both his wrists before he could move. She was very, very strong, and when she put her hand on the back of his head and pushed down, he had to let her tilt it or his neck would break in half.

One Robin showed him what she held. It was a yellowish insect with large eyes and transparent, fluttering wings. Instead of jaws, it had two bright blades, and its legs came to fine, needlelike points.

"This is a hornet," she said. "If you leave our domain, it will kill you."

She set the hornet on the back of his neck. Six sharp pins jabbed him. He sucked in his breath.

One Robin knelt down to his level and, as he gasped and shuddered, took his chin in her soft hand. "I am truly truly sorry," she said, lifting his head so he could meet her eyes. "None of this is what I want. Now, if you pass the walls of the beekeeper courts, the hornet will drive its mandibles into your neck, snipping your spinal cord like a rose stem. If you try to take the hornet off your neck, it will drive its mandibles in, snipping your spinal cord like a rose stem. If anyone else tries to take it off—well, I think you get the idea."

She waited as he got his breathing under control. "Do you understand why this is happening?"

After a moment, he nodded.

"I would hate for you to hold this against me," said One Robin. "I truly would. But I understand if you do." To Thirty Robin, she added, "Has he made friendly with anyone at all?"

Thirty shrugged. "He spent a little time with Frin."

"Right. Have Frin shadow him as much as possible." To Kew, she said, "Frin is going to try to keep you alive. Do you understand?"

He nodded.

"I am sorry," said One. "I can only say it so much, but I am. Now we wait for the Lady."

"How long?" said Kew, through loose, shivering lips. The hornet hurt more than he could have ever imagined.

"Perhaps two weeks," said One. She sat down at her desk again. "You can help out as needed in the time you're with us. And please do not hold what I've done against any of my people. I decided to do this for them; that don't mean they would have wanted me to."

It turned out to be fifty-four days. He tallied them with marks on his bedpost. On the first night, he stood with the beekeepers watching the tower. Visible through its tiny windows, a thread of light was making its way from cellar to throne, and he knew he had missed the Sparrows' dance. On the fourteenth day, he went to a window overlooking the Passage and thought about jumping. It was not too far down. The hornet's legs tensed up as he stood there, and he wondered if it would be very painful to have one's spinal cord cut. Was it the sort of thing you could survive?

Hawthorn's face came to him. If he left now, he would surely die. If he stayed, he might live long enough to reach the tower. A Guardian must protect, but a Guardian must also know how to read a fucking situation. Hawthorn herself had said that one day, when Kew had tried to protect another child from bullies and had been soundly beaten for his trouble. It was not her most inspiring maxim, but it had stuck with him. He turned and went back to the court.

His stay was not unpleasant. The court was a place of eternal spring, where flowers bloomed constantly, and a place of eternal autumn, where fruit was always ripening. And *trees,* living trees! The spindly dead things of Grey Tower could not have prepared him for their lush greenery, the sheer fragrant life of them. It was almost worth being imprisoned.

Every day he practiced the fighting forms Hawthorn had drilled into his skull. Frin found him an old barrel stave, and with this meager weapon he put his body through each set of movements. There were few of them, at least compared to the endless droning chants he'd always heard the girls practicing, but each was demanding and rigorous. The Beast could look like anything when it came; the one who fought it had to be equally adaptable.

Every week or so, a Butler Itinerant arrived on a hollowman and was loaded up with casks of honey to take to those who, by ancient custom, were owed it. Despite his curiosity (or perhaps because of it), the beekeepers didn't let Kew help with loading; all he saw of the fabled hollowman was a curve of dull white flesh. And every two weeks, a delegation arrived from Black Tower itself to collect a barrel of honey for the Willow Lady, ineffable ruler of the whole palace. Kew, who could read and figure, unlike many beekeepers, found himself unexpectedly useful in these encounters. This helped distract him from the anxiety haunting every hour: that the Beast was coming, and it could be here tomorrow, or it could arrive a year from now.

Between these arrivals he helped Ten Robin with inventory. The previous One Robin had left things in a shambles, and the current One had spent the first three years of her regime trying to clean everything up. There were, it seemed, several different kinds of honey. To Kew, who had grown up only with what honey the little court of beekeepers in Ginkgo's district produced, this was an astonishing development. Every flower made its own flavor, which the beekeepers carefully managed. The hives were pastured in set places and times to produce specific blends, and these were prescribed by tradition and need: the Order of Transit, for instance, required one yearly cask of apple blossom honey, so there always needed to be two or three of them on hand in case of a bad year. Other groups or places had their own requirements, from the buckwheat honey sent to Red Tower's Sisterhood of the Hearth, to the clover honey for the farmers of Yellow's outer mansions. The Library of Black Tower got a little beribboned cask of azalea all its own. To a boy who had spent his entire life accumulating facts, it was all fascinating.

More than all those details, though, he learned a great secret of the beekeepers, entirely by accident. Ten had sent him down to Cellar 37 to count the casks there, and as he totted them up, he heard someone coming. Not being in the mood to talk, he ducked behind a rack of empty casks, and saw One Robin pass by, accompanied by Fifteen and Three.

"We can't keep doing this," said Three. "It's running out."

"We can dilute it with orange blossom," said One. "She won't know. And if she figures it out, we'll say someone must have siphoned off the missing bit."

"The Ebony Lady's cleverer than you think," said Three. "And if this arrangement breaks down—"

"You don't need to tell me," said One.

The three of them stopped before a blank wall, and One pushed on a stone about halfway up. A section of the wall swung away. Tiptoeing forward, Kew saw that the beekeepers had gone down a few steps into a smaller room off the main cellar. Wooden racks lined its four walls, and on the racks were glass bottles of honey. But not just any honey. There were bottles labeled Apple, Thistle, Bellflower, Lily, even Hellebore. Each bottle was meticulously dated. A deep thrill ran through Kew's body. Some of this honey was older than parts of the palace. Some of it had been bottled when there was a Lady in Grey. Some of it might even have been bottled in the lifetimes of the five sisters.

"It's the only thing keeping her a Lady," said Three. "She'll notice, I tell you."

One took a bottle of Thistle Era honey and tipped some of its contents into a jar. Even from outside the room, and even surrounded as he was by honey, Kew could smell it: the most delicious thing possible, golden-sweet and heavy as joy.

"If she's as clever as you say—or as clever as she thinks she is—she'll know we can't spend our entire store on her," said One. "She needs it, we have it, she'll do anything for it. If that means accepting a diluted supply, she will." She passed the jar to Fifteen. "Take this and fill the rest with orange blossom, then put it in the casket for Her Ebony Ladyship." She took down a nearly empty jar of thick, treacly Hellebore honey and spooned a bit into a green glass vial. This she handed to Fifteen with no explanation; presumably *that* was all business as usual.

Kew hid again as the beekeepers left the cellar. What had One meant? No point in investigating. He knew better than to meddle with the hidden room, but he stored it up carefully in his memory.

10. Winter Is Bad and Time Passes

All the dwellings of Grey had been on summer rations before the seasons collapsed on each other. The bounty of spring had already faded when winter came unannounced, and the fields and orchards were not ready for harvest, and in fact were in danger of being frozen away. Most of the fruit trees had been dead for years, and the snow was likely to finish off the remaining few. In Grey House, the women and girls continued for a good while yet, and all the people who made signs at them to avert ill fortune came crawling up the great steps to beg.

Pell had never seen most of them before. Though the cloisters of Grey spread wide around the tower, its population had always been small and scattered, requiring the services of the women for only two events in their lives, and when tithe-tide came every three months the same three representatives had always arrived to deposit their offerings of grain, fruit, and fodder.

Ginkgo LXXVII, steward of the south cloisters of Grey, was a tall, broad-shouldered woman with a puff of yellow hair where a bird or two nested. Before, she had brought sacks of wheat and barley and bundles of herbs and given them with quiet haughtiness. Now she was thin and concerned, and around her huddled a dozen withered people with the stooped backs of that region's farm laborers, like chicks around a hen.

Oak LXXIV, steward of the north cloisters of Grey, was a little man in lace. His ears rose up in feathery pink points over his head, though now they were bundled up in a large scarf printed all over with elephants.

Before, he had brought bales of hay and cords of firewood, and given them with many speeches and thanks, as if Yarrow and Arnica were Ladies of Grey Tower and not merely two old women who handled life and death. Now he was sallow and silent, and behind him in a short line were husky northerners.

There was a space between Ginkgo and Oak wide enough for another retinue, which they maintained in memory of the west cloisters. Nobody had lived in the west cloisters since the Bellflower Era.

Madrona LXXV, steward of the east cloisters of Grey, was an otter-furred person of middling height in a brown robe. As warden of the East Passage, they kept watch on the bridge and any trade flowing between Grey and the courts of Red and Blue. There was precious little of it, and Madrona's people depended on the other Grey districts as much as the house itself did. They brought a chipped dish of antique design, which even Pell could see meant that nothing had crossed the bridge in months.

Yarrow and Arnica received them in the great hall of Grey House. Yarrow explained to Pell that this was meant to reinforce the authority of the house over its satellites: though the women in grey were only the last tattered remnants of a vibrant, sacred court, they were still the legal successors to the Ladies. She (Yarrow) had long suspected the outlying cloisters of tithing their second-best to the house, and she knew for certain they were not providing the proper complement of children for the women in grey; she wanted to remind them that they existed on the house's sufferance, not vice versa. Pell approved.

Despite Yarrow's grand plan, custom forbade her or Arnica's use of the Lady's throne, which rose atop a dais of many steps, and all that sat enthroned there was dust. The chair itself was too large for a normal behind. When the Ladies had stopped being quite so large, a much smaller chair had been set up on the throne, reached by a flight of stone stairs, but even that chair and those steps were coated in dust, for the Ladies of Grey were no more.

Both women seated themselves on the second-lowest tier of the dais, and Pell sat at their feet. Light sifted down through the holes in the roof. Snow lay here and there, collected among the flagstones or piled up in corners by the drafts. Though the hall was ruinous and very cold, it was still impressive. The grandeur was a bit undercut when the outer court people arrived and the wind roared in through the open door, rustling the shredded tapestries and pulling one of them down entirely. But when the door was shut, the hall was full of awesome majesty once more, and since the women took no notice of the mishap, Pell would not either.

"Speak your piece and begone," said Yarrow in a bored voice. This was not only hauteur: the Ladies and their successors had used this formula to open their audiences since time immemorial.

"If this winter holds any longer, we'll have no food," said Ginkgo. "The orchards may be lost already, and the barley won't survive much longer." Even the birds in her hair were sober as she spoke.

"The arrested growing season and cold weather will deplete our stores of wood," said Oak. "It has killed the new saplings from Blue, and in the proper order of things we cannot get more for another year."

"And this," said Ginkgo (the birds in her hair fluttered), "is leaving aside the problem we've spoken of to you before, Mother. The cloisters no longer produce even a tenth of what they used to."

"The very soil is sour," said Oak. "It began in my father's grandfather's day, and the Mothers did nothing. Now we are lucky to get one year of growth before the trees die."

"We know," said Arnica.

"It is why the western cloisters were abandoned," said Yarrow. "The women remember." Pell was very proud of the grand melancholy with which Yarrow said this.

"The women remember but do not act," said Ginkgo, her tone supplying the respect her words lacked. "More than the west was abandoned in my grandmother's day, and all the women did was make a song."

"Grey cannot continue like this, Mother," said Oak, his tone supplying the disrespect his words lacked. "If the women refuse—"

Yarrow sat upright, the prickles on her hands standing at attention. Her eyes met Oak's. He was silent but defiant.

"We must appeal to Black Tower," said Madrona. "I've no doubt this is punishment."

"Perhaps we have been Ladyless too long," said Ginkgo.

"If that is the crime, then it took them a hundred summers to realize it," said Oak. (He was wrong, of course; the songs of Grey House told the real number, which was far greater.)

"Then it must be something else," said Madrona. "This wouldn't happen for no reason."

"We will not appeal to Black Tower," said Yarrow. Arnica sniffed derisively at the same time. "Grey has done nothing wrong, and I think it's likely this is the result of other courts' infighting."

"So we'll suffer for a crime we did not commit," said Ginkgo.

"The lot of Grey is to bear," said Yarrow. The spines on her hands and the back of her neck were stiff with dignity. "The lot of Black is to rule, the lot of Blue is to make, the lot of Yellow is to take, the lot of Red is to see and send, but beneath all these is Grey, the bedrock of the palace. And the bedrock does not say to the foot, 'Why do you tread on me?'"

"We learned the catechism as well as you, Mother Yarrow," said Ginkgo. "But it will not make our children cry the less from hunger, and it will not put the more grain into our bushels."

"The winter will end soon, I am sure," said Yarrow.

"We've had two months and more," said Oak. "And no sign of spring to be seen, I'll add."

"And there is no guardian," said Ginkgo. "They say after Hawthorn died, her apprentice left. Where is he? Find him, Mother! Confirm him in her place!"

"Why?" said Yarrow coolly. Nobody from outside the house knew how much Yarrow and Arnica disliked the old guardian. After the talk at the tombs, she seemed willing to let the office lapse just to avoid the trouble of a new one. With how much the women and girls had to do even without all that, Pell couldn't blame her.

"The songs all say winter heralds the Beast," said Madrona. Everyone made the sign to avert evil.

"If that were true, it would have come every time the wheel's wobbled," said Yarrow. "If the guardian's apprentice has chosen to neglect his duty, I've no power to summon him back and *make* him do it."

"But this winter," said Oak. "If he has neglected his duty and ended his line, is that not a crime? Might that not bring punishment?"

"No," said Yarrow. "If that were so, it would have happened with the end of the tutors and of the doctors. Yet we know it did not, and they were more useful in their time than the guardians."

The audience was not going the way she wished. Who were these farmers to question the Mother? Pell could see Yarrow dearly wanted to make these people say their catechisms and go to bed without dinner. That was only right, and yet they wouldn't be here if something wasn't very wrong. But Yarrow had to know best. She and her forebears had steered Grey through worse things than an errant winter.

"If it lasts—" said Oak.

"No one season has ever lasted longer than the span of three," said Yarrow. "Except when the Ladies took it into their heads to punish, and Grey has done nothing. Perhaps they wish to favor a different tower with a longer summer, but even then, such a gift must end soon, before it becomes a punishment in its turn. The wheel will move, and winter will end, and you will all feel foolish for your fear and panic. Go. To the glory of the Lady."

There was nothing more for the others to say, not if they wished their young born and their dead buried, so they took their leave. A swirl of snow followed them out the door. With brow knotted, Yarrow rose stiffly from her place and dusted her bum.

"I almost believed you myself," said Arnica.

"Damn this winter," Yarrow said, stretching backward. Her spine went *pop pop pop* like a set of knuckles. "Fuck it South *and* North."

Cursing! In the hall? Pell stifled a noise of disapproval. Arnica seemed to hear it anyway and gave her a crabbed grin and a wink.

"What's to do about it?" said Arnica.

"Pell, take the other two and make a full inventory of larder and granary." Yarrow bent forward, and her spine made the same popping noises in reverse. "Servant will have the keys. Bring me the tallies and we'll go over them. If there's extra, as I'm sure there's not, we'll send it to the outer cloisters with our compliments."

It was on the tip of Pell's tongue to ask about the sour soil. Nobody had mentioned it in her hearing before. But then, the business of the women was birth and death. They would only act if extraordinary circumstances required it. Since they hadn't acted in this matter, nothing must be required of them. Anyway, Yarrow was always a little touchy after tithe-tide. How much touchier she'd be after *this* mess!

The girls spent the rest of the day following Yarrow's orders. A surprising amount of food lay hidden in the recesses of the larder, though some of it was so old that Ban was certain nobody could eat it and live. Past the shelves of fresher fare they found jars of figs preserved in honey, olives in brine, cheese in waxed wrappings, heels of bread, sacks of nuts and dried fruit, crock after crock of pickles. There were also several small dusty miracles: crimson bread on a silver plate, a jug with a mouse running endless circles inside it, a little wooden bee. Ban tried to pick up the bread, but it screamed and writhed and bled, so they left it and the other miracles alone.

The figs were still good—over Pell's protests, Grith opened one jar "to try some" and wound up eating the contents with Ban's help—and they had some hope of the olives; but the cheese had shrunk to wrinkled, moldy disks; the bread was of course wholly inedible; and while the nuts and fruit seemed all right, the pickles were of such a vintage that, when opened, the air itself turned to noxious vinegar. Ban found a small crock half-full of meat preserved in honey, but none of them could read the label, and the bits of meat were too small and few to be useful. So the larder did not come out very well, all things considered. But in the granary, they had enough sacks of meal and unmilled grain to last Grey House through nearly a year.

Yarrow had them pack up food (more than Pell expected her to give away) and load it onto Monkshood's little fish-drawn cart. The old man drove it off through the long white afternoon, and the women and girls went back to their lives.

Winter or no, there was much to be done around Grey House. Some rooms were cleaned for convenience's sake, others for tradition's. The Lady's Bedchamber, for example, must be swept once every seven days and the chamber pots ritualistically emptied out of the window. They never contained anything but dust and the occasional spider. One of them had been broken in ages past and replaced by a dented copper pot; Yarrow always said it was the action that mattered.

The bed in the chamber was huge, as big as a room all its own, but its deep, soft mattresses and quilts were sagging and rotten, and the silvery hangings faded and moth-eaten. Forty could have slept in the bed; in the old days, they did so for warmth, with the women clustered around the great Lady like kittens around their mother. But nobody slept there now. Every night, Arnica closed the bedcurtains, humming the minor-key tune of The Lullaby of Reeds. Every morning, Yarrow mounted the stairs and opened the bedcurtains, saying in a desultory voice, "Wake, Lady, and look."

This room was at the top of one of Grey House's turrets, and its three windows faced north across the cloisters' slate roofs to Black Tower. Pell would always take a moment from her sweeping and lean on the windowsill, her eyes fixed on the dark thorny mass from whence all power in the palace flowed. Its huge buttresses, its arched windows like yawning mouths, its banners and its intricate spires, its crown lost in mist, all frightened her. But generations of Ladies and their handmaidens and children had worn the sills down until they were soft as silk; initials were carved in corners or pilasters, in writing so old that even if Pell could read, she wouldn't understand them. All that history was a great comfort. If her tower was the heart of the palace, Grey House was the heart of the tower, and the Bedchamber was the heart of the house.

If she wasn't cleaning the Bedchamber, Pell was helping clean the rooms they *did* use: the kitchen, the southern side-hall, the dormitory and schoolroom, the Mother's study, and the long upper hall. Other rooms were half-kept up, like the southern turret chamber where every nine days Arnica went to the window and looked for a flag to be raised over Yellow. There never was a flag, and Arnica didn't know why she had to look for one, but look she did, and so there must be a path for her to walk. On either side of her path was the debris of years that filled most of the house. There were miracles and spinning wheels and old chests and broken statuary. Some of these things had names all their own, as if they were important once, like the Serpentine Girl whose hair held flowers. None of that meant anything now to the life of the house. Sometimes Yarrow would take it into her head to set some disused room or other in order, and she, Arnica, the girls, and Servant would tie cloths over their mouths and rummage through the dust and cobwebs, poking any miracles they found with the leg of a chair to be sure they were dead. None of these attempts lasted beyond a day: not even Yarrow relished dealing with all the pleading spiders, or the miracles that could make your eyes bleed, or the choking dust. Anyway, nothing could be gotten rid of: it was all sacred for some reason or other.

On fine days, Pell and Ban had to work in the garden, tucked in a courtyard beside the house. That was generally pleasant, though sometimes things crawled out of the ground. It was up to Ban to smash those between two rocks, and there were more and more as the days went on—though no rats, thankfully.

When there were no chores, there were lessons. The three girls sat together at a desk in the long, empty schoolroom while Yarrow or Arnica drilled them in lore, herbs, body parts. There were books in the schoolroom, but the women in grey had never written down their trade, and so Pell and the others never learned what the mildewy pages contained. The women possessed ancient arts of memory—taught to them, it was said, by the Lady herself. You had to make a place in yourself for knowledge, a little palace, and populate it with striking images. To remember the use of *arnica,* you might think of a person beaten black and blue, and from their bruises grew the tiny yellow flowers of that herb. The litanies helped; you would sing them to yourself as you walked the corridors of the palace in your memory. Some things, like slabroom lore, were striking enough on their own that Pell didn't need to add them to her memory so carefully, but she did it anyway, and the rooms of her mind were soon lined with bright caskets full of bodies. You would get a rap on the knuckles for poor memorization, but if you did particularly well, Arnica might give you a bit of candied angelica. Ban was best at sums, and Grith was best at herbs, but Pell was best at anatomy and recitation.

After lessons ended at noon, the other girls had a few free hours. Pell, however, was taken to the slabroom for more instruction. Yarrow had marked her out as a successor, which was a great honor, but Pell found she missed playtime with Grith and Ban. Though they were no longer small children, they still had games to play in the vast rooms of Grey House: hide-and-seek in the Gallery of Images, tag in the courtyards, featherball in the upper hall. Now Pell was to be a woman sooner than the others, and must leave games behind.

In place of the games, Yarrow would sometimes tell Pell things about the house's past. The court had been more populous when Yarrow was a small child. There was no Lady even then, but the women in grey had numbered a full score, and the girls twice that. There had still been tutors in Grey House, and a chamberlain—small and mean though he was—and a butler, and even a doctor, who was pleased to take a glass of honey wine with Yarrow's predecessor of an evening.

It was not all dull. The more Pell learned about the passages and chambers of the body, the more she wanted to know, and Yarrow was pleased to teach her—as pleased as Yarrow ever was about anything. For most of her life, Pell had thought Yarrow was strict and parsimonious simply because adults needed to be strict. Now she began to realize that Yarrow truly loved Grey Tower, and under her stern outside, the woman felt a child's unreasoning fear of the court crumbling away entirely. Rules were the means to shore up her home: even if Yarrow broke them herself, she would ensure the next generation followed them to the letter. Teaching the function of the gallbladder or the proper song for a dead tutor made Yarrow a little less afraid for the future, and so Pell learned it.

About six weeks into winter, lessons came to an abrupt end when Yarrow slipped on some ice in the courtyard. Inside the kitchen, the girls heard the *whump* and the scream, and they raced out. Yarrow had fallen against the fountain, striking her spine right in its center then sliding heavily to the ground. Between the girls and the stricken woman was a smooth sheet of ice where they had spent a glorious hour sliding the day before. Now they had to cross it with tiny careful steps, waving their arms like dolls held in a careless hand, and meanwhile Yarrow lay just ahead of them and moaned and cried.

Pell told Grith and Ban not to move Yarrow. She sent Grith to find Arnica and took her own cloak off to cover Yarrow. Ban did so as well. Yarrow cursed volubly.

After half an hour Grith and Arnica returned, moving with the same ridiculous gait across the ice. Arnica felt about on Yarrow's body and looked very grave.

"Get Monkshood and his barrow," she said, and Grith set off again across the ice.

"Doesn't look good, does it," said Yarrow through gritted teeth.

"Bout as bad as ever I've seen," said Arnica.

"I'm sorry," said Yarrow.

"Not sorrier than I," said Arnica.

It seemed hours before Monkshood and Grith returned, pushing the wheelbarrow before them.

"It's sorry I am, so so sorry," said Monkshood. "It's only that it wanted cleaning out first, it being full of dry leaves—Mother."

"We'll slide a cloak under her," said Arnica. "Two, more like. Then we'll each take a corner and heave-ho into the barrow and get her up the stairs. Yarrow, it'll hurt like fuckall."

Yarrow nodded, her face very red with two tiny tears frosted over in the corners of her eyes.

Getting Yarrow into the wheelbarrow was no easy task: she was by far the tallest person in the house, and her lower half was limp. She screamed and cried whenever they touched her, which was very horrible and pitiful to hear. But at last they succeeded, though her calves dangled out the front, and push-pulled her carefully over the ice, up the stairs, and into her own bed. Arnica left to get a dose of poppy for her, while the girls and Monkshood lined up against the wall, uncertain what to do.

"Everyone out," said Yarrow, her voice now low and hoarse. "Except you, Pell."

They obeyed quickly and with an obvious sense of relief.

"Come here," said Yarrow. Her hands resting on the thick coverlet were still and pale; when she raised one to beckon, it fell back down again as if it weighed ten tons.

"What is it, Mother Yarrow?" said Pell. "Do you need anything?"

"There is no way this turns out well for me," said Yarrow. "I fear bleeding inside, and my spine slides around itself. Even if I live, I'll never be able to go about my duties."

Pell said nothing. She sensed something enormous on the horizon, and feared to speak lest it recede again, or worse, speed up.

"I am Yarrow LXXV," said Yarrow. "Before this winter ends, maybe even this week, you will be Yarrow LXXVI, Mother of Grey House."

11. The Apprentice Meets a Lady and He Is Given a Quest

On the fifty-fifth day of Kew's imprisonment, Thirty Robin and her friend Twenty-Nine joined him after breakfast and took him to the garden. It was a beautiful sunny morning, and the flowers glowed like gems amid the enamel-green grass. Fruit trees bloomed here and there, wafting their fragrance about as they stirred in a gentle breeze. Above the courtyard roof, Black Tower shone as dark as a snake's scales, its windows bright as eyes. Banners broke from its spires, yellow and red and white, echoing the flowers below.

In the midst of the garden, the hives wandered. They varied somewhat in size, but all of them were more than a head taller than Kew. The fur on their bodies was glossy and smooth, but shaggy at the neck and tail. Dainty ebony hooves flashed in the sunlight. All of them had pyramidal spires for heads, as tall again as themselves. They were pierced with small windows through which bees came and went like lanterns from the tower.

"Ladyship should be here soon," said Thirty Robin.

"And you can leave," said Twenty-Nine Robin to Kew. She scratched her beard in agitation.

"Don't mind Two Nine," said Thirty Robin. "She just don't want to get back on Her Ladyship's bad side."

"How did you get on her bad side before?" said Kew.

"Harbored a traveler through the West Passage," said Twenty-Nine. "*They* were a no-name from Yellow, whilst *you* claim to be an apprentice from Grey, but still. Everyone from outside's a 'spy' to Her Ladyship. She thinks you'll keep her from ever reaching the tower."

She made a reflexive gesture of her right hand, aiming middle and ring fingers at the black mass above the rooftops.

"Reaching the tower?" said Kew.

"A moment," said Thirty. "Under the apple tree. It's dropping."

She ran back inside. Twenty-Nine ran forward. Kew whirled between them for a moment as if pulled by two opposing ropes, then followed Twenty-Nine to see if he could help. She was headed for the tree, where a fat dappled hive was spreading its back legs.

"Bucket bucket bucket bucket," Twenty-Nine was saying as she got behind the hive. She cupped her hands below its rear. "Bucket bucket bucket."

"Bucket bucket bucket," came an answer from behind Kew, and he dodged aside just as Thirty ran up with a wooden pail in each hand. "Bucket bucket bucket."

The hive's bees buzzed in unison, like a groan. Twenty-Nine held the bucket with one hand and patted the hive's flank with the other. The bees buzzed again. With a wet *splut,* the hive's urethra opened and a stream of thin, clear honey oozed down its fur and into the bucket.

"Good girl," said Twenty-Nine. "That's it."

"Looks a bit early," said Thirty, bending over to look at the trickle. "Kind of pale *if* you ask me."

"Nobody did. Still—" Twenty-Nine swiped some up on her index finger and held it up to the light critically. "Could be thicker and goldener."

"They should've held on to it longer." Thirty leaned over to the hive's head. "You should've held on to it longer."

"Oh, hush," said Twenty-Nine. She licked her finger and hummed with pleasure. "Still good. Could be better, but still good. Her Obsidian Ladyship'll be pleased."

"Aw, shit," said Thirty. "Aw, *shit*. Just remembered. One had a message before breakfast."

"What of it?" said Twenty-Nine.

"*She'll* be here tonight! She'll want her proper sip!"

Twenty-Nine huffed a sigh. "Get her cup then. No, you soothe the queen, see if we can keep this coming. You, Kew. Go inside and ask anyone where the Lady's cup is and bring it here directly."

Kew looked at Thirty, who nodded. He obeyed. Frin was just inside the door with a diagram of bees, mouthing words to himself as if memorizing. Kew explained the situation to him.

"The cup is in the safe," said Frin. "Come with me. We'll see if Fifteen will open it for you."

Fifteen Robin was very old and a little hard of hearing, and she nearly tripped over her own white beard when she went to open the safe, but open it she did. Inside, amid a lot of objects of clearly ceremonial use, was a simple wooden cup.

"Careful with it, Grey apprentice," said Fifteen. "Thank North *I* won't be responsible for the consequences if *you* lose or break it—or worse, drink from it."

Kew and Frin ran back to the garden. The bucket was about half-full, and the trickle of honey had slowed to a thread of sticky droplets. Twenty-Nine took the cup and dipped up a little of the honey. When that was done, she and Thirty sighed with relief.

"It'd *never* do if you told Her Ladyship a hive had dropped and there was none for her," said Thirty. "Not even if you sang it to her with a golden voice."

"Ah, why'd you come, Grey-boy," said Twenty-Nine. "She'll think you came from Ebony, she will. And Obsidian and Ebony aren't exactly sisterly-loving at the moment."

The wind had been steadily rising as she spoke, which at first Kew took no notice of, but soon it was whipping everyone's clothes about and playing havoc with the trees' blossoms. A horn blew a deep call that throbbed in the stones of the walls and the very ground itself.

"Ah," said Thirty calmly. "She's early."

Twenty-Nine thrust the cup of honey into Kew's hands as if it were too hot to hold. "Here," she said. "Her Ladyship'll know you're not one of us, but if you offer her a treat she won't bite your head off. Immediately."

"She what," said Kew.

"Hush, hush!" said Thirty. "Follow us!"

On their way inside, Twenty-Nine paused a moment to leave the bucket of honey in the kitchen. Grabbing a towel to clean her hands with, she led the other beekeeper and the two apprentices through the mess hall and into a large cobwebby hall of polished but dusty stone. At its end was a great wooden door studded with bronze. Two guards stood on either side of it, sheathed in black chitinous armor like Sparrow's, and they held thin needly spears. The other beekeepers and apprentices were filing in as well, some of them still getting dressed or toweling themselves dry after a bath.

There was a change in the air. It did not come from the crowd, though at first it seemed to. A kind of hum or drone vibrated in the floorboards and into Kew's very bones. It grew louder and stronger until the door itself seemed to be shaking.

"What is that?" he whispered to Thirty. His voice was very loud in a room gone suddenly quiet.

Her, Thirty mouthed.

The door opened. Two immense hands crept into the hall, sleek and black as stag beetles. There was a suggestion of transparency at their edges, as if they were molded of glass. They moved like hunting jackals, attached to slender arms jangling with jewelry. One hand contracted until its index finger pointed down the length of the hall. All the beekeepers and apprentices turned their heads to follow it, and stepped aside as they did so, until Kew stood alone at one end of the hall, cup in hand, with that gigantic finger aimed directly at him.

"You'd better go in," said Thirty. "Don't worry. We'll go after."

He swallowed. Forcing his feet to walk was the hardest thing he had ever made himself do. To go farther into that *sound* . . . But the Lady might punish the beekeepers for his disobedience.

Sworn to protect.

The crowd closed in behind him as he walked toward the hands, which withdrew behind a veil of gauzy black curtains. He passed through the door, and the crowd followed him. Beyond the curtains was a room even higher and broader than the first, which now seemed reduced to the status of vestibule. There were tall, narrow, diamond-paned windows, but their light was baffled and scattered by many hangings of more black gauze. The hands retreated as Kew advanced, shifting the hangings aside but never revealing more than the long, glassy arms and the immense bangles at the wrists. Finally, the hands halted. One faced him, palm up, and he stopped walking. After a moment, the other came toward him, thumb and forefinger extended. Kew held out the cup. The great fingers closed on it delicately. An odor rose from them like cedar and lavender. At that proximity, the gems in the bangles were clearly visible. Each was a crystal orb inside which tiny red and yellow birds fluttered ceaselessly.

The hand took the cup and slipped into the shadows beyond the hangings. Slurps resounded throughout the room, and the beekeepers looked at each other nervously, like students awaiting the results of an exam. Soon the hand set the cup down on the stone floor, heavily slimed.

It is sufficient, said the Lady, but it tastes foreign. It is like the dust of graves. Who has given it to me?

"An apprentice from Grey," said One Robin. "We took him in for a night, and—"

Oh? said the Lady. How interesting. How *unexpected*. Especially after the last time.

Quick as thought, her hand shot back out and grabbed One Robin around the chest and began squeezing. She swelled up like a bubble. In a moment, the beekeeper would burst from the pressure.

"They rescued me," said Kew.

The hand paused but did not release One Robin.

I see, said the Lady. I must punish them anyway. They have been bribing Ebony behind my back. As if I could not defend my own fief, they buy her off with *my honey*.

"I am traveling to Black Tower with a message for the Willow Lady," said Kew. "I will give it to you if you like."

I have no interest in messages from Grey, said the Lady.

One Robin looked about to faint.

"It is of vital importance to the palace," said Kew. "You will be the first of the Ladies to hear it."

First of my sisters? said the Lady. I see what you are doing. But happily for you, my curiosity is piqued.

She set down One Robin, who immediately collapsed, gasping and choking. Nobody went to her aid, but Frin and Thirty stepped an inch or two forward as if they were on the verge of doing so.

Come in here, Grey apprentice, said the Lady, beckoning to him with one finger. It slipped away; Kew followed. The beekeepers murmured among themselves as he passed them. One Robin nodded to him, her face purple.

Beyond the last hangings was a great palanquin of black glass ten or twelve yards high, and nearly as wide as it was tall. Its roof was a web of spun glass rising to a flowerlike finial. Its linings and curtains were black lace and blacker velvet. Almost a tower in its own right, it was staggering to think of the power that could move such a thing.

In ranks on either side of the palanquin stood people in yellow robes. Obsidian plaques festooned their necks and wrists, and many of them wore long surcoats or veils of black. Three or four wore tall, spire-like hats, lined with openings in which goldfinches perched. None of the courtiers said anything to him, or even acknowledged his presence. The only sound in the room was a little dragonfly, buzzing in the window above the palanquin to land on the glass.

As he approached, the curtains parted. There was the Obsidian Lady. She wore a simple shift of black, but around her neck was a court's worth of gold. Her head was a cube of some dark substance like a talon, and many yellow eyes opened in its sides. Its base rested on three ornate pillars of the same substance. Three corresponding shoulders sprouted beneath them, leading to three arms, though one was severed just above the elbow and capped with chased gold. The parts of her that were not talon-like were the same glassy material as her hands. She sat cross-legged (or perhaps her lower body was naturally tetrahedral) upon mounds of black and purple silk, fringed with gold. On a perch dangling from the palanquin's roof, a bird with a long yellow tail swung to her left.

Kew averted his eyes.

"I will speak to you like this," said the bird in high, silvery tones. "I cannot hide my proper voice, and I do not wish this conversation to reach other ears than ours."

"I understand, Your Ladyship," said Kew.

"What is your news?" said the Lady.

"The Beast rises," said Kew.

Her several eyes blinked with a dry sucking noise. "I had wondered."

"Apologies, Your Ladyship, I had thought my news was fresh."

"Winter lies over Grey and spreads toward Blue. That means that either the wheel has been turned, or the Beast has awakened once more. You have confirmed this. I am in your debt."

"Surely your sisters must know." At the same time, he thought *Winter?*

The bird's voice carried some dry amusement. "The fiefs of Obsidian are outermost. I hear what happens in the palace long before them, if they ever hear at all. Those that do hear, likely do not care. I do not care either, except that I can use this to my advantage. Tell me. You taste of books and the grave. To whom are you apprenticed?"

"The Guardian of the West Passage."

The Lady sighed with her natural voice. The blood in Kew's body grew thick for a moment. The courtiers' eyes rolled back in their skulls. Some of them licked their lips.

"And she has sent you here."

"Yes."

"She did not come herself?"

"She is dead."

The Lady sighed again. "I am too young to remember the last gap in the chain of succession. It is not good to let the guardianship lapse."

"I had hoped—" Kew swallowed. "I had hoped an edict from Black Tower would instate me to the office and name of Hawthorn, in—in gratitude for my fulfillment of her order."

Her eyes narrowed in a kind of cosmic merriment. So might the stars be amused by a flash of lightning. "A small concern for a small person. What a mayfly you are. By the time I next draw breath, you will be dust."

"I know, Your Ladyship. And I am sorry to bother you with my concerns."

"You say I am the first Lady of Black to receive this news. If you complete one task for me, I will grant you what you seek."

"Yes, Your Ladyship, anything." The instant he spoke, Kew regretted it. Used to dealing with his own Ladyless Grey, he had forgotten: a bargain with a Lady should not be undertaken lightly. Promise them nothing, accept no promises from them: either obey only, or run. And yet, if winter lay over Grey . . . The courtiers whispered behind upraised hands.

She sighed a third time. Kew's vision swam with white spots. "Go to the next fief. Tell the Ebony Lady that the Beast rises and has granted my wish, and that I will ride it to the conquest of Black Tower."

"Will she believe me?" said Kew.

"She will believe that you believe it. She will pass you along to the next Lady, and the next, and so on, and so you will confuse my sisters in the tower" (her hand made the same gesture as Twenty-Nine in the garden) "and they will be unprepared, and I will follow in your wake, and they will be too distracted to oppose me."

"How can I believe it when I know it is not true?"

The silks beneath the Lady shifted aside. A long, wet, pink tongue emerged, studded along its length with pale beads or blisters. The scent of honey breathed throughout the chamber. Many courtiers gasped. Kew shuddered as the tongue came nearer.

Do not run, said the Lady. And Kew could not run.

The tongue-tip touched his head, right where Frin had stared earlier. A drop of her saliva slid down his forehead. With a murmur of delight, the courtiers admired the tableau.

"You bear a stain of our lantern light," said the Lady. "One of the oldest miracles. They say it makes one malleable and receptive. And so I can make you believe it."

Of course. So powerful and beautiful a Lady, so alive to the doings of the palace, unlike her insular sisters, would naturally know of the Beast and how to ally herself with it. So clever and wonderful a Lady, and so merciful. How fit to become the highest Lady of Black Tower, to rule the palace. The Beast was no danger. She had it on a chain like a fierce dog, and it would bite only at her command. He was honored to stand in the presence of such power.

"Oh, not so much as all that," said the Lady, and her tongue touched him again. His head cleared a little. What rubbish he had been thinking. She would ride the Beast, but it of course had its own plans and appetites, ill-suited to her own.

"I will use the Beast's wish to conquer the tower. And when you are Guardian," said the Lady, "you will rid me of the Beast. That is the truth."

"That is the truth," said Kew. The bird's feathers rustled. The dragonfly whirred out the window.

"Now go and deliver your message," said the Lady. "And do not be distracted by the delights within the tower. You will become everything you dream if you keep your wits about you."

"My Lady," said Kew. "You are the best and cleverest of Ladies."

I am, said the Lady.

A Story Told by the Mothers in Grey House: How Yarrow Got Her Name

This is holy and ancient knowledge.

There have been women in grey in the house for as long as the house has been, but they did not always have their names. When the First Lady of Grey Tower died, she had no name, for it had been taken, but her daughter, who ate of her flesh, became known as Madam Carrion. And the women in grey tended to her body. And when Madam Carrion died of yew-tree poison, her daughter, who ate of her flesh, became known as Yew. And the women in grey tended to her body. And so it was for years. Every Lady took a name; the name died with her.

The Lady named Yarrow lived in the Lily Era. She was a very great Lady: in her was the First seen again. For she took back the name of nameless Grey, and in it ruled well. All loved her, and she was very beautiful, and a powerful singer. But then Yarrow took sick one day. A plague had come from Red Tower, and all the palace groaned with the sorrow and pain of it. And Yarrow grew sicker and sicker.

One of her women, seeing this, determined to help her. This woman ate only honey for seven times seven days, until her excrement was honey, until her sweat was honey, until her tears were honey. Then she had the other women put her in a casket of honey, where she drowned in honey. And after seven times seven days, the flesh of her body was given to the Lady Yarrow to eat. The Lady grew strong again and her gratitude was boundless. In death, the woman was given the name Yarrow, and her apprentice took it as well, and so it has been passed down in a long chain of Yarrows through the long ages.

That is how all the women's names came to be. They are gifts for the worthy. And only the worthy may bear them.

12. Pell Becomes the Seventy-Sixth Yarrow and Arnica Has Something to Say

The Mother of Grey House? But I'm too young, Pell almost protested. But would you argue with a woman who thought she was dying? No, Yarrow must be spared that debate. Even if she would never walk again, she could teach songs and anatomy from her bedside or from a chair. The role of Mother was not dependent on the use of one's legs. It might still be all right.

Then again, Yarrow was not given to exaggeration or overreaction.

"Ar—" Pell swallowed and began again. "Arnica?"

"Arnica is an Arnica, and a good one. But of all the people in this house, you are the only one who can become a Yarrow."

"Why?"

"Only you care as much about Grey House as I do."

Pell doubted that was true—no one could care as much as Yarrow—but even at the best of times there was no point in arguing with Yarrow. And it all felt like her fault, as if she had somehow made the woman fall by wishing to become the next Yarrow. She took one of the woman's nerveless hands in her own and smiled. "You've spoken. I'll obey."

Arnica arrived, holding a small white cup half-full of dark liquid. "Drink up," she said brusquely, holding it to Yarrow's lips.

The poppy took effect almost immediately, and Yarrow fell into a stupor. Arnica pulled back the coverlet and began feeling around Yarrow's body with less delicacy than she had used in the courtyard.

"Spine cracked, of course," said Arnica. "Two or three ribs snapped, probably." She lifted Yarrow's shift a bit. There was a large, dark bruise all along Yarrow's right side, and the sharp quills that covered the woman's back had been broken or driven into the flesh. Even to Pell's less experienced eye there was clearly something wrong with Yarrow's rib cage. "Feel her skin, girl."

Yarrow was cold and clammy to the touch.

"That's bleeding inside, that is," said Arnica. "Poor Mother. North, I wish we still had a doctor about. Us women in grey are just for birth and death, not life."

Us women. Despite the horror and grief of the day, Pell felt a small thrill of pleasure and pride at Arnica including her in that statement.

"Can't we do anything?" said Pell.

"Keep her dosed with poppy and wait, is all," said Arnica. "If we had a bit of mellified man we might fix this right up, but it's been ages since any man went into the casket for another."

"Aren't there doctors in other courts?" said Pell. "Apothecaries, even?"

"Ain't an apothecary alive who could fix this," said Arnica. As she resettled the shift and coverlet, she added, "Ain't you or I know the way to one, either. Like as not we'd find an apothecary but get back to find Yarrow three weeks dead."

"You don't know how to find one?" said Pell. That couldn't be right.

"We're called to the outer cloisters as needed, girl," said Arnica. "We do our job, we come back. Ain't wandering around in the halls looking for anyone."

Pell stared at Yarrow, feeling the same sense of helpless shock she'd had when the mask broke. "So Yarrow dies."

"Don't pity her too much," said Arnica, using the corner of the sheet to mop Yarrow's brow. "She gets to leave all this mess behind." Her other hand made a gesture that took in, not the injured woman as Pell might expect, but the wall, the window, the white-shrouded roofs.

Yarrow grunted as if in assent.

Arnica left to find some water for her. Pell stood by the bedside and waited to be dismissed. The dismissal never came, not from Yarrow. Arnica sent her off to eat much later, and then the two of them traded off standing vigil by Yarrow's still form.

The old woman lasted about seven days. It was a dreadful thing to watch, and far fouler than Pell had any notion of. Yarrow seemed better on the third day, but then some illness set in that made her flushed with fever; she tried to toss and turn, injuring herself further until

Arnica used an old sheet to tie her down. The bed itself was soiled frequently: Yarrow's stool turned black with blood then vanished entirely, as she was unable to eat anything more than broth or the thinnest of gruels. The air in the small bedroom was nearly unbreathable, and Arnica came there less and less, either unable or unwilling to watch her old friend disintegrate.

Pell stayed. She owed Yarrow everything, and though she could not claim to be fond of the stern woman, she was accustomed to her as to a tricky step in a stairwell. Looking at the dying face in its nest of spines, she regretted much: not thinking better of Yarrow, or gossiping about her with the girls, or her tiny everyday disobediences that did not become a girl of Grey House. How pitiful Yarrow looked. How much better a girl Pell should have been to her. On the fifth day she began to hold Yarrow's hand.

Yarrow herself wandered in and out of consciousness. She was kept well-dosed with poppy, and even when awake her eyes seemed to be looking through a film of jelly. But she talked more than Pell had ever heard. There was so much to impart to her successor, and Yarrow knew that there was practically no time for it. The songs and lore inside her seemed to know it as well, for even when she was not fully conscious Pell heard her singing, in a voice now weak and tuneless, the proper verses for a dead crofter or a new child, as if the traditions she contained yearned for release.

With time even this subsided, and Yarrow's eyes became permanently wet with tears as she thought of all the knowledge that would die with her. Pell would sing back to her, at first to repeat what Yarrow passed on, then to soothe her. Surely, among all the songs of the house, there was one that would bring oblivion. But nothing helped Yarrow rest.

"You must swear," said Yarrow suddenly at noon on the sixth day. Though a quivering restlessness had seized her in the morning, she had barely spoken since the previous night, and her voice startled Pell out of a light doze.

"Yes, of course," said Pell in confusion. "Of course I will. Swear what?"

"To me, not to the house. The house takes its own oath. I ask something special of you, girl."

"What should I swear?" said Pell, wiping her sticky eyes with the cuff of her sleeve.

"To save them," said Yarrow. "From winter."

"How?"

Yarrow made a small but fretful movement of her chin. "Send to Black Tower. I was wrong not to. They will know. The Lady there can help. I was too stubborn. Swear to save the house, Pell."

"I do," said Pell. She put both her hands on Yarrow's. "I do."

Yarrow nodded, and with her restlessness calmed, she lapsed into sleep. At some point after sunrise, she was dead.

There were a lot of rituals to perform when a Mother of Grey House passed. Pell went through them at Arnica's instruction; they mostly had to do with cleaning, it seemed. Once clean, the body must be laid on the floor of the great hall and the girls must troop around it singing and waving small boughs of lavender. (The lavender was quite old and shed its leaves troublesomely.) Then it must be moved to the steps outside, and the girls must troop around it in the opposite direction, silently and with empty hands. Then it must be moved to the door of the tower, and once more the girls must troop around it in alternating directions, dropping grains of myrrh and shouting Yarrow's name. (Ban kept getting her directions mixed up and colliding with Grith.) Then the featureless slate mask of the Mothers was strapped over Yarrow's face, and they put her on a bier and carried her up the inside of the tower.

The air atop Grey Tower was as cold and stern as Yarrow herself. A few random flakes of snow fell, giving the mask a ridiculous cock-eyed face as they shifted the body up the steps of the Hand. In brief glimpses, Pell could see that winter lay over much of the palace; only Yellow and Black looked to be in summer still. That was something to worry about later.

At the top, Arnica nudged Pell. It was hard to whistle in the cold. Pell's first attempts were more like raspy breaths. But at last she managed the five notes, and soon the crows descended in a flurry of black against the white sky. As they feasted, Arnica drew Pell aside.

"I'm leaving, Mother," she said.

Pell stifled a sob. Was she to lose Arnica, too? The only person who knew what had died with Yarrow?

Arnica put a consoling hand on her shoulder. "Not quite yet," she added. "Ain't *that* selfish. But I always wanted to see the wide world. Never got to. I'm sorry for you and the girls, but there it is. I won't stay here to be frozen or starved or broken by winter. Rather die in some unknown corridor than here."

"But," said Pell, and found she could manage no other words. Could an Arnica even leave?

"One month," said Arnica. "I'll stay one month to tell you all I know, then I'm gone. What's here anyway but a dead tower and a dying house? Not just now, but for years and years gone. The Mothers ain't let me leave—beat me, even, when I tried. Then they died and *she* ain't let me leave. Don't be so hard as all them, Mother. Let me be as I am, and that's not a woman in grey. No matter how long I've been one, I won't ever *be* one. Ain't like you, who's born to it. But only forget to be a woman in grey for just a small moment and say I can go. Say I can, please, Mother."

Pell's mouth pressed into a thin line like a crease in a wimple. Arnica's pleading face embarrassed her. A woman four or five times her own age calling her "Mother" embarrassed her. Yarrow had died and left her with this weak old woman, this *problem,* and that embarrassed her too, with the knowledge that she was not ready, and that she was more alone than she had thought. The only thing to do was to end the conversation as quickly as possible.

"Go, then," said Pell. "Abandon us, if that's in your conscience."

Arnica smiled in pitiful relief. Her red-rimmed eyes now brimmed with tears of gratitude. She was the happiest anyone had been in Grey House for decades. Pell felt this, and it did nothing to make her friendlier to Arnica. How dare the notion of leaving bring such joy? Did years of dedication mean nothing?

The crows went on their way. Yarrow's bones dropped into the South Passage to lie with her foremothers. No butterflies came; it was too cold for them. Pell and Arnica gathered up the bloody stinking scraps of the shroud and returned to the tower's still heart.

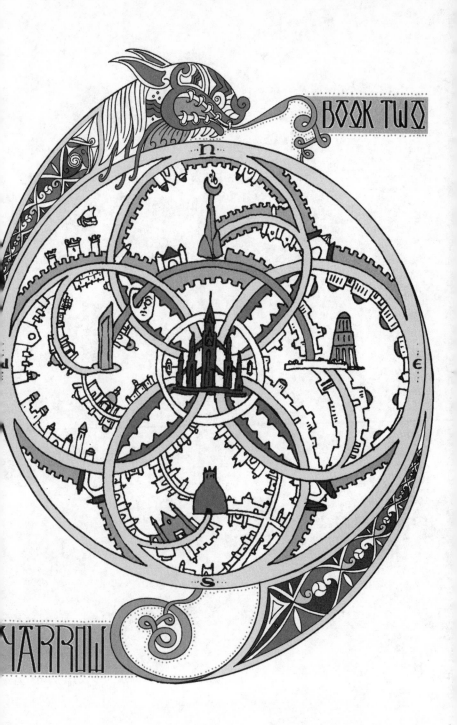

BOOK TWO

YARROW

13. Yarrow Does Some Gardening and Arnica Follows a Dream

There was a brief ceremony to instate Pell as the new Yarrow. She sat on the dais at the chair's foot and Arnica had her swear a brief oath, then dressed her in gown and wimple like a real woman, and handed her the rusty Keys of Grey House. Grith, small and frightened, brought a fresh-made leather apron and tied it around the new Yarrow. In fact, so we must call her now: no longer Pell but Yarrow LXXVI, Mother of Grey House, mistress of life and death, overseer of the Thousand Cloisters. She was perhaps sixteen.

Before the ceremony, she'd thought that maybe there were secrets she would learn once she was a woman in grey. Maybe there were locked rooms deep in the house that her new keys would open, where the treasures of the Ladies lay in dingy grandeur. Maybe there were hidden practices of the slabroom that Arnica would reveal to her, or Servant would tell her of a subterranean passage to the outer cloisters. Or maybe she would finally understand the purpose of all the disused chambers in Grey Tower.

The first night she was Yarrow, she lay awake in the women's bed, smelling the faint lingering smells of the Mother's death, hearing Arnica snore, and wondering what novelties the morning would bring. The first morning she was Yarrow, she had the same chores as ever. Why had she never noticed that, by and large, the women did the same tasks as the girls, just in different parts of the house?

But then she had to discipline Ban. That *was* a novelty, and an unpleasant one at that.

The rules of the house said that the Mother's orders had to be obeyed unquestioningly. The girls had frequently disobeyed the old Yarrow, when they thought she couldn't see or wouldn't find out. But the new Yarrow, having been so lately a girl herself, knew all the tricks, and the lax discipline of the house would not slacken even further under her regime.

"Go check the storeroom again," she said to Ban when they finished breakfast. "I want to see what's left after we sent food to the outer cloisters."

She waited half an hour, then went to the storeroom herself. As suspected, Ban was sitting on a sack of grain and eating figs.

"How *dare* you?" said Yarrow. "When we have so little—!" She gave Ban a resounding smack on the ear. "Go. *Go*. I'll finish this myself."

Ban slunk out of the storeroom, rubbing her ear. Yarrow closed the jar of figs and replaced the sack. Her hand stung. She went and raked the garden. When doctors had lived in the house, the garden had been full of healing herbs, but now the plants were as sparse as hair on Monkshood's head. There were clumps of yarrow, arnica, lavender, rue, mugwort, betony, and a few other things used for the women's duties, as well as sometimes in the kitchen. Everything else was dry stems, leafless trees. When the cold air had numbed her hand, she went back inside.

The second day she was Yarrow, she punished Grith for lackadaisical sweeping. The kitchen floor had to be clean, as clean as Yarrow had kept it when she was Pell. When scolded, Grith muttered *The old one was nicer* under her breath, and Yarrow cuffed her. Another garden bed was raked, this time around the great stone half-face in the eastern corner.

The third day she was Yarrow, she called Servant to the musty washroom to steam and wind her hair. The twigs of it needed to be softened and coiled up as they grew, or they would go out straight and stiff all about her head like a thicket. Each twig bore several leaves that dried and withered as soon as they sprouted, and had to be picked out. The steaming and picking had always been Servant's job. Before, she had done it by holding Yarrow's head over a bowl of hot water and jerking the twigs about until Yarrow cried from the pain. Now she wrapped soft hot towels around Yarrow's head and waited silently for them to do their work, and when she went about the winding, she did it gently and even reverently, weaving the twigs into fine basketwork close to Yarrow's skull.

"I am not used to this," said Yarrow stiffly. It wouldn't do to imply Servant didn't know her own work, but—why the change? Did Yarrow actually *miss* the roughness, because it meant she was no longer a girl?

"A Servant must never pain a Mother," said Servant. Her voice was crackly as old porcelain; Yarrow had barely ever heard her speak at all except to say *Yes, Mother,* or *No, Mother.* She took up a little jar of sweet oil (only slightly rancid) and worked it into the drying twigs with a flannel.

"A good rule," said Yarrow. There might be pleasant things to this, after all.

The fourth day she was Yarrow, she reprimanded Arnica for some slight fault, a fault she instantly forgot in the rush of having spoken harshly to a woman in grey. Would Arnica be offended? Had the new Yarrow overstepped? Memories of the schoolroom, of Arnica standing on the platform just a few weeks ago and teaching her, rose and choked her.

Arnica drew herself up to her full height, which was only an inch or two taller than the new Yarrow. She had no spines like the old Yarrow, no claws like Ban, no fur like Grith, no twigs for hair like the new Yarrow. She was simple flesh and bone, but nothing was more frightening than her anger. In a house of the old, it was the first new thing in years.

"Don't you try that on me," said Arnica. "Mother you are now, and Mother you'll remain, so you'd best learn now how far your power goes." She moved her hand up and down between her and Yarrow, as if running it over an invisible wall. "This far and no farther."

Yarrow drew herself up in turn and looked down her short nose at Arnica. The older woman was right, but if Yarrow did not insist on her authority now, it would erode away like Grey Tower itself.

Arnica only laughed. "Ain't it a sight," she said. Her anger was swallowed up in her amusement. "A girl just the other day, now she thinks she's the Lady herself. Well, Yarrow LXXVI, do you know what we are? The coals of a spent fire. That's your realm. That's all you are: a mother of ashes. Ain't any glory to be had here, nor any power neither. Grey's a heart all right, but one that don't beat, and nobody's yet put it to rest. Enjoy your rules, for soon that's all you'll have."

Laughing once more, she turned and left the room. In an hour or two, Yarrow would need to join Arnica and the girls in the refectory for dinner. A poor meal it would be: thinned-down gruel, no curds, only some dried fruit. Servant knew how to stretch out the meal and other staples, but from the schoolroom lore rose the specter of scurvy. It had not struck Grey House in decades, but the old stories kindled fear in Yarrow's stomach.

Arnica was right. But more importantly, she was wrong. This heart still beat. If the lot of Grey was to bear, then let it bear. Since stories began, the Yarrows had made sure of that. So this Yarrow, chilly with determination, went to wash for dinner. There was much to do.

Yarrow had half expected Arnica to storm off that evening, but the old woman was in the refectory when Yarrow entered. Arnica was not the sort to remember offenses very long, and seemed to have burned through all her anger simply by laughing.

When Servant brought the honey wine, Yarrow asked her to stay a moment. Then Yarrow rose. Everyone looked at her, and though she already had their attention, she rapped her spoon on the table as if to get it. Eight eyes stared at her, and for a moment her resolve wavered. But she was Yarrow, so she mastered herself.

"I shall leave in the morning," she said. "Someone must go and plead our case to the great Lady at Black Tower for the restoration of summer. Arnica has made it clear she wishes to leave our house, so I shall not burden her with the task. Girls, you will stay here in Servant's care. Ban, I will name you the temporary Yarrow, and Grith, if Arnica leaves before I come back, you will assume her place. I hope it will not take more than a week to reach Black and return, and no births are expected in that time, so you will be spared that duty. For any deaths, you both know what to do. Arnica, I do not ask you to delay your own departure, but please instruct them both as much as you can before then. Now let us drink our wine and be about our business. I have packing to do."

Arnica raised her glass to the North, then to Yarrow. "Mother," she said, and downed the wine.

Yarrow still was not used to the taste and effects of wine, but she followed suit, and Arnica laughed at her sputtering.

"Careful," said Arnica. "Don't want to find out what happens if *you* drink too much."

Grey House went to sleep, except for Yarrow. She found an old leather knapsack in one of the storerooms and packed it with her extra robe and wimple. In the larder, she filled a small cloth bag with dried fruit, a jar of preserved figs, and the little flat biscuits that were the only bread a Mother might eat. After a moment of thought, she added the jar of honeyed meat. It might be useful along the way, to trade if nothing else. Meat might not be plentiful elsewhere, either.

She laid her shoes and clothes out at the foot of her bed and attempted to go to sleep. There was no precedent in her emotional world for a Mother leaving Grey House. Of course it had happened, but not in decades, and the old Yarrow had told her no stories about it, only a song or two. Though it was meant to help the house, it felt like a betrayal. *Forgive me,* she wanted to whisper to the dark corners of the room. *I'll be back. Be good. Stay alive.*

But all that night the house creaked and settled, heedless of her. And Arnica snored.

In the morning, she took leave of Arnica, Servant, and the girls. They stood in the great hall and she said a few parting words. A speech seemed appropriate, but nothing grand enough came to mind, so Yarrow's chattering teeth only managed one sentence.

"I'll be back."

Arnica hugged her tightly, and she hugged Arnica back. Then she curtsied to Ban and Grith, who curtsied back after a moment. In the old days they might have hugged as well, but there was rank to be preserved, after all. Then Yarrow pulled her heavy cloak about herself, shouldered her knapsack, and was off.

A month later, with no Yarrow to be seen, Arnica left in the same way, and only two girls and an ancient handmaiden were left in the wintry darkness of Grey House.

14. Yarrow Is in the West Passage and So Are Some Other People

The first thing Yarrow did was climb the tower. She had no maps of the palace, and the top of Grey Tower seemed like a good place to get her bearings. It was very cold, and snow had buried the floor of the atrium up to the fourth step. At the top, Yarrow walked around the parapet, hoping to see an easy way through the cloisters to the South Passage. Yes—she'd reach it if she just headed directly south. Easy enough.

She placed the route carefully in the halls of her memory and went back down the stairs and into the Room of Masks. Respects must be paid to the mask of the Mothers. For her to leave, she needed to do them proper obeisance, all those generations of Yarrows before her. She was doing this for them. If they were conscious of her actions at all, she hoped they were pleased.

The mask of the Mothers was there, but the green mask of the guardians was not.

A great rage welled up from the soles of her feet to the top of her head. The worst sacrilege! Yarrow clenched her fists and two tiny hot tears came to her eyes. Who could have done this? Who *would* have done this? The mask *belonged* to Grey Tower! It had not left it once in all the long eras. Who would *dare* steal it?

She stalked out, rigid with anger. The mask had to be returned. No matter how difficult it might be to track down, no matter how far across the palace it had traveled, Yarrow would find the mask and bring it back.

Two duties burdened her now, one practical, one sacred. Yarrow was good at her duties. She was even better at doing them angrily. Fresh purpose came into her step and a granite gleam into her eye. And off she went toward Black Tower.

Rather than follow the first bit of her journey, let us look at what she did wrong. Her first mistake was heading south. To leave Grey, the only thing to do was head north. The old women had never bothered to tell her this most important principle of travel, so Yarrow, alone and ignorant, passed through ten cloisters before she suspected anything, and only when she came through a door to a broad open space did she know something was fully wrong.

She stood in an arched doorway decorated with grinning horned heads. Ahead of her, a long statue-lined avenue stretched into the distance. High walls flanked it, their turrets and crenellations gnawing at the sky, their stones blanketed by ivy. The statues themselves were all identical: old women, left hands raised with palm outward, right hands cradling a book. They stood on harsh green grass. The avenue itself was smooth stone.

Hot tears of shame and dread burned Yarrow's eyes. She was miles away from the river. She stood at the start of the West Passage, and Black Tower was nowhere in sight. Only Yellow rose before her, blade-edged enough to cut the eye.

When she turned to go back, the door had locked itself. Things like that happened in parts of the palace, she had heard: there were ancient stories of women in grey getting lost in the Passage attempting to get to Yellow or Black for births and funerals. Usually the stories ended with their bones being found by other women years later. But Yarrow had been so careful. She had taken the right road and everything, but here she was. For a moment, she nearly cried.

Then she squared her shoulders, tilted her chin up, and set one foot in front of the other. What good was there in waiting around? At least this way she would get *somewhere*. And perhaps this would work to her advantage: the Passage was a clear shot out of Grey, so there'd be no need to navigate the warren of cloisters and colonnades. The only cause for anxiety lay directly ahead: *The lot of Yellow is to take,* the saying went. The carrion crows came from there. Yellow Tower was not built to give an air of friendliness, but more than that: according to the old Yarrow, there was still the ancient Lady seated within.

A feeling of unease crept over her as she moved through the Passage.

It wasn't the silence; everything in Grey was quiet. It wasn't the lack of people. It wasn't the horizon, though she'd rarely seen one from ground-level before.

There. Once you noticed it, it was impossible to escape: the Passage was clear. No trash or loose stones scattered about. No husks of miracles in out-of-the-way corners. Parts of the walls had fallen in, but the piles of rubble had been removed. And the granite pavement had no potholes. There was nothing but her, the statues, and the pale tower ahead.

Though it grew no closer as she walked, she was able to see Yellow in some detail, certainly more than she ever had before. Its base was hidden from her by the Passage's convergence on the horizon, so there was no telling what lay around it. The tower seemed to have three sides and rise several hundred feet in the air. Its top was sheared off at a hard slant, with none of the turrets or crenellations that marked the other towers. No ivy or moss blanketed its walls; instead, a grooved border was incised along each of its edges, as if a giant had taken a pencil and underlined its harsh angles. Its few windows were dark and scattered randomly over the pus-colored stone. A few white birds fluttered about it, no bigger than dust motes in the morning sun.

The statues petered out and came to an end, though pedestals for many more marched along both sides of the road for some way. The smooth pavement roughened and became cobblestones. In some places, they were worn away to the ground, which a recent rain had turned into mud. The walls of the Passage grew ever taller and began to be pocked with windows and prickled with turrets. No faces looked out of the windows, many of which were closed with wooden shutters, or gaping open like dead mouths.

Crows lined the walls and wheeled overhead. Perhaps this was where they nested when the women in grey did not require their services. They called to each other, their rough voices echoing off the stones. Many stared at the little woman making her way down the empty road.

Yarrow did not like any of this. She liked it less when she came to a mud puddle laid across the road, and she liked it still less when in the mud she saw a handprint.

Not a reasonably sized print. It belonged to no hand you could comfortably shake. At least seven feet from heel to fingertip, it made five long ditches in the wet ground. Some considerable weight had pressed up the mud into ridges, all crackled and dry on their top edges. Worse than that, the near side of the mud was dented with a few crescents, as if the fingers of a second hand had been pressed there: each was as wide as Yarrow's torso. And still worse, prints were left on the dry stone beyond, getting less distinct as the dirt wore off, but continuing on in a straight line toward Yellow Tower. There were no corresponding footprints. Whatever had passed this way seemed to walk on two hands like a monstrous acrobat.

Going home looked like the safest option. Yarrow turned around and had actually taken a few steps when she saw the grey sky over Grey Tower. Nothing ever looked colder than that small, ancient pinnacle of dark stone, holding up its five turrets like fingers to ward off a blow.

Yarrow faced Yellow Tower and resumed walking. Her stomach rumbled. She had eaten nothing since early morning, so she sat on one of the empty pedestals and opened her sack. She planned to allow herself one biscuit and one fig. While rummaging for the figs, her fingers brushed something hard and flat in her spare robe. Biscuit in one hand, she searched the robe with the other and discovered the guardian's book still in her sleeve, along with candied angelica and a few buttons. She ate some angelica. The book she had no immediate use for, but as something that came from Grey House, leaving it behind would be unbearable. She replaced it in the sleeve. Someone she met might know what it meant.

After eating, with angelica-flavored honey gumming up her mouth, Yarrow was very thirsty. She had brought no water. The enormity of this mistake slid right past her brain: like the handprints, she could not fully comprehend it, only sense its passing. Perhaps farther down the Passage she might find some fountains. Grey had them all over the place, many of them scummy and disused, but nonetheless there.

She set off again. The air was still cold, but with more of a tingling springtime chill than the numbing deadness of winter. Yarrow gritted her teeth. It was quite shameful somehow that Yellow had spring while Grey's summer had been cut short.

The pedestals ended, leaving only two shoulders of brown grass on either side of the road. Lichen and moss spread over the walls. No longer smooth, they bulged with bartizans, bay windows, machicolations, oriels. They were much taller now, so that as wide as the avenue was, it felt more like an alley. After some time they began to hang over the grass, then the road. Yarrow came to a place where two buildings met in an enclosed bridge, pierced with lattices, and after that bridges and walkways were commonplace. The grass vanished, replaced with dark, vigorous ivy. The road went straight as straight, but the buildings pushed out of the wall and onto its stones, making Yarrow zigzag. They rose up in spires and crenellations and vast windows, as if the walls were dissolving into the air. But even as the buildings became livelier, the air, though warm, was dead. Yellow Tower with its white birds was lost beyond the profusion of roofs and bridges. No crows were to be seen. No laundry hung between walls. No footstep was heard but her own. No doors opened to let her out.

The ivy hung down in curtains from the bridges, intermixed with creeping thyme, which blossomed bright pink. Yarrow came to a place where the draped ivy completely filled the road with a tapestry of green. Butterflies moved in and out between the waving tendrils as if among the ribs of a corpse, perching here and there on slim pale limbs. Some of them had court dress on, others wore nothing at all. Their beauty transfixed her, and tears came to her eyes for some reason she dared not think about.

As she watched, a hand darted out of the ivy, snatched a butterfly, and withdrew. The sounds of chewing were heard. Yarrow gripped her bag, ready to run.

The leaves parted, and a red ape came out. A white chaperon covered its head; the dangling liripipe was soiled and frayed. Over its hairy body it wore an ill-fitting, pinkish scholar's robe. The ragged blue ends of a butterfly's wing protruded from its lips for a moment before it swallowed. After nodding solemnly at Yarrow, it proceeded to gather butterflies one after another and cram them into its mouth. Dribbling saliva soaked the front of its robe.

Yarrow pressed her lips together in thought. Could it talk? No way to tell just by looking.

"Good day," she said.

The ape looked over its shoulder at her, its tiny dark eyes completely expressionless as it chewed its iridescent snack.

"Could you perhaps—" Oh, confound it, how did the old Yarrow talk? How did she summon up that reserve of dignity? "—if it please you, show me where I might find some water?" She curtseyed quickly at the end. It was probably too much respect to show to this creature, but better safe than sorry.

Keeping its eyes on hers, the ape stuffed another handful of fluttering insects into its mouth. It chewed a moment, then showed its teeth in a grin full of butterfly guts and bright shreds of wing and gown. The ape swept another hand through the air, indiscriminately gathering butterflies and thyme sprigs alike, filled its mouth once more, then went back through the ivy. Was that a good sign? She waited.

The ape thrust its head out of the leaves and gibbered at her. It waved clumsily, then withdrew again. Presumably she was meant to follow.

Yarrow slid into the swaying plants. Ivy snagged on her clothes and wimple: she had to hold it in place as she pushed through. Thyme leaves rubbed their spiciness off on her. As she came out the other side of the vine-hung bridge, a blue butterfly landed on her nose and spread its wings, blindfolding her. A moment later it was gone: the ape had eaten it.

The ape and the woman stood regarding each other. They were in a sort of plaza formed by the corners of four buildings thrusting out into the West Passage. Beyond, the Passage rose up a hill to the clear sky, where the tip of Yellow Tower glowed in the noon sun. Between the plaza and the hilltop was a warren of buildings more ramshackle and looming than any Yarrow had yet seen. Instead of grey granite, they had become a warm brown sandstone. Delicate carvings flowered around the doors and eaves, and makeshift awnings of pink or blue or white fabric shaded the windows. Some of the windows had glass rather than lattice, though a lot of the glass was broken.

But there were still no people.

"Water?" said Yarrow.

The ape loped away from her on its short legs and long arms. For a moment of near-delirium she thought perhaps it was responsible for the handprints, but it walked not on splayed fingers but curled-up knuckles, and of course it was far too small. She had never been so thirsty in her life.

Straight on under more overgrown bridges went the ape, past empty windows and lichen-bearded walls, its limbs making soft flabby noises on the cobblestones. Straight on went Yarrow in its trail, trying not to think of cold water from the house well, or the drops she had caught on her tongue on rainy days, or the milk the women gave her as a child. Even the after-dinner wine would have been welcome. Her mouth and throat burned, and her head ached. Still the ape went on, at a steady, moderate pace, occasionally treading on the hem of its own gown, now and then snagging a butterfly to munch.

Yarrow did not for a moment think it could lead her astray: it was a relief to have someone to follow again.

They passed under another curtain of ivy, but when Yarrow emerged the ape had vanished. The crest of the hill was a few yards away, framed by two mismatched towers. Assuming she would see the ape from there, she went forward.

The Passage fell away before her feet at a sheer angle, so steep that for a moment she thought it was vertical. Stairs flanked it on both sides as it plunged to the bottom of a great circular valley, then continued on straight to Yellow. For the first time, she saw the foot of the hideous tower.

All around the vertiginous sides of the valley were mansions and courts of buttery stone, even more ornately carved than those in the Passage, and roofed with green copper. Many of them held fields or orchards, much like those around Grey, but these were flourishing. The courts were arranged in nine large rings, enclosing and enclosed by gardens full of lawns and topiaries and pavilions. Promenades and avenues linked them up; Yarrow thought she could see tiny figures moving along the roads. As she stood there, a white bird took flight from a nearby roof, drawing her eye along the valley floor.

In the center of the ringed courts was a wide maze of green, living hedges. Nine pools were scattered through the maze in no apparent pattern. Every one sported the white plume of a fountain, like an egret's feather in a cerulean beret. From each pool, a thin stream ran with uncanny straightness into the wide, still lake at Yellow's foot. A corbel-arched portal stood out from the tower's side. A sleek, dark boat was moored there, for the tower rose right out of the water. The bird winged up and up, and Yarrow took a simple pleasure in its flight. Then it passed in front of Yellow Tower and she realized that something was off. Aside from the familiar, violent ugliness of Yellow, some small element in the valley was amiss, as if the place were sick and didn't yet realize it.

The tower cast no reflection. The pools in the maze showed only sky and hedges; the lake held clouds in its deep blue, and quicksilver images of the white birds, even the high, thin bow and stern of the boat; but neither pools nor lake reflected the tower.

A horrid noise behind her startled Yarrow. The ape was poking its head out of an open window and making some awful *hoo hoo hoo* racket to get her attention. Eagerly, she turned her back to the bright sickness of the valley and went to the window.

"Water?" she said.

The ape retreated into the building. Yarrow waited. A door opened that she had not noticed, and the ape stood just inside, clearly expecting her to enter as well. She stepped over the threshold and out of the West Passage.

15. Yarrow Has a Drink

Inside, the place was furnished with the same dusty, decaying grandeur as Grey House. She and the ape were walking through what might once have been a sitting room, its furniture mostly threadbare damask and careworn walnut. A portrait on the wall showed a man with long white hair and fingers like scallions. The ape saluted it in passing with the automatic, perfunctory observance familiar to Yarrow from daily life in the house, where ritual was inscribed on the very bones of the inhabitants.

The ape led her into a short passage and then out a wooden door into a stone-paved courtyard. In the center was a stinking green pool fed by a sluggish fountain. Dozens of other apes were already there, each in a scholar's robe and chaperon. Two of them were grooming each other. One was defecating. All of them turned to look at Yarrow, then went back to what they were doing, except the defecating one. It kept its eyes on her absently while it finished its business. She stared back. At last it broke eye contact and waddled off to a sunnier corner of the courtyard, where it sat down with its feet in front of it and its long arms lying at strange angles like a broken doll, an expression of witless contentment on its face.

Yarrow's ape seemed to think its task was done. Surely she was not expected to drink the scum in the fountain's pool. It reeked of rot, and gnats flitted around it.

"Water?" she said. Then, more loudly and very hoarsely, "*Water?*"

"Oh my," said another voice. "Oh *my.*"

From a door on the other side of the courtyard stepped an elderly, owlish person with a staff of pampas grass stalks. They looked about with slow eagerness, their wrinkled head turning nearly all the way around to take in every angle of the yard. They wore a dark blue robe with huge bell sleeves and a high, rigid collar that nearly swallowed their skull. From within the edifice of this robe their thin wrists, thin bare feet, and thin neck protruded. They were bald, except for tufts of flour-white hair in two curling points on either side of their head, and their nose was flat and thin, coming to a delicate beaky point just above their upper lip. Thick saucer-sized spectacles magnified their golden eyes, which were already quite large and round, until their face seemed to be all eyes. When they saw Yarrow, their eyes became even wider, threatening to absorb the nose and mouth entirely.

"You're not one of mine," said the owlish person. Their teeth were very small and white. The tufts of hair quivered with some emotion, as did the knobby hand which clutched the staff, and the tufts atop the grass stalks quivered in their turn, until the entire person vibrated in the stiff blue shell of their robe, which itself remained unmoved. "I did think—" said the person. "For a moment—" they said. "But *no*."

They snaked their hand into their robe and took out a brass bell, which they rang three times. The apes all came to some sort of attention, though it did not stop them scratching themselves or eating each other's lice. At a second set of three rings, they shuffled into the door behind the owlish person.

"How dare you," said the person, quivering, quivering. "How *dare* you!" They struck the ground with their staff, and their eyes were wet with rage.

Yarrow curtseyed very deeply. "My apologies," she said, keeping her eyes on the stones. "I am Yarrow LXXVI, Mother of Grey House."

"I am Jasper, the Last Schoolmaster," said the owlish person. He chopped each syllable between the little adzes of his teeth. "And I say how *dare* you."

"If I have given offense, I am truly sorry, and ask how I may rectify it," said Yarrow.

"I thought they had finally spoken," said Jasper. "You made me think they had spoken. My life's work, achieved at last. But *no*."

"You're teaching the apes to talk?" said Yarrow.

"Why not?" Jasper frowned. "I taught them to write."

"I had thought—" Yarrow paused, coughing. "May I have some water? I've been on a long journey, and I have none."

Jasper sucked his lips into his mouth and chewed them for a

moment. Then he nodded once, grudgingly, and put the bell back in his robe. "Come inside."

She followed him. When he moved, the bell tolled softly within his clothes. They came into a large room with walls of white plaster and tall windows that opened on the courtyard. The apes all sat at wooden desks, parchment scrolls open before them, writing industriously with quill pens—except one, which was chewing on its hat.

"What are they doing?" said Yarrow.

"None of your business," said Jasper. As if to punctuate his reply, one ape farted loudly.

As they passed the hat-chewing ape, Jasper whacked it soundly across the head with his staff, and the ape left off chewing and picked up a pen. As they passed the farting ape, Jasper tweaked its ear, and it hooted. On the other side of the room was a second courtyard, much smaller, with a fountain of bright water in a clear pool.

"You may drink," said Jasper grandly, and stepped aside.

Imagine! A clean running fountain. Yarrow tore off her wimple and plunged her entire head in. The water was cold and pure, and she drank until her lungs burned for air. She surfaced, gasped for breath, and returned to the water. At last she was satisfied, and seated herself on the basin's edge to let her hair dry in the sun.

Jasper regarded her with something like curiosity. "Did you say you were from Grey House?"

"Yes," said Yarrow, wiping her dripping lips with the back of her hand.

"Hmph," said Jasper. "Didn't know anyone still lived in that ruin."

"People from Blue and Black and Red know of us," said Yarrow grandly, or as grandly as she could with her breath still coming in harsh lumps and water streaming from her hair.

"Perhaps it's as you say," said Jasper. "News passes me by; I am so busy with my work."

"Work?" said Yarrow. "You mean the apes—writing?"

"Writing is the first step," said Jasper.

"And speaking is second?"

Jasper sighed. There was a three-legged stool near the fountain, and he went to it. His robe enveloped it completely, and did not bend with him when he sat. It stayed rigid and tall, so his nose and eyes peered out from the lower edge of his collar, and his hands hung, caught in the armholes. There must have been some framework inside it, or perhaps it was starched to a degree not even Servant could manage.

"I am the Last Schoolmaster of Yellow Tower," said Jasper. "There were many before me. There will be many after me, as long as the palace endures."

"But if you are the last—"

"Silence, child. I am the Last Schoolmaster because when you leave the tower and pass east toward Grey, there are no schoolmasters beyond me. There have been no children in this district for many a long year. But a schoolmaster must teach."

"So you took on apes as pupils," said Yarrow.

Jasper's magnified eyes turned into angry yellow slits. "Have the goodness not to interrupt."

"I apologize," said Yarrow.

"As you say, I took on apes as pupils. But this was not on a whim. I teach them so they may, in turn, teach me." He paused, keeping his narrowed eyes on her to see if she would interrupt, then went on. "One day in my youth, as I bemoaned the lack of students for my school, I was walking on Cleric's Bridge, between Ramshead and the Maid, and I saw there an ape in a nest of ivy. It was a gibbon of the rufous sort, and it sat with immense gravity in its leafy nest, with one hand upraised. And upon its upraised hand was an upraised finger. And upon the upraised finger was a white butterfly of exquisite beauty, which it watched with dark eyes."

Jasper shut his own eyes as if the image were engraved on the inner skin of his lids. "I saw upon the ape's face a contentment and peace that I have never known. It is not to be found on the faces of the people in Yellow, nor those I have seen from Blue or Black or Red, and I see it is not to be found on yours, O Mother of Grey House. The ape, I believed, must know the secret of happiness.

"For a time I thought that, in order to find happiness, I must live as the apes do. I ran wild among the bridges and rooftops of the West Passage, sleeping in nests at night, foraging among the stones in daylight. This brought me nothing except splintered fingernails and cold nights. So the secret must not be how the apes lived, but something deep within them, some innate quality of the ape which I lacked."

A large tear spotted the edge of the collar. Jasper tried to wipe his eyes on his sleeve but could not move his hand far enough to reach. Yarrow took her own handkerchief and held it to his face.

"Much obliged," he said, and blew his nose, though she had only intended to mop up his tears. "Anyway, my time was not entirely wasted, for I befriended those noble creatures. There are many of them in this part of the palace: not just gibbons, as you can see, but the chimpanzee, the orangutan, even the gorilla, all live along the rim of Yellow. I soon learned that they can be taught to do simple tasks. From there I was able to teach them to wear clothes and make signs to indicate what they wanted. At first I feared I would corrupt their beautiful peace, but they kept it no matter what they learned. That is when I knew they had a secret, and they might be able to tell me if they could only speak."

"So you taught them to write?" said Yarrow. It seemed backward, since she had learned to speak but never to write, but you couldn't say that to someone so obviously learned.

"Yes. The first ones did not take to it as I had hoped, but their children learned more easily, and the grandchildren of my first students are now able to form simple sentences now and then. Though, sadly, I must admit that they largely produce gibberish."

"And soon they'll learn to speak?"

"That is my hope." Jasper sniffled. "And it is why I am still angry with you. Can you imagine what it is like to have one dream for decades, and believe for one glorious moment that it has been fulfilled, only to have it dashed by a dusty little intruder?"

"I can," said Yarrow, thinking obscurely of Arnica leaving.

"I no longer need to imagine," said Jasper. "It happened to me."

The peevish tone of him! She rose. "I feel I needn't trouble you any longer. Thank you for your hospitality. Can you direct me to Black Tower, please? And then I'll be gone."

Jasper's eyebrows executed a complicated sequence of movements. "Leave?" he said, his voice suddenly high and querulous.

"Yes," said Yarrow. She pinned her wimple around her still-damp hair. "I'm on an important mission for Grey House, but I've become turned around in the passages. If you could help . . ."

"But you—" Jasper began, then snipped the sentence with his thin lips and thought. "I can't tell you the way," he said, in his former dusty tone. "I know the rooms and mansions around Yellow well enough, but I have never ventured out beyond the rim, certainly not all the way to Black. I can tell you the names of all things vegetable, animal, and mineral within the palace walls; I can describe the movements of the forty-seven constellations; I can spell every word you know and a great deal you don't; but I cannot tell you the way to Black Tower."

"Then how am I to get there?" said Yarrow, the tone of her voice becoming more polite to counteract her rising anger.

"In a week or two, Peregrine will be along," said Jasper. "He can tell you, or even take you."

"And who is Peregrine?" said Yarrow.

"A Black Tower trader—one of the Butlers Itinerant—who makes a circuit of the palace every month." Jasper drew himself up proudly. "It is an ancient privilege of the Last Schoolmaster to be supplied with one bottle of mead *per mensis* from Black's cellars."

"And of the Mothers of Grey House as well," said Yarrow. Jasper's hand gripped the staff more tightly; her words may not have been tactful. "You did mean each year, correct?"

"No, little fool," said Jasper. "Each month." His hand relaxed. "It is a reward for a service performed to the Lady of Yellow back in the Thistle Era."

"I can't wait for this butler," said Yarrow. "Winter's fallen on us out of season, and Grey will starve before long. I *must* get to Black Tower."

"I expect Peregrine within one week," said Jasper. "I promise you that if you leave here without guidance, you'll be lost in the palace halls until some footman finds your bones in a cobwebby corner and sweeps you up with a broom. How much use will you be to the house then?"

He maneuvered himself back into a standing position, as slowly and with as much crackling as if he needed to move each bone individually. "In the meantime, you can help me with the apes in exchange for room and board."

Yarrow's shoulders sagged. "A week?"

"Or less," said Jasper.

"All right," said Yarrow.

"Excellent." Jasper and his architectural robe moved away from the stool. In its center was a gleaming white egg. He picked it up and handed it to her. The warm, damp shell stuck to her fingers. "Then you can put that in the kitchen with the others. Everything else you need should be there. The apes and I prefer breakfast at ten o'clock in the west parlor."

A Story Told by the Tutors in Grey House (But as the Tutors Are Dead, It Is Forgotten): How Yellow Tower Came to Be

*W*hen the Hellebore Era began, the towers of the palace were three: Grey Tower, the heart; Black Tower, the head; and Blue Tower, the hand. The Beast came and ended the Hellebores, and the rule of the palace passed to the Lilies. At the end of the Hellebore Era, the towers of the palace were four: Grey, Black, Blue, and Red Tower: the eye.

At that time, Wasp the Bloodhand was given the rule of Red Tower. Of the five sisters who founded the palace, only Citrine of the Bright Eyes remained without her proper tower. She lived in Black Tower with the Lily Lady, and all were glad, and the palace flourished. Trees and flowers grew, and the song of the nightingale was heard, and the wheel of the seasons turned smoothly. Then, after many years, winter fell on all, and the Beast arose once more.

In battle fell Wasp the Bloodhand, and the Beast prevailed. The tenth Lily Lady was cast down, and her era ended with her. The guardians of Grey were left to stand alone. The oncoming of the Beast had been so swift and terrible that they were cut off from their tower, and the steel of Wasp the Bloodhand was not with them, but in Grey House.

Then Citrine of the Bright Eyes came from Black Tower, driving flocks of Sparrows before her. With one hand she brought up the steel of Wasp the Bloodhand, with the second she strengthened the guardians, and with the third she grappled the Beast. All down the West Passage she drove the Beast and the Sparrows, until they came to the place called Nine Fountains. There she cast down the Beast, and mourned. And in the place called Nine Fountains, Citrine of the Bright Eyes built her tower of Yellow, and rested from her labors.

16. Yarrow Becomes a Schoolmistress and Like All Teachers Is Taught by Her Pupils in Turn

The Last Schoolhouse was like Grey House, in that it was large, ruinous, and packed to the rafters with old, moldering furniture and a few broken miracles, but there all points of comparison ceased. Though the House looked like several chapels leaning on each other for support, it was a single structure built around one ancient core. The Schoolhouse was more like a district: a set of courtyards, corridors, and rooms in the warren around Yellow Tower. Jasper was mostly uncommunicative about the place's history, but it seemed to have been chartered by a Lady of the Bellflower Era to provide schooling for children along the rim. Despite being very jealous of the privileges attached to it, Jasper did not seem to know much, and resented his own lack of knowledge when questioned, so Yarrow learned before noon the next day that if she wanted to learn something, she had to find it out for herself.

She slept in an attic over the schoolroom. At one end was the door she came and went by. At the other was a door that Jasper waspishly told her never to open. A clean path through the dust showed that someone regularly used that door, but he did not comment and she did not ask. The raftered ceiling tilted up from the floor to a sharp peak, and one side of it was crowded with dormer windows. Shrouded furniture filled about half of it. The rest was all odds and ends: old dishes, discarded clothes, miracles. Yarrow's bed was an old sofa, made as comfortable as possible with a pile of tattered robes. From it, she could see out the windows to the blade of Yellow Tower, which was unfortunate, but there was nowhere else to move the bed, and Jasper said there were no other rooms.

At night, greenish lights came and went in the windows of Yellow Tower. No warm candlelight or lamplight or firelight, just a wavering, sickly glow that passed along the windows as if something inside were moving in ceaseless circles. Yarrow had to put a robe over her head to shut out the sight. She slept poorly, with poor dreams, but awoke somehow refreshed (if a bit cloth-tongued and aching).

She had eaten gruel and milk in the kitchen the night before, so she knew her way there. It was staffed by three reddish apes with huge purple faces, and though they knew where all the utensils and cookware were, they had no idea how to cook porridge. It was a pity that this whole time, Jasper and his scholars had been putting up with burnt slop every morning. She showed them how to do it better, and they were fast learners.

Jasper's egg had been put in a wire casket with dozens of others just like it. She boiled these until the yolks were soft but set, and put them in egg cups for the table. The table itself was a crusty mess, and she and the smallest ape spent nearly half an hour scrubbing it until it shone.

The breakfast parlor was a large room with white plaster walls. Down the center was the plain, rough wooden table, now damp from washing. Morning light came through large windows facing a flowering courtyard. Yarrow was surprised her first morning in Yellow had passed so pleasantly. Then she rang the gong for the meal.

Within moments, the parlor filled with chattering apes. They fought each other for food, splashed porridge on the table, threw eggs about. Jasper appeared a little later. Instead of stopping them, he joined in, wielding his staff to defend himself with one hand and slopping porridge into his mouth with the other. Yarrow clenched her fists and her jaw. Silently, she rose and went back to the kitchen, where she stood at a granite counter and ate her breakfast. To treat her this way—! As if she were Servant.

A little later the gong rang again. Shuffling feet passed the kitchen door, and Yarrow ran to see the apes filing in two long, porridgy lines down the hall to the schoolroom. Jasper followed, flicking bits of egg from his robe. He paused near the door to lay another egg, then moved on after his pupils. Sighing, Yarrow picked up the egg and put it in the cellar, then went to the schoolroom to see what was happening there.

"Ah, excellent," said Jasper when she entered. "Saves me the trouble of shouting for you. The apes will need their pens trimmed and inkwells refilled; please attend to that as needed. Otherwise, I will expect you to sit quietly on that stool in the corner."

That was no problem. Yarrow was used to being quiet and out of the way. Jasper went up and down the aisles, checking the apes' work. After a little while, he went to a large slate slab at the front of the room and wrote a great many words. The apes stopped what they were doing to watch. When he finished, as one they discarded the scrolls they had been writing, took up blank parchment, and started again. Over the shoulder of the ape nearest her, Yarrow saw that they were copying from the board.

Jasper sat at his own desk and promptly fell asleep. The smallest ape chittered, holding up its pen. Yarrow darted over to help. She had never trimmed a pen, but its end looked a bit bent and ragged, so she pared that part away. When the ape went back to writing, she stayed to watch.

After a moment, it looked up at her questioningly and pointed to a word. She shrugged. It pointed to another.

"I can't read," she said.

The ape chuffed with irritation and picked up the discarded parchment. On the blank back, it wrote a few signs and pointed to her.

"Me? You?" she said. "Yarrow?"

The ape nodded.

"Well, which is it?" said Yarrow. "Is it my name?"

The ape nodded more aggressively. It wrote a set of several small signs and pointed around the room. *Book. Chair. Table. Robe.* Yarrow tried to commit them to memory, but they were a little slippery and wouldn't quite stick. Impatiently, she drew out the guardian's book.

"Can you read this?" she said.

The ape was about to take it when the grass staff whisked down and slapped its wrist.

"No no no," said Jasper. "My apes must not be corrupted by outside knowledge. Their wisdom comes from within. Put that away."

The second day was much the same: messy breakfast, hours spent sitting in the schoolroom, talking to the apes when Jasper napped, remaining still and quiet when he was awake. Yarrow learned her own name, and a few important words like *food* and *water*, but she had so much trouble remembering anything more that she almost started crying. She had always been good at memorization. The songs were easy, the rituals more complicated but comforting: rhythmic, and always the same. But written words shifted shape, sometimes looking one way, sometimes another. Even *food* and *water* did not always look the same. The signs would jumble around and melt together. Perhaps that would go away with time. Perhaps not. Either way, she had more important things to do.

The third day, Jasper slept so long into the afternoon that the apes rose on their own and left the schoolroom (in two lines, always in two lines) and went out to the courtyard for playtime. Yarrow, for her part, tiptoed up to her attic and opened the other door. She needed time away from the apes and from taking orders, and the schoolmaster was not to forbid her *everything*. The door creaked alarmingly and she hesitated. What if Jasper had heard? But after a few moments of silence, she stepped over the threshold.

On the other side was a long gallery, all windows on one wall, all fresco on the other. Yellow Tower glared through each of the windows, so she turned her attention to the fresco. It was faded and flaking, but mostly intelligible. She soon realized it was a kind of map of the palace—or, if not a map, at least a representation of its districts. And the images it bore were of the same shocking, strange nature as those made in the art of memory.

Closest to the door was Red Tower with its light. A smudge of blue was the sea, which she had heard about, but had never seen, and neither had anyone in Grey. Around the tiers of Red fluttered bluish pigeons. Next to it, nearly as tall as itself, was a being she instantly knew for a Lady, hands upraised in warning or blessing, eyes shut in contemplation. The Lady wore crimson armor and a chestnut cloak striped with black. Her head rose in overlapping leaves and turrets and thorny vines, out of which birds came and went, or perched, preening and shitting. Beneath her feet was a pile of eggs.

A noise disturbed the silent room. Yarrow started, expecting Jasper, but the smallest ape stood there, and behind it several of the others. They entered, ignoring her, and went past her to the center of the wall where a greyish blot took up the heart of the fresco. Something went cold in Yarrow's stomach.

After Red Tower came Blue, rising from its courts of white-plastered walls, its azure dome floating like a smaller sky beneath the larger. Honeycreepers and swallows fed among the flowering vines on its flanks. And beside it was a Lady in a simple white shift over cerulean hose. Her head was a lapis turret, flecked with windows and warty with balconies. In one hand she held blobs of translucent blue. The faded paint was hard to grasp; perhaps they were frogs' eggs.

Certainly the Lady, with another hand, was drawing forth something small and slimy from them. With a third hand, she was placing a little froggy creature in a balcony on her head. Several others were already peering from its windows or holding out their hands to feed birds.

So it was the Five Sisters. Yarrow held her hands together to stop a sudden tremble. How did they come to be painted *here*? Now she knew she shouldn't look in the center. Custom, prohibition, tradition, all were against it.

A dull little *click* echoed in the room. The apes had seated themselves in a semicircle at the foot of the fresco, their eyes fixed on the grey bit. One of them was placidly scratching its nethers. As Yarrow watched, the smallest ape opened its mouth as wide as it could, then brought its teeth together in the same *click* as before. The others followed suit. Not taking their eyes from the fresco, they sat there and clicked their teeth, nearly in unison, and clicked again, and again.

She had to walk around them to reach the other side of the fresco. Yarrow averted her eyes as she passed. What lay in the middle of the painting was something she was not meant to see. The others, yes. Not this.

The Red and Blue Ladies had faced the door, with the towers to their left. Here, the Ladies of Yellow and Black faced the other direction, with the towers to their right. Presumably, Grey faced the viewer. Nothing would induce her to look.

The Lady of Yellow Tower wore a saffron gown and a high collar of greenish lace. She had a bird's head, which was all right—Ban was feathered, and there were people in the cloisters with beaks or bird's heads or wings. But her beak was biting into a person, whose struggling legs stuck out wildly. One hand held the person there lightly as if they were a delicacy. Another held a writing tablet, while a third wrote something upon it. The tower's white birds speckled her. All around the Lady were bones, broken eggshells, dirty platters with crumbs or rinds still upon them. She was the holiest thing Yarrow had ever seen.

The apes kept clicking and clicking. They groomed each other or themselves, or simply sat still, but their gaze did not stray from the center, from Grey. Yarrow wanted to scream.

Black Tower thrust upward from the slate roofs around it, like a spear aimed at the heart of heaven. She knew it well, its buttresses flying out to satellite towers, which in turn were buttressed by smaller ones. She knew its huge thorny spire and abyssal windows. She knew every pinnacle and clerestory.

The Lady of Black Tower was clothed in stag beetles. Her bodice was of woven snakeskins. Her seven ebony arms held the emblems of the other four towers, plus three unique to Black: the *wheel*, the *apple*, and the *flail*. Her head was like a complex of ruined walls, and fires burned in them, and sparrows flew about them. She was crowned with the moon, and beneath her feet was a disc of flaking gold leaf. She was very holy.

Yarrow stepped away to go back into the attic, but the smallest ape, unbeknownst to her, had come up beside her. It took her hand. She resisted, but it pulled her into the semicircle with awful strength, and she saw Grey Tower and the Grey Lady, because her eyes would not close and her head would not turn.

There should have been effigies around the foot of Grey. But there were none, and the tower looked young and fresh and new as it had not for centuries, for era upon era. The fresco had either been painted when the palace was built—which was not likely, since Yellow was far younger than Grey—or was a copy of a copy, like a memory of a song. The crows and yellow butterflies were there, swirling about the pale stones as they had for ages. And seated cross-legged at its base, where effigies now stood, was the Lady of Grey Tower.

Her dark robe was Yarrow's own, and so was her wimple. Two pale arms emerged from her sleeves and split into four wrists, each with its proper hand. Each hand held a mask: the guardians' green mask, the Mothers' blue slate mask, the yellow oaken mask of the doctors, and the red jasper mask of the tutors. Beneath her, the earth gaped in a great angry mouth, and a creature lay coiled within it, a creature of wings and tails and teeth, all its eyes closed, and a chain wrapped around its limbs. That chain ran up and up, and Yarrow, who had managed to avoid the Lady's face thus far, felt her gaze drawn along it, as it passed behind the guardian's mask and up to the holy head.

The Lady had no face. There was only a fall of loose ash-colored fabric from under the wimple, and the chain vanished under it. Upon the fabric was written the word that the ape had said was Yarrow's own name. Yarrow clicked her teeth.

A Story Told by the Mothers in Grey House: The Hellebore Lady Visits

This is holy and ancient knowledge. In the Hellebore Era, the Sparrows first arose, and brought knowledge forth from Black Tower, and back to Black Tower. They had not far to go, for Yellow Tower and Red Tower had not yet arisen. In the Hellebore Era, stories were first written down. The Lady of Black Tower, granddaughter of the first Hellebore Lady, took the signs for writing from the Lady of Blue, and they became the seed of the Library. The Hellebore Lady went out with the Sparrows, bringing knowledge forth from Black Tower, and back to Black Tower. The Hellebore Lady desired that all should know and use these signs, and to her will and her Sparrows bowed Blue.

But Grey did not bow. The Lady said, Memory is the greatest wonder. The Lady said, To remember is to engrave knowledge in one's flesh. Sparrow after Sparrow was sent to her, but the Lady broke them and sent them back, saying, We will not remove knowledge from our bodies.

At last the Hellebore Lady arose with her Sparrows and came to see her sister. Citrine the Yellow accompanied her, for it was Citrine of Yellow who had long been the arms and hands of Black Tower. Wasp the Red accompanied her, for it was Wasp of Red who had long been the spear and shield of Black Tower. The three of them stood in the court before Grey House and said, Come out, sister.

At this time the Lady of Grey was the one who had always been: the Lady of the Rose Era. Citrine the Yellow and Wasp the Red were of the Roses, too: her true sisters. But Hellebore of Black was not. Dynasties had risen and fallen since the Roses, and Hellebore was new, and arrogant, and young.

And the Lady of Grey came out in the presence of her women and offered them water. They drank. She offered them bread and salt. They ate. And she sang. They listened.

The Lady of Grey sang a song of sleep, and Citrine the Yellow fell.

She sang a song of stillness, and Wasp the Red moved not. And to Hellebore she did not sing, but lifted her veil to meet the proud eyes of the Lady of Black Tower. Then the Lady of Grey took the miraculous knife of Wasp the Red, and gave it to the guardians as their sword. Then the Lady of Grey took the miraculous mirror of Citrine the Yellow, and gave it to the doctors to strengthen their sight. Then in the presence of her women, the Lady of Grey said to Hellebore, No.

And never again did Sparrows come to Grey, for terrible in the sight of Hellebore were the eyes of the Lady of Grey. After the Hellebores fell, the guardians learned to read, and the doctors, and the tutors. But the women in grey: never.

17. Yarrow Remains Calm in the Face of Revelation and Peregrine Arrives

If there was one thing Yarrow knew how to do, it was to resume her duties. She helped in the kitchen and schoolroom, gathered up Jasper's eggs as needed, dusted and swept. Two or three days passed. She did not visit the painted room again.

She should never have gone in. The Lady chained to the creature returned in her dreams. Sometimes she was the Lady, sometimes the creature, sometimes a small girl again, clinging to the skirts of an adult as something horrible happened. Yellow Tower almost ceased to frighten her: the real fear lay behind, at home. For though the fresco had not been true to life in many respects (the veiled Lady was from the Lily Era, as everyone knew), the guardians existed for a reason. Arnica and Old Yarrow had said as much: *The evil that comes through the Passage.* But they hadn't said where it came from. Whether they had suspected it, Yarrow didn't know, but she now believed that under Grey something ancient and awful was captive. She was, as we know, perfectly right.

She awakened from nightmares so many times that at last she determined to tell Jasper. He would be angry, of course, and might even banish her from the Last Schoolhouse, but Yarrow had been raised to confess. It would help if she spoke.

His face turned quite purple when she did.

"You what?" he said. And again, "You *what*?," slamming his staff into the floor as punctuation to his outrage.

"I am sorry," said Yarrow. Now that the confession was past, she was herself once more: Mother of Grey House, and his equal.

"Sorry! You're sorry! You're *sorry*?"

They were in the fountain court on a cloudy afternoon. He stumbled backward onto his stool, his robes crackling as he sat carelessly.

"I am," said Yarrow. "I went in, and I regret it. I saw something that upset me, and I wish I hadn't."

"But you're not sorry for breaking the rules."

"They aren't *my* rules," said Yarrow. "Perhaps I could have respected them more, yes, but—"

"The painted room was entrusted to *our* care, and nobody— nobody—is allowed in except the Last Schoolmaster."

"What about the apes?" said Yarrow thoughtlessly.

Jasper's eyes narrowed. "Did you let them in?"

"No."

"Did they go in of themselves?"

Yarrow hesitated, which was answer enough.

"I'll lock the door," said Jasper. "I'll put chairs in front of it. I'll beat them, if nothing else suffices."

"Leave them alone," said Yarrow. "I'll bet they didn't know what they were doing."

"Of course they know! They always know! Haven't I told you again and again about their wisdom? But you went in! You saw the name! How could you do this?"

Yarrow rose and went to her room. She packed up her things and went to the door of the Schoolhouse. Jasper was there, locking it. He swept over to lock the door of the front room with the shuttered, glassless windows that were the only other means of egress.

"I won't let you leave," he said, his voice and body trembling even as he defied her. "The name in the painted room is secret. It's not to be seen or said, except by the Lady. You'll speak of it, I know you will. You'll tell people. They'll come. They'll see the name. They'll disturb the Schoolhouse and Lady knows what else. You aren't leaving, not now, not with Peregrine, not ever. I won't allow it. I won't, I say."

In his excess of emotion, an egg must have fallen out of him, for Yarrow heard the crunch and splat. She left him there and went back to the attic. She did not come down the next day, or the day after, not even when the smallest ape brought her a tray and stood by the door, motioning for her to follow. The breakfast table must have been in a sorry state by then, even though she'd trained the apes to clean it much more thoroughly. And nobody, likely, would pick up Jasper's eggs or do the sweeping. That was fine by her. They got along without her before she came; they could get along without her now.

Jasper could not keep her locked up forever. He would relent, or she would outsmart him. But there was a way out, if not through the school door, then through the schoolmaster.

She passed the time by reciting as much of the Grey House lore as she could remember. There were the Lullaby of Reeds, the Ninety-Eight Dirges, the Forty Birthing-Songs, the One Hundred and Ninety-Two Botanical Rhymes, the morning and evening rites, the Order of Cleanliness, and that was just the start. She even dug up some old nursery rhyme about the Sisters Six; it went with a clapping game, and at the end someone was supposed to fall down. *That,* however, she stopped reciting very quickly. It reminded her too much of Ban and Grith.

More surfaced in her mind the longer she went, and she said the rules aloud and sang the songs at the top of her voice. It was blasphemy and desecration, out here so far from the house, but if she was to die in the Last Schoolhouse, she would first make it hear as much of her as she could.

As she sang, she also sorted through the furniture, bric-a-brac, and miracles in the attic. Work was a comfort, even (or especially) meaningless work. The chairs were stacked *here*, the tables shoved *there*, the candelabra and dishes and silverware and basins arranged according to type, then by color, then by whether they were still usable. And the miracles, well, one had to be more careful with them.

Many miracles lay abandoned and useless in the corners and attics of Grey, and though they were all more or less worn out and dead, occasionally they went off. There was a spool of silvery thread that once made Grith's hand vanish, then reappear at sunrise. There was a broken dulcimer whose pegs were pale men and, when bumped one day, it played of itself a jangling tune that compelled the girls to dance, and was only stopped when Old Yarrow, hearing the commotion, jigged over to it and smashed it with her foot. The little men rolled their eyes in fright and died.

Where did miracles come from? Gifts of the Ladies, of course. At least, that was what everyone knew. But an old story of the Mothers said that the Ladies produced them of their own bodies— uncontrollably, instinctively, like a cat coughing up a hairball—in response to the wishes of their most faithful servants, or simply because the stars were right. The dulcimer had been a fingernail of a Grey Lady, pulled off and given to a minstrel who had no instrument. The thread had been plucked from the scalp of another Lady and given to a Mother whose greatest wish was not to be seen. And there were dozens, hundreds of others, most with no story anyone now remembered.

The miracles of Yellow were different from those of Grey. Naturally: another lineage of Ladies had made them. But they were likewise odd: a knife whose handle was blanketed with two soft, warm ears; a bowl holding a chilly marble-white hand and a single die; a pink bagpipe with threads of steam rising from its mouthpiece. Yarrow used a snapped-off table leg to prod each miracle before touching it with her hands. None of them reacted strongly; the worst was a slight twitch from the white hand. That was good. No miracles that came from this horrible tower could possibly be pleasant.

When Yarrow woke up without ever quite having fallen asleep, she realized one of the miracles in the room was still active. There was a telltale tingle in the air. It must have been one of those she'd disturbed. Groggily, navigating solely by the strengthening or weakening of the tingling aura, she found it: a crystal rod with a string of egg yolks sealed down its center. The egg at the end opened when she poked it, revealing a tawny eye. Drowsiness filtered through her brain, but not as much as before: likely there were not many uses left in it. But she stored it in her sleeve, and thought.

On the third day, she was too hungry to stay in the attic any longer, and she resumed her duties as if nothing had happened. But she watched Jasper closely now. He was not observant at all, so she was able to follow him around the Schoolhouse while sweeping or dusting and not raise his suspicions. If he had been a slightly different kind of selfish, he would have known instantly what she was doing, but from morning to night he was focused on getting the apes to talk. She once watched him walk right over the shards of a dropped bowl without breaking his stride, all because he thought he heard the albino ape utter a syllable.

First there was the matter of the keys. She had never seen them until he locked the doors. They must be in his robe somewhere. But he did not take them out again while she was watching, and time was running out, so she contrived to bump into him in a corridor to see if she could feel where they might be. Though she only meant to brush against him, he tottered and nearly fell, and Yarrow had to put out a hand to steady him. As he angrily shook himself, there was a faint jingling on his right, near his midsection. Since Yarrow was no pickpocket—

and was not even familiar with the concept, there being no thieves in Grey—she had to think carefully about how to procure them.

Then there was the matter of the apes. Would they try to stop her? The smallest one was a friend, and would run to her if Jasper mistreated it, but the others more or less followed his orders (as much as apes ever would). While Jasper slept, she began praising their writing. *How beautiful it looks. How elegantly you formed that word.* And she gave them little treats: a hardboiled egg for finishing a scroll, a honeyed fig for finishing three.

Peregrine had not come yet. Jasper had promised Yarrow at the beginning of her stay that he would arrive within a week, but that week had ended on the day Jasper locked her in the Schoolhouse, and still no Peregrine. Three more days passed. If the butler did not show his face soon, would she need to wrest control of the Schoolhouse by force?

On her eleventh morning in the Schoolhouse, she made breakfast as usual. The apes now sat quietly and used spoons, while Jasper scrabbled food out of his bowl with gnarled hands and belched. After breakfast, Yarrow and the smallest ape cleared the table and washed it. She stroked the ape's head gently as they went into the schoolroom. It took her hand and held it on the way to its seat.

Jasper's eyes were wet and smiling as he began class. "Did you see them at breakfast?" he said to Yarrow. "At last I am making progress. At last. They'll speak any day now. I know it."

He fell asleep for an hour or two. The apes wrote industriously. Yarrow dozed herself, waking only when she heard Jasper's harsh caw.

"What are you doing?" he shouted. "What is this?" He stood over the smallest ape, brandishing a scroll in its face. "I did not tell you to write this. What are you doing? Tell me!"

He struck it on the head with his staff. Yarrow was out of her chair in an instant and threw herself between Jasper and the ape.

"Leave it alone!" she shouted.

Jasper shoved the parchment at her. "This is your fault!"

Written all over it in neat rows was her name.

"I didn't do anything," said Yarrow. "You know I can't read."

"They got this from the painted room!" said Jasper. "You must have let them in again. They *never* wrote it before you!"

"It's just my name!" said Yarrow. "Isn't it?"

Jasper's staff slashed her across the stomach. "No, fool! It's the name of the Lady of Grey Tower. Absolutely forbidden! What have you done? *Why?*"

He struck her again and again. She cowered, raising her hands against the blows. All at once they stopped, and there was a horrible cry and gurgle.

The smallest ape had jumped onto Jasper's back and was digging its hands into his throat. Its teeth clicked together so fast it sounded like a rattle, and Jasper kept gurgling. He was going blue. The staff clattered from his twitching hands.

"Let him go," she said to the ape. "It's all right. Let him go."

The ape released Jasper and leaped onto its desk. Jasper collapsed to the floor, moaning. All the apes watched expressionlessly. Yarrow got to her knees, her arms and back stinging from the beating. It was fortunate the old man had no strength in him.

Taking the crystal rod from her sleeve, she crawled over to Jasper, who lay among the ruins of his robes, struggling to breathe. He had fallen on his right side, so she turned him onto his back. He tried to fight her, but the shock of the ape's rebellion made him weep, and the miraculous drowsiness made him choke on his weeping. Yarrow snaked her hand into his sleeve, through wickerwork struts and folds of fabric, until she felt flesh. Under the robes, Jasper was soft and damp, like a slug's underbelly, and her hand slid over him without resistance. He seemed to have a leather belt around his rib cage. Following it with her fingers, she found the keys and pulled them out. Trails of odorless slime hung from them, then broke.

"I'm going," she said, drying the keys on his robe. "I'll leave the keys inside the door."

Curling his limbs up like a dead spider, Jasper kept crying the weak, sodden cry of an unwell old man. His round eyes were squeezed shut as Yarrow stood, and he did not see what happened next, but he must have heard it.

The apes had all left their desks and crowded around her. "I'm leaving," she said to them. "You can stay or go. Up to you."

She went upstairs and got her things. When she reached the antechamber by the front door, all the apes were there, many of them having discarded their scholar's robes. Their fur was long and lustrous as they huddled around her, stroking her hands. Yarrow unlocked the doors, and the apes filed out in two lines.

Jasper would likely find someone else to teach. One needed duty, order, purpose. Still, she didn't feel too badly for him as, true to her word, she set the keys and worn-out miracle down on the floor and closed the door of the Last Schoolhouse behind her.

The open air was warm and drowsy. Yellow Tower shimmered in the summer haze, and its lake glittered. One by one the apes scattered, climbing walls and swinging up vines. They made no sound and spoke no words, for they were, after all, only apes. Only the smallest one remained. Yarrow squatted down to its level.

"Do you want to come with me?" she said, stroking the long, rusty fur on its head.

For one mad moment she was sure it was about to say something, but then a yellow butterfly flickered past her, and the ape turned to chase it. The two of them vanished into the ivy, and the ape did not look back.

Shouldering her pack, Yarrow continued down the West Passage.

The road was steep and straight, still crossed by bridges and walkways. Around her, the buildings turned from brownish-yellow to plain yellow, prickled over in places with green ivy. Every window was still empty, every door still closed. The air grew warmer and calmer as she went, until she was sweating profusely. About halfway down the hill she realized she had, once more, forgotten to pack water. Ahead were the pools of Yellow Tower, but she would die of thirst before drinking from *them*. Perhaps she would come to a fountain before long.

Yarrow was so dizzy with thirst and the sky so crowded with bridges that she did not see the darkness falling over her until it was almost too late. She flung herself out of the looming shadow a second before a great palm and fingers slammed into the road.

Heart pounding, she looked up. And up. And up.

The hand was at the end of a long pale arm, lightly fuzzed with yellow hair, that attached to a huge torso. At the front of the torso was a large face with vacant eyes and a distant smile, half-shrouded by chin-length blond curls. On top of the torso's head and back was a wide white platform, lashed to the figure with multiple ropes and bearing a tall pink tent. The whole thing, creature and edifice, had just emerged from the hanging ivy behind her.

"Hold it, hold it," said a voice, and the figure, which had been raising its other hand to take a step, halted, chuckling to itself in tones that rumbled in Yarrow's chest. A head looked out over the platform's edge and saw her. "I thought I heard someone down there," said the head. "Where are you going?"

"Black Tower. Where are you coming from?" said Yarrow.

"I'm a Butler Itinerant on my rounds," said the head. "Where are *you* coming from, if I might ask? The Last Schoolmaster was full of curses for a little girl in grey who ruined his life."

Yarrow drew herself up. "He ruined it himself," she said. "And I am a *woman* in grey. You must be Peregrine. He told me you were coming days ago."

"He told *me* to avoid you, though you look harmless enough," said Peregrine. "If you're bound for Black Tower, I'm headed there myself, and Tertius won't mind another passenger. I warn you, though, it can be a bouncy ride."

"I don't mind," said Yarrow. "I've been through worse."

Peregrine laughed and vanished. A moment later, a rope ladder fell down the side of the torso. Climbing up, Yarrow found herself on a flat white surface, pitted like bone. The pink tent extended over the creature's head—Tertius, she supposed it was called. Toward the platform's rear were two smaller tents. And directly in front of her was Peregrine.

He was much taller than her, wearing a white hood and a close-fitting garment of iridescent green that wrapped his legs and made his breasts and hips bright and prominent. Yarrow had never seen anything like it and found it very odd. How could you wear something that didn't slip easily over your head? That didn't have sleeves to store things in?

Peregrine bowed to her, and she curtseyed to him.

"Yarrow LXXVI, Mother of Grey House," she said.

"Three Peregrine Borealis," he said. "I didn't know there was still a Mother of Grey. North, you must be barely eighteen."

"Sixteen, they told me," said Yarrow. "There were some unfortunate circumstances."

"I won't ask if you don't want to tell," said Peregrine. "Some of these old offices get passed on through circumstances more unfortunate than I care to mention." He raised his voice. "On, Tertius."

The platform jolted and started moving.

"How long until Black Tower?" said Yarrow. "I'm on an errand of some urgency."

"Oh," said Peregrine, stretching himself out on the sunny platform and closing his eyes. "No more than five days. Don't worry, little Mother, I'll have you there safely."

Tertius jounced and bounced down the hill, deeper into the valley of Yellow Tower.

18. Yarrow Gets Too Close to Yellow Tower and Tertius Gets Its Hands Wet

Peregrine called Tertius a hollowman, and seemed confused that Yarrow had never heard of or seen one before. "A Mother must *know* of them," he said. "We itinerants take them all over Black and Red, and other places too."

"Not to Grey," said Yarrow. She looked over her shoulder. The West Passage rose up behind them to the edge of the hill, cutting off any glimpse she might have had of the top of her tower. "You never come to Grey."

"*I* don't, but some other butler must."

"Never. The wine arrives by fish-cart."

"Ah, well." Peregrine put a wad of leaves into his mouth and chewed them, then spat bright emerald juice over Tertius's side. "Maybe the Master of Privileges knows why. I sure as South don't."

The Passage went up a little hump, and through a dip in the left-hand rim of the valley, Blue Tower loomed through chilly mists. Yarrow shivered.

"Do you know why winter's fallen?" she asked. "We were in summer before the snow came. We did nothing wrong."

"I've been over in Red for a month," said Peregrine. "It was winter there, and meant to be, but I heard a rumor that the seasons had come out of joint for Blue and Grey."

"Did we do anything to displease Black?" The broken mask flashed into her mind, but Yarrow would not confess to that sin unless necessary. The Willow Lady could only punish you if she knew you'd done wrong, and as powerful as she was, how could she have seen that slip in the heart of Grey?

Peregrine shrugged. "I stopped at Black long enough to restock on wine, but not on gossip. Take comfort, though, little Mother: if Grey had committed some sin bad enough to warrant wintering, the whole palace would have heard. No, I think it's more likely that the wheel has stuck or been meddled with."

This was not reassuring. If the wheel of the seasons was so easily disturbed, it meant people all over the palace had been suffering or dying over some slight mistake in Black.

"That's horrible," said Yarrow.

Peregrine shrugged again and spat purple onto the road below. "It's how things are."

Tertius reached the level part of Yellow and its gait became smoother. The pools and parks around the tower disappeared behind roofs and walls, but the tower itself still surged into the sky like a jet of vomit. Bridges dwindled and vanished, while the buildings became tall and smooth and orderly. Stone traceries framed their arched glass windows. Wrought iron railings and balconies sprouted everywhere like vines. The green copper roofs were warm as leaves in summer. The humid air glued Yarrow's robe and wimple to her.

Something rustled above her head. When Yarrow looked up, she saw the smallest ape peering over a flower-carved cornice. She waved at it, and it imitated her. As Tertius moved on, the ape kept pace with it, and Yarrow felt a little better. At least she would have a friend of sorts here.

They came to a crossroads where a broad, white avenue intersected the West Passage. Peregrine rapped on the platform three times. Tertius halted.

"To the Lady's Lakehouse," said Peregrine, enunciating each syllable with the abstracted precision of someone performing a ritual for the hundredth time. Tertius let out its deep chuckle and turned right. As they left the crossroads, Peregrine spat orange.

"What's at the Lakehouse?" said Yarrow.

"Sardonyx, the Keeper of the Ferry, is owed one bottle of claret every seventy-five days," said Peregrine. "In recognition of his services during the Night of Bones at the end of the Apple Era."

"What services?"

Peregrine shrugged. "The Master of Records would know. I'm not even sure what the Night of Bones was; I just deliver wine."

Old Yarrow had told the story once, though it was on her deathbed and incomplete. Something about factions of Grey and Red aligning with each other to overthrow the Bellflowers. The third ruling Lady used to progress from tower to tower, and at each she would demand tribute. Great Citrine of Yellow was her ally, and took a tithe of the tribute to enrich Yellow itself. And the guardians of Grey, overzealous in their duty, put their ancient weapon at the disposal of fractious Red. It came to pass that the Bellflower Lady was staying in unfortified Yellow, and the conspiracy saw their chance. In a single night, with the aid of an unnamed miracle of Red, thousands of Bellflower partisans died, and the guardian's weapon killed the Bellflower Lady. They did not achieve their aim: her daughter was in Black and took the throne at once, and an answering miracle of Yellow devastated Red for three generations. And so order was restored. The house had stayed aloof from the conflict and so Grey was spared the punishment that fell on Red. And that, Old Yarrow said, was another reason not to trust the guardians, who would betray even their home in the pursuit of their duty.

But Arnica, in the room to check Old Yarrow's pulse, disagreed. Red had stolen the weapon. The guardians were never involved.

And Jasper, teaching the apes, had read a very long poem lauding Citrine for killing her tyrant sister with the guardians' steel, and taking the uncountable wealth of Bellflower for Yellow.

So Yarrow did not see any point in telling Peregrine about the Night of Bones.

They began to pass people at last. Many of them had glistening amphibian skin and long spiny tails, but just as many had feathered heads like Ban's, and a few like Peregrine were simple flesh. As the hollowman came to a plaza with a fountain, it paused and laboriously settled down onto its elbows and uttered a low call. Standing up, Yarrow could see that Tertius appeared to do honor to a group of three blue-robed figures, whose faces protruded like long silver spoons from their hoods. Each of them trilled a high note, and Tertius got back to its feet and went on.

"Brothers of the Order of Transit," said Peregrine, when Yarrow gave him a questioning look. "They made the hollowmen back in the Bellflower Era, so Tertius is bound to acknowledge them whenever they enter its sight." He spat brown. "Mostly they run the trains these days, though. There's hardly any hollowmen left, just those in service of Black Tower, and not many of them either. Trains are faster and need less maintenance, so most of the towers turned to them ages ago." He patted the platform and Tertius rumbled. "Tertius is one of the originals."

Peregrine's face was so proud that Yarrow assumed his use of Tertius was an honor accorded to him. She made a noise of interest as the hollowman swung right onto a narrow passage between two long rows of houses. The platform scraped a wall, sending a little shower of stone dust onto the pavement. The walls all along the passage were marked like that; some of the gouges had clearly eroded. The Apple Era was ages past, and Yarrow felt a thrill of awe at just how long the Butlers Itinerant had been making this journey to Sardonyx. Tertius alone had probably done it thousands of times. But as old as the custom was, her own were even older.

The passage made a long, graceful curve to the left. Yarrow's awe faded as the pit of her stomach twisted. A low drone thrummed in the passage, and it grew louder as the passage went on. The drone rose and fell, wavering like a sick person's breath, but never going entirely away. Yarrow's hands were cold with sweat, and she knotted her fingers around her sleeves. Please don't let it be what I think, she said to no one. Please, let it not be. Her breath began to match the uneven throb in the air.

Tertius entered a path between high green hedges. Too high, too green. But over the trimmed tops hung the branches of dead trees, almost comforting in their homey barrenness. Tertius turned right and left and left and right and kept turning until Yarrow was lost. All the time she thought, Let it be somewhere else, let it be one of the pools. Not the lake. Do not take me there. The Lady of Yellow Tower has never died. The drone grew louder and louder. It's only insects, Yarrow told herself. Nobody can come close to Yellow Tower, not even Peregrine. The Lady is one of the five, older than the palace. She has never died. She is too holy.

The hedge rustled. Alarmed, Yarrow glanced to the side. The little ape was swinging among the green, green branches. It did not seem affected by the droning. That was some comfort. Surely an animal would know if there was any harm ahead.

The maze debouched onto a wide terrace. Directly ahead was calm blue water, and beyond that, Yellow's roofs and the hazy spikes of Black and Red. Then Tertius turned right, and Yellow Tower was before them, rancid. The stones themselves seemed to sweat. Green algae fringed its windows and the pits of its incised decoration. The windows gleamed as slick as oil. A sickly rotten smell like compost breathed from the lake at its foot. Yarrow's stomach flipped and she doubled over.

"A bit of a shock, isn't it?" said Peregrine, not unkindly, and patted her shoulder. "It's all right, little Mother. You get used to it."

The sickening drone lay around Yellow Tower like a fog. Whether it came from the tower itself, or rose from the water as a fume, or was just Yarrow's own panic at being so near the Lady, could not be told. She kept her mind on breathing. She sang the Thirty-First Birthing-Song without making a sound, and made her lungs go in and out with its rhythm, instead of the nauseous chaos of the tower's drone. Peregrine spat on the terrace, red as blood, and touched her shoulder.

"We won't be here for long," he said. "Just to deliver the bottle, and then we're gone."

"Why is it like that?" Yarrow gasped. "Oh, why is it *like* that?"

Peregrine shrugged. "It's just holiness, little Mother. All the Ladies give that off, though normally it's endurable. My master once told me it's the weight of their dreams. And the old one there, she has thousands of years of 'em."

Tertius had kept moving this whole time, and like a cat stepping from a stool to the floor, went over the terrace's marble balustrade and down to the green shore of the lake. Before them was a little house, also of marble, built entirely of scrollwork and lattice and situated beneath two weeping willows, dead and dry but so covered with ivy that they seemed alive. If she'd come across it anywhere else, Yarrow would have called it a pleasant little place. The ape followed, and got immediately into one of the willows, where it snatched at dragonflies. Tertius came to a halt.

Peregrine leaned into the pink tent and produced a small brass horn, which he blew. The echoes were swallowed up by the drone. A door in the little house opened and a man in marigold robes came out. Meanwhile, Peregrine took a wooden pole with a brass hook on its end and went to the rope ladder.

"Welcome," said the man, bowing.

"Thank you," said Peregrine, bowing and unrolling the ladder at the same time. Since nobody told Yarrow not to follow, she did. Being on steady ground might clear her head and settle her stomach.

Peregrine went around to the back of the hollowman. At the end of its rib cage was a flap of ivory flesh, buttoned at the top two corners. With the pole, Peregrine unfastened it and the flap came open.

The inside of Tertius was all red and moist, like lips, its ribs visible through cloudy membranes. The cavernous space was full of bundles and packages and trunks. Peregrine hooked a satchel with the pole and brought it out. By then, the Keeper of the Ferry had joined them, yawning and scratching himself.

"Slow day?" said Peregrine wryly, opening the satchel.

"Always," said Sardonyx.

Peregrine drew out a dark glass bottle and began to say something about rewards and nights of bones, but Yarrow's attention was drawn away. Near the top of the tower, on its shady side, a round yellow-green light was pulsing and winking in a window. She stepped forward. Everything around her faded into grey except that pus-colored light, dancing and skipping like a guttering candle. Its motion gradually stopped, and the sphere came into focus and *turned*.

It was *looking* at her.

Yarrow screamed. Peregrine stopped in the middle of his ceremony, and both he and Sardonyx looked faintly annoyed. Just then, the ape, hearing her scream, bounded down out of the tree and toward her. Tertius made its witless chuckle and slammed its hand onto the ape. There was a squelch, and a lot of red and purple. Tertius lifted its hand and, still chuckling, began to lick the squashy remnants of the ape from its dirty palm.

Sardonyx sighed in annoyance. "That's a month of paperwork for old Bismuth, right there," he said.

Yarrow screamed again and sank to her knees. Peregrine followed, trying to quiet her, but she would not be quieted. All the ape wanted was to follow her. It only wanted to see if she was all right. She'd *asked* it to come.

The drone rose until the air and ground throbbed with it. Yarrow fell forward onto her hands and vomited, her stomach moving to the tuneless tune. Peregrine clutched his own stomach. Even Sardonyx looked a little green. The sound cut off abruptly, leaving only the quiet splashing noises of the lake.

"*She's* calling," he said.

"*What?*" said Peregrine, almost shouting.

"Who?" said Yarrow. The drone returned, gradually rising in volume.

"You're to come up immediately," Sardonyx said. "The girl, at least, though she didn't say no to the Butler Itinerant."

"She can't mean it," said Peregrine. "The Mother didn't know the rules. She's not to blame. I'll go instead. I shouldn't have brought her this far."

Sardonyx shook his head. "She said the girl. You can go if you want, but the girl for sure."

Peregrine turned to Yarrow. "I'm sorry," he said. "I'm so, so sorry."

"Who wants me?" said Yarrow, wiping her mouth on her sleeve. "Who's called?" She knew the answer before she spoke, and the look on Peregrine's face confirmed it.

"The Lady of Yellow Tower," said Peregrine. "She's called, and you'll go."

As if in reply, the green light in the window winked and went out.

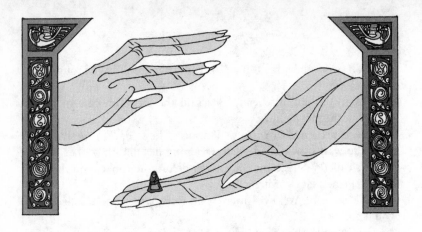

19. They Take a Ferry and Yarrow Does a Favor for the Lady

I can't go," said Yarrow. "Grey Tower is depending on me. I *can't*."

She dug her heels into the grass, but only left two brown trenches as Sardonyx pushed her to the ferry. Peregrine, meanwhile, lashed Tertius to one of the willows with the ladder.

"She's called," Sardonyx said, and gritted his teeth as Yarrow's feet hit a root and she had to be lifted over it.

Yarrow was well aware that the Lady had called. The noise of it still vibrated in her bones. They ached with a sick, feverish ache, and that was all that kept her from struggling with any strength. She would throw up again if she went out on the hot, stinking water. If she touched the tower, she would vomit until her intestines unspooled from her mouth. If the Lady spoke again, Yarrow would beg to be killed just to unhear that voice. O, for the empty Bedchamber!

Sardonyx dragged her down the short marble quay and, when her legs would not let her into the ferry, tore a strip from his robe to lash her feet together. Peregrine arrived, and though he too was weak and shaking, between the two of them Yarrow was lowered into the boat and set up against its high carved stern, propped like a rolled-up rug.

"Why is this happening?" said Yarrow. Her teeth were chattering. Ants seemed to be crawling under her skin. Tears flowed from her eyes and snot dribbled from her nose. It tickled, and she wanted to wipe it, but her hand wouldn't quite obey her. The taste of bile burned in her mouth. And in the back of her mind, over and over, she saw Tertius casually crushing the ape. "Why does it feel like this? What's *wrong* with the tower?"

"I told you, little Mother," said Peregrine. "The Lady's dreams."

Sardonyx, in the middle of shoving off from the quay, shook his head. "Not quite."

With a long black pole, he punted the ferry out onto the lake. The rotten odor was stronger, but there was more of a breeze. Yarrow could breathe a little easier, though only in time to the pulsing air. Yellow Tower still left no reflection in the water; against the sky, the wheeling white birds were dark.

"It was never safe to approach the Ladies in the old days," Sardonyx said. Then, as if remembering this was a sacred story, he tuned his voice to a singsong register and said, "When the petals of the Rose Era were not yet fallen—"

In the midst of everything, that formula was some small comfort. Children's stories began that way in Grey House. Yarrow heard the women speaking it as they boiled laundry or told, in their perfunctory, elliptical way, the beginnings of Grey Tower.

"Are you listening?" said Sardonyx sternly.

"Yes," said Yarrow. The lake was very calm, but even so, the boat's motion did her stomach no favors, and she put her hand over her mouth.

"When the petals of the Rose Era were not yet fallen, every Lady of every tower was a luminous being. All loved them, and they loved all, with a love so strong and incandescent that it burned those who approached. The Ladies are the lights of the palace, and its hearts."

Sardonyx's voice slipped into his normal register. "I don't remember all the lore. It goes on for quite a while. But of the five Ladies, the originals, four are gone. Dead or departed, it doesn't matter. Only Citrine the Golden, she of Yellow Tower, is left from those days. And she wasn't always like this."

They were nearly halfway across the lake. The drone had not grown louder, but it was steadier, and Yarrow found herself thinking of *sleep* and *rest*. Her hand, she discovered, was trailing in the lukewarm water. How nice it would be to slip over the side and rest in that warmth. The dark green water would close over her head. The swaying lakeweed would be the softest of beds. She'd never hear the birds again, never be disturbed by the bilious sun or troubled by the choleric moon. To forget the North and the South, to let her vast body slip the shackles of East and West—

A hand shook her, and Yarrow blinked. She was leaning over the side, with her face practically in the water. Peregrine's hand tightened on her shoulder and he pulled her back to rest against the stern.

"*Her* holiness has curdled," said Sardonyx. "The valley has been full of it for centuries, like a pan of sour milk. She's been this way since Thistle for certain, possibly since Bellflower—maybe even since Lily, if anyone can tell a true story from that far back. The other Ladies have gone, but *she* continues, and it gets worse and worse. By now most people have moved to Red or Black, I think. Those of us who know our duty to her remain, and we are few."

"What went wrong?" said Yarrow.

"The Night of Bones, my predecessor told me. But our Mistress of the Library says it was the comet at the end of Lily, as recorded on the starry ceiling of her reading room. And the Father of the Cellars says it was the earthquake midway through Bellflower that did it. Some disaster shook the tower, and her great foot slipped, maybe, or in her fear she acted rashly. However it happened, she killed her minstrel."

"And?" said Yarrow. The ferry bumped against a pillar of the tower's portal.

"He had no apprentice yet, so his music was forgotten. After that she could not sleep," said the Keeper, making the ferry fast against the worn stone steps. "She has not slept in ages and ages. And it has driven her mad."

The droning was less on the short dock under the corbel arch. Yarrow could stand and walk, though her stomach and head felt full of tadpoles. The portal opened onto a blank, bone-colored wall. A passage ran away to the right, dimly illuminated by globes of some warm, flameless light. The walls and floor sweated. Yarrow turned on the threshold. Sardonyx was already casting off.

"Don't keep her waiting," he said, poling the boat so fast he was rapidly going out of earshot. "Get it over with as soon as possible."

Peregrine grinned mirthlessly at her. "The Lady banned loud voices in the valley centuries ago," he said. "She punishes anyone who disturbs her repose, whether it was intentional or not."

"Has anyone *ever* done it intentionally?"

"It's one way out of the valley."

Yarrow repeated the Litany of Roots under her breath, getting up to *mandrake* before her legs steadied enough for her to walk. She went into the passage.

The sunlight was swallowed up instantly, leaving only the gold light from the globes. The passage hit the corner of the tower and turned sharply left. Its walls went up to dizzying heights, perhaps all the way to the roof, which was lost in darkness.

A footstep sounded behind her. Yarrow jerked in shock. The Lady—? No. Peregrine had followed her. She almost told him to go back, but to go on alone . . . impossible. And this way, if she gave out, someone could, well, could make sure the Lady's will was done.

As they walked, the air became warmer and the dampness thicker and stickier. Their feet squelched in it, and it stretched in gooey bridges from sole to floor with their steps. The passage turned again. Clear jelly now coated the walls and floor and wrapped around the globes, dimming them. There was a dark blot against the bright circle of the nearest globe, and Yarrow paused to investigate it.

A tiny, coiled figure floated in the jelly. Like a little woman, it wore a simple dress with a stiff, bell-shaped skirt. Instead of a head, a horn or talon grew between its shoulders. A thin brown vein connected its abdomen with the globe.

"It's an embryo," said Yarrow.

They moved on. All the globes now had a small woman within them, and as they went farther, the lights were dimmer and the embryos larger. Their horns began to have little divots, and the dresses sprouted the beginnings of lace and ruching. At last they came to a turn beyond which all was darkness, and the last globe was wavering. Yarrow leaned toward it.

The embryo before her was roughly the size of a chicken and far more developed than the others. There was lace and embroidery on its gown, and its little hands were perfectly formed. It even moved a little, stirring as if in uneasy dreams. As Yarrow's face came near it, her breath shivered on the surface of the jelly, and the divots in the horn opened, revealing dozens of miniscule eyes. All of them rotated to look at her.

Yarrow jumped back and slipped. Peregrine had to catch her, and while they grappled, trying not to fall into the slime, the egg sac burst and the baby fell to the ground. They froze. The baby squeaked and struggled in the slime.

"I have to help it," said Yarrow. There were no birthing songs for Ladies of Yellow Tower—when she'd asked Old Yarrow why, she was brushed off, and now she knew the reason. The Lady of Yellow Tower had never needed help giving birth. So Yarrow sang, in a low but melodious voice, the song for Ladies of Grey Tower, and helped the baby stand up and scrape off the worst of the slime from its delicate, pretty dress.

The baby shook itself and, on unsteady legs, curtsied most beautifully to Yarrow, then to Peregrine. It toddled off through the slime and, before they could lose it in the darkness, they followed. It turned the corner and led them down the shadowy passage. Little lights pulsed under its skin and within its eyes: not enough for Yarrow and Peregrine to see by, but enough to lead them. It was picking up speed.

The first time it rounded a corner, Yarrow nearly screamed again and stopped walking, for the lights seemed to wink out. What if something had happened to it? But a moment later they appeared again: the baby was beckoning to them. The second time it happened, Yarrow was prepared, and they did not stop. The third time, a faint light was growing and the baby was visible against it. They were getting close to the Lady.

After the turn, before either of them was prepared, they stumbled over a low sill in the floor and fell into the warm heart of Yellow Tower: a high, wide space filling the entire triangular center of the building.

The baby trotted ahead, past mountains of bright jellied globes, toward a blank wall of dim yellow. It was laughing. The laugh was so infectious that Yarrow smiled, but her smile died in the making as the wall shifted. It was in fact no wall. She was looking at the skirts of the Lady.

Yarrow had thought the fresco was symbolic. Perhaps exaggerated, at worst. But no.

A hand bigger than the great hall of Grey House lowered from the heights. It gleamed like polished ivory, its portcullis-sized nails shining and perfect. The baby scrambled up its side, using the ridges of its fingerprints as handholds. As the hand lifted back up, the baby waved to them, as small in proportion to the hand as a grain of sand to Yarrow's own.

The hand went up and up, past acres of yellow silk fringed with forests of lace. The Lady appeared to be sitting with her knees drawn up to her chin, if Yarrow was seeing correctly—if anything so small could perceive anything so huge. Past the knees were ropes of pearls, each as big as a house, resting on landscapes of embroidery broken by ranges of ruffles. Then the collar began.

While she wore a green lace collar like her image in the Last Schoolhouse, it was not neat and symmetrical. It seemed to grow from her skin like ivy, and had woven its way into the very fabric of the tower. There was enough slack for her to move her head and shoulders about—if she chose, she could stoop down to the floor—but she could not leave the tower without tearing it. Every fine strand of the lace shone with unsteady fungal light, and interspersed along them were huge wet eyes. Some of these eyes were pressed to openings in the walls. Others were shut. Others rolled here and there. It was only a matter of time before she would see Yarrow and Peregrine.

From this nimbus of watchful green, the Lady's head loomed. It was birdlike, covered with feathers that were each bigger than the ferry. There were two eyes in the head as well, but gold rather than luminous green, and they reflected the others as a myriad of starry pinpricks. The beak was as big as the hands, and gleamed like polished copper. It opened as the hand came nearer, showing slick pink insides, and the bright speck of the baby vanished within it.

Yarrow let out a gasp. It echoed up the core of the tower, and the piles of eggs shuddered as the Lady's bulk shifted. Her three hands were upraised, one to the ceiling, one to each wall beside her, and every eye turned to Yarrow.

It's you, said the Lady. Welcome, sister. I love you. It has been ages.

Yarrow curtsied. "You're very kind," she said. "But I'm no sister of the Ladies."

Then you and your noise are subject to punishment, said the Lady. It is my law.

One great hand drifted down toward them, thumb and forefinger outstretched to pluck them from the floor.

"May I ask a question first?" said Yarrow quickly. "In memory of the Grey Sister."

The hand slowed and stopped just above her head. The Lady's own head rotated and pointed down, and she bent over them. One hand came down on a pile of eggs, extinguishing them and releasing a smell like moldy bread. The other came down near a second pile, shaking the eggs out of their pyramid and into a shapeless blob of lights. The third came down beyond Yarrow and Peregrine. The beak and golden eyes were above them. If they squinted, they could see their reflections in the Lady's eye, as if she held them in her mind.

You know the way to my heart, said the Lady. Are you certain you are not my sister? *There were six sisters to cross the river.*

"Quite sure," said Yarrow. How was the Lady speaking? Her beak did not move. There was no voice to be heard. She simply communicated.

Then in her memory I will answer, said the Lady. And to her memory I will dedicate the savor of your flesh.

"Why has winter fallen on Grey Tower?" Peregrine's hand gripped her arm, whether in fear or warning she did not know.

"Ahh," sighed the Lady. It was the first sound she had made, proper, *real* sound with the breath of her body, and the gale of it nearly bowled Yarrow and Peregrine over. All around the tower, she blinked her golden eyes.

"Please," said Yarrow. "I must know. And I need to know if those still there can undo whatever they've done to be punished."

The Beast, said the Lady. Winter falls; the Beast rises. It is the way of things.

"What beast?" said Yarrow.

The Beast, said the Lady. Soon she will break the surface and go down the West Passage, devouring as she moves, and the guardian of the West Passage will stop her, and all will be as it was before. It is the way of things. Why, sister, epitaph-bearer, do you not know this?

"I'm not your sister," said Yarrow. Peregrine's hand tightened briefly, as if to say *Pretend to be, it's your only way out.* But Yarrow could not lie to a Lady.

If you were ten times my sister, I would yet devour you. Oh, I am so tired. A bite before bed. Perhaps they will bring me a sip of milk, too. Be still. You are honored. The pain you will feel in my mouth is a sacrament. It is love. None of my true sisters felt that love. Let me punish you. Let me love you. Let me love you for disturbing me.

A hand stretched above them again, as if the ceiling of the great hall meant to grasp them. Peregrine was crying. Yarrow was not. She knew death too well to fear it. But she would not die without trying again.

"You're tired," said Yarrow. "Don't you want to sleep?"

The hand hesitated.

How can you help me sleep? said the Lady. You are nothing except loved and desired. If the stars cannot sing me to sleep, how can you?

Yarrow was gambling, and the risk made her head swim, but she answered. "There is a lullaby. We sang it to your sister. I can sing it for you."

"Lullaby?" said Peregrine.

Lullaby, said the Lady. (The hand relaxed and sagged to the floor.) She sang that to me once. My proper song. I can't sleep without it. Help me sleep and I won't punish you.

Proper song chilled Yarrow. The Lullaby of Reeds might be specific to Grey Tower. It might not work here. Or perhaps it wouldn't have long ago, but now, with a Lady mad from fatigue, it might. Regardless, she had nothing to lose by trying.

"I'll do it," said Yarrow. "If you let me and him go, I will sing for you."

I want to sleep, said the Lady fretfully. Help me sleep and I will give you the key to the wheel of the seasons. I will give you the crown of Yellow Tower and its orb. I will make you my true sister if you help me sleep. I want to sleep.

Her eyes filled with tears. One of them welled over and fell, splashing a pond's worth of hot salty water over Yarrow and Peregrine.

"I will," said Yarrow.

The Lady lowered her hand. Come closer to my face.

Swallowing her nerves, Yarrow stepped onto the hand. The yellow dress flowed past her, then the pearls and embroidery, then the head rising into place as the Lady resumed her position in the corner of the tower. The lace collar and its eyes settled into cobwebby shreds around her shoulders.

Sing, said the Lady.

There were words to the song that the old Yarrow had recited for her. Neither Yarrow had ever sung them. The words and music were not to be put together unless the song was performed for a Lady, which had not happened in Grey House since eras long gone. But it was a simple melody with simple words, not terribly hard to figure out.

> *Hush now, little girl*
> *In the waving reeds*
> *Mother's gone to fetch the moon*
> *Father's gone to sow the stars*
> *Sleep now, little girl*
> *In the waving reeds*
> *For the river sings*
> *All the song you need*

As she sang, the Lady's collar paled from green to yellow. The golden eyes closed, the heavy lids slipping like mudslides. The lullaby curled back on itself and repeated.

> *Hush now, little girl*

The green eyes twisted shut and winked out. Bit by bit the collar turned white and withdrew its tendrils, sinking back into itself until it was a ruff of symmetrical rays around her mighty neck. The hand holding Yarrow sank back to the floor, and Yarrow climbed down it, still singing.

Sleep now, little girl

The Lady's body sagged. Freed from her restraints, she slumped toward her knees; then, with a sigh, rolled onto her side, crushing the remaining eggs. Yarrow and Peregrine leaped back as her limp arms fell like rafters, *boom, boom, boom*. Last of all her head hit the floor, ruffling its feathers with the wind of its impact. The beak struck the stones, and the whole tower trembled from its foundation to its crown.

Silence fell. Shafts of sunlight came in through the windows. The great sleeping form of the Lady lay curled up like one of her embryos. Her indrawn breath broke the silence. She did not exhale. Her chest expanded further and further. Yarrow and Peregrine stepped back.

Stitches like hawsers snapped in her bodice. Pearls tumbled and rolled like boulders, grinding the remains of the eggs into a yellow-brown paste. Still she kept inhaling. Yarrow and Peregrine ducked into the passage, peeping around its edge to see what came next.

At last her inhalation slowed and stopped. With another vast sigh, the Lady burst into ivory-colored birds. They whirled like a cyclone, filling the tower with the deafening rustle of their wings and the sharp sweetness of their voices. Some of them foraged among the squashed eggs for a moment, but most wheeled up, up through calm beams of sunlight and out the windows, and in another moment they were gone.

The empty dress of the Lady was left in hills and valleys of yellow silk, spotted white with bird shit. Nothing remained of her body except the beak, sharp and glistening on the sticky floor. And that was the end of the Lady of Yellow Tower.

20. Tertius Moves On and So Do We

Outside, the suffocating haze had lifted and the drone had gone silent for good. The lake smelled fetid still, but the wind was blowing sweetly from the east. Peregrine whistled for Tertius, who waded through the water to them. Peregrine washed himself in the lake, but Yarrow could not bring herself to, messy as she was. And she could hardly bear to board Tertius again. Around its lips was a rusty scum of ape blood.

When it reached the far shore, Yarrow spoke. "I'll go the rest of the way by myself."

"Are you sure, little Mother?" said Peregrine.

"I am." She did not give her reasons. Whatever Peregrine knew or guessed, he did not say. He only passed her pack to her.

"Maybe we'll meet again," he said.

"I would like that," said Yarrow.

"So would I." Peregrine rummaged in the pink tent for a moment and took out a bottle. "This is mine, but I think you need it more than I do right now."

Yarrow stored it in her pack. "Thank you." She curtsied. "And thank you for your help, Butler Itinerant."

"Thank you for the most interesting journey I've had yet, Mother of Grey House." Peregrine laughed, but the bright shape of Yellow Tower caught his attention and he sighed. "They'll want to know what happened here. Over at Black, they'll ask."

"I'll tell them the truth," said Yarrow. "They can't do worse to Grey than what's already going on."

"You have to tell the guardian of the Passage," said Peregrine. "Only she can handle the Beast. According to the songs."

"There is no guardian till I make one," said Yarrow. Among the women, the knowledge of the Beast belonged to the Goldenseals; Yarrows had no part of it.

"Try guarding the Passage yourself," said Peregrine. "What's one more deed for Yarrow LXXVI?" He rapped on the platform and Tertius got up from its elbows. "But I suppose it would need to be a new day for a Mother to do that."

Yarrow laughed bitterly. Indeed. Things needed to go back to the way they were. If you had enough old days, who needed new ones?

"If you want to shorten the way, you can take the train from Angel's Head," said Peregrine. He flipped a little disc to her. "That token will get you to Black, if you're sure you don't want a ride."

Yarrow thanked him, slipping the token into her sleeve. They waved to each other as long as Tertius was in view. Then Yarrow turned and, of course, the West Passage yawned before her. She looked over her shoulder for one last glimpse of Yellow Tower.

At first nothing seemed odd. Then she saw: in the rippling lake, the golden reflection of the tower shimmered. A grey flag broke from its pinnacle. Yarrow smiled, set her jaw, and went on her way.

An Interlude in Blue Tower

Azure Vole 3 awakened before the light of dawn. There was no reason to, except habit. The Company of Illuminators had little work these days. He washed his face and hands and donned his indigo robe over his linen shirt. Though spotted with pigment and streaked with gesso, it was nicer than any his brethren had: he'd traded a painting to the Master of the Silk Rooms for it.

All the Voles slept on the floor of the scriptorium. The great room was a mass of shadows. Made for dozens, even a hundred illuminators, it now held only four, plus two apprentices, and the many empty desks and chairs were dark hazards to navigate in the blue hour before sunrise. To get to the dining hall for breakfast, he had to tiptoe over and around his three compatriots: Vermillion 1, Verdigris 2, and Ochre 5. (Ochre tended to sleep with his hands flung out, a different position every morning, very difficult to plan for and avoid.) There had been a fourth Vole, but he'd left one day and never returned (due to boredom, Ochre claimed), and the tower census takers hadn't gotten around to renumbering them.

It was early spring. Through the windows in the corridor came chilly air, laden with the scent of green. The vines all over the tower were in bloom, but until the sun rose, you wouldn't smell them at all. Against the ultramarine sky, Black Tower was drawn in charcoal. Its lamps were beginning to be lighted.

To see by, the dining hall had only candles and a great fireplace at one end, large and hot enough to roast a whole ox. There were seven long tables, and a dais with the high table for the Lady. Each office had its own assigned seat, intended to prevent scrambling at mealtimes, but now fully half the benches stood empty even on holidays, and at the high table, only three of the Masters had bothered to arrive for breakfast.

The Lady herself never came. She was old, even for one of her august sisterhood, and Vole had never seen her except as a shadowy form in a curtained palanquin, carried here and there through the great rooms of the tower. Her two daughters likewise never attended a meal, the tension between them always on the verge of erupting into a fight.

Azure took his seat. Servers moved along the tables, dishing out barley pottage. It was a little too thick today, and had too many leeks, but at least he was in time to get a chunk of bread; the kitchens usually ran out quickly, and felt no need to make more. This he ate with a very sharp cheese and a lot of small beer.

He lingered over his empty bowl. There was nothing much to do that day. He might go down to the library and look at some of the printed books, or wander up to the Archives and admire old manuscripts. Verdigris was at work on a little book of poems for a Master in Red, but the other Illuminators would probably just get drunk around midday—Vole himself included.

His own Master, who had passed the cognomen *Azure* to him, had bemoaned the sorry state of the Company, and drunk himself to death. That should have been a cautionary tale, but there were days when Azure saw the bottom of his cup and accepted that he and the others were likely to ignore the warning. There were so few people left, and with the palace trees dead or dying, what everyone needed from Blue Tower was not beautiful books but food.

Leaving the dining hall, he passed Verdigris and Vermilion coming in. Both of them smelled of ale already, which renewed Azure's thirst, and he went back upstairs to the scriptorium. In one corner, framed by two empty desks and backed by a high shelf of manuscripts, Ochre sat by a cask, dressed in only his shirt, finishing off the last of a row of three mugs. Upon seeing Azure, he filled one from the cask and passed it over, heady with yarrow and juniper.

"I'm getting rusty," said Azure after his second mug. "I just want to work again."

Ochre laughed, belched, and laughed. "Drink up."

"I don't want to drink; I want something to work on."

"We already break most of the rules anyway. Why not break the one on materials and make your own book?"

"I can't do that. I don't have anything to put in one."

They had this conversation often, and after the ale clouded their memories, they never fully recalled it. Ochre was content to sit around, take the occasional task that came his way, and otherwise drink and piss out the window, among other amusements. Though to a casual observer Azure might seem to be doing the same, in his chest was a wide-ranging restlessness: he needed some *work,* or he was not happy. And unlike Vermilion and Verdigris, he would not waste the scriptorium's supplies on doodles or little projects of his own. Azure was, more or less, a follower of rules, no matter how often Ochre urged him otherwise.

Ochre went to the window to relieve himself. He liked to brag that he was the reason the vines grew so profusely on the west side of the tower. The stock response from his brethren was *But we're on the east side,* to which he'd respond *Exactly.* This time Azure did not play his part. Some days, the ale made him dull and a little weepy, and even when Ochre repeated his joke a little louder, Azure ignored it. With a sigh, Ochre stumbled back to the little nook by the cask and dropped to his knees before Vole.

"Poor little boy," said Ochre with a pout. "Having a sad day again?"

There was a familiar eager brightness in his eyes. Down the sagging front of his shirt, Azure could see that the ale was stirring his blood. Some days, it did that to Ochre. That was usually a pleasant diversion, so Azure assented this time as well, allowed Ochre to tug up his robe, tumble a bit there in the corner by the cask, stain the indigo silk with a little more spilled ale. Ochre was simple flesh, which was a strange thing to lie with: soft here, hard there, smooth here, hairy there. Azure himself had a bird's head, which meant there were pleasures Ochre could give him that he couldn't give Ochre—and vice versa, if Ochre was in certain moods. He was not in one of those moods today, which was just as well; Azure had barely enough energy for the task at hand.

When they were done, Azure cast aside his robe entirely and collapsed backward on the floor in shirt and open hose, fanning his sweat away. Ochre, now entirely naked, lay next to him and attempted to drink more. He ended up slopping it on both of them. Azure was irritated a moment—how dare he be so careless—but that irritation was swallowed up in a wave of discontent so powerful that it spilled out of his eyes in large, hot tears. It had not been a pleasant diversion after all.

"Are you crying because you love me?" said Ochre lightly.

"Yes," said Azure.

"Good man," said Ochre, sitting up and reaching between Azure's legs to squeeze him gently. Filling another mug, he passed it to Azure, who sat up to drink and lay back down.

Dust drifted through the scriptorium, visible only in the light from the windows, but it was so thick in that light that you wondered how much you were breathing in. You could almost feel it settling on you. A thick coating of dust, turning you into another piece of disused furniture in a half-abandoned room.

Vermilion and Verdigris returned soon. Ochre slid the sleeve of his shirt over his crotch and kept drinking. Azure still lay on the floor, but as he had already been more or less dressed, he made no move to do anything at all.

"Can't you do that somewhere else?" said Verdigris, as he always did. Ochre made a rude gesture, as *he* always did. Anyway, Verdigris had been caught with Ochre himself once or twice, and with Vermilion several times. He was not one to talk, but had to protest for decency's sake.

"Order's come in," said Vermilion, entering just behind Verdigris and brandishing a piece of paper. "From Grey House, oddly enough. Guardian wants a copy of *Goodlie Instruction for Tender Wits,* or at least one page of it. Ochre, rhymes. That's you."

Ochre put out a hand for the paper, then stopped. "Give it to Azure this time."

"Are you sure?" said Vermilion. "It would give you something to do besides turning this room into a bawdy house."

"It takes two or more for that," said Ochre, "and if *you're* all busy . . ." He winked as he drank again.

Vermilion sighed and tossed the paper onto Azure's belly. "Get on it," he said. "She wants it as soon as possible."

Azure did not immediately obey. His eyes remained on the ceiling: flaking white plaster, dark beams, a cobweb every foot or so. *Work.* But only one page? What was the point of that? It would amuse him for a week at most.

Ochre's face floated into view. He was grinning. "Come on," he said. "You wanted something to do."

He spiked the paper on Azure's beak and went away. At last, with a groan, Azure got up, shrugged on his robe, and staggered to his desk. The ale was doing unkind things to his head and stomach. The paper,

written in the heavy black lettering still used in Grey, asked for a page
from *Goodlie Instruction*: the rhyme beginning *There were six sisters
to cross the river*. Why would the guardian need that? Moreover, if she
knew the first line, why not the rest of it? The rhyme was common
enough.

Well, it was work, and it was the role of the Company of Illuminators to fulfill such requests. He sent an apprentice to the Archives
for the book, and when it came, opened to the page requested. In the
same black letters as the guardian's note, the rhyme ran:

> *There were six sisters to cross the river*
> *One fell down in the cold, cold ground*
> *There were five sisters to cross the river*
> *One with thorns and iron was crown'd*
> *There were four sisters to cross the river*
> *One stood guard at the mouth of the sea*
> *There were three sisters to cross the river*
> *One ate gold and jewels with glee*
> *There were two sisters to cross the river*
> *One taught frogs their chorus to sing*
> *There was one sister to cross the river*
> *One caught death in a reedy ring*
> *There were no sisters to cross the river*
> *One springs up from the cold, cold ground*
> *Who'll she catch when her time comes round?*

He'd heard this once as a child. It was a counting, clapping sort of
game that nobody played anymore, but older generations reminisced
about the fun of chasing each other at the end. Like other such things,
you'd find it referenced in texts but with many variations: a different
order for the sisters, different acts that kept them from crossing the
river. Most of them had only five, though. What possible use could a
guardian have for this nonsense?

Urgent, said the request, so once an apprentice brought up parchment nicely tacked to a board, Azure got Ochre to start on the lettering. He was by far the fastest and most accurate, while Azure himself
might labor for days and still not get it right. Meanwhile, Azure began
grinding pigments. An apprentice fetched some distemper, and between the two of them, they blended the paint as Ochre wrote away.

The page in *Goodlie Instruction* was illuminated with five roundels and much fine tracery. Azure studied it carefully. Despite the skill, it was obviously a Lily reworking of a Thistle original. Too much white space—these periods of stylistic transition were always a little clumsy. A Thistle artist would never have left that awkward blank at the bottom right. In each of the roundels was one of the Five Sisters who founded the palace. Naturally: if anyone thought of the rhyme nowadays, they ascribed it to a folk tradition about the very beginning of everything. In versions of the rhyme with six sisters, the sixth was taken to mean the earth, which cycles between the rising fruitfulness of spring and the falling decay of autumn.

Ochre passed him the page, neatly and perfectly lettered. "I think she only *really* wants the rhyme itself," he said wryly to Azure. "You don't *need* to illuminate it."

Azure gave him a look, perhaps more severe than intended, and Ochre smiled an easy smile and went back to the cask. With pencil and ruler in hand, Azure laid out the horizontal lines for the little friezes, then the vertical where the roundels and traceries would swirl. Down the vertical, he marked off a point every two inches for a total of five, then took up a compass to draw the roundels, centered on each point. The page was still unbalanced, though. After a moment of thought, he added a sixth. Better that way—much more natural.

Then came the business of drawing, gilding, and painting. There was very little gold leaf at hand, but the page needed little, so that was all right. The apprentice had already made up some fresh garlic juice, with which Azure picked out tiny bits of foliage and the eyes of the Ladies. It was hardly dry before he applied the leaf: it did not look very good, but a rush job was a rush job. Time to paint. An even middle tone to start, then the darker shades, then fine lines of white lead to pick out the highlights. The Ladies took shape under his brush, exact copies of their sisters in the original; Azure was the best at imitating older styles. He left the sixth circle empty as long as possible, afraid of his own boldness.

Why had he done it? To Azure, the truest answer was probably that it looked better and he wanted more to do. There may have been another answer he was not aware of, but who could say, after all? It could not be avoided now that it was begun, anyway.

The other Ladies had each their model in the older page. But the sixth one, this sister in the ground, what would she look like? That question brought his brush up short. Last time he'd painted something original had been, oh, years ago. He'd been an apprentice still. Did he even remember how?

He had to remember, for there were no representations of the sixth sister in the Archives, she being at most a regional variant, but he could not leave the roundel blank or fill it with something off-theme. And he had to remember soon, for the guardian wanted this and he'd already delayed its completion. Black had her beetles and moon, Grey her stones and veil, Blue her tower and frogs, what would do for the sixth? Well, she *was* the earth after all.

Azure took up some verdigris and yellow ochre and thinned them down. He put an ochre face in the center of the roundel. He gave her a green dress, the sleeves dagged like oak leaves. For adornment, she wore vines. As they twined around her arms, a slip of the brush brought them outside the roundel. For a moment Azure was aghast: *a mistake!* But he rather liked the effect, so he joined the vines up with the tracery and added even more, so that all the decoration on the page stemmed from her. He touched it up with white highlights and set it to dry.

Ochre saw it and raised his eyebrows. "What have you done?"

"Something new," said Azure, and drained a cup of room-warm ale. The sun was rising now. Or setting. What day was it?

A courier came to collect the page and take it off to Grey. Unbeknownst to Azure, his first original work in years would be the last thing Hawthorn the Guardian saw before she died. He planned to make more, but soon word came that the Lady of Yellow had died, and at the news, her distant sister who ruled Blue expired of shock, and the two daughters both decided to take their mother's place.

book three

HAWTHORN

21. Kew and Frin Start Walking

Kew and Frin left the Obsidian courts after breakfast the next day. During the night, the Lady had progressed to another of her mansions, but she'd left orders that Kew should take a no-name with him as a squire. *What's a squire?* the beekeepers and apprentices asked themselves, but nobody would dare ask the Lady. A servant? No, since both would be no-names, free of rank and its concerns, a squire must mean a kind of friend for Kew, and that in turn meant Frin.

Frin did not want to leave the court he had known his whole life. His parents were beekeepers; he had grown up playing among the slow-striding hives; he had expected to become a beekeeper himself within a year or two. Now all that was in jeopardy, merely because this stranger had somehow charmed the Lady into granting him a favor. Everyone in the courts of Black knew that people who went to the tower rarely returned. It was a place of marvels so exquisite that they became dangers, and of dangers so exquisite they became marvels. You might stay for love of it, or you might die for love of it. Either way, you would remain.

As a parting gift, One Robin gave Frin a bee sleeping in a red wooden box.

"If you open it, she'll wake up," said One. "Give her any message and send her back to us. Likely we won't be able to help, but we'll—we'll leastways know what you wanted."

In her hand she held the hornet; it had been removed from Kew that morning. It curled up in her palm like a tiny cat, and she stroked it absently.

Frin put the bee in a green cloth bag along with his spare tunic, hood, and puttees, and as much water, bread, and dried fruit as he could fit. He joined Kew near the door. They would not be taking the West Passage: the rubbish made it nearly impassable. One Robin had sketched a quick map to guide them through the halls.

Take the Long Gallery until you come to the seventh red door on the right. The Gallery ran nearly the length of the Passage walls, and it was lined with portraits of Obsidian Ladies, going all the way back to the lineage's foundation at the end of Apple, when the Guardians' steel had been used to kill the last Apple Lady. Frin did not look at them, only at the frayed remnants of the carpet on the floor. Kew stared openly at the paintings, but his expression was as blank as if the wall itself had been.

"You all right?" said Frin.

"My head feels a little odd," said Kew. "I suppose I should have gotten more sleep."

"We can stop in here if you want," said Frin, making as if to take off his pack. "You ain't walked much lately."

"No, no," said Kew. They passed another painting of an Obsidian, great hands splayed. A shudder ran up Kew's spine, hit his skull, and became a terrible headache. He didn't say anything to Frin.

Go through the red door and take the upper colonnade north. Already they were out of Frin's knowledge. The door opened onto a landing looking out over a marble courtyard full of statues. To the right, a stone staircase went down to a colonnade. To the left, it went up to another, identical in every respect except location. Both were lined with caryatids in rhythmic dancers' poses. Kew felt a twinge of memory: their swaying postures echoed the Labyrinth Dance that Hawthorn and the women had done every spring on a worn-away track in one of the courtyards of Grey. Frin felt a similar twinge: the caryatids looked like the keepers dancing to awaken the bees at the end of winter.

"It must be Lady-day by now," said Kew. "I don't like losing track of time."

"What's Lady-day?" said Frin.

"You don't have it? I thought it was celebrated all over the palace."

"Neh. We've got the quarter days, of course, and the intercalaries, and—" Frin noticed Kew's expression and let his sentence melt away into a shrug. After a moment of walking, Frin went on, "I guess Lady-day is for your own Lady?"

"Yes, I think so. Hawthorn had a book about it, but she said the book didn't tell the whole story."

"What *was* the whole story?" said Frin, feeling that a good squire must be able to converse about such things.

"There was a Grey Lady who—I don't know. She bent the West Passage as if she were making a miracle. I understand directions well enough, but this had something to do with—changing them. That day was celebrated as Lady-day. I don't really know why. The book was missing a lot of pages."

On the colonnade's open side was Black Tower. This was the closest Kew had ever been to it. The tower's height could not be guessed. From Grey you could see the great piers and flying buttresses that held it up, but now Kew could tell that the piers sprouted from a spherical base, then angled upward like the petals of a flower. While he had only ever known it to have three such "arms," at this new angle he saw that it had five. Each pier was buttressed in turn by a smaller one, and so on, making this vast structure a lacy filigree of stone. Every time he saw Black Tower, it showed him a new face.

Perhaps because he was looking at these faces so intently, he got them lost.

22. Kew and Frin See the Stars

Upon the rough hide of the palace we see two boys crawling like insects upon an old cow. The one insect is tall and thin, mantis-like. The other insect is short and round, beetle-like. They are not speaking much as they navigate the cracks and crevices of this ancient skin. We whir closer to investigate.

We can see that they do not know what to make of each other. The tall one does not understand the sociable world of the other, nor his air of quiet good cheer. The short one is in awe of the other, with whom a Lady has meddled. It does not make for easy conversation as they scramble through ruins and half-ruins.

The West Passage is, of course, choked with the wreckage of feasts. Were it not, how much easier would their journey be! For though the corridors and courtyards around Black Tower are clearer than in Grey, there are more rooms to go through: grand, dismal rooms, built for the courtiers of Ladies, long-abandoned. Here is a chamber painted with bird-headed figures surrounding a crowned Lady with three and a half arms. And here is a room walled and floored with amber. And there is a chamber whose ribbed vaulting is carved into stacks of tiny people upholding a rosette in the ceiling center; the rosette is a miracle, for silver liquid wells up in its center, beads, and falls in a constant stream of sour-smelling droplets. The boys know better than to touch it, and give a wide berth to the ebony basin in which the liquid pools.

Now they come to a fork in the corridors. The left fork goes up. The right continues at one level and bends out of sight. At last, the short one speaks.

"One said that if we wanted a quicker way, we'd go by the Alchemists' Turret. But only if the weather is fine."

They both look out a nearby window. The weather is fine.

"I don't know the alchemists," says the one—Kew, his name is, as we remember.

"There ain't none anymore," says the other—Frin, his name is, as we remember. "Not since—oh, I forget. Lily, I guess. Or Thistle. Point is, we won't meet them. But the place is still named after them."

We see Kew shrug, rather slowly and lopsidedly. He is curious, perhaps, but afraid to show it: if he expresses an interest in something, Frin will go along with it, and that makes Kew rather afraid of imposing his will upon Frin.

"If it gets us there more quickly," Kew says. "Why not?"

Frin smiles and nods. Perhaps he thinks Kew is hiding his curiosity because it will get him laughed at. Certainly before now he has seen Kew come at his own wishes slantwise. And so they go left.

We see them now going up a long, long staircase. They are in the outer shell of a great hall. The inside, which they do not see, is full of old furniture moldering in shafts of dusty light. A little greenish creature snores curled up on an ironwood chair. They do not see that either. Much later, at sunset, the creature will wake up, stretch, put on an upside-down funnel for a hat, and go about her work sweeping cobwebs out of one corner of the hall. The rest of the mess is someone else's duty.

At the top of the staircase, the boys come out into sunlight. They stand on a small square terrace with a mostly intact balustrade. Black Tower is there, quite suddenly and grimly. Banners with the crest of the Willow dynasty fly from its many spires. They ignore it as best they can: it may be that Frin is too used to it to care; it may be that Kew is overcome by visions not his own, and must look somewhere else. At the other end of the terrace, another staircase plunges down. Much farther down.

They are now in the outer shell of another building. This one is an old hall divided into living quarters for the unnamed people who served the guards of Black Tower. The hall no longer serves its original function; neither do the living quarters, the unnamed people, nor the guards. The outer wall of this staircase is very recent, dating perhaps to just before the rise of Willow. We know this because of a certain solidity about the stonework: it is less delicate or flashy than some other eras, hearkening back to the unobtrusive elegance of Apple. It is possible that Kew notices this as well, for he keeps pausing to examine it and must be urged along. The inner wall of this staircase is quite different, and it is probably this that draws Kew's interest to the outer, for why would they be so mismatched?

The inner wall is lined with niches, each with a statue of a Lady. They are quite weathered, and the names are faded away, at least near the stairs. The stonework there is elaborate and finely detailed, at least as far as we can tell under the veil of age. It might be Lily; it might be Thistle. Both eras are known for the omnipresent ornament of their architecture. It is impossible to say. Our eyes might be compared to the hands of an apothecary running over a quilted comforter, trying to diagnose the broken ankle beneath.

We can at least see that the niches change the farther the boys descend. The statuary becomes more geometric and stylized. The shapes are so clear and strongly marked that even with their great age, it is not hard to see how beautiful they once were. Where the Ladies above are locked in swirling motion, flinging out wings, arms, eyes, and tongues over passersby, the Ladies here are calmer, pensive, folding their limbs in on their varied bodies like dead spiders. The stones of the wall are large and irregular; if they were polished once, they are not now. Likely, this part reminds Kew of Grey, for there are many similarities. He may even think of the room in Grey Tower full of identical veiled figures labeled *Yarrow*.

We can theorize that this place was a memorial, though certain of its features complicate such an idea. Firstly, though a dynasty might destroy or ignore physical remnants of its predecessors, it would not preserve them like this. Those who rule from Black Tower keep things that serve their purposes, like the Irises' wheel of seasons, and nothing else. Secondly, the proper place of remembrance for departed Ladies is upon the grounds of Grey Tower. Thirdly, the names seem to occupy roughly the same space on each niche, allowing for stylistic differences across the eras.

At last, on the lowest level, where the staircase smooths out into a long walk between high walls, we see Kew stop. He bends to look in a corner where erosion has left one name alone.

"What is it?" Frin says.

Kew points.

Hawthorn, it says.

Kew's eyes move sidewise, upwise, downwise. His lips move, shaping what looks like the name—his future name, if he is worthy of taking it. If this place is a memorial, then it memorializes the long, long line of Guardians and the Ladies they served. He might hope that when his name is joined with the Willow Lady's image, hers will be more impressive than some of these monuments. We feel the weight of history, perilously suspended, bear down upon us.

"Let's keep moving," says Kew. His expression is grim.

"Are you all right?" says Frin. "I—I don't know what that says." He hurries after a suddenly energetic Kew.

While Kew explains, let us move back a little to take in the rest of their journey. A second staircase rises from this bottom level and climbs to the top of a broken-backed roofline. From there, a walkway meanders between gables and turrets until it reaches a long, level battlement of the West Passage. At the other end of the battlement, makeshift lantern tracks bypass a—but no, let us first look slightly beyond. After the battlement, the way plunges through a series of corridors, loggias, and stairwells until it reaches the territory of Ebony. From there, a clear path is swept to the great jet-toothed gate of Black Tower, guarded by forty Sparrows Minor and watched by many eyes. A lantern is leaving the tower and passing back toward us; let us follow it along the track until it comes to the bypass. Here the Sparrow within changes their whistling to a slower tempo: the tracks are rickety and in poor repair, and require careful handling.

The lantern switches to the newer track, running in a wobbly semicircle under the blank, blackened gaze of scorched pilasters and burst windows. A few moments later, it reaches the safe harbor—the saf*er* harbor, anyway—of the old track, and the Sparrow picks up the pace. Soon the lantern is whizzing away down the West Passage. Perhaps we shall see it later. For now, we must look at what the Sparrow avoided: the ruins of the Alchemists' Spire.

If the records are to be believed, this compound right beneath the Great Tower was devoted to the Owls, royal alchemists to the Thistles. In the dormitories lived their acolytes and servants; in the halls they ate; in the storerooms they kept their strange substances and tools; in the workshops they bent to their labor. It seems remarkable that such powerful Ladies as the Thistles would need the assistance of anyone, let alone the alchemists and their dubious achievements, but that toward the end of their era, the Thistles and their miracles were exhausted and fading. The brief flare of wonders before the end was possibly due to the alchemists' efforts. Regardless, it was only a false renewal, like the last flicker of a dying candle. And the Owls themselves are gone. The only physical remnants left of them are collected upon the burned floor of the Spire's central chamber, open to the elements for years upon uncounted years. The truth is here, whatever it was. Here, amid the shards of old roofs and walls, Kew and Frin stumble out of a half-choked stairway, their faces and hands grubby with soot, and blink in the dimming sunlight.

"What is this place?" says Frin.

Kew can only guess that it is the Alchemists' Spire, but when he says so, the pitch of his voice goes up and he rubs the back of his neck. Frin smiles, not quite looking in Kew's direction.

Against the bluing sky, we see the ruined vaulting of the spire, black and sparse like dry branches. Something erupted out of the north and west walls, leaving only burnt-clean stone, and destabilized the south wall, which has collapsed into rubble. The north wall is largely intact, along with a portion of the tall, sharp roof. A haze of ultramarine still shimmers on the ceiling, and two or three gilded stars still cling to it. Lower down, upon shelves built into the walls themselves, are glittering fragments of instruments and glass vessels. Between the shelves are carved pillars, each an allegorical figure. Some of them we might recognize: there is Sir Lacklady, who signifies uncertainty; there is Madame Frogwit, who signifies eloquence. There are others we do not: a hooded creature with a single curious gauntlet on; a nubile person cupping a naked breast in one hand, the other holding a sword: at its foot, a meager fountain bubbles into a cracked basin. Kew stares for a moment, furrows his brow, and looks away.

Closer to the south wall, the shelves give way to a frieze, which in turn gives way to rubble. It is bordered with leaves and birds and frogs, all quite weathered but retaining a buoyant charm. (Frin traces the age-softened head of a frog with his finger.) Within the frieze are set many tiny, random circles of metal, once gilded. Each of them is labeled, and Frin is about to call Kew over to read them when he sees Kew standing on the very edge of the western wall, a dark shape against the greater darkness of the Great Tower.

Kew's lips are moving. Listening carefully, we hear a faint whisper. "The Beast rises, and she will ride it to the conquest of Black Tower. She is the cleverest, most glorious of Ladies. The Beast obeys her. It obeys nobody else." That is news indeed for us to carry.

Frin's hand grips his arm. Kew shakes his head. "What was I saying?"

"I don't know," Frin asks. "But come away from the ledge. Come." He tugs. "Please," he adds, for Kew's feet don't move. He puts his free hand on Kew's back. At that, as if it were a signal, Kew turns and comes with Frin back to the floor.

Frin urges Kew to sit down. He wets a kerchief in the fountain to scrub at his hands and face. Meanwhile, Kew sits upon what appears to be a disused furnace and clasps his hands to his knees, which seem to be shaking.

"You missed a spot," Kew says eventually.

Frin sighs. "Ain't a mirror to check in."

"Come here." Kew's tone is mildly exasperated. He takes the cloth and scrubs at Frin's jawline.

"You're filthy, too," says Frin. "Here, I'll—" He rinses out the kerchief and hands it back to Kew.

While Kew washes himself, Frin picks up a piece of stone and plugs the basin as well as possible. It fills. Frin unlaces his cotehardie and slips it off, along with his hood. He takes up handfuls of water and splashes himself, puffing and blowing against the chill. Kew shifts in his seat. Growing up in the robed and wimpled and gowned environs of Grey, he may not be used to someone so casually removing clothing. He scrubs at himself even harder, and—is he?—he *is* looking at Frin now and then, and looking away, and looking back, as if he has never seen such a sight.

It is a common enough sight, a young man rinsing himself off. Frin is quite average for a beekeeper's apprentice: short, with a soft body and sinewy hands, dark where the sun has darkened him, somewhat paler where it hasn't. His black hair is close-cropped but would be curly if it grew out. The short velvety fur of his ears does not continue anywhere else that we can see. If Kew is fascinated, it must be by Frin's evident comfort with being himself. Certainly *we* see nothing of interest.

Though there is something odd here. A black spot against Frin's chest, which one might think was part of him if it wasn't bobbing around like a pendant. Even then, it could still be part of him. Kew seems to be gathering the courage to ask.

"All yours," says Frin, turning around and shaking water off his limbs and out of his hair.

At the fountain, Kew hesitates. At last, he removes his long overgown and rolls up his sleeves.

We observe a repetition of this curious staring and not-staring, but from Frin. And again, the Grey apprentice is a common enough sight. Skinny, knobbly, tall, Kew seems whipped together from old twigs; if a bone *can* stick out, it does. The sun has never touched his skin. He is simple flesh, as far as we can see, and his eyes are the large bright eyes of Grey. To Frin, they must seem miraculous. To Kew, perhaps Frin's small dark eyes are the miracles.

"What's that around your neck?" says Kew as he splashes and rinses.

"An old miracle," says Frin. "One Robin lends it to travelers sometimes, says it's for luck. Here, look."

As he leans over, the pendant swings away from his neck, and Kew catches it. Kew's brow furrows—it must be hard to pick out details in the dimming light, especially on an item this dark—and he draws the pendant closer to his eyes, pulling Frin's face toward him as well. Kew does not seem to notice. After a moment in which we see Frin's eyes dart from side to side, the muscles in his shoulders relax as he waits for Kew to finish the examination. His patience is admirable, if patience it is.

What Kew sees: a bulbous vial of onyx about as large as two walnuts. Overlapping triangles are incised all over it, giving it the appearance of thin, tight petals, or perhaps spines. At the narrow neck, they turn into parallel grooves and end in a similarly grooved stopper, also of onyx. At the back of the vial is a projecting horizontal cylinder, through which the slender chain passes. There are signs of wear all over the object: tiny chips on the edges of the cylinder and stopper, a few very slight scratches wrapping around the base, as if the vial has been kept upon a stand and rotated ungently. But overall, it is in excellent condition.

Now Kew looks up from the vial and may realize how close Frin is, for he releases it gently and sits back. Frin straightens up and stretches. It cannot have been easy for Kew with his childhood, never being close to anyone: obviously the only other children nearby were the girls in the house. And Hawthorn, though by all accounts protective and more or less loving toward her apprentice, was by those same accounts not particularly affectionate, nor did she see much point in giving him any time to make friends. And so we might think, as we watch Kew watch Frin stretch, that Kew has never learned what a normal interaction is, and that almost everything a person does is charged with a meaning for Kew that may not necessarily be intended. We cannot know for sure; we may only surmise.

"Look!" Frin says, pointing up. "Stars!"

In the close-packed towering warrens of Grey, Kew would never have seen more than a small rectangle of the night sky. In the broader but heavily planted courts of Black, Frin would not have seen much more. Now their eyes roam the sky, unimpeded by walls as their bodies never shall be.

"Do they have names?" Frin asks.

Kew hesitates. "If they do, I never learned them." He stands beside Frin.

Far away, the beacon of Red smudges out many of them in smoke and hazy orange light, but nearer, only the filigree of burnt roofbeams stands between them and the stars. There is a long river of sparkling light running across the sky from north to south, blotted here and there with dark patches like rocks, and on either side of it are close-packed stars like the lamplit windows of the palace. The boys do not seem to be breathing. At last Frin remembers to inhale. The sound breaks the silence, and Kew inhales too.

We do not know the names of the stars, either, if names they have. Nobody has ever asked them, and surely not even the Ladies of Black would dare to give a name to a star. But our attention, like the boys', might be drawn to a particular cluster almost directly overhead where the "river" narrows before broadening again.

Kew points here. There are six of them just on the west side of the narrows, each quite brilliant, and immediately across to the east is a seventh, far brighter, and burning a cold, bitter green. Frin takes a moment to see it. His vision may be less acute than Kew's.

"I would think if any of them had names, it would be those," says Kew. He sounds as if he is trying to discover some fact, as if by hinting that the fact exists, he can call it up.

Frin shrugs. He goes to his pack, which he has left by the basin, muttering something about being hungry. Kew remains staring upward until Frin calls him over.

Frin points at the wall. "Can you tell me what that says?"

Though rubble still blocks most of it, we can see that a florid frame is carved into the wall, extending for many feet beneath the debris. Within the frame are little words, lines, and dots, all forming geometric figures. Many of the dots have a few rays. A few dots have many,

perhaps indicating brightness. To Frin, it is probably meaningless, but
to Kew, who now begins to look from the frame to the sky and back
again, it may appear to be what we have already concluded it is: an as-
tronomical map.

We see Kew kneel beside the rubble. His finger moves across a
grid, blurred by age and choked with dust.

"Those stars," he says, pointing to four dots arranged in a square,
"are called the Casket. And those," he gestures to a ring of five with a
tail of two, "are the Key."

We see Frin nod. His eyes are on Kew rather than the sky.

Kew's finger moves along a swarm of tiny dots running diagonally
across the map, corresponding in shape to the river of stars. "Now I'm
really curious about the bright ones," he says. But his finger runs into
the pile of fallen stones and crumbling mortar. He sighs.

Frin scampers toward him. "We can clear those in no time," he
says, climbing halfway up the pile and taking up a large piece of fallen
molding.

Kew sits back on his heels and watches Frin eagerly shifting stones
away. Some of them roll off the edge of this high aerie and plummet
into the remains of banquets at the foot of the Great Tower. Most land
harmlessly in fruitcake, waterlogged pastry, a haunch of withered
meat. One shatters the last blue wineglass from the Hellebore Era.
There is a small custodian with a garlic-shaped body and ducklike
feet whose job it is to collect unbroken dishes; he sees the wineglass
break and shrieks.

Kew, who has joined Frin in the job of clearing, jumps at the sound.
This startles Frin, who slips on a loose rock. His body slams into the
star map and goes right through.

Kew gasps and darts forward. We and Kew can now see that the
map is also a door. One half of it has swung inward, letting Frin, a
little shower of rock chips, and sandy mortar into a dark chamber.

"Frin?" says Kew, stepping down. "Frin, are you all right?"

There is a low whistle. Then there is light. It comes from a basin
held in a stone hand. The stone hand is attached to a stone arm. The
stone arm is attached to a flesh torso. The flesh torso is imprisoned in
a carapace of spires, arches, pillars, and walls of black stone. The stone
is sprouting from the floor. Atop the flesh torso is a half-stone head. A
crown of stone pinnacles wraps around and through it. One eye is
blank stone. The other is green and wet. The other arm attached to
the torso is flesh, except for the fingertips, which are stone. The fin-

gertips are attached to long threads of stone, also sprouting from the floor. The legs are invisible within the carapace. All in all, it looks as if this being is in the middle of getting devoured by the palace. At their feet, Frin is sprawled, blinking up with a dazed expression, his body smeared with dust and dirt.

"Who are you?" Kew asks, helping Frin up. Still dazed, Frin staggers. Kew puts an arm around his shoulders to support him.

"Ten Owl. I am an alchemist to Her Ladyship." He speaks in a voice that seems to come through clouds of dust. A third arm emerges from the carapace and gestures at the walls. "If you had looked around, you would have known for yourself."

All around the chamber are wooden tables with glass vessels, books, glittering tools. There is surprisingly little dust, aside from what the boys accidentally brought in.

"There aren't any alchemists," says Kew. "Not since—"

"Hush, hush," says Owl, waving his free arm. "Show me your palm. Words take too long."

After looking at Frin, Kew shrugs and holds out his palm. Owl takes it and brings it closer to his eye. Whenever Owl speaks, the skin of his cheek and lips pulls against the stone. It looks uncomfortable, as if it might tear away, but Owl does not appear to notice.

"Tell me your name," says Owl. Kew looks at Frin again, but obeys. Owl shuts his eyes. "Yes, yes, I see," he whispers. "Grey. Orphan. Alone. No name. The Hawthorn dead. The mother dead, too."

Kew grimaces slightly, as if he resents that his palm should know anything about the women in grey.

"And you on a quest to defeat the Eternal Enemy," says Owl. "Interfered with, I see. A promise that may or may not bear fruit." His flesh eye swivels to meet Kew's. His stone eye turns more slowly, releasing a little shower of sand. "And no alchemists. I had expected it. The others must have died in the experiment." His thumb presses deeply into the center of Kew's palm. "Yes, dead for generations. I see. The experiment was a partial success, then."

"Success?" says Kew. "If they're dead?"

"*I* am still alive. Your turn, boy."

With a glance at Kew as if for permission, Frin gives the alchemist his name and his hand.

"You are not simple flesh," says the alchemist, prodding and pressing. "This place is written upon you more strongly. Its future, even. *Here.*" He squeezes; Frin winces. "A great thing will fall. Another will end."

"End?" says Frin. His eyes meet Kew's. "What will end?"

"A possibility," says the alchemist. He lets go of Frin and stretches his fingers toward the vial, though he does not touch it. "What is this you carry, boy?"

"We don't know," says Kew.

"I do," says the alchemist. A crafty look comes into his flesh eye. "It will free me. Will you give it to me?"

Frin seems about to, but hesitates. "I don't know. It ain't mine to give."

"I offer information in exchange," says Owl.

"What information could possibly be worth that?" says Kew. His body language is different from what we are accustomed to. He is acting more sure of himself. We would have last seen this confidence when the Obsidian Lady imparted it to him.

Frin looks at him, alarmed for a moment, then seeming to recognize what is going on, relaxes.

"The Beast rises," says the alchemist. "It rose in my day as well. I was an apprentice then. I saw the end of the Thistles, but I also saw the end of the Eternal Enemy, and I can tell you how to end it once more."

Kew frowns. His eyes narrow, then widen. "When the Beast rises, the Obsidian Lady will ride it to victory over the Great Tower," he says tonelessly.

"Need it come to that?" says the alchemist. "Think you the towers of this palace came into being by the labor of hands? Is the never-drying river the work of the rains alone? For generations, I have been walled up alive like an oblate of Grey, but I know more of this place than you. There is a thing at the Beast's heart. A wish, a song, a name, many have called it by many words, but there is one truth about it: to the victor it goes, to the vanquisher of the Beast goes this power. What a failure of imagination you show. Victory over the Great Tower? The Great Tower *is* victory. The Great Tower is a sword. Why be the sword when you can be the wielder?"

"That," says Kew, and stops, and shakes himself. He looks like someone who is unsure whether his foot is about to cramp. "That's Ladies' business. I'm Hawthorn's apprentice. I can't—*do* that."

Owl blinks his flesh eye. Much more slowly, the stone lid of his stone eye grinds down and back up. "They are the dreamer, we the dreamed. Does the dreamer guide the dream, or the dream the dreamer? Give me the vial so I can free myself, and I will show you what to do."

"I know what to do," says Kew. His right hand tightens as if gripping the handle of an invisible blade.

"No doubt you believe that," says Owl. "But I can see for myself there is some veil laid upon your mind. The Guardian is the first defense against the Beast. Why else are they in Grey? In my time, the Beast rose, and the Guardian failed in her task, and the monster came down the West Passage, devouring and crushing and burning as it went, until it reached the Great Tower. The last Thistle Lady, old and wily, had commanded us to brew such tinctures and philters as we could, and she drank of them and her strength was renewed, and she and her daughters fought the Beast here, in Black itself, and lost their lives one after another. Last of all stood the youngest daughter, and it was she who vanquished the Beast with our help, and her name was Bellflower, and from her rose the new dynasty."

"And did she imprison you, then?" Kew says, with a skeptical quirk of his brow. "To keep her secrets from the others?"

"By no means," says Owl. "Those of us who remained were commanded once more to go about our business: pursuing immortality. All the Great Ladies since the beginning of everything have sought to stave off the one thing their tongues cannot command: death itself. For if they do not die, their power does not die. And so we stoked our ovens and set up our alembics and gathered our materials. And we found one material that showed promise. Something of Hellebore's, very precious. Through refinement and sublimation we concentrated its essence. When it had passed to its purest form, we tested a drop on a cat. The results were promising. We drew lots, and it fell to me to try it upon my own flesh."

He stops.

"Well?" says Frin. "What happened?"

"I remember a great light. It was in and around me. Then a great darkness and a great noise, and I thought they, too, were in and around me. Maybe they were. Then I awakened. I thought perhaps I was dead. I thought so until you broke through that wall. The silence and darkness and waiting are what some of us thought death was. Others have said death is a river, sweeping us away into oblivion." He blinks his eyes, one rapidly, one less rapidly. "But enough of that. I know what I need in order to recover. The last and least ingredient, as is always the way. Give me that vial. Please."

Kew and Frin share a long look. While they do, Owl licks his lips.

A trickle of muddy saliva leaks from the corner of his mouth. We stir, but we cannot intervene.

"All right," says Frin. "But least or not, it *is* a miracle. I ain't responsible for what happens when you open it."

Why does Frin agree, when the item is so precious to the beekeepers? Perhaps even he knows that the alchemists were masters of change and healing. Perhaps he sees in Kew's face the thing put there by the Obsidian Lady, and hopes the alchemist's gratitude will extend to removing it. Perhaps he is curious about the thing he carries and thinks, As well the alchemist open it as another. We may never know.

He lifts the chain from around his neck and holds it out to Owl. Kew's eyes track the motion of his hands. Trembling slightly, Owl's fingers close around the stopper and strongly (but gently) twist it off.

A fragrance fills the room: all-pervading, heavy, but relieving its weight with its sweetness, and relieving its sweetness with its wild tang. Kew's eyes, which have been squinting as if in anxiety, open wide, and his pupils become large and black.

"Should it just be given away like that?" Kew asks.

The alchemist's eyes narrow. "Do not question the great work!"

"What?" says Frin, looking from Owl to Kew and back. "What is it?"

"You don't know?" says Kew.

"Quiet!" says the alchemist. One of his hands snatches at the vial, but Frin takes a step back.

"Thistle honey," says Kew. Frin goes very pale. Kew asks, "What does it do?"

"None of your concern," says the alchemist. He lunges for Frin, but his carapace of stone prevents him. "It shouldn't be carried by such as you. *I* know how to use it. Give it to me."

Frin dodges anyway. "Last? *Least?* You—you were lying. To get this?"

"Give it to me!" says the alchemist. He lunges again. Some of the stone filigree cracks. At almost the same time, Kew seizes the stopper from Owl's waving hand and gives it to Frin.

"You *lied*?" says Frin. "For *Thistle honey*?"

Owl begins to say many things that we need not listen to. We have all heard the ravings of a thwarted alchemist, or if not, we can easily imagine them. What is important, and what Kew's eyes fix on, is that as Owl flails and lurches against his imprisoning stone, it is starting to crumble.

"Come on!" says Kew, grabbing Frin's hand and scrambling toward the opening in the wall.

Behind them, the alchemist roars and there is a shuddering grating noise of falling rocks. Just as the boys reach the open floor, the star map bursts from within, sending fragments flying. The turret trembles under the blow, sending the boys sprawling.

A large, roughly triangular piece of the map skids to a halt right beside Kew's head. It is unclear if he sees it, though it sits exactly where he *could*. We see it, either way. There are six stars, carved with many more rays than the others: one, across the river, has even more rays than that. Beside the remaining five is a dark deep-bored dot. The brightest star bears the label *The Mother*. The others are unnamed. Beside the dot is the word *beware*.

But we are getting distracted. Kew and Frin are up and running, though there is nowhere really to run to. The alchemist has gotten out, or at least some of him has. Long articulated legs of stone haul a pale fleshy body, supported here and there by filigrees and arches. In the midst of the body, dangling like a doll in a careless embrace, are the head, neck, and remaining flesh-arms of the alchemist. Ribbons of soft skin trail behind him into the chamber like the roots of a freshly pulled weed. He is still saying many things, but more importantly, he is blocking the stairs.

Kew looks around. While he does, the alchemist's hands catch Frin up. Two of them pinion him against a broad thigh of jet molding. Two others creep about his body. *Where is the vial* they seem to say, feeling for it here and there.

Where *is* the vial? Even as we think this, Owl shrieks the question into the evening air. A little casement in Black Tower opens, and a sleepy head pokes out to listen.

A Guardian protects. That is their duty. And not only from the Beast. All enemies that threaten the residents of the palace are within the Guardian's purview. Kew knows this, but what will he do about it?

His eyes lock on something. Hard to tell what. He begins to edge around the wall of the crumbling room. (Owl's legs are twitching and stamping in fury. The ancient architecture can't withstand it much longer.) Frin shrieks. Abandoning caution, Kew runs to the now-broken statue with the sword. The sword itself is broken, too, the fresh, sharp edges ironically making it far more suitable as a weapon. It cannot be anything like the sword Kew trained with, but he picks it up easily and brandishes it in warning.

"Let him go," Kew says.

With a wet tearing noise, the flesh half of Owl's head turns to look at him. The stone half watches Frin; the arms are still searching him, nails digging into soft skin. Frin shrieks again.

Kew rushes between Owl's stone legs and drives the sword into the flesh body. Owl gasps and shudders. Dropping Frin, he dances in pain. His body drops, driving the sword farther in, and Owl screams. Black mud spurts from his mouth. In his agony, he stumbles over the edge of the ruined wall and falls. The lantern tracks catch him. His weight bends them. His weight breaks them. He falls again. The thin roots of flesh whip out of the chamber after him, pull taut, and tear. A moment or two later, there is a horrible crash. The little casement in Black Tower shuts.

Silence. We are grateful, Kew and Frin probably more so. They lie on the cracked floor, panting.

"Are you all right?" Kew says at last. He sits up. "Did he hurt you much? I'm sorry I wasn't faster."

Frin shakes his head, nods, shrugs. "No worse than a few stings."

Their packs have been kicked about and the contents scattered. Some of the food is missing. Kew picks up everything he can, repacks it, and hands Frin his shirt.

"I dropped it," says Frin quietly. He does not meet Kew's eyes. "The—miracle. I dropped it. I can't find it."

Kew reaches into his pocket and takes out the vial. "I caught it."

Now Frin meets Kew's eyes. "You *caught* it?"

"Hawthorn trained me," says Kew with a shrug. This may not explain anything to Frin, but we understand. "I'm sorry, I didn't know he'd go after you like that."

"It's all right," says Frin. "What are squires for?"

They both chuckle a little. They seem too sleepy to know whether either of them truly found it funny. Kew says they should leave: parts of the floor are creaking ominously. They return to the half-choked stairs and go on their way. They find a little alcove in some building or other and make camp for the night. It is cold. They spread out one blanket, lie back to back, and pull the other over themselves.

We cannot linger. We have other places to be. The eyes of Red Tower see many things, and those things must be reported. We spread our wings and buzz away into the sky. Seven stars twinkle down upon two boys, one tall, one short, both fast asleep within the hide of the palace.

23. The Apprentices Meet a Lady

The next morning, Frin got up first, moving slowly and pain-fully. The alchemist had bruised him more than he'd let on. The aches worked themselves away, though, or so he told Kew, who woke up with another headache and a fuzzy, dusty taste in his mouth. One set of miseries was enough for the both of them. After a quick bite of bread and dried apples, they were off again. The tower was very close now, stretching up into the mists, so tall it weighed the air down.

When you come to a red archway, take the stairs up to Last Lily. A long onyx walkway arcing over the North Passage, Last Lily had the form of a person stretching out with her toes on one walltop and her fingers on the opposite. The story went that the last Lady of the Lily Era had turned herself into this bridge, escaping the violent downfall of her dynasty and the rise of the Hellebores. She had done a poor job of it; the hills and valleys of her clothes must have been nearly im-passable in those early years, until generations of feet wore a track through them. Kew paused in the small of her back to gaze up the North Passage. At one end was Grey Tower, half-shrouded by snow. He turned around.

When you have crossed Last Lily, you will be in Ebony. Don't linger there, but go down the grand staircase to the tower.

Kew went up the stairs.

"What are you doing?" said Frin, running after him. "One said *down* the stairs." He caught at Kew's hand, but Kew jerked it out of his grasp.

"I'm to deliver my message to the Ebony Lady," said Kew.

"I can't go with you," said Frin. "I'm one of Her Ladyship's crofters. If Ebony and her people catch me here, I could be killed."

"I'm here with you, though," said Kew. "You're under my protection, I suppose."

They stared at each other, neither comprehending. To Frin, the patchwork of fiefdoms around the tower was a maze of shifting allegiances whose constantly redrawn boundaries brought death with the stroke of a pen. To Kew, who knew only how things worked once upon a time, the battles between the outer Ladies of Black Tower were nothing more than the little rivalries between Guardian and mother, or between the north and south cloisters of Grey. Frin gave in, believing that Kew was far better informed. Kew was acting on behalf of the Obsidian Lady. That surely gave him some kind of immunity, as these things went.

At the top of the stairs, a wide mezzanine overlooked a rectangular courtyard. Tables had been laid there, and people were eating. By a white balustrade stood a person in a black kirtle, gazing out over the meal. They turned when Kew and Frin left the stairs. One side of their pale face had burst open to show smooth ebony, carved with butterflies and flowers, and amid the traceries was a quatrefoil window holding four blue eyes. The air crawled with holiness.

Who are you? said the Ebony Lady. And why are you here?

One of her eyes swiveled and focused on Frin, who grabbed Kew's arm.

"My Lady," said Kew, bowing. "I'm Kew of Grey Tower, apprentice-Guardian of the West Passage, and I am here to inform you that the Beast comes; more than that, your sister Obsidian has aligned herself with it, and will use it to conquer the Great Tower."

The four eyes blinked.

Come, said the Lady, eat with us.

She led them down into the courtyard and stood behind them as her people set places, setting out trenchers and ladling on thick stews and boiled, buttered vegetables. But with the Lady right there, smelling of hot steel, neither of them could eat.

Finally she took a seat in a high-backed chair carved all over with leaves and thorns. Please, she said, have a bite. Little beekeeper, you have nothing to fear from me—the Robins and I have an agreement, and you are my guests.

Kew worried down a pinch of something in a sour brownish sauce. Frin ate a leaf of spinach.

Ah, I see that you are what you say, said the Lady. She folded her hands together. I do not see why you are saying it. I do not like this news. The balance of power is delicate. Your coming signals a dangerous shift in the fiefs, whether or not what you say is true. What of the Guardian? Is she prepared to do her duty?

"The Guardian is dead," said Kew. "Many days ago now. I will take her place."

The Lady looked at her hands.

We all know nothing can tame the Beast except the Guardian, she said. The Guardian herself would not have done it for Obsidian. You are not the Guardian and cannot have done it. It is obvious that this is a lie on Obsidian's part. If she truly had possession of the wish, she would have built her own tower. She is foolish and does not know the ancient mysteries. She wants to sow doubt among us. I will not let that happen.

"The Beast *is* rising," said Kew. "Hawthorn knew it, and winter's fallen on Grey. I must tell the others as well."

You will not, said the Lady; Kew's forehead burned as she spoke. Obsidian was always too quicksilver. It is those instincts that have led to the fall of dynasties. Her chaos ends with me.

While her voice whispered in the air around them, their vision began to go dark. Only her four eyes were visible like a cluster of blue stars.

I am sending you to the tower, said the Lady; her cold hands came out of the darkness and a thumb touched each of them on the lips as if wiping away a bit of sauce. You will speak to nobody except the Willow Lady. She will decide what to do with you. The line of Guardians is too valuable to lose; you had better hope she does not punish your companion in your stead. I will see to Obsidian myself.

Her eyes closed, and the boys' vision brightened. Kew and Frin were at the bottom of a broad onyx staircase in a black hall. Rubbish and the remains of banners littered it. Dust and spiderwebs were everywhere. The staircase swept upward to a huge bull's-eye window, split, and ascended to galleries on either side of the room. Beyond the glass was one of the piers.

They were inside Black Tower, and they had a long way to go.

24. Kew and Frin Go to the Ballroom and Join the Revels

Kew tried to ask Frin where to go, but his mouth and throat would not form the words. Frin tried to say something as well, but had the same problem. They met each other's eyes in horror.

You will not speak to anyone but the Willow Lady. It had not been a command, but a promise. Neither of them had any idea where the Willow Lady was, though, nor how long it would take to reach her. And this level of the tower seemed completely abandoned.

Seeing huge swathes of the palace empty was nothing new to either of them. Grey's cloisters were nearly empty; Kew had grown up at one of the last hearthfires there. Frin hailed from a small community on the edge of a disused thoroughfare, separated by long walks from everything else around. They knew the palace was depopulated just as they knew air was for breathing. But all their lives, both of them had believed Black Tower itself still thrived. At night, it glowed with life; the West Passage was full of its debris. So where was everyone?

With nothing else to do, Kew started up the stairs. Frin followed. At the top, they paused to look out the window. Perhaps getting their bearings would help.

Beyond the piers, Red Tower smoldered. Kew had never been so near it: windows were visible in its sides, and the light of its beacon licked along the edges of the piers. Snow blew toward it: winter, it seemed, was encroaching from Grey. With a shiver, he turned to go up the left-hand staircase. There was a faint glimmering trail up it, like the light left by a spilled lantern. Immediately Kew decided that this was the way to go. He got Frin's attention and pointed.

Frin did not understand. He thought Kew was simply indicating a direction. The light was invisible to him. But he was relieved that someone had made a decision.

The two boys made their way up to the galleries. Kew followed the trail through narrow halls, up more stairs (several floors' worth, all lined with niches of moldering cobwebbed statuary), and finally through a pointed-arched door onto a mezzanine. The trail seemed to end there.

The mezzanine lay about halfway up the wall of an immense room. Its ceiling was curved; had they reached the upper part of the tower's base? Five stained-glass windows lined the outer wall, rich with deeds of the Ladies. The central one was very large, even in a room that could hold hundreds. It depicted Grey Tower, and beneath it, a coiled creature shrouded in grey.

The Beast. It had to be. It was shrouded, but eyes peered out from its ashen wrappings, and it had many claws and mismatched green wings that corresponded to several pictures of it in the Bestiaries. A chain around its neck wound up to settle around the tower's own neck, as if the Beast were simply a bauble for Grey Tower to wear. All around the two, dozens of tinier figures crowded, arms upraised in fear or gratitude. Among them were women in grey, Guardians in their fierce thorny armor (the same armor Hawthorn donned for solemn ceremonies), doctors, tutors, and the other named citizens of Grey.

It took him a moment to see that behind the tower was a third figure: a black-veiled Lady, her thirteen arms outstretched as if about to catch or embrace the tower itself. In the center of her veil was a great yellow eye.

Frin was tugging on Kew's sleeve, shaking his head emphatically. He pointed along the mezzanine to a narrow staircase rising to the domed ceiling. Having nothing better to do, Kew followed. As they went, he noticed that the trail of light had not vanished: it ran along the balustrade, as if whatever left it had walked the railing. They passed a large arch leading deeper into the tower, but the trail did not go there, so Kew ignored it. Where the balustrade joined the stairs, the trail left it and went up the steps, occasionally venturing onto the wall as if seeking variety.

A voice broke the silence. It was quiet and seemed to come from someplace far away and high above, and what it said was incomprehensible. The boys came to a halt and looked at each other questioningly.

After a moment, the voice stopped speaking. They waited, but it spoke no further words. They went on.

The stairs themselves slipped through a small arch and up, up, up, winding like a thread around the bobbin of the tower. Here and there, the white plaster walls were broken by huge ribs of black stone: the inner structure of the tower itself. They seemed smooth, but bore infinitesimal pitting, like the surface of a bone. The ravages of time, Kew supposed. Occasional round windows (rather dirty, and dotted with the husks of spiders) let them see out over the center of the palace: the Black courts, full of green, and the other towers with their buildings of vermillion, cerulean, golden—and cloud-grey. They were already much higher than the highest point of Grey Tower, and for the first time in their lives, they saw the edges of the palace. Beyond its ragged fringes of wall and quadrangle were distant blue hills and white mountains. That vista did not change no matter how far they went. Meanwhile, the palace rotated, constantly bringing new aspects of itself into view.

They had been walking for hours, so though Frin had been snacking at regular intervals, he opened his pack and they munched bread and fruit while sitting side by side on a windowsill, their backs to the needle of Yellow Tower. Both of them were used to chatting while they ate, Frin with the other apprentices and beekeepers, Kew with Hawthorn. Even though they were exhausted and out of breath, they still felt the urge to talk. But their throats could only make lumps of sound like misborn animals. Finally, Frin gently squeezed Kew's hand. Kew squeezed back. That was all the conversation they could make.

The voice spoke again. It was a little clearer, and the diction sounded like a proclamation, but they could understand nothing it said. Still, it was a relief to hear someone speaking at all.

After they'd walked for perhaps half an hour more, faint music began to trickle down the stairs toward them. Frin knew it as a tune that often emanated from the windows midway up the tower. Kew hardly recognized it as music at all, except that it contained the same four-note motif Sparrow used to make the lantern go. Neither of them wanted to get any closer, but they had passed no doors, and going all the way back down to the room of stained glass would mean undoing the walking of half a day.

They stopped again, partly out of hesitation and partly to relieve themselves. Kew watched the stream of his urine flow down the stairs. Just a day or two ago such a desecration would have been unthinkable. Now it was hard to imagine treating Black Tower any worse than its owners did.

Why was he there? To tell the Willow Lady about the Beast, yes. But his memory of the last few days was confused. Someone seemed to have put his brain in a jar and given it a good shake. The Obsidian Lady had tamed the Beast and would ride it to the conquest of Black Tower, because she was noble and good and deserving. But also, Hawthorn had died, and with her dying words commanded him to warn the tower. They could not both be equally true. Frin could not help him, for they could not speak to each other. His whole life, Kew had depended on his own knowledge, and even this small crack in the foundation unnerved him.

The trail of light, though ... His memories of Sparrow and the lantern were unclouded. *Those* at least were trustworthy, if not as a guide, then as a sign the world still made some kind of sense. And on a level below words, he owed it to Sparrow to follow this light. Whether it would lead him to an opportunity to repay their self-sacrifice, there was no telling. But if he stood still, Sparrow's death would surely be in vain.

Frin did not know about Sparrow. Kew wanted to tell Frin all about them, though there was very little for him to tell. Someone else should know about Sparrow. Someone else should remember. The mothers' penchant for recording everything in song made sense to him, now that something had actually happened in his life besides memorization and meals.

The music grew louder and louder. Frin tried to breathe normally. To him, of course, the four notes did not say "Sparrow." They said, "Here is the Ballroom, where you have been warned never to go."

Soon the music filled the air till they could not hear themselves breathe. Around one more turn of the stairs was a small oak door, dark with age. The music flowed from behind it, and the trail vanished under it. They looked at each other. Kew shrugged. Frin shrugged. They grinned mirthlessly. Kew opened the door.

Beyond was the biggest room either of them had ever seen. If the windows were any guide, it filled one entire floor of the tower. Red-gold light streamed from several chandeliers, and red velvet draperies lined the walls. The parquet floor shone like water. On a gallery around the top of the room, musicians played viols, dulcimers, harps, drums. On the main floor, hundreds of people were dancing. And in the center of the floor was a Lady.

The Lady towered over the other dancers. She had several arms, each outstretched to hold the hand of a partner. Her head was a spoked wheel of eyes, laid on its side with a wavering flame in the center. An exquisite black gown clung tightly to her torso, then flared out into a bell-like skirt, nearly the size of a courtyard, leaving her arms and shoulders bare. All manner of frills and laces and fringes and bobbles and trimmings covered the skirt, like growths of ivy and weeds. The wheel and her skin alike were made of a black stone shot through with red and yellow lightning. Her presence hummed throughout the room, rising and falling with the music.

The Lady's partners were half as tall as her. They were fashioned of the same black stone, and wore suits or gowns of similar intricacy to hers. For a moment, nothing seemed particularly odd about them, until Kew realized that the eye-wheel and skirt were revolving one way, her torso and partners the other. As Kew and Frin stood there, the music changed to a different brisk piece—still based on the four-note motif—and the partners stopped, bowed to the Lady and each other, and reversed direction. The wheel and gown reversed as well.

All the other dancers were an assortment of normal palace people, and they danced their own complicated set of steps and figures. Even these coincided with the movements of the Lady's group, forming great patterns on the floor so that one moment a star of dancers matched its inner points with the position of the Lady's partners; the next, several nested rings of them corresponded to the many-rayed gaze of her eyes.

Kew glanced around for the trail. It ran about a third of the way along the side of the room to a small door. Directly across from them, alternately hidden and revealed by the Lady's motion, was the grand entrance of the Ballroom, laced here and there with cobwebs.

It was then that he noticed they were being watched. Scattered about the room were motionless spectators, holding glasses of long-evaporated honey wine. Only their eyes shifted, and they had all shifted to stare at Kew and Frin, and from the nearest to the farthest, a sheen of tears was visible in every eye.

The atmosphere of the room changed. Everywhere he looked, Kew saw tears. Even the Lady wept, steam rising from her eyes, the drops splashing and running off her gown like rain. The floor shone like water because she had drowned it in her distress.

Kew tapped Frin's shoulder. He pointed at the musicians' gallery, then made a chopping motion with his hand. Frin shook his head and

pointed at the door. Kew mimed tears flowing from his eyes and ges-
tured at the whole Ballroom. After a moment, Frin nodded dubiously.

But how to get to the gallery? They stepped farther into the room.
Though every eye was still upon them, nobody left their place to do
anything about it. As they moved, their feet fell into the rhythm of
the dance. We'll be caught if we aren't fast, Kew thought, and saw in
Frin's eyes that he knew it, too.

There was no obvious way up to the gallery, unless the side door
where the trail led were it. Kew followed the light, and Frin followed
Kew. The door revealed another little set of stairs (*very* dusty and cobwebby) that headed right to the musicians.

Dozens of them were ranged all around the gallery. They played
deftly, their hands in swift, easy motion, their bodies still as stone.
Over their heads, hiding their faces entirely, were dusty black hoods
marked with a yellow eye. Kew shrugged and went to the nearest musician, a harpist, though Kew didn't know the instrument's name.
He yanked off the hood. The harpist gave him a fearful gaze even as
their fingers kept moving. Trails of dry salt marked their cheeks with
white. Kew tried to still their hands, but it was like trying to halt the
sun. The strings would not snap. He could not even budge the instrument itself. The longer he stood there, the more his breath and pulse
slipped into the rhythm. Perhaps Frin could try.

Frin was eating bread and trying not to look at anything. Kew went
to snatch the bread from his hands when he heard the harpist play a
dissonant note. They were staring at the food, and something about it
made their hands falter. When Kew touched the bread, the pressure
of the rhythm faded away. Kew and Frin shared a questioning glance.

Frin brought the half-eaten bread closer to the harpist. Their hands
slowed, breaking the chain of four notes for just a moment. Out of the
corner of his eye, Kew saw the Lady falter. Her wheel wobbled in its
rotation, and all her eyes fixed on him. Her hum changed key, as if in
anticipation or relief.

Kew tore the bread in half, leaving part with Frin, and started
down the circle of musicians, passing out crumbs. Each player left off
playing to take the food and eat. The music quieted but did not stop:
there were so many. He motioned to Frin for more. All around the
room they went, tearing their bread into smaller and smaller pieces,
then moving on to the dried fruit, then to crumbs from the wrinkles
in Frin's tunic. Soon there was only a single dulcimer pounding out
the four notes. It was hardly audible over the rustling and stomping of

the dancers. Their heads could turn now, but their feet and hands still moved, on and on and on, catching and releasing each other, tapping out the same figures and rounds that they had for so, so long.

There was nothing left for the dulcimer player. They wept and wept, but even the crumbs were eaten. Kew spread his hands in despair.

Frin remembered the Thistle honey. He had only a little, and it was precious, but even a tiny dab might work. He uncorked the vial.

The perfume of a thousand summers filled the ballroom. Nothing had ever smelled so delicious as that honey, the essence perhaps of flowers that had been dust since the time of songs. Kew felt a chill. The Lady's eyes shed tears like fountains: among the embroidery on her gown were hundreds of thistles; who could even say what the fragrance meant to her?

Frin took a tiny drop of honey on his finger, warm and heavy as afternoon sunlight, and brought it to the musician's lips. They swallowed it and a smile of contentment spread across their face. Their hands went still. The dance ceased. The Ballroom was entirely silent.

Poof. One by one, the dancers fell to dust. Their clothes unraveled and shredded as if centuries were passing in a moment. Each of them sighed in ecstasy as they went. Dust swirled on the watery Ballroom floor. The musicians dissolved as well, the taste of food still on their lips. The yellow-eyed hoods remained. The dulcimer player lingered. Golden light flickered from their lips, struggling against the slow collapse. They started to scream just as their body finally gave in. The light died.

The Lady alone was left with her partners. Now it was clear that her "partners" were but extensions of herself, for their eyes moved with hers, and their legs walked her over to the gallery where the two boys stood.

I cannot thank you, she said as her presence filled the room, thick and rich like honey. There are no words to thank you.

Kew tried to answer her. Frin did as well. Finally they just bowed.

Why can you not speak? said the Lady. Please, answer me. I know I am not dreaming this time. Why will you say nothing? Does my sister still lie sleepless in Yellow? Does the beacon of Red still burn? Am I a song, or a story?

Kew rippled his fingers to mimic musical notes.

Please tell me, said the Lady. She released her partners' hands, and they crumbled like charcoal. All her own hands were held out to the boys, like a bouquet of flowers offered by a pleading lover. The sound of her weeping replaced the silence. Her eyes closed over her steaming tears.

With a crack, her body split asunder and fell. Her dress peeled apart into ash and soot. Her hands dropped like rotten apples to break on the floor. The wheel of eyes remained in the air a moment more, then its flame went out and it toppled, coming to rest upon her remains. The eyes froze into stony carvings.

Kew and Frin met each other's eyes. Had they—had they *killed* a Lady of Black Tower? Or simply released her from some punishment? Would she be back? Could the Ladies even *come* back? It was impossible that this act would not bring them grief later, and surely someone would be along soon, wondering what had happened.

The only thing to do was to keep moving. The trail led to a door in the musicians' gallery and up yet more stairs. They began to climb again.

25. Kew and Frin Go to the Oculus and See What There Is to See

Night soon fell on the palace. The only light in the stairs came from the small, scattered windows, and from the trail that only Kew could see, so when darkness came, they had to stop moving. They were hungry, but all they had was water. Each of them took a sparing drink. The night was very cold, so they curled up together against the wall, and Frin spread his extra clothes over them, and Kew spread his overgown on top of that. Before they slept, Frin squeezed his hand. He patted Frin's shoulder. Outside, the moon rose as chilly winds blew winter out of Grey, around Black, and into Blue and Red.

They were awakened not by sunrise but by their stomachs gnawing. In the dry environment of the tower, there were not even mushrooms to be had, and though they might eventually stoop to eating insects and spiders, all those they found were merely empty carapaces. After stamping and swinging their arms about for a bit to get the blood flowing, the boys resumed their climb.

The windows were larger and more frequent, but there was less to see. Fog blanketed much of the palace, with merely the tops of the highest towers visible. Only in Yellow was there sunlight.

A voice said *Attention, loyal subjects.* The boys skidded to a stop. There was a small brass tube coming out of the wall. The voice emanated from it.

On this twelfth day of the third month of the three hundred and fortieth year of the Willow Era, Her Ladyship has decreed that all residents of the palace must wear a yellow ribbon pinned to their left sleeve, in memory of those who fell fighting the forces of Blue Tower in the one hundred and eighth year of the Willow Era.

The announcement ended. Neither Kew nor Frin had anything yellow on them, but they tore a small strip from Kew's pale doublet and divided it between themselves to wear. How many other such decrees had they missed? Hopefully, everyone would understand that they were newcomers to the tower. And they went on.

To Kew's frustration, the trail began to meander. It ran up the walls, looped around, doubled back on itself, even ventured onto the ceiling of struts above them. As long as they were going in its general direction, he would not allow himself to worry too much, but even as he followed it intently, he resented his own determination.

They passed some doors. A few were locked. Some opened only on darkness. One led to a disused study piled with books and paper. Excitedly, Kew ran in, grabbed a pencil, and began to write a note to Frin on a scrap of parchment.

I'm following a trail. I know you can't see it, but I think if we keep

Frin interrupted by gently putting a hand over Kew's. He pointed at the paper, shrugged, and shook his head. Did nobody in the palace read except the Guardians?

Signing to let Frin know the next note was not for him, Kew took a different scrap of parchment and wrote *We are looking for the Willow Lady. Can you help?* This he folded and put in his pocket. Even if nobody ever read it, it was a relief to get it out. He had gone too long without communicating in words.

Some of the books struck him as odd. They were written in regular, geometric characters, quite unlike the books in Grey's small Archives, and they lacked pictures except for a black line drawing here and there—none of the extensive, beautiful illumination he was used to. He compared the word *fire* on one page to another instance of it on the page opposite. Except for some slight pooling of ink, they were identical. They seemed to have been stamped. The laboriousness of the process was absurd. Why not just write?

In the front of every book was another imprint. *If found, return to the Library on Swan Level, North Face,* then the familiar symbol of the eye. Knowing the location of the tower library felt good. It would be nice to be surrounded by books again—perhaps the trail would lead them there. And if not, maybe they could leave the trail.

Whoever had used the study left nothing more immediately useful.

One or two empty green vials, but no food, no water, just signs of its occupant going out one day and never returning. Among the books piled on the desk was *Being a True et Accurate Mirror of the Black Tower,* written rather than stamped, and in it was a map. The light in the study was poor, so Kew motioned that they should go back to the staircase.

By the chill light of the winter sky he examined the map of Black Tower. It folded out to several times the size of the book, and had been added to and amended over many, many years by many, many different hands. All the principal chambers were clearly marked, including the Ballroom—but more important, the great central kitchens, and more important still, the throne room. The book only seemed to go up to the Apple Era, since it referred to the ruler of the tower by that name, but the Willow Lady likely used the same throne room. It was at worst a starting place.

Kew could not even begin to convey all this to Frin by signs, but he tapped the throne room on the map and started walking. The kitchens lay on the way; perhaps they could beg a dish, or even just some scraps. He did not pay much attention to the other great rooms, and only briefly wondered what the Oculus might be, though it was in their way. With some relief, he could now disregard the trail.

Another announcement began. They seemed to be getting closer to whoever was speaking; it was a little louder and clearer than before.

On this twelfth day of the third month of the three hundred and fortieth year of the Willow Era, Her Ladyship has decreed that every member of the Order of Websters be caned upon the left hand.

Grateful that this did not apply to them, the boys continued. The map, though detailed, did not show the staircase they were using. It seemed too insignificant for the cartographer, and had probably been built for maintenance, then forgotten. According to the map, the main route from the tower's bottom to its top was a much grander staircase called the Spine, and it looked more direct. Perhaps they could find their way to it.

Kew had to guess at where they were in the tower. Based on how many rounds they had already made, plus the distance since the Ballroom, he judged they were more or less on the level of the kitchens already, so the next time they came to a door, he tried it.

From the vibration in the air he instantly knew it was a mistake. But the door shut behind them and locked, trapping them in the same room as a Lady.

Kew and Frin found themselves on a narrow ledge before a chasm. On either side, the ledge sloped down and around the walls to meet on the far side of a vast space, as if they stood on the uppermost edge of a tilted hoop. Five banners hung from the shadowy walls above the hoop, one in each of the tower colors. Sunlight shone on them from an open circle a hundred or so feet up and across the chamber. It was, of course, the Oculus. The rays were divided by a gigantic head: a Lady, molded of jet and gilded. Had it not been for a thrum in the air, they would have taken her for a statue.

Her head had four faces, each pointing a different direction. Her eight eyes were closed. A three-tiered crown floated above them, as big as a house. Each face had once had its proper arm, but like the Obsidian Lady's, something had shortened them, and they were capped by gold filigree just below the shoulder. Heavy iron chains swooped from these caps to four equidistant points along the ledge where the boys stood. As their eyes adjusted, they saw that the ledge was marked all around with little golden lines and delicate words, but only Kew could read them and recognize the room for what it was.

They stood on the rim of the wheel of seasons itself. Almost as soon as he realized this, the Lady rotated her bulk just a bit. The chains clanked along. The wheel turned one tick, jarring them. Kew almost fell, but Frin caught him and pulled him back. The Lady took no notice. At best, they were ants to her. She was so large that her feet were lost in shadow far below, but her waist seemed level with the Ballroom: they had climbed for more than a day and only barely reached the level of her head.

Who did this to you? Kew wondered. Or did you volunteer? Was this the only way to bring the seasons under the tower's control? Perhaps she could slow or halt the Beast. Winter signaled its coming; if she turned the wheel back, forcing Grey into an earlier part of summer, that might buy them time. There was no knowing how long they had, but any little bit would help.

Kew started banging on the wall. Panicked, Frin grabbed his hand, but it was too late. Her eyes opened, each the size of a moon, and the hum in the air grew stronger.

Do you bring word from my sister? said the Lady. Whom am I to punish or reward?

Kew knew at once that he had not thought this through. Hurriedly, he flipped through *Goodlie Instruction*, hoping it would say something about the Beast. Nothing. He put it in his bag and took out the

Grand Bestiary of Blue Tower. Somewhere in there was a picture of the Beast—yes! He held it up before her.

The Lady squinted. It was such a human thing to do that Kew and Frin nearly retched.

It comes, she said. That has not happened since last I saw the moon. What does my sister wish? Are we to take up arms against it? Why do the Guardians not act?

For a moment Kew felt the two memories at war within him, saw the Obsidian Lady riding the Beast to the ruin of Black Tower. No. Whatever the truth was, it had nothing to do with what he meant to tell her. He pointed to the grey banner, then to the part of the wheel marked *summer,* and mimed turning it backward.

Hush, she said, though he'd been entirely soundless. You confuse me. There is a light on your forehead that I can see. Let me reach you through it.

One of her pupils opened like a door, and a long dark tendril reached toward him. Frin flinched, but Kew felt oddly calm, as if this had been done to him before. He must have gotten some of the spilled light on himself, despite Sparrow's warning. How odd that nobody had mentioned it. The tendril reached his forehead, and all the vibrations in the air now seemed to emanate from his own skin.

Someone has been repainting your memory, she said. But I cannot tell you how without knowing what has already happened to you.

Her faces frowned in concentration.

Move the wheel *back*? she said. I cannot without consulting the will of my sister. My sister is the Willow Lady. She is of a different dynasty than I. She is Willow. I am Iris. Iris no longer rules this palace. I have no say. You must ask her permission to shift the seasons. Do you understand?

He did.

I will let you take a message to her, then. Remember this, along with everything else.

As clear as an illumination in a book, he felt the memory of this encounter inscribed on his mind.

She will see this and know what you and I have said to each other. But, little Guardian, you will have already displeased her. You have released the Last Thistle from her punishment in the Ballroom. You have spoken to Ebony. And you have bargained with Obsidian. Whatever her daughter has promised you, whatever you have promised her daughter, she will not like it. The outer fiefs have no authority. Her daughter's actions, whatever the truth of them, are sedition. Unhappy the messenger who brings news of rebellion. I do not believe we will speak again.

The tendril brushed the hair back from his forehead.

There is an ancient kinship between us, said the Lady. The Towers of Grey and Black with their Ladies, the line of the Guardians, the Beast. It is an ancient mystery. I cannot tell you the truth of it, for it belongs to the Roses, to the time of songs. My heart aches with it. Yours will as well.

She withdrew her tendril. Her pupil closed again.

I cannot see the future, but the shape of the future is the shape of the past. The seasons are not the only wheel at work in the palace. I tell you what has happened before so that you may know what happens again. I turn this wheel with my own turning. But that other wheel you will turn with heartache.

The Lady closed her eyes, and the Oculus was silent in the cold sunlight.

A Story Told by the Mothers in Grey House:
How the Seasons Came to Be

This is holy and ancient knowledge.

In the Rose Era, the seasons moved on their own, and lay upon the whole of the palace. This was a great marvel of the Ladies. Sometimes great storms arose and flooded the palace. Sometimes great snow buried it. Sometimes great droughts starved it. Then, as the palace grew, and a Lady's voice could no longer be heard over the whole of it at once, the Iris Lady gave thought to this troublesome matter. She took no food, heard no lullabies, listened to no petitions. She sat in the top of Black Tower and thought.

A power such as the seasons could not be constrained by any force except a Lady's. But to exercise such power, a Lady could do nothing else. The rule of the palace would crumble. The Iris Lady thought and thought, and in the depths of winter a new thought came to her. She took one of her daughters and said, You are the Lady now, if you help me.

Then the two Ladies dug out a great room in Black Tower, and opened an eye overlooking the whole of the palace, and they built there a great wheel, and the Iris Lady stood in the center and said, You are the Lady now, if you take my arms.

Then the younger Lady cut off her mother's arms and from them made Black Tower's five piers.

The Iris Lady said, You are the Lady now, if you chain me to the great wheel.

Then the younger Lady chained her mother to the wheel, and at once winter fell on Grey, spring on Blue, summer on Red, and autumn on Yellow, and the hub of the seasons was Black. And the new Iris Lady went on her way rejoicing in her new virtue, and the old Lady began to turn. At first, she turned too quickly, and summer flickered over the palace like lightning, and winter breathed a single cold breath. Then she slowed, and learned the proper round of days. And ever since, she turns the wheel of the seasons, and watches the whole of the palace. As she laid down her virtue, the rise and fall of dynasties does not trouble her: she follows the will of the Lady of Black Tower. But sometimes she sees a person in need of a summer's day, or another yearning for the cool of winter, and she grants it to them. This too is a great marvel of the Ladies.

26. Kew and Frin Go to the Kitchen and Assist with the Baking of Bread

As they left the Oculus, another announcement was just ending. *—shall abstain from the eating of damsons.*

Kew's head ached and he did not spare a thought for this. Frin was glad that they had already given away their food, just in case. He had to lead the way up the stairs, for Kew only stumbled along, wondering what in North's name he was supposed to do now.

They were dizzy with hunger, and more than once Frin took the vial of honey out and pondered it, licking his lips. But Thistle honey was a powerful thing. It came from the time of songs. The flowers that went into it no longer existed. The bees that had made it were of a legendary, extinct lineage. And then of course when they had fed a drop to the musician, something strange had begun to happen before they died. There would be food somewhere in the tower. There would be no more Thistle honey.

Soon the smell of baking bread wafted down the stairs toward them. Their mouths watered, and even Kew found his pace quickening. If the map was accurate, the kitchen was not far above the Oculus. They only needed to keep going a bit longer.

On this twelfth day of the third month of the three hundred and fortieth year of the Willow Era, Her Ladyship has decreed that every resident of the palace must be still for half an hour, in memory of the first Willow Lady and her death in the one hundred and tenth year of the Willow Era.

The boys unwillingly stopped. Their stomachs were practically turning inside out, and a top was spinning in their heads, but the decree had been made. Why had these decrees never reached the rest of the palace? Frin assumed the squabbling fiefs outside the tower had kept messengers from going out. Kew assumed Grey was too neglected by the other towers to be worth communicating with. But they could not compare notes.

As the staircase had no clock, they waited for a go-ahead to move. A shaft of light came through the window a short ways up the stairs. They watched it move, sliding fingerwidth by fingerwidth. Meanwhile their stomachs ached and they were so hungry they nearly vomited.

At last Kew stood up. It may have been long enough, it may not have, but Frin was drooping noticeably. If either of them stayed on the stairs a minute longer, they would have no energy to keep on. He tugged Frin up to a standing position and fairly pulled him step by step toward the smell of bread.

There was a narrow wooden door, bound with bronze, and beyond it was the clatter and bustle of cooking. The smell of bread was so strong and sweet, it practically fed them just to breathe it. Kew pushed the door open and dragged Frin into the kitchen of Black Tower.

Like the Ballroom, it seemed to fill an entire level. They stood between two pillars, on either side of which were iron stoves. Cooks in tattered white jackets were stirring pots of sauce and soup. They ignored the boys, even as Kew and Frin tried to get their attention. One ladled up a boat of some red gravy and passed it to a person in a grey jacket, who hurried it deeper into the kitchen. The boys followed.

White pillars filled the kitchen, hung with utensils and vessels and built around with work tables where meat was sliced and salads composed. The grey-jacketed person turned aside, revealing a table where bakers in blue jackets were kneading bread. Beyond that were ranks of roaring ovens where loaves were shoveled in and out. The aromas were so delicious the boys could hardly stand it.

One of the cooks shoved a platter of sliced pork into Kew's arms. Another passed Frin a bowl of delicately arranged lettuce and tomato, garnished with bright nasturtiums. They looked at each other, shrugged, and dug in. In Grey, when food was passed to you, the implication was that it was *for* you. In the court of the beekeepers, all food was shared. It never occurred to either of them that they ought not eat it, until a massive hand descended on each of their heads and jerked them into the center of the kitchen.

"Thieves," said a deep voice, as the hands rotated their heads up to look at the speaker. "Thieves in *my* kitchen?"

The person was large and round, with no hair, only a scalp of red rind. Their eyes were dark and bright as dewdrops, and their limbs were thick and powerful from years of kneading and chopping and stirring and carrying.

Frin shook his head emphatically. Kew followed suit. The person's eyes flashed over them, taking in every detail of their travelworn clothing and dust-streaked hands and faces.

"Travelers from down-tower?"

They shrugged and nodded.

"Don't you know?"

Kew pointed toward one of the windows.

"From *outside*?" said the person, their voice rolling with surprise. They nodded.

"Then I'll forgive you provisionally. Why are you here?"

Kew took the piece of paper from his pocket. The person read it and guffawed. "You're off to Her Ladyship? Have you left your senses?"

They shook their heads.

"Oh, of course you don't think so. But you have, if you think the Lady will see you." They put out a hand to each of them. "I am Kestrel, chef of Her Ladyship's kitchens. To make up for your theft, you will help prepare the banquet. If you do a good job, I might let you stay, or I'll point you to the throne room. Though that would not be much reward. Do you agree?"

Since there was no other choice, the boys nodded.

"The ovens need tending," she said. "That's labor unskilled enough for you. Mynah will show you where the wood is. Be off with you."

Mynah, a man as short and thin as Kestrel was tall and fat, took them over to the ovens. An alcove nearby was stacked floor to ceiling with cut wood.

"Softwood for the pastries," said Mynah. "Hardwood for the bread. Only feed the fires when asked. I'll tell you when to rake them."

This part is not exciting. We only need to know that they did well, both boys having been raised to follow orders. We might also state that it was torture watching the bakers at work. There were cream puffs, large and golden and crisp, that were taken away and filled with cold custard and topped with pink icing. There was white bread, its crust crunchy and brown, its insides as soft and warm as love. There were swirls of pastry full of dragonfruit and pomegranate conserve and glazed with sugar. There were knotted rolls well flavored with rosemary and sprinkled with coarse salt. There were tiny tarts filled with sliced strawberries and piped cream. There were cakes the size of sparrows, covered with pastry cream domes and sheets of emerald-green marchpane. There were little meat pies steaming with the good brown smell of their gravy. There were bigger pies of songbirds with herbs. There were subtleties of crisp dough baked in individual pieces: scrollwork and oblongs and feathers, assembled to form towers with birds perched atop them. And most delicate of all, one baker drew out a cheese soufflé, shining and as light as a child's joy.

In the ovens just down the way there were joints and roasts sizzling. Potatoes had been set to roast and were taken out for buttering and salting, then browned under salamanders and sprinkled with herbs. Whole chickens were slipped out on trays, basted, and put back in to become crackling and golden. Fish were nestled among onions and lemons and broiled. Skewers of larks turned on rotisseries, and freshly drowned ortolans were put in little clay dishes to cook delicately.

Running from a window down the middle of the kitchen was a broad wooden table. There was some mechanism under its center that Kew could not discover the purpose of, but it was semicircular and had a lever. Upon the age-polished surface were set the finished dishes, all in fine porcelain or upon gleaming silver. Tureens and covered dishes marched along its length, with smaller plates and baskets around them like the courts clustered about the towers. Crystal bowls of honey-preserved fruit were put out. Glasses of wine and cordial were poured and set out, bright and sparkling, as if the banqueters would eat in the kitchen.

The sun was going down. Music played somewhere above the kitchen and came in through the open windows. The festal atmosphere excited the boys. There must be a holiday on, of some sort peculiar to the Great Tower.

Kestrel bustled around the table, making minute adjustments, garnishing things with parsley, sliced lemons, or chives. The businesslike delight she took in her work was beautiful to see. She went around the ovens and stoves, tasting everything and telling everyone how to fix the food. (Mostly she recommended more salt.) Everyone took pastries to her for finishing touches. She would fan out sliced poached quinces atop tarts, or add a little cream or a drizzle of honey. When she only told them to put it directly on the table, the baker whose work was so approved looked as happy as if the Lady herself had complimented it.

As the boys labored, they were fed. Crunchy ends of roasts, half-burnt or misshapen pastries, the scrapings of saucepans. It was more food than they had ever seen in one place. Feasts in Grey Tower meant everyone got more porridge than usual. Feasts in the Obsidian Lady's court meant white bread rather than brown. The boys' fingers were sticky and their mouths smeared with sauce. They shared glances of satisfaction and laughed for sheer joy.

At last everything was ready. The cooks and bakers and sauciers assembled at the head of the table, facing the window. Kestrel stood at the center, near the mechanism. Kew and Frin were both flushed with excitement, eager to see what marvel would send the food up to the feasters. Or perhaps *they* were the feasters. How wonderful that would be!

But everyone else looked sober. All the kitchen staff seemed apprehensive. They shifted uneasily, looking at the floor or each other, not at the food. Kestrel alone looked at the food. Why was her face sad?

The music played on. The sun dropped behind the hills. Still they waited.

A door opened, and someone came in. They wore dingy black livery with a gold medallion in the shape of an eye, and their long, spoon-shaped face had the slight frown of a person discharging a mildly disagreeable duty for the thousandth time.

"The feast will not be required today," they said, as if reading from a paper. "The Lady thanks you for your service."

They waited. Kestrel, her face expressionless, pulled the lever. The table tilted toward the window. All the fabulous dishes slid out, cascading down, down, down into the West Passage. The wind of their going blew back into the kitchen, delicious and sad. Where anything still clung to the table or windowsill, the cooks swept it off.

"Well," said Kestrel, "that's that. Mynah, Swallow, Blackbird, I commend you on another job well done. Let's plan the menu for tomorrow. Sir." She bowed to the newcomer, who returned it and left. The three of her staff whom she had named followed her toward a little office built out from the side of the tower. A desk and several chairs were set there.

Unsure what else to do, the boys followed. They stood in the office doorway as Kestrel settled into an armchair with a sigh, and her cooks took their own seats.

"Instead of varied courses tomorrow," she said, "I say we do something with apples. Roasts with applesauce, apple tarts, that kind of thing." She uncorked a bottle of something and poured it into heavy earthenware mugs that she passed to her staff. "May it tempt her appetite."

"May it tempt her appetite," they said, raising their mugs. As they drank, Kestrel noticed the boys.

"Well, friends," she said, slamming down her drained cup. "Do you feel up to talking now that you've fed?"

They demonstrated that they could not.

"I see," said Kestrel. "Well, no matter. I cannot say the ovens were the best-stoked they've ever been, but you served well enough, and freed some of our apprentices up for other tasks. You can stay if you wish. And you should, if it were my advice you asked. The throne room is not kind to those from out-tower."

Kew took out the piece of paper and pointed at it emphatically.

"A pity," Kestrel sighed. "Can't say I'll be sorry to lose you, exactly, you being so new, but I'm always sorry to see anything happen to soft fools. Mynah, have one of your folk guide them as far as the grand stairs. Friends, if you ever turn back this way, drop in and say hello."

Mynah accompanied them back to the kitchen and called a little apprentice in a grey jacket over as their guide. He had Frin open his pack and filled it with extra rolls, a few heels of bread, and a flask of water. Then, hesitating, he added a jar of honey. Apple blossom honey, Frin could tell, and from the viscosity, a very good year.

"If you speak to the Lady," he said, "ask her just once to taste our food. *We* daren't speak. But you—"

He did not say they were expendable, though he clearly thought so. To make up for it, he gave them little flaky pastries filled with sweet cheese. These they ate as they followed the apprentice back into the narrow stairs, up just a short way, and out.

For the first time since the Ballroom, the boys saw the proper inside of Black Tower. A long, vaulted corridor stretched before them to a broad staircase, lined with lamps. Above the stairs was a round window of blue, red, and yellow glass arranged like lily petals. On either side of the corridor were iron doors, each marked with words so old Kew could not read them. The floor, walls, and ceiling were all onyx so dark that it was like walking on the back of a black cat.

The apprentice took them to the stairs but refused to go farther.

"I can tell you're no-names like me," she said. "Be careful. I've never been upstairs, but they tell stories about it in the kitchen. The Library's always open, so I think you just go in. You mustn't touch anything there. At the end of the Library is the Great Way. I don't know how you go up it, but at its top is the throne room. But you must be so careful. The Sparrows guard the throne room, and they are not kind to bakers. They upset our baskets and eat our crusts and laugh at us."

She bobbed a curtsy, and they bowed, and she flitted away back to the kitchen. After their long day, the boys were exhausted, so they crawled into the corner of the stairs and slept. The throne room could wait.

27. Kew and Frin Go to the Library and Avoid Getting Crumbs on Anything

The sun awoke them. All the angles and curves of the corridor were altered in the morning light. Rich velvety colors streamed from the stained glass and turned the onyx into a dark mirror. The boys ate some bread and took the grand staircase up. It spiraled three times, but the steps were clean and unbroken. After toiling through the skin of the tower for days, it was easy. The stairs terminated in double doors of carved ebony, hung just slightly open.

Frin wanted to go right in, but Kew paused to look at the carvings. Each door showed Black Tower, with the mansions at its foot and the sun over its pinnacle. But in the center of the tower, something had been viciously hacked away and replaced with a gold eye. It was this that had caught Kew's attention.

The Willows' symbol was the eye, and like every other dynasty, they had forcibly replaced their predecessors, the Hemlocks. But it was one thing to know that, and another to see evidence of it gouged into the tower itself. Was there no transfer of power that did not involve destroying the old? It seemed now that everything he knew about the palace's history was the merest thread in a tapestry bigger than his mind could encompass.

The Hemlock Era had been a time of stasis. Apple Era had been a time of peace. The Thistle Era had been a time of wonder. The Bellflower Era had been a time of prosperity. And so on back to the Roses. Each era had its overriding virtue. What did Willow have? Did they *do* anything? If Hawthorn was correct, the palace had been crumbling since the fall of the Thistles, but two succeeding dynasties had attempted, in their own ways, to mitigate it.

He was on the verge of thinking sacrilege of the Willow Ladies, and he stopped himself. With the light still etched on his head, he could not risk adding that to the heap of memories. And besides, Frin was pulling on his sleeve.

The Library was dim and quiet. Smaller in diameter than the kitchens, but three times as tall, it filled yet another level. High windows all around opened on empty sky. The domed ceiling was painted in shades of grey and black, showing the deeds of some winged Lady whose name and story were unknown to the boys. The floor was filled with high bookcases, and all around the walls were tiers and tiers of books. Everything was coated in a layer of dust. At the far end was a pillared and manteled opening like a fireplace. That, presumably, was the Great Way. Frin was heading toward it when he realized Kew was not following.

The Guardian-apprentice was distracted by *books*. The Archives of Grey Tower would fit in one-quarter of one tier of the Library. Kew had never seen so many books, nor dreamed that they could exist. Volume after volume of poetry, history, songs, fables, botany, medicine. All the knowledge Hawthorn or the women could impart would hardly fill a shelf. He could stay here for days. Months. The rest of his life. And spend it on *one* bookcase.

In his pack he held nearly the sum total of the Guardians' wisdom. Faced with this wealth, he could hardly bear the poverty he had been raised with. There hadn't even been a way of knowing it *was* poverty until now. All at once he remembered: he did not have *The Downfall of the Thistles*. If he could find a copy here, though it would not have Hawthorn's notes, he would take it. They would never know. Nobody ever came here, clearly. And it would help against the Beast. Even if it did not help—and without Hawthorn's annotations, it might not—he would take it. He was owed it. How could the people of the tower hoard this? Why did these books never come as far as Grey? Did the *other* towers have as many? Grey Tower needed that book. But more important, Kew did. It was justice.

"Can I help you?"

Startled, the boys looked around. A person in a pink scholar's robe stood in the center of the floor. On their head they wore a flat, square, white hat, veiled in front with long strips of calligraphed paper. Their hands were simple flesh, but whatever could be glimpsed of their face was dark, thorny, and complex.

Kew took out some paper and wrote. *I'm looking for* The Downfall of the Thistles.

"I am Rook, Librarian of Black Tower." They bowed. Their paper veil rustled like tree boughs; how had the boys not heard them coming?

Kew bowed in return. *I am Kew, Guardian-apprentice of the West Passage. This is Frin, an apprentice of the beekeepers.*

Rook evinced no surprise or interest. "The Library sees few visitors these days. I have heard of your journey through the tower, and I know you did not come here for that book. I know your master. She has a copy; go home and read it. The Great Way welcomes you. Please have the goodness to move on."

I need that book.

"What use is *Downfall* to a boy?"

The last Thistle Lady defeated the Beast. The book tells of it, and my master died without completing my apprenticeship. I need all the information I can get.

"Hawthorn is dead? My condolences." Rook spread their arms. "The Library holds every book I know of—and I know of every book. Here you may find treatises on the Beast, bestiaries, songs and stories of Guardians who faced the same danger as you. Why is *Downfall* so important to you?"

Kew swallowed. Because he needed it, of course!

No. That was not the whole reason.

Because my master had a copy, and it was taken from her deathbed. Would the conversation go much longer? He was running out of paper.

Arms still outstretched, Rook moved a step closer to him. "Thank you for doing me the honor of telling the truth."

In the place where the Librarian had stood, there was a pool of light. A wandering trail led away from it into the shelves. Kew swallowed again.

What do you want?

"A book," they answered.

A specific book? He was almost out of paper. This had to end soon.

"No." He heard the smile in their voice. "But you carry two or three, do you not? Immense rarities, manuscripts from the very Archives of Grey Tower. I should like to have one."

In exchange for?

Frin could not see the light—indeed, did not even know there was light to see—but as the Librarian came closer his skin prickled, and a vibration filtered through the air around them, felt rather than heard.

"Access to the Library," said Rook. "Information is not free. Your master and I were friends after a fashion, but she understood the value of my time. I also wish to know more of what has happened in Grey over the years."

Kew's forehead stung. *I can just tell you.*

"Not good enough." Rook moved between the boys, with their back to Frin. A sweet, musty odor accompanied them, like the opening of an old room where incense has been kept. Light flickered in their path. Rook seemed to notice Kew watching it. "The lantern light is an ancient miracle of the Hellebores. It has its source here, in the tower. Some of us who are associated with it cannot help but absorb it over time. Very helpful, as it opens the mind, but very dangerous for the same reason, unless you can balance it. You have not. It is a powerful thing, but rare to begin with, and rarer now. Outside of a lantern, few people can even see it. I think you have come here by way of the Luminous Name."

As they spoke, their hand floated toward Kew's head, pausing just before it touched him. "Everything your master could have taught you resides here in a purer form. Let me give it to you in exchange for one book and a handful of memories."

A hand slipped into Kew's. Frin had moved around Rook and was by his side once more.

All right, said Kew.

Rook laid their hand on his forehead. Even Frin could see the light that spilled out then. Kew felt nothing except cool pressure.

"And the book?" said the Librarian.

Kew opened his pack. Rook sorted through the volumes inside and took out *Campanula.*

"Our copy is not nearly so beautifully illuminated," they said, one finger tracing the scrolling vines in its margins. "Thank you. For one hour, you have free use of the Library."

That's it?

Rook's posture showed surprise. "What did you expect?"

Kew was honestly unsure. But he had an hour with the books, and he needed to make use of it. Rook showed him where books concerning the Beast might be found, and he and Frin carried them all to a reading desk. Frin snacked while Kew read.

There was not much he did not already know. The Beast only

appeared at long intervals—entire eras, in some cases. Only certain people could stop it. What gave him pause was learning that Guardians sometimes failed. At the end of the Bellflower Era, the Beast managed to *kill* the Lady of Grey. Hawthorn had never mentioned that. She taught him very little history, saying that was the tutors' domain, and the tutors were all dead. During Bellflower, there had been an entire corps of Guardians, so the others were able to stop the destruction, but Grey never recovered.

He had always attributed the desolation of Grey Tower to the mothers' mismanagement. They did, after all, care for nothing beyond birth and death and their songs. Kew's face grew hot. A *Guardian* had failed in her most sacred duty. And Hawthorn herself had failed him in a sense. It was not enough to get your name and title. You must also be worthy of it. All the reading in the palace would not help. It hadn't helped that Hawthorn long ago. It would not help Kew now.

He tossed that book aside and picked up another at random, flipping through it without really seeing anything until a word caught his eye. He looked at the cover. *The Downfall of the Thistles.*

Turning back to the third chapter, Kew read four paragraphs very carefully. He rapped on the table to get Rook's attention.

What's mellified man?

28. The Great Way Takes Them to the Willow Lady

When the hour was up, the boys went to the portal of the Great Way. It opened onto a shaft, running down into darkness and up into light. Frin clapped his hands together three times, which Rook had told them to do. Soon, a lantern glided up from the depths and its door opened. A Sparrow listlessly motioned them inside and began whistling. Up went the lantern, moving much more smoothly than those in the West Passage.

There was no mellified man in Black Tower. Rook knew of none in the palace at all. "It's long since any man went into the casket for another," they said.

To become mellified, a man must, of his own free will, live upon nothing but honey for years, until he pissed and shat and sweated it. When he was saturated with it, he would be drowned in honey, then entombed in a casket full of it. After a suitable time had passed, his flesh would be carved up. Its powers of healing were miraculous. In *Downfall*, the Thistle Lady had fed upon mellified man and grown strong enough, in the absence of Guardians, to defeat the Beast by herself. Kew was no Lady, but if he could just eat some of it, combined with the chants and the Guardian's steel, he knew he could handle the Beast.

But there was none in the whole palace.

While Kew thought, Frin looked out the lantern window as they passed room after room. Rook had said that everything above the Library was the Lady's own. Her quarters were here, her parlors and dining salon and study, and at the very top of the tower, her throne room.

In one room, people in fine robes lounged on divans, feasting on spiders they speared from the floor with sharpened sticks. A harpist played while six beautiful young dancers in gossamer twirled. The song sounded like the one the beekeepers sang to welcome apple blossoms.

In another room, several people with spoonlike faces were mopping a tile floor. They moved in patterns, mopping the same places over and over, while piles of dust between their strokes showed that the same figures had been mopped for years and years. A ritual, then, whose purpose was probably forgotten.

I wish I'd seen more of the tower, thought Frin. To be warned against temptations and then encounter none is quite a hardship.

He squeezed Kew's hand, who squeezed back.

The lantern slowed to a halt, and the Sparrow opened the door. Frin handed them a bun from the kitchen (only slightly burnt), and their eyes lit up. As the boys walked away and the lantern closed again, they heard the sounds of frenzied chewing.

A short hall led them to an antechamber of dull lava blocks, where a bored-looking official took their names and places of origin. They were directed to a second antechamber of glossy black stone, this one very tall, apparently reaching up to the top of the tower, and very wide, extending from the north face to the south face, but very short, with hardly room for four people to stand lined up between the outer and inner doors. And it was crowded.

A gold and crimson carpet (dingy and worn) led between the two doors. Since nobody was standing on it, it was probably sacred, so Kew and Frin pushed in among the people already there. This did not win them any friends.

"Absolutely rude," said a frog-faced person in a red doublet.

"The idea," said a ferret-bodied person wearing only ropes of amber beads.

"We were here first," said a mouse-headed person with a huge lace headdress, under which smaller but clearly older mouse-headed people crowded.

"I'm going to die here," said an ancient person of simple flesh who wore a pilgrim's badge from Red Tower. Their tone was plaintive and accusatory, as if Kew and Frin should be held responsible for their imminent demise.

A soft bell chimed. The boys straightened up, thinking it might mean something, but the other petitioners only looked bored. The huge inner doors opened a crack, and a person with an ibis's head slipped into the antechamber. Going to a brass tube in the wall, they cleared their throat and said,

On this thirteenth day of the third month of the three hundred and fortieth year of the Willow Era, Her Ladyship has decreed that all eggs laid in the last fortnight are to be smashed against a stone, as an offering to those lost during the downfall of the Lily dynasty.

They cleared their throat again and went back into the inner chamber.

"It's never anything that applies to us," said the pilgrim fretfully.

"Nor to anyone else either," said the mouse-headed person. "I never once heard tell of these decrees before coming here."

"Not even the towerfolk follow them," said the frog-faced person. "I came through the Chocolate Rooms, and not a one of those speeches did they heed. Not. A. One." They punctuated their words by digging their left forefinger into their right palm.

"Then we needn't?" said the ferret-bodied person, holding a round bluish egg in their hands that they had, apparently, just laid.

"I say smash it," said the pilgrim. "I could do with a snack."

The ferret shrugged and cracked the egg open. The shell and its contents were passed around on that side of the rug, but never reached the boys.

Are you hungry? Kew wrote on one of his last slips of paper, and held it up for all to see.

In a clamoring rush, everyone on their side of the rug agreed. Frin began to tear up and distribute bread.

"Ah," said the mouse-headed person, passing out hunks of it to the nest in their headdress. "That's proper food, that is. Not the stuff they give us while we wait."

"This came from the great kitchens, didn't it," said the frog-faced person, chewing. "Nobody I ever talked to knew how to get there. I s'pose, seeing as how you wrote that down, neither of you do much in the way of talking?"

Frin shook his head.

"Pity. You might've traded the knowledge for favors. What way *did* you two come up by? You have the look of people who didn't have to toil like the rest of us. Ah, never mind. I spose the answer would take too much paper."

Indeed it would. Kew took more bread across the rug, then quickly returned, lest he stay too long on it. As bread was chewed and swallowed, the mood of the room turned somewhat in their favor. This, however, began to fade again, as hours went on and nothing more happened, and the supply of bread turned out to be finite.

The door opened again and the ibis-headed person came out and went through the whole process of throat-clearing. Kew tapped his pencil on his paper and cleared his own throat. The long black bill turned a degree or two in his direction.

Let us in, Kew wrote.

The official ignored his note and spoke into the tube.

On this thirteenth day of the third month of the three hundred and fortieth year of the Willow Era, Her Ladyship has decreed that butter shall no longer be used on bread, in order to relieve the strain on the palace's dairy herds.

They repeated their throat-clearing and returned to the throne room, once more ignoring Kew's sign.

"No good, that," said the mouse-headed person. "They don't listen to anything."

Kew made a motion as if to say *Then how do you get in,* and it was apparently understood, for the mouse-headed person said, "They just . . . call you."

"Doesn't happen often, though, I can tell you," said the frog-headed person. "I've been here a week and I've only seen *one* brought into Her Ladyship's presence."

A *week*? Kew was no tutor and did not know the more arcane laws of the palace, but surely the Lady of Black Tower was bound to see her subjects, by honor if by nothing else.

Another hour or two wore on. A small coterie of officials entered from the outer door, buckets in hand, and moved among the crowd so people could relieve themselves. Most of them did it with scarcely a thought; only those who were new, like the boys and the ferret, blushed and tried to hide their indignity.

Another hour passed. The mouse-headed people fell asleep, the big one supported by the small ones. The frog-faced person yawned. Kew wrote a single sentence and waited for the official to return with the next nonsensical decree.

At last, the inner door swung open again. Kew thrust the note directly into the official's path. They stopped short, coughed, choked, and coughed again. Singing an urgent, tuneless *da da da da* to themselves, they whisked back into the throne room and the door banged shut.

"Oi, what did you say?" said the frog-faced person, with a return of resentment and suspicion. "I've been here a *week*."

"Oh hush," said the mouse-headed person, stirring. "We've been here *two*."

"*I've* been here a *month*," said the pilgrim. "They'll be wondering back home what's become of me. I suppose I'll die here, and then the Lady will be pleased. I suppose *that's* what she *wa*—"

The ibis head poked into the antechamber and the pilgrim clammed up immediately. "You, come in," they said, pointing. The frog-faced person, right next to Kew, acted as if the official meant them, and started forward. "No," said the official, and consulted a list held in their pink feathery hand. "Kew, of Grey Tower, and Frin, of the Bee-keepers."

The boys started forward. Frin urgently poked Kew in the arm, then jabbed his finger at the paper, hoping for an explanation, but none could be given with signs. The throne room door opened wider to admit them, then closed with a marrow-shaking *boom*. Kew and Frin stood in the throne room of the Willow Lady, ultimate ruler of the palace, and the light blinded them so that they could not see her when she first spoke. But they felt the hum of her holiness, lilting and vertiginous.

Explain yourselves to me, she said. Is the report correct? Do you have it?

"Yes." Kew's voice came out cracked and hideous, and he coughed. "Yes," he said, closer to normal. "We do." He raised his voice. "Your Ladyship, we come bearing Thistle honey for you."

29. Kew and Frin Meet the Willow Lady

If it had not been for the Lady so near, Frin would have shouted at Kew. By the time that urge passed, their vision had cleared, and they could see the throne room and its occupants.

The semicircular wall slanted inward, and dozens of high, narrow windows lined it, throwing harsh sunlight. A polished onyx floor reflected them, as if the boys were floating amid white bars. Traceries of onyx formed the ceiling, where the glass turned yellow, and in the center of the ceiling was the eye of the Willow dynasty, staring at its own reflection two or three hundred feet below. Masses of courtiers and officials stood around the perimeter, all in black robes or gowns, all sparkling with gold jewelry. And in the center of the wall, directly across from the door and the boys, was the throne.

It was even bigger than the Obsidian Lady's palanquin. It was possibly as tall as Grey Tower itself. The throne's arms held their velvet cushions fifty or sixty feet off the floor, and the proud spines of its back reached nearly to the ceiling. Rose canes twisted together to form its arms and legs, and interlaced for its seat and back. They were made of iron, and iron thorns thrust out from them, and iron flowers bloomed on them. At the throne's apex, the vines wound around five spires like the tower's, with the central and largest one bearing a calm face with closed eyes.

The throne's occupant was on a much lesser scale. She was, in fact, hardly bigger than Frin. Wearing a puffy black dress and a white ruff, the Willow Lady sat on the throne with her feet sticking out before her, like a baby in its parent's chair. Her skin had a strange texture that only became apparent when she motioned for the boys to come closer: she seemed woven together of cords. Kew soon saw that, instead of cords, she was made of willow charcoal. Among the dry, crackling sticks of her flesh, she had a single golden eye, placed roughly where a nose should be.

How do you come to have Thistle honey? the Willow Lady asked. There has been so little for so long, and I know the others take whatever they can find. Obsidian keeps her own. Ebony found a cache years ago. She's a Lady now. Sometimes more is found and Ebony takes it before I can get to it. I wish to have my own. I am the true Lady. I am the ruler here. If it can make her a Lady, it can make of me a greater Lady. My lineage is true. My rule is legitimate. She is a petty princess of a petty fief. I am the ruler of the palace. I will have that honey.

"Of course, Your Ladyship," said Kew, bowing.

"Kew—" said Frin. "What—"

"Silence, squire," said Kew. "My Lady, I am the Guardian-apprentice of Grey Tower. And before we negotiate for the honey, I must warn you."

He paused. What was he to warn her of? The smell of the Obsidian Lady rushed over him. He saw the eyes of Ebony. He felt the touch of Rook's hand.

Meanwhile the Willow Lady laughed. The charcoal of her face split diagonally, and a dusty rasp came out. The court laughed with her.

Negotiate! I, negotiate!

"Pardon," said Kew. Vertigo nearly made him stumble. "I meant only to say that I hope to be rewarded for this favor."

Rewarded? I suppose that is proper for the Lady of Black Tower. She turned to the ibis-headed official. Tell the palace that I will reward those who bring me gifts. Tell them I want gifts. Tell them I am owed gifts. I have spoken.

The official scuttled out of the throne room—to the speaking tube, one must assume.

What do you want as your *reward*? said the Lady.

"I want to be named Hawthorn. My master is dead. The palace is without a Guardian, and the Beast—" Vertigo seized him again. "—the Beast rises. Obsidian—no, that's wrong. The Beast rises, and a Guardian is needed."

Silence, said the Lady.

The whole court went still. She raised her hand. A small shower of dust fell as she moved.

When this boy has given me my gift, I will grant his wish, said the Lady. He will become Hawthorn, Guardian of Grey Tower and of the palace's heart.

"Kew," said Frin, trembling and nearly crying. "Kew, *don't*. Not to her. Not this one."

Silence him, said the Lady. Or I will.

Kew gripped Frin by the face and jerked him closer. "I said *silence*." At the same time, his other hand gently squeezed Frin's shoulder.

Frin's trembling eased but did not stop. Kew released him and opened the pack. He drew out the jar of apple blossom honey.

Yes, said the Lady with a sigh that was a puff of dust. Bring it to me.

Kew took a step toward the throne. *The Beast rises and I have made peace with it, and will ride it to the conquest of Black Tower*—had he spoken? Yellow feathers seemed to rustle in his mind. Was he speaking *now*?

"Kew?" said Frin, and he realized he was listing to one side.

The Lady had cocked her head. Is there a problem? she said.

"Thistle honey is a wondrous thing," said Kew, rubbing one hand across his eyes. The floor was tilting wildly. He took another step. "It is too powerful for me." He nearly fell, but he kept walking. His stomach was doing flips. "But for one of your lineage—for the Willow Lady—"

Yes, said the Lady. Yes, yes, yes. For me, it will be perfect.

She sighed again, and Kew, at the foot of the throne, felt a soft rain of soot on his face. The Lady stood up on the edge of her seat and jumped. Her skirt ballooned out, making her fall slow and graceful. She landed right in front of him, and her eye gleamed into his.

I have never seen a light like I see in you, she said. You are a fitting giver of gifts. She put out a hand like a bundle of singed twigs. Give it to me.

He set the jar in her hand. The Lady was laughing.

Your wish is granted, she said as she uncorked the jar. Let it be known that Kew of Grey Tower, he who has brought me this miracle, is henceforth Hawthorn, Guardian of the Grey Tower and a Knight of the Lady, and let all do her honor.

The floor turned upside down, and Hawthorn slid, her body pressing itself onto what was now the ceiling. Frin's face bent over her, swimming.

"Kew—" said Frin. *"Hawthorn!"*

In the background, she saw the Lady extend a wet pink tongue to lick up the contents of the jar. The hum in the air took on a higher pitch. She was giggling, spewing dust into the honey even as she drank it. Hawthorn convulsed. In a voice not her own, she said,

"The Beast rises and I, the Obsidian Lady, have made peace with it, and will ride it to the conquest of Black Tower."

The Lady began to scream with rage. Hawthorn's vision dwindled to Frin's face. Weeping, Frin guttered like a candle and went out.

An Interlude in Yellow Tower

There came a morning when everything was different, in a place where mornings had been the same forever. It began like any other, however. A servant woke Bismuth at about three hours past sunrise, and helped him to the close stool, and waited patiently as the great prince pissed. In Bismuth's grandmother's day, honorable people of the court had sought this position; now it was filled by no-names—though they were, as Bismuth had gradually, unconsciously learned over his long years, not the less honorable for that.

Afterward, Bismuth was helped to a chair, and this same servant, whose name was Lally, consulted with him about the choice of clothes for the morning. The gamboge silk doublet with white leather jerkin, yes, and hose to match the doublet, and an overgown of pale weld-dyed wool. And of course the chains of office and the Lady-ring. Lally fussed over Bismuth's white hair, combing and smoothing it with scented oils, as if this were an important day instead of just another morning, until Bismuth finally waved her away with a kind of pleased irritation.

Through the triple window, Yellow Tower was brilliant in the morning light: spare and elegant amidst its cupolaed and ironworked pavilions. At the same time, it was the worst place in the entire palace. You could live in the presence of the other Ladies. But Citrine, well, only her mad old ferry-keeper willingly stayed within the grounds of the Nine Fountains. Bismuth went there four times a year for certain rites and obeisances, and that was quite enough for him.

A pink tent wobbled and bounced past the windows. That would be the butler Peregrine on his way to the ferry. Was it that time of the month already? Bismuth's mouth watered, thinking of the fiery wines that Peregrine would bring before the day was over, and he called for his staff.

His leg allowed him to move just as often as it didn't. This day was one of the former cases, but for longer walks, Bismuth still preferred his staff. It had some ancient name, and truly was not meant for supporting him, but the scrollwork grip fitted his hand precisely, and it looked well when he walked with it. Particularly now, as all the halls and rooms of Nonesuch House were aglow with the noonday sun.

Built by Citrine before the Night of Bones, Nonesuch House was a miniature palace within the greater. She called it Nonesuch both for the yellow-flowered clover she had carved everywhere, and because there was no other residence like it in the palace. Forested with spires and turrets, it sat with one face in the pavilions and mansions of Yellow and one in the parklands of the Nine Fountains. A wide plaza separated it from the courts, but nothing separated it from the Fountains. Nobody lived on that side of the house, of course.

Nonesuch was intended as a retreat, and such it had become in a very literal sense. The Bismuth princes fled there after Citrine's decline began, and there they preserved such bits of Yellow Tower's government as had survived. Now, eras later, there were only three ministers, and they with Bismuth formed the entire leadership of Yellow.

Topaz, the Mistress of the Yellow Library, was waiting for Bismuth in the Privy Chamber, near the table laid for breakfast. She wore a long tight-sleeved gown of saffron cotton, buttoned from floor to neck with peridot spheres. The streaks of ink on her face, carefully painted each morning by Lally, were a little too close together today, making her look as if she'd been whacked on the cheek with a stick. She curtsied to Bismuth, kissing the air just above the Lady-ring, and rose slightly before his bidding. He smiled.

Galena, the Prime Minister, entered a moment later. His greying hair had been teased into a high, beribboned tower where tiny pearl pins peeped, and he had taken very little care with his makeup. His rhubarb-dyed jacket was ironed, but his breeches were not, and the less said about his white waistcoat, the better. He bowed, kissed the Lady-ring, and rose when bidden.

Silver, the Master of Arms, was late. When she finally appeared, it was with one pauldron unfastened and Lally hurrying after her, trying to finish buckling it. However, when she stood in the traditional pose (one arm behind her back, one foot slightly forward), and Lally had set everything aright, she was impressive.

"Let us take our seats," said Bismuth.

Lally returned with a tray. Cook had sent up white bread, only slightly stale, soft-boiled eggs, and a little pyramid of peaches, only slightly unripe. The ministers drank small beer; Bismuth had a green glass of yellow honeyed wine with spices in, which the apothecary had assured him would help his leg. A chicken had followed Lally in and wandered about as she came and went, its scaly tail hissing on the marble floor. Everyone ignored it. It was a pleasant breakfast; the open, arched outer wall of the chamber looked out on the well-tended garden, where Lally and Herth grew herbs, vegetables, and flowers in profusion, and a warm breeze bore their scent continually into the spacious room.

"To business," said Bismuth, when he was done but nobody else quite was. Only Topaz groaned as Lally cleared away the unfinished meal. (At that moment, Tertius and its two passengers had just reached the end of the green maze.)

"I've none," said Galena. It was unclear to everyone, most of all Galena, precisely what a prime minister was meant to do, so he spent his days handling incoming and outgoing messages, conducting the occasional guest to their rooms, that sort of thing.

"The Golden Army is ready for inspection when Your Highness has a moment," said Silver.

"I've finally got to the bottom of my requisition list," said Topaz, producing a long scrap of parchment. "Grey wants to borrow a copy of Your Highness's ancestor's *A History of the Yellow Sister,* if that's agreeable."

Bismuth blinked. "Of course, but why ask me?"

"It's in the glass cabinet, and Your Highness has the key."

Bismuth sighed. "I can't find the key. Lally's looked for it, too, and it's simply nowhere to be found."

"Maybe the chicken stole it," said Galena dryly.

"A possibility," said Bismuth, just as dryly. "I'll have Lally inspect the coop later. In the meantime, Topaz, what if we can't find it? Do we smash the glass?"

She consulted her parchment. "The request came several months ago with no follow-up from Grey. I doubt the guardian has noticed our little slip."

"Then I suppose she can wait some days longer. However long it might take the chicken to pass the key."

"And if it doesn't?" said Galena.

"Soup," said Silver.

The air shifted, stirred by some massive sound or movement near the tower. They all shuddered.

"I see Her Ladyship has been disturbed," said Galena.

"North, I hope it isn't a child again," said Silver.

A silence fell, broken only by the chicken trotting in, then right back out.

"We should put up a sign," said Silver. "That's the third disturbance in a month."

"Oh, the other two were dares," said Galena. "Silly young folks being silly and young. No sign'll stop that."

Silence fell again. They were all thinking of Sardonyx's inflexibility: all violators went straight to Her Ladyship, never to be seen again.

(Yarrow and Peregrine had reached the island.)

"If there's nothing more to do," said Bismuth, "I'll go inspect Her Ladyship's army."

He stood, and Topaz and Galena went about their separate business as Silver walked with Bismuth to the grassy parade ground in the center of Nonesuch. It would have been a lovely place to sit in the sun and daydream. A square colonnade surrounded it, and lavender beds lined it, laden with flowers no matter the season. Warm breezes stirred the dry palm trees that shaded it. Over its western edge, Yellow Tower shone. In the evening, the point of its shadow touched a block of rhyolite in the parade ground's center, and some ritual or other was meant to happen then, but could not, for half of the ground was inside the sphere of discomfort.

If you walked west past the yellow stone, you would feel a little uneasy, as if someone was watching you. If you kept going, this feeling deepened. Your heart would race. Your hands would shake. You would want to leave the parade ground forever. Eventually you would turn and run. It was possible to become accustomed to this feeling—indeed, there were some among the Lady's subjects who sought it out as a test of endurance and means of spiritual purification, and the Sardonyxes had always lived under its influence—but nobody in Nonesuch House was particularly interested in doing so.

The Golden Army had once filled the parade ground. Now it was three lads in ill-fitting helmets, their ostrich plumes a little ragged, but they cheered like anything when Silver and Bismuth came out onto the balcony. Bismuth raised his hand in benediction. At the same moment, there was a distant rumble. Everyone paused. A summer storm? But the sky remained clear.

A moment later the air stirred. A great weight seemed to lift from Bismuth's shoulders. He felt young again, and smiled with a relief he did not understand. Then the birds came.

Huge white gulls, the Lady's own favored creatures, streamed from the tower's windows in numbers unseen for generations. The noise was terrible, even before the birds reached Nonesuch. They filled the parade ground like hail, driving the Golden Army into shelter, colliding with walls, and breaking whatever windows remained whole. At that point Bismuth's leg gave out, and Silver had to help him inside and back to his chamber.

"Peregrine is here," said Lally as she brought in a little bowl of frumenty some hours later. "He says he has quite a tale to tell you."

"Show him in," said Bismuth, propping himself up in bed. "Did he bring any of that sweet wine from the south of Blue?"

"Just a bottle, sire," said Peregrine, entering as Lally handed the bowl to Bismuth. "There was a poor harvest ten years ago, I'm sorry to say."

"Ah, well." Bismuth pointed the butler to a chair. "What tale is this? A new play? I will be sorely disappointed if you come only to tell me of the Blue Sisters fighting, for that is already over, and I owe Silver a new doublet for predicting the winner."

"Is it over? I hadn't heard. No, this is something that affects you more directly."

"If it's the birds, I was there when they appeared. Some new miracle of our Lady, no doubt. She likes a little joke now and then." His bad leg twitched at the memory of the last one.

According to ancient records, the princely line of Yellow Tower had been founded by Citrine when she came across a pitiful creature in the mud of the river and adopted him as her own. He ran away three times, only to return to her bearing some great gift; the third time, it was a wife, who bore him a son, who was therefore Citrine's grandson, and ever since the Bismuths had ruled alongside or on behalf of the last living founder of the palace. According to other, equally ancient records, Citrine had gone and captured her adoptive son all three times, and finally induced him to stay by breeding him like a stallion and holding his first son hostage. Either way, it was an

honor, but the Bismuths had held an ambivalent view of their great
patroness all these long years.

"It has to do with the birds," said Peregrine. Something in his voice
stilled the jokiness in Bismuth. Peregrine proceeded to tell the prince
what we already know: that Citrine the Yellow had finally gone to
sleep.

"So," said Bismuth, when Peregrine was finally done and the silence
had become unbearable. He stirred his frumenty without appetite.
"We offered rewards. Minstrels came from all over. Doctors brewed
potions. One young girl went to fetch a sip of water from the mountains at the world's end. Citrine ate her for her trouble. And all the
while, a little ditty from a Ladyless tower would have solved everything."

"It seems so," said Peregrine. He squeezed Bismuth's hand, a gesture
that none of the court, for all their sardonic familiarity, would have
made.

"And there's no heir. Her Ladyship never bore children of her own
body."

Peregrine hesitated. "No," he said. "No heir."

"Then we are Ladyless too," said Bismuth. Outside in the long
summer sunset, Yellow Tower was darkening, and for the first time in
centuries, no lights glowed in its windows. That, more than anything
else, convinced Bismuth that Peregrine was telling the truth. "What
do we do?" he said. "What are we without *her*?"

Peregrine shrugged, pouring some wine. "I'm just a Butler Itinerant,
sire. Have a drink."

It went down as sweet and hot as incense smoke. After a bit, Bismuth
began to smile.

"There may be claimants," he said. "Ladies from Black who see no
chance for advancement under Willow. The tower must be secured."

"Naturally," said Peregrine, nipping a bit directly from the bottle.
"Though this is a sad day, I suppose it must be nice to know that your
long guardianship is nearly over." His eyes twinkled. "You might take
up rulership of the tower yourself, sire. Become the new Lady."

Bismuth shook his head. "I'm too old for that. And I have no
children. But I will defend the tower as long as I may. After that—who
knows?"

"I've seen new things today," said Peregrine. "I never expected to,
you know."

Yellow Tower was fading into the sky. Bismuth, watching it, shook his head. Nothing had truly changed for him. He had never in his life laid eyes on the Lady, only felt her dreadful presence from afar. The government would remain exiled in Nonesuch for now. The present was the same as the past. The future did not seem likely to differ.

Peregrine stood. "I must, unfortunately, take my leave. There are deliveries to make elsewhere. But, Your Highness, it has been, as always, a pleasure."

He bent to kiss the Lady-ring. Bismuth withdrew it. "Let us ignore protocol this time," the prince said. "What does the ring mean, with no Lady in Yellow Tower?"

After Peregrine had gone, Bismuth held the ring up to the lamplight, asking that question of himself over and over. He thought it would make him sadder, but it did not. Yellow Tower had been de facto without a Lady for over a millennium. She had mattered only to those in Nonesuch House, or to anyone who happened to wander into the Nine Fountains. The other towers only sent such embassages and gifts as tradition required, but they all came to Nonesuch and not the tower.

Bismuth was free to act as he chose, until Black Tower took notice—if they ever did, and the Willows rarely showed much interest in the larger palace. But he had been Prince Bismuth, Viceroy of Her Ladyship, for so long that he was not sure how to be anything else. He rang the bell for Lally, and while he waited, drained the glass.

"Go find Topaz. Tell her to break open the cabinet and send that Grey guardian the book."

He poured himself more wine as Lally ran off. A little scratching noise made him look at the door. The chicken was there, staring at him with a beady golden eye. It was in the process of swallowing a little silver key.

BOOK FOUR

YARROW AGAIN

30. Yarrow Catches a Train and Meets One or Two Fellow Passengers

Angel's Head overlooked the circular valley of Yellow Tower from the western rim. Lying just off the West Passage, it was a large face of orange rock, the features quite eroded, and through its hollow left eye, the train ran toward Black Tower. Yarrow reached it after perhaps half an hour of climbing. It would have been less, but she was exhausted, still covered in egg slime (which had dried to a clear, sharp-smelling crust), and had stopped to rest several times along the way. Her bag was heavy, her feet were stones, her head drooped like an overripe apple on the branch.

Behind the face was a platform with benches, and she gratefully flung herself onto one. With a groan, she stretched her legs this way and that, keeping a wary watch on the station. From where she sat, Black Tower formed an upright pupil in the angel's eye. Yarrow shifted in her seat and looked somewhere else. In the other direction was Red Tower, fuming. Across the track was another platform, where some people were sitting on benches and reading books or rocking babies or simply staring, as Yarrow was. Beyond that, Yellow's outer courts mounted up a hill, terrace upon terrace, to one of the old inner walls that still interrupted parts of the palace. Banners of the Lady fluttered from staves all along the wall. Something caught deep within Yarrow, and she looked away. The urge to cry had to be fought down.

There were no words in her mind for what she had done. Yarrow was stuffed full of songs and even fuller of lore, but no song or litany could help her understand. The Lady of Yellow Tower had been one of the five original Ladies. Citrine the Deathless, one of *the sisters*, shadowy figures of legend, builders of the palace, peerless creatures of fierce wisdom and power. Yet if they had relied so on the one lullaby to help them sleep, no wonder their rule ended. Or perhaps the Lullaby of Reeds had simply not been meant for that Lady. Or only for a young Lady. Or. Or. Or many possibilities, all of them some fatal misunderstanding. Yarrow had no way of knowing, and it galled her. She was used to knowing. Or rather, she was used to knowing the limits of her own knowledge. But what happened in the tower lay so far beyond the bounds of her life that she could only call it holy.

Holiness was a strange and terrible thing.

There was a whistle in the distance. The train was coming. Noiselessly, it slid along the track and came to a stop, steam venting from the blowhole in its helmeted head. It had no eyes, but perhaps it didn't need them with those great silver-scaled arms pulling it along, hand over hand. Surely it could feel its way where it needed to go. Strapped to the back of its neck was a white platform where a Brother of the Order of Transit held the reins, his blue robes tied with twine at the wrists and knees so as not to flap in the wind.

Behind the train's sleek head were seven or eight steel coaches, held together by clasped hands. Doors opened and passengers exited, carrying luggage, leading children, or just meandering, hands in pockets, toward the stairs. From the rearmost coach, porters in blue caps unloaded parcels and chests. Yarrow got up and moved on stiff legs toward the nearest door.

"Usually I hate Angel's Head," one passenger said to their companion as they passed Yarrow. "Always feels sick somehow. But today the air's different."

"Wind must've changed," said their companion.

Another Brother of the Order stood at the coach door, checking tokens for embarking passengers. His eyebrow cocked at Yarrow holding a Butler token, and his eyes took in her crusty robe with a frisson of disgust, but he let her on and wished her a pleasant journey.

The coach had double rows of benches with an aisle down the middle. Every surface was upholstered with worn, stained crimson velvet. About half the seats were empty, and Yarrow stopped short, fingering the strap of her bag. Could a person boarding a train take any seat they wanted? Did you just . . . sit down wherever?

"Keep moving," said the brother.

There was an empty bench near the center of the coach. Yarrow sat down and scooted over to the window. Ash and dirt streaked the glass, but there was a pretty clear view of the terraces. It would be lovely to see the rest of the palace as the train moved.

A pale-skinned person edged into the seat next to her, their head and upper body entirely covered with an upside-down red flower, their lower body bare. The petal nearest Yarrow brushed up against her and her bag, and she compressed herself into the side of the train. With a shudder and a whispery noise like a hand sliding over stone, they began to move.

The terraces slipped away. A vista of the Yellow mansions replaced them, crossed here and there by the inner walls. Between Yellow and Red, the South Passage cut its watery, bony path. The train was running along the hill that Yarrow had crested to reach the Schoolhouse. Though she was on the right side, and Grey Tower would be on the left, she might be able to get a glimpse of it as they went.

But the train turned down a viaduct, taking it into the lower districts of Yellow and toward the South Passage bridge. Her tower was lost behind crumbling golden walls. For a moment it stared at her through a window. Then it was gone. She blinked sleepily.

"Can you make your bag stop moving?" said her seatmate.

"Oh, I apologize," said Yarrow, shifting it away from them. The ride had been fairly smooth so far, but maybe they were touchy about personal space. Perfectly understandable.

The train came to a stop between a pair of stone hands. Some people got off and some people got on. How did you know when it was your time? Nobody had said where the train was, but the buildings were still yellowish, so she probably wasn't in Black yet.

"So where are you from?" said her seatmate.

"Grey Tower." Yarrow could not keep a touch of pride out of her voice.

"Huh. I didn't know anyone still lived there."

Didn't know—!

"We do."

Her voice must have conveyed some of her displeasure, for the flower said nothing as the train pulled out of the station and headed down to the bridge. Tilted buildings and overhanging roofs shadowed its way. Here and there a pigeon fluttered.

As it went over the South Passage, Yarrow looked down. The river shimmered beneath her. Its banks were piles of bones. A single crow perched on a stone and seemed to meet her eyes. She smiled.

Farther down, a hollowman—Tertius?—was splashing through the river toward a dark, gaping mouth in the deep Passage. Not Tertius: the tents on its back were russet. A pity. She would have liked to wave to Peregrine from up here. A twinge of homesickness made her grimace, though it had only been a little while.

"Your bag is moving again," said the flower.

"I'm sorry," Yarrow said, putting it on her lap. Wait—moving?

"You keep a baby in there or something?" said the flower.

"Of course not," said Yarrow. The bag wobbled and stretched.

"A pet?" said the flower.

"Not as far as I know." Her hand hesitated on the clasp. A small voice cried out from inside, muffled by the old leather. A locust, maybe? They sometimes tried to steal things, Arnica had said once. With her other hand ready to swat the interloper, she opened the bag.

Nestled among her extra robe and wimple was a small creature in a marigold gown. Its head was a four-sided spire of brownish stone lined with six tawny-golden eyes along each face. They blinked and looked up at her, and the cry came again.

It was unmistakably a Lady.

Yarrow stared as the Lady sat up, ran tiny, segmented hands along her bodice as if grooming herself, and began to cry. The noise was piercing, carried on a wave of vibration like the one that had filled Yellow Tower. Every passenger clapped their hands over their ears.

"Stop now!" said Yarrow. "Please stop!"

The Lady went on crying.

"Make it shut up!" said the flower person.

The windowpane cracked.

"I don't know how!" said Yarrow.

"For North's sake, put something in its mouth!"

"I don't even know where her mouth *is*," said Yarrow, picking the Lady up by her waist like a doll. Turning her around, she saw no mouth at all. Maybe under her skirts? She flipped the struggling Lady upside down. The crying grew louder, and the crack spread over the window.

"Don't you even—" said the flower, but the crying had stopped.

A warm, wet cavity had swallowed Yarrow's thumb. Two sharp hands like grasshopper legs had latched onto her hand. When she turned the Lady the right way up, she saw that the base of the spire opened like a hinge, and inside was dark maroon flesh. The Lady's eyes swiveled to meet hers.

"I hate this," said Yarrow.

31. There Is a Form of New Life to Be Cared for and Nobody Knows How

The train roared into a tunnel beneath overhanging buildings of blue slate. Yarrow yanked her thumb out of the Lady's mouth, and she started crying again.

"Just let it suck on your thumb," said the flower.

"It's disgusting!" said Yarrow. "Let her suck on your petal and see how you like it!"

Before she could stop the Lady, the infant put her mouth on the nearest petal. Yarrow sucked in her breath. With a high-pitched cough, the Lady spat the petal back out just before the flower shrieked and jerked away. The crying resumed, and a fine network of cracks turned the window opaque, while the window just ahead of them gave an ominous groan. Yarrow put her thumb back in the Lady's mouth and tried to think things through.

The infant Lady must have crawled into Yarrow's pack in the tower, perhaps to avoid the collapse of her sleeping mother. There was no way Yarrow could take her along. How would she explain showing up at Black Tower with the daughter of a dead Lady? A Lady *she herself had accidentally killed*, no less? She still didn't know how she'd explain *that*, either.

And yet the rules were clear. If a baby was delivered by a woman in grey, but the parents died or were otherwise unable to care for it, she was duty bound to get that baby to an appropriate caretaker. Yarrow *had* to do something with this infant.

"What the fuck is it?" said the flower. "And where did you get it?"

"I found it," said Yarrow. "In the West Passage."

The flower shuddered. "Well, if things like that are around, I'm glad I always followed my da's advice. *Never take the West Passage,* he said, and I never have."

A sheet-covered cart came down the aisle, pushed by a very short person with very large eyes. "Refreshments!" they called. "Refreshments!"

When the flower asked to see what they had, they pulled off the sheet. There were trays of fruit, bread, and roasted songbirds, with little cups for water or chamomile tea.

"Ah," said the flower regretfully. "I only have a Blue Tower token."

The vendor passed them some bread and an apple.

"I have a Black Tower token," said Yarrow. "What will *that* get me?"

"Anything you want," said the vendor with a low bow that hid them below the seat.

"Songbirds, then," said Yarrow. "And tea and fruit."

The vendor produced a steel tray from the lower level of the cart and loaded it up with her order. They passed it to her with their compliments and moved on.

"Would you like anything?" said Yarrow.

The flower's petals swayed as they shook their head. "The Brothers look a bit dim on passengers sharing. Bread 'n apple's enough for me."

Yarrow picked up an ortolan and breathed in the savory aroma. She popped it into her mouth and crunched down. The flavor permeated her body like summer heat, and she relaxed with a long sigh. Her eyes closed in bliss.

"Good?" said the flower dryly.

"They're a treat in Grey House," said Yarrow, her eyes still closed. "The only meat we're allowed, and we only have them on Lady-days."

"In a moment, you won't have any today either," said the flower.

Yarrow opened her eyes. The Lady had clambered on top of the tray and was devouring an ortolan.

"*No!*" said Yarrow, snatching her up. Before she could cry, Yarrow (with a shudder) put a thumb back in the Lady's mouth while she looked for a less precious replacement. The baby might like some grapes or something. There was no milk to be had, but then an infant Lady probably didn't drink milk. Yarrow tried feeding her a grape. The Lady narrowed her eyes and kept her head clamped where it was. Yarrow proffered an orange. The Lady closed her eyes entirely. With a sigh, Yarrow took up the half-gnawed ortolan and gave it to her. With a squeal of pleasure, the baby set to munching. She gummed the bird's flesh into a damp paste, swallowed it, and spat out the bones. It was a long, disgusting process.

While she was occupied, Yarrow shoved down the rest of the ortolans, nearly gagging on bones several times. South take her if this *child* ate the thing she loved most in the world. As it turned out, she need not have bothered. Whatever the other powers of the infant, she did not have an internal capacity larger than a whole ortolan. When it was finished, she licked her fingers like an ant cleaning its feelers and curled up against Yarrow's side.

"Adorable," said the flower wryly. "Is it wearing a diaper, or is it just going to shit on the seat?"

Yarrow did not reply. What answer could she give? Scattered ends of disused Lady-lore filled the corners of her mind, but they all assumed that one was dealing with an adult Lady. Offer this sort of reverence in this chamber, speak with the utmost respect, behave in such and such a way around a Lady of Black, all that sort of thing. The notion of encountering an *infant* Lady had never occurred to her, nor to generation upon generation of Yarrows before. Other towers might have infant Ladies, but since Bellflower, Grey had not.

As for diapers, well, a woman in grey was for two things: birth and death. Childcare was for *parents*, tutors in a pinch. Tithelings weren't even accepted into the house until they were old enough to use a latrine. Old Yarrow once said that in the old days many had joined the women in grey specifically to avoid raising children. Grey House was no place for them, Yarrow's lap even less so.

"Do you want her?" she said to the flower.

"Want . . . *that*?" they answered, pointing to the baby.

"Yes."

"Can't say as I do," said the flower. "Anyway, look, she's taken to you."

There was no evidence of that. Yarrow was about to argue when the coach jolted.

The tray leapt from her lap as the train shuddered to a halt. Wheels screeched. She barely caught the Lady and herself, jamming one foot against the seat before her to brace them. The flower flew forward and banged their head on the seatback. Passengers shouted as they were thrown about. With a liquid crash, the broken window shattered and rained down around Yarrow's shoulders.

Hissing and creaking, the train settled into silence.

"The fuck?" the flower said, sitting up amid the glass. "The *fuck*?"

32. Yarrow Disembarks Before Her Scheduled Stop

Outside the empty window frame, the domed roofs of Blue brushed the cloudy sky. Green vines twined around their walls, bearing clusters of flowers in red, orange, yellow. People were setting themselves right, gathering scattered belongings, or pressing eyes to windows to see the cause of the disaster. Yarrow tried to ignore them.

"Are you hurt?" she said, setting the baby aside and bending over to help the flower back onto the bench. They kept repeating *the fuck* over and over, but aside from bruises and scrapes, they seemed all right.

Yarrow leaned out the window to look down the line. The train had been in the middle of a leftward turn along a viaduct, so the track ahead was hidden from her. Before her eyes were bare, snow-whitened tree-tops full of bright birds, and above that, tier on tier, was Blue Tower. Beyond it, along the top of the South Passage, sat the cloisters of Grey from which she had so often looked at Blue, but the near tower hid her own. That was just as well. Homesickness already laid cold fingertips on her heart. It would never do to let it get a stronger grip.

One of the Brothers came into the coach, checking passengers for injuries, hearing their complaints. When he had seen everyone, he went to the front and raised his voice.

"This train will not be completing its journey," he said. From the belt of his robe, he took a dark cylindrical object. "Ice has disrupted the line ahead, and we cannot continue farther." He unwound several long leather strands from what now appeared to be a handle. At the end of each strand was a sparkling shard of obsidian. "The Order of Transit apologizes for any inconvenience this may cause."

He shook the strands out, and with no hesitation, swung them back to flog himself. The obsidian slashed through his robe and into his skin. "We apologize," he said, and flogged himself again. All in all, he went through the rite twelve times. By the end, he was shaking and tears were running down his cheeks, but his voice was steady.

"What are we to do, then?" said a businesslike person with smooth rose-pink skin.

"The Brothers will assist you off the train. From within Blue, you may arrange transportation to your destination or continue on foot. Train service resumes at Prince Margay Station near the Court of Weavers."

Most of the passengers groaned. Yarrow furrowed her brow.

"How do I get to Black Tower?" she said.

The Brother inclined his head. "The disruption has made it impossible for any Angel Circuit trains to reach Black Tower. From Margay, you may take the Gatehouse Circuit to Red, which will circle back within a day or two."

"I can't wait that long," said Yarrow. "How can I get there sooner?"

"Foot traffic is outside the purview of the Order," said the Brother. He was sweating and trembling, but he stiffened right up when someone else started to ask another question. "I am only permitted to give three answers," he said. "The rest of the Brothers will be along shortly."

When he was gone, the other passengers grumbled to and about Yarrow. She sat and looked out the window, her face burning. How was she supposed to know the rules?

In the abstract, Yarrow had no problem with rules. In Grey House, she knew all of them. She *enforced* them, for North's sake. And everyone around her had known them, taught them to her, followed them, reverenced them. But out here in the rest of the palace—

The flower nudged her. "Your pet just went out the window."

"She *what*?"

The flower pointed. Yarrow leaned through the window frame. On puffed-out skirts, the Lady was drifting downward like a dandelion seed. She looked up at Yarrow and waved.

Sighing, Yarrow slumped back into her seat.

"You're not going after her?" said the flower. "You didn't seem interested, but—"

Yarrow sighed again, more heavily. "She's not mine. I just picked her up accidentally."

The flower shrugged, making all their petals jiggle.

Yarrow chewed her thumb. It would be more convenient to travel without the Lady. The creature was maturing rapidly: she was no longer a newborn. (Probably.) As a woman in grey, it was not Yarrow's responsibility to care for a *child*. The Lady was making decisions, jumping out of trains, waving: not exactly newborn behavior. It was tricky, but Yarrow was perfectly justified leaving the Lady behind. (Possibly.)

But in a flash she saw herself ascending the steps of Black Tower and having to admit, first of all, that she had destroyed the Yellow Lady, and second, that she had abandoned the Lady's own daughter and heir to die in Blue. However the first was judged, the second was a serious dereliction of duty. They would never turn the wheel for someone so neglectful. And they'd certainly punish her. All the more harshly if she lied—and there went any chance of lifting winter.

Sighing a third time, she got her pack and stood. Many of the passengers had already left. Two Brothers of the Order flanked the train door to assist people out.

A Brother with several eyes handed her down. When she reached the track, it rapidly became clear that she was going to hate whatever happened next. The viaduct ran along huge piers of rough dark stone. Though the other passengers were sidling along the track's broad curb, there was no obvious way off. She could climb down the stones, perhaps, but they would tear her fingers to bits. And she was so, so tired.

"Can you help me down?" she said.

"Foot traffic is outside the purview of the Order," said the many-eyed Brother.

Below, the bright gown of the Lady vanished under the trees. Yarrow gritted her teeth and held up the Black Tower token.

"I only want to get to the *ground*," she said. "You don't have to touch it. Just help me down if you can."

The Brother blinked. It took a while. "Do you understand that you assume full personal responsibility for yourself and your goods and chattels *as soon as* you leave our track?"

"Yes," said Yarrow.

"And do you swear to absolve the Order of all culpability in any harm that may come to you or your goods and chattels?"

"Yes," said Yarrow. Why did they make things so *difficult*? She brandished the token. *"Yes!"*

Whether because of the token or the promise, he whistled. A third Brother joined them. His large hands had bulbous scaly fingers, their ends padded and wrinkled. At his instruction, she climbed on his back, and he descended the pier. The skin of his fingers caught and held on the stone, allowing him to move with ease.

The pier was surprisingly high, even allowing for the trees obscuring the distance to the ground. By the time they reached the grass, the train was hidden behind the treetops. The winter in Blue was lighter than in Grey, and hardly any snow had accumulated, especially beneath the ivy-hung trees. The air grew stiller and warmer as they descended, until it almost seemed as if Blue stood poised on the verge of spring.

From her brief glimpse atop Grey Tower, Yarrow had known that winter covered much of the palace, but after spending so much time in Yellow, she had forgotten how uncanny it was. Peregrine, the Keeper, and Old Yarrow had all believed something was truly wrong. Some part of her had still thought it was punishment. It was easier that way. The wheel could *not* break so thoroughly. It couldn't. There was a reason for this, surely.

But Blue was the tower of peace. It alone had never spawned a rebellion against Black: Red Tower, at least once per era; Yellow, during Bellflower; even Grey had asserted its autonomy during Lily. Blue was the place of artisans, flowers, birds. What could it have done to merit this?

She asked the Brother the way to Prince Margay Station, but he shook his head and went back up the pier, leaving Yarrow shivering and looking for the Lady. All about her were tall, straight trees and neatly mown grass, as unlike the stony cloisters of Grey as one could imagine. But even here the trees were dead, green only with ivy, and in many places the grass was patchy brown. Birds flashed from bough to bough, chattering and fighting over seeds and insects. The Lady's cry could not be heard, and among the birds, her yellow gown would not stand out.

"Hello?" said Yarrow. "Are you up there somewhere?"

There was no reply, but farther down the viaduct birds flapped and shrieked in a sudden commotion. Yarrow hiked up her skirts and ran.

Near the next pier, things had already settled down. Halfway up a beech tree, the Lady clung to the bark with one prickly hand. The other clutched a tattered goldfinch carcass, which she was devouring with eager speed. Drops of blood spattered her dress and dripped from the bird's bent and broken tail. The grass and snow were sprayed with red.

"Hey!" said Yarrow. "Put that down!"

The Lady's eyes swiveled toward her, but the child kept munching. When had she developed teeth? Had they been there the whole time, sheathed like a cat's claws?

Keeping back revulsion, Yarrow held up her arms. "Come down from there."

The Lady's teeth caught on a gristly bit and began gnawing. She did not move.

"Come on," said Yarrow. "Or I'll leave you here."

The gristle came out with a wet rip, and the Lady swallowed what appeared to be a chunk of the bird's spine. Yarrow's stomach turned. Women in grey were forbidden to handle raw meat; Servant had always cooked the Lady-day ortolans, and no other meat was permitted in Grey House. This violence was unfamiliar and obscene.

She tried again and again to coax the Lady out of the tree, but it seemed the little creature, having tasted fresh goldfinch, was determined to stay there until she caught more. Not for biscuits would she come down, and not for the few figs Yarrow had left. And Yarrow would *not* go catch a bird to lure her. Face burning with frustration, Yarrow threw herself down on the cold ground and crossed her arms.

Maybe if the Lullaby of the Reeds were sung, it would put her to sleep. But that was a huge risk. If it worked, she caught the Lady and could resume her journey. If it destroyed the child the way it destroyed the mother, Yarrow was no worse off. Others must have survived: the place had been plastered with eggs. This one would be no great loss.

At that thought, Yarrow stood and was about to leave. Let her stay here eating! What did it matter? But no. The Lady had a distinct fondness for meat. Only a finger in her mouth had kept her silent, and she would eat nothing but birds. Left alone, would she grow to hunt bigger game? A woman in grey must not be responsible for death. Blue had Ladies; *someone* here must know what to do with the baby.

With a groan, she began the Lullaby. From the first note, the baby was transfixed. Her eyes grew heavy. She nodded, jerked back awake, and nodded again. At last her grip on the tree slackened. Yarrow moved forward and caught her as she fell, sleeping peacefully. With great care, as if packing a piece of porcelain, she put the Lady in her pack. That did not feel secure enough, so she took the Lady back out, wrapped her in the extra wimple, and pinned it tightly so the Lady could not wiggle free. Then she turned toward the obscured face of Blue Tower and, once more, began walking.

*A Question Posed by the Tutors in Grey House
(But as the Tutors Are Dead, It Is Forgotten):
What Is the True Name of Blue Tower?*

So Eglantine XLIV asked of his apprentice, and the apprentice answered *It is the House of Frogs,* and Eglantine was well pleased.

33. Yarrow Continues on Foot and Feeds a Baby

Like every part of the palace except the four Passages, the courts of Blue were difficult to traverse. In Grey, to get to Madrona's district, you had to cross the Court of the Tower to the northern wall; go in at the side door; walk up a staircase to a long gallery; follow that to a crumbling mezzanine in a court where half of a huge stone face glowered; pick your way along the mezzanine, which grew crumblier every year; take the left-hand door in the far wall; go down a short corridor, and come out on the parapet of the wall known as Hand-maidens' Fall. You would end nearly back where you started, only higher up.

Once, there had been more direct routes through Grey, but collapsed arches or toppled walls now blocked them, and new structures had been built over, around, or through those ruins. Then those structures had collapsed in their turn, and so on. Now the clearest paths lay through disused rooms or ancient galleries where once only members of the Lady's court had been permitted. There were apologies to make upon entry, or in some rooms you had to walk along only one wall so as not to disturb people who had been dead for an era and weren't in the room anyway.

Blue was newer and more populous, but it still resisted the traveler. All of its white-plastered walls looked the same; every door was the same cerulean blue; new buildings had been constructed straddling others or jutting out at strange angles. It seemed *made* to confuse, where Grey had only *lapsed* into confusion. Also, the land around Blue was wrinkly with valleys and hills. Yarrow had never known that. From a distance, Blue's rooflines baffled the eye and made the district seem like a single smooth hill. But the same primeval forces that had carved the South Passage seemed to have crumpled Blue up like a napkin. More than once, Yarrow entered a building by one door, then exited by another many floors below, or the reverse, so that after an hour or two of walking she was exhausted and had made hardly any progress at all.

Every room or corridor was empty of people. Unsure of the protocol, she whispered a ritual apology each time, even though the emptiness was that of a crow-picked skull. In Grey and Yellow, emptiness was still cluttered. Decaying furniture, shredded tapestries, moldering ornamentation, abandoned miracles: it was an airless, overstuffed quality. In Blue there was nothing at all, not a stick of furniture or a film of dust. Even the windows were empty, wooden shutters open wide without even a lattice. The whole place seemed scoured. In one room she found a dead fly, and the shock of seeing anything at all nearly made her scream.

After that, she began to find other things. Not furniture, decoration, or miracles: concatenations of metal and wood, full of struts and gears and pulleys. These things must be machines. Yarrow had never seen machines, but Grith had told her of them: great mechanical beasts with flesh and innards of clockwork, Grith said. Moved by water, wind, or muscle, Grith said.

As to what they did, well, there were straightforward ones, and there were less straightforward ones. Yarrow saw what had to be looms, though they were nothing like the looms on which Arnica wove. She saw large presses for fruit and mills for grain. And she saw a curious machine that seemed to make pages and pages of writing. Jasper's library kept a few books like that, but Yarrow had always thought they were the work of a particularly finicky scribe.

But in one tall, narrow atrium was a vast machine turned by a creature: nothing but bulky greyish legs walking around and around a track, which its feet had worn smooth. Where something else might keep its genitals, this had a horizontal metal pole attached to the machine, transferring its motion to stacks upon stacks of interlocking gears, which filled the atrium up to the circle of winter-white sky at the top. The creature had to be a miracle; nothing else could be that tireless.

It was the first living (or quasi-living) thing she had seen since leaving the trees, and she stood a while and watched it. Where was everyone? Even Grey was not this empty.

Something rumbled underground, and the machine shuddered. The miracle did not cease walking. After a moment, chutes swung down from the machine's rotating sides, and several dozen spheres of clear jelly poured out. Yarrow skipped back, avoiding the splashes as the spheres burst around her. Each one left behind some object: from this one a wheelbarrow, from that one a sapling, from another a mirror. All around the walls were bins marked with symbols: wheelbarrows, trees, mirrors, lambs, potatoes, as if the things now piling up on the floor were to be sorted into them. But there was nobody to do the work, and at last the stream of spheres stopped. All around were useful things: if she had been heading back to Grey, Yarrow would have filled a wheelbarrow with whatever they needed there. The creature continued its walking, smashing a mirror with one foot, crushing a steel pot with another, snapping the neck of a bleating lamb, and so on. There was another lamb in the track, and Yarrow pulled it out of the way before the miracle got to it. It kept bleating, and the Lady started whining in time with it, so Yarrow left. The echoes of the lamb's cries followed her, and she shivered. Surely someone would be along for all of it eventually.

A long corridor and a rickety wooden staircase brought her out onto a broad walltop. The tower was very close now, and she had to lean back to see its top. A little tributary of the river wound past the foot of the wall and fell down a short cascade, where it turned a dented, rusty wheel. Yarrow closed her eyes against the keen wind and breathed deep. One got so used to stale air. The Lady squirmed and grunted, and Yarrow shushed her.

The other end of the walltop brought her into an enfilade of four rooms, each filled with machines. In the first, iron arms twisted sheets of metal into huge lantern-shapes like Servant folding laundry. The Lady hissed at the clanging and screeching, and Yarrow hurried on, following the lanterns as they rolled into the next room, where delicate silver fingers etched them with a hellebore flower. In the next room, a bronze fist stamped the Willow eye over the flower. In the final room, the lanterns were piling up. All the while the machines labored noisily on. One of the litanies said to avoid lanterns, and that was no problem for Yarrow. After a few more stairs, she shoved through a particularly stubborn door into a fan-shaped room.

She sighed with relief at the silence and the light. Here were many high windows, and the clamor of machines was muffled by many more cobwebs than any place she'd been in Blue. But there were still no furnishings, and the room was nearly empty. At its narrow end was a broad pedestal, or perhaps a dais, with a dusty curtain of brown velvet veiling its top. A rope hung to one side.

On Lady-day in Grey, the players presented their mystery plays on stages with curtains like this, and ropes to draw them. Refreshed by her time in the wind, Yarrow felt she had earned a break. There certainly weren't any players about, but the stage might have some cunningly painted scenery. *That* would be pleasant to look at. The Lady had lapsed into sullen sleep, so Yarrow tugged at the rope until, with a puff of dust and a sour smell, the heavy folds of the curtain drew up and the stage was revealed.

There was scenery, but it was a plain panorama of the palace with the five towers. It reminded Yarrow of the schoolhouse fresco, and she squirmed uncomfortably. Above it was a black hole like a chimney. There was a bit of a draft from it—very unpleasant, especially as the air made the scenery quiver as if the towers were twitching, pulsing, like things hatching. She was about to leave when a little body clattered out of the chimney onto the stage.

Was it—*alive*? She edged closer. It was metal and wood, but was there any *flesh*? She poked at it. No, it wasn't alive. She found fine black threads for moving it—only a puppet. Then it twitched and unfolded and stood. The blue costume it wore didn't look like anything she knew.

Yarrow leaned over the edge of the stage and looked up. In the chimney was an assemblage of iron gears, arms, strings—and more puppets dropping toward her. She stumbled back just as one hit the stage, followed by several more, *clackety clack-clack*. Then, grandly, a Lady in a black robe.

A tinkly little tune began. Yarrow peered around the back of the stage. More machinery, this for making music. A bellows began expanding and contracting, and a terrible, reedy imitation of a voice started up.

"Eh uh uh *eh*-eh-eh ay-ee ih eer," it said, and from the waving of the little blue-robe's arms, Yarrow could tell it must be the one talking. "Oo ah ah uh ai-ee eh oh uh ah ee-air-eh-ee."

It was an awful, incomprehensible racket. But Yarrow sat and watched, resting her feet and relieved to have some sound that, grating as it was, still wasn't the baby's crying. An argument, it sounded like, which was only resolved when the Lady herself spoke. Her voice was a gong, not loud but very deep and hollow. The whole group began an up-and-down motion while the panorama behind them rolled past, bringing Grey into closer view. And there they were joined by a tall bird-headed Lady in yellow and a turret-headed Lady in red. Yarrow flinched.

Was it—it couldn't be. Was it a story told by the Mothers?

Yes: the Hellebore Lady's defeat at Grey long, long ago. Not only had a story of the house been taken, it had been *recorded*. Though whatever machinery drove these puppets was not sacrilegious writing, it wasn't flesh, either. And worse than all of that, it was a grotesque parody of the actual tale. The Lady of Grey (at whom Yarrow couldn't *quite* look) was a bumbling noisemaker accompanied by three wimpled women who echoed whatever she said in voices even reedier and more terrible than the other puppets'. And in a complete departure from the truth, Hellebore took a lantern from within her robes and poured its light upon Grey, making it and its inhabitants stand still and listen to her. Then she sang: crystalline notes like a finger on a wineglass's rim.

The Lady and people of Grey capered stiffly and sang along to Hellebore's tune. They flapped about and rolled their tiny puppet eyes. Their horrible voices screeched in Yarrow's ears. At last they stopped and bowed to Hellebore, speaking words that were nonsense even compared to the rest.

That had certainly never happened. As the Mothers knew, the lantern light in its liquid form made you receptive, even pliant in mind as well as body, which was why the Hellebores had sent it out to unite the palace factions under their banner. There were other, less predictable effects, too, especially if it were diluted. Thankfully, once the Lady defied Hellebore, no lantern track had ever reached Grey Tower. After that era, successive dynasties found it useful, though by the dawn of Willow it must surely have been depleted. If the Hellebores had actually deployed it in Grey, the Mothers would remember.

Yarrow stood with fists clenched. So this is what Blue thought of them. This is what the *palace* thought of them, more than likely. Stiff, bumbling repeaters. Toys of Black. Fools, even. Their stories free for the taking, free for reworking, free for mocking the Lady and the Mothers and the house and *everything*. Here, where anyone could see them, where nobody could correct them, where nobody knew Blue was passing this brackish water off as wine.

The machinery came to a squealing halt, and every puppet went limp. She picked up the Lady, who was drowsily awake, and left.

Yarrow's duty now was to show that Grey was nobody's puppet. They would see her guiding the new Lady of Yellow. They would know the long learning of the house was for some purpose.

Despite her determination, there was a very long way to go still, and she was very lost.

At last, tired and footsore, she found herself in a court of mown grass with an apple tree planted in its center—a *living* apple tree, very black and gnarled under the darkening sky. Beneath the tree was a stone, carved into no particular shape but smooth and polished: the oldest effigies of Grey were like that, too. Despite the cold and the scattering of snow, the tree still bore some puckered-up apples. Yarrow gathered a few. On the other side of the tree was a door: the only way out besides the way she'd come in. Through it was another bare room, this one long and narrow, its white ceiling plainly and simply vaulted. Slender windows on the far wall overlooked the spreading apron of Blue Tower, the teeth of Black, and the beacon of Red. As the blue of evening settled over the palace, amber lights sparkled here and there.

What with curfew, and funerals only taking place at noon, Yarrow had never been up high enough at night to see the beacon, nor close enough to see details of Red Tower's shape. The main mass of the tower was an irregular cone, bolstered by structures like tilted slabs of stone. At the pinnacle was a sort of husk, like half of a burst seed-pod. Thin spines seemed to cover it, though she couldn't tell for sure in the dim light. In the cup of the husk, the beacon burned. It was a great flame, disastrously great: a conflagration that could devour all of Grey House in a moment, and it billowed and swirled like the costume of a player. But the light it cast was warm and homely. There was a song that spoke of Red Tower as the hearth of the palace. She could almost understand why.

Nearer, its lamps like a swarm of fireflies, Black Tower brooded. Its familiar shape was wrong, somehow. She felt as if she'd reentered a room to find that her cup had been moved a few inches. Ah, *there* was the difference: some windows at its pinnacle had lighted up. Normally, the top of the tower was as dark as anything, but there, where the Willow Lady was said to hold court, someone was awake.

Curious, but unconcerned, Yarrow went back to the corner where she had left her pack and ate a scant meal of two biscuits and an apple. The apple core was hollow and full of black mold, but the rest was acceptable. Fresh fruit was not to be disdained, however poor it might

be. She took the baby out of the pack and laid her on the floor, then
curled up next to her and tried to sleep. It was not easy. The loathsome
eh eh ah ah of the puppets echoed in her mind. And Blue was the
friendliest of the towers to Grey. Better the vast indifference of Yellow
than this—this—this . . .

Yarrow slept.

The Lady's cries woke her in the night. Groggy and unthinking,
Yarrow put her finger in the baby's mouth to quiet her and went back
to sleep.

Around sunrise, Yarrow awoke with a sharp pain in her finger. She
jerked upright. What a fool, to make such a mistake! The baby had to
be shaken off. When she was finally detached, she ran to the corner
and sulked. Yarrow's finger was mostly intact. The Lady had not done
much more than break the skin: there were two tiny, bloody semicir-
cles of teethmarks, but that was all. If Yarrow had been just a bit more
deeply asleep, it is hard to say what would have happened.

"You little—" Yarrow began, stanching the wounds with the edge
of her sleeve. What was a bad word she could use? Before she thought
of one, the Lady began to wail. "I'm not feeding you. There's nothing
here except me."

She started to sing the lullaby, but though the crying settled to a
whimper, the Lady was, it seemed, too hungry to sleep. Yarrow gritted her teeth. After yesterday's success, she had assumed the lullaby
would be of great help. Apparently, it had its limits.

"Here," she said, tossing the baby a fig. Her crying ramped back up,
and she kicked the fig back to Yarrow. *"Here,"* said Yarrow, throwing
a biscuit over. Screaming with rage and hunger, the Lady ran to the
biscuit and stomped it to pieces. "I *hate* you," said Yarrow. "I hate you
so much."

They glared at each other, the one with more eyes than the other.

"This is not my role," said Yarrow. "I'm *the* Mother, not *a* mother.
Why are you even here? Why didn't you stay in the tower? Why
weren't you *smashed*? I hate you. *I hate you.*"

The baby resumed crying, but Yarrow did not feel the least bit of regret. She picked up the wimple and, after chasing the Lady around the
empty room for several minutes, captured her again and pinned her
up tightly. The Lady did not stop crying, so Yarrow took a handkerchief from her sleeve and tied it around the small, loud mouth. This
dampened, but did not entirely muffle, the noise. Yarrow jammed the

Lady into her pack and ate her own breakfast. There was little left: the destroyed biscuit had been a loss she could ill afford.

The Lady would only eat flesh, and there was just one kind of flesh to give her. Yarrow took out the jar of honeyed meat and unstoppered it. The smell was sweet and delicious and heavy with rot, like the wine she had drunk at dinner in Grey House. There were five bits of meat inside: rather small, unfortunately, but if the Lady would accept a snack it might be enough until something better came along. She gave one chunk to the Lady, who ate it greedily, and wiped the honey off on the handkerchief before tying it back around the Lady's mouth.

Her injured finger throbbed more than she had expected, and the skin around it was red and beginning to burn. Was it infected? Or did Ladies have venom? She ripped up another handkerchief and bound the wound securely, but if something was seriously wrong, there was nothing more she could do for herself. There might still be a doctor in Blue somewhere, but the abandoned state of the courts so far did not inspire confidence.

Opening the outer door of the room, she went down a whitewashed staircase for several minutes until she reached a wide parkland of gently rolling grass, dotted with tall brown conifers. Stumps showed that this court was a source of lumber or firewood. Wandering here and there were cattle, nibbling at the grass. Their horns were tied with blue and yellow ribbons. Their gills flared and contracted as they breathed. They ignored Yarrow.

When she had got across the park, there was yet another white wall with a short staircase. Above it, Blue Tower filled the sky. Its three receding tiers were of marble the color of a cloud's shadowed side. Their parapets and windows were trimmed with a much darker stone that iridesced deep blue and bright gold. Despite the cold, vines bloomed all over its walls, and dark ivy coiled about it. Hummingbirds with yellow throats buzzed about, sipping nectar, and grey pigeons cooed in the niches and crevices. Seeing the birds, the Lady squalled, and Yarrow was forced to feed her another piece of meat. She seemed to have grown: the wimple restraining her was stretched tighter than it had been, and either Yarrow was very tired, or the pack was heavier as well.

At the top of the stairs, Yarrow found a broad terrace of marble tiles, interrupted here and there by short trees trimmed into cubes of grey sticks. Another planted terrace rose a distance away, and another, and another, curving around the tower and diminishing as they went, until they ended in a large portico that must be the entrance to the tower. Her heart sank. It was still so far away. But if she wanted directions, she needed to talk to someone, and there must be people in the tower proper. Yarrow resumed walking.

After a while she was quite warm. The sun was shining, and though a chill wind swept across the terrace, she was overheating in her dark cloak and gown. Her hand throbbed, too, and had grown red and swollen, with angry hot streaks running up her arm. Though no doctor, she knew enough to grasp that this was not good. She tied her last clean handkerchief around her arm just under the elbow, slowing the blood flow; that might keep infection at bay a little longer. Just until she got to the tower. She fed the Lady again; there were only two pieces of meat left. The Lady seemed to have gotten very heavy, and barely fit in the pack at all.

The roofs and lapis domes of Blue loomed over the first terrace but as she climbed to the second, she drew level with them. And when she stopped for breath on the third, she stood higher than at any point since leaving the train. Yarrow had come around the side of the tower and expected to see home across the South Passage. A blizzard had obscured it. Snow drifted against the outermost cloister and fell in pale showers from the dark canyon edge. The near roofs were blanketed too deeply: as she watched, one ridgepole snapped and collapsed in a puff of white. The walls tumbled after it, and the whole building slid into the Passage to rest with the other bones of the palace. A moment later, the noise of it echoed in Blue. The expanding storm swallowed the Passage and advanced.

Grey was not built for this, Yarrow thought. I am failing them. I *have* failed them. The house will be so cold and hungry. The orchards are dead. There will be no harvest. I am the last Mother of Grey, and I've failed.

She got up and walked. Heat throbbed along her aching arm: the handkerchief was not doing its job. The blizzard was moving toward Blue, and she was nowhere near shelter. That was just as well. If there was no more Grey, there need be no more Mother. And without Grey, she thought, without the Motherhood, I am nothing.

The first flakes reached her before she'd gone more than a dozen steps. A wave of bitter, bone-gnawing cold swamped her. She was ice, and her arm was fire, and her vision was going dark. Bile burned her throat. Heavy as effigies, her feet no longer moved. She dropped to her knees on the frozen stone, then onto her back. Snow piled against her side and her pack. The Lady squealed at the cold. Yarrow let her eyes close as above her the storm swallowed Blue Tower, where the windows glowed as its people lighted lamps against the dark.

34. A Moment of Reassurance for Those Fearful or Despondent

Though the hungry Lady wriggles out of her restraints, and the storm is very bad, Yarrow does not die here. There is a house beyond the trees—a shack, really—which she could not see, and even as we turn our attention elsewhere, that house's inhabitant is scurrying home to escape the snow. Yarrow is in their path, and will be found. This is not to say something bad will not happen to Yarrow later: the Beast, after all, is on its way. It is only to say that, at the moment, Yarrow is safer than we may have feared.

The Beast rises, bit by bit, its mind and appetite sharpening. It remembers the crunch of stone between its teeth. It remembers the Ladies. It tugs against the luminous chain around its neck. The heat beneath propels it; the cold above, which it has created, calls to it. Those statements are all approximate, for to truly know the Beast would be to open a void in the mind.

In a dark place in Black Tower, Frin keeps watch over Hawthorn. He feels a shard of cold in his heart and mistakes it for worry. In her sleep, Hawthorn feels it as well, and it is part and parcel of the nightmare she now wanders in. She shivers, and Frin puts a hand on her shoulder to warm and quiet her.

Asleep before a fire in a shack, the same chill threads its way through Yarrow's dreams, but her fever takes it up and spins it into other forms. She tosses, her skin slick with sweat, half her mind pinned by the hot pain that stretches toward her heart, the other wandering in that cold tangle of fear.

In Grey House, huddled in the kitchen where a low fire consumes sticks of furniture, Arnica, the girls, and Servant feel it, and mistake it for another tooth in winter's maw. Arnica throws a table leg on the fire: she knows there is little left in the house that is safe to burn, and she also knows she will leave soon. Perhaps she will head to Red Tower, where it is still spring or summer. Perhaps she will explore what is beyond the walls. Ban and Grith see the departure in her eyes. It is another bit of their life falling away.

In the West Passage, where Peregrine and Tertius have made camp, Peregrine senses a change in the wind, and above the walls the blizzard roars toward Red Tower. Nothing has ever extinguished that beacon, not war or famine or revolution. But Peregrine fears this winter storm, and shivers in his pink tent.

In Blue and Red and Black and Yellow, lamps burn amid the storm. There is no light in Grey Tower, and never has been. But in all the courts and mansions of the palace, including those in Grey, there are lights. And Yarrow is as safe as she can be.

BOOK FIVE: HAWTHORN AGAIN

35. Hawthorn Wakes Up and There Is Snow on the Ground

Hawthorn woke up. She was not entirely sure where she was, only that the space was dim and cold, and that Frin was nearby, asleep in a shaft of pallid light. They were somewhere in Black Tower, but competing versions of her memory made it unclear where exactly.

She was Hawthorn now, though. *The* Hawthorn. If she clung to that, she might be able to put the other pieces back together. Trying made her head hurt.

Stiffly, she rose and walked around to stretch out. The room was long and narrow. She had been lying at one end with her back to a locked iron door, the tiny window of which was barred. At the other was a round window in a deep embrasure, low enough in the wall to see through, but too small to climb out of. It looked over the center of the palace: none of Black Tower was visible, but in the distance she spotted the gash of the South Passage and the tiny finger of Grey. Blanketing everything was a thick layer of snow. The sky was blue and clear, the sun high enough to tell her it was midmorning.

Her stomach rumbled. How long had it been since she last ate? There was no way of knowing, but she had eaten so little for days before that it made no difference.

She still had her pack and her books. Frin still had his vial of Thistle honey. Everything seemed to be intact. Had the Willow Lady discovered the deception and locked them in here? Somehow, Hawthorn doubted the Lady would have let them both live if she knew. They were locked away for some other reason. Frin might know. If he did not, Hawthorn doubted it would be pleasant waiting to find out.

Should she wake Frin up? He had been through so much, the poor boy. Pestering him with questions would be thoughtless. She sat beside Frin and leaned against the wall. Since it was so cold, she pulled him closer to keep him warm, and dozed off herself.

Much later, she awakened again when Frin stirred. The boy blinked and groaned and sat up. His hands felt automatically for the onyx vial, and he relaxed as soon as he had made sure it was still there.

"Good to see you up," he said with a yawn. "I was wondering if you'd ever wake."

"What happened?" said Hawthorn. "When did it snow?"

"There was a blizzard. I ain't never seen weather so bad. It must've lasted two or three days at least. I hope the orchards are still safe."

Grey must be practically buried. The food had been low already; anyone still in the house and cloisters could be starving. The Beast is coming, Hawthorn thought. I've already failed. Next there will be tremors. Then the sun will stand still. Then the earth of the West Passage will burst open and it will come. We have no time.

As if her thoughts had summoned it, a shudder ran through Black Tower. The piers swayed like the women in grey dancing, and kept swaying long after the tremor ended. Hawthorn huddled against the wall. Frin's fingers clenched as if he could find purchase and security in the smooth floor, but he did not seem surprised.

"That's been happening for a while," he said. "You slept through the others."

"We have to get out of here," said Hawthorn, bracing herself as the swaying slowed. "There might be time—if I can get to Grey Tower and retrieve the steel—" But the enormity of the task squashed the rest of her words, and she sighed.

"I can call for help," said Frin. "At least I can try." He took out the red box. "We'll get a message to the beekeepers."

"Will they storm the tower?" said Hawthorn dryly. "Will they ride to our rescue on the hives?"

"No," said Frin shortly. "But if you want the steel so badly, they might be able to bring it here. We are beekeepers. We take care of our own. Meanwhile, you and I can try to get out."

Hawthorn was about to speak, but thought better of it. "Go ahead," she said, sagging against the stones behind her. "Though I don't know what good it will do."

Frin opened the box. The bee shook herself awake and looked at him with bright, alert eyes.

"Tell One Robin that Frin and Hawthorn are imprisoned in Black Tower," he said. "Someone must go to Grey and get the Guardian's steel. It must be brought here."

The bee circled his palm three times, rubbed her head with her forelegs, and buzzed away out the window. She was quickly lost in the winter-blue sky. When Frin turned back to Hawthorn, she had drawn her knees up to her chest and was resting her forehead on them.

What was a squire for? Frin had never been sure, and still wasn't. But they certainly wouldn't let their knight give in to despair.

"There *is* a way out," he said.

"Is there," said Hawthorn, her voice flat and muffled by her knees.

"I can climb out the window," said Frin. "For one thing."

She looked up. Why had she not considered that? Frin was much smaller than she was, and the window was unobstructed.

"And if I can climb out the window, I can climb *in* another," said Frin. "The problem is I don't know where I'll end up. Do you still have the map?"

Hawthorn paused in the act of getting it out. "Why haven't you left already?"

"I'm your squire," said Frin. "And I may not know the right meaning of the word, or be of any use otherwise, but I know it means I don't leave you."

Despite everything, Hawthorn found herself grinning.

36. An Escape Is Made and Birds Are Seen

From the map, old and much altered as it was, Hawthorn determined they were in the southwest pier of Black Tower. If Frin climbed out the window, he should be able to reenter by a balcony in a chamber called Wasp's Eye. From there, he would simply have to go up some stairs to reach the corridor of cells. Then he could let out Hawthorn, and the two of them could exit the pier by one of the little posterns at its base.

"However," said Hawthorn, attempting with little success to refold the map, "there is the possibility that we're in one of the spines. That would make it much more dangerous."

Frin went to the window. Its embrasure gave him a place to prop himself while he peered out. The air nipped at his face, and for a moment he reeled, seeing the ground hundreds of feet below, with nothing at all between.

"We are," he said calmly. "We're in the tip of a spine."

Hawthorn laced her fingers and eyebrows together. "You don't *have* to do this, Frin."

"*Someone* has to," said Frin. "It's better than waiting for the Lady to decide what to do with us."

When Hawthorn had swooned, the Lady had been furious. She saw Hawthorn as an agent of Obsidian or Ebony or both; she issued a dozen contradicting verdicts on their fate in as many seconds. Finally her courtiers were able to calm her and guide her to her bedchamber, where she would wait for the honey to take effect, and One Sparrow had ordered Frin and Hawthorn imprisoned until the Lady made up her mind.

It was only a matter of time until the Lady realized she had been given ordinary honey. Delusional though she was, even she would soon notice the lack of changes in her body. When she did, death was the best Frin and Hawthorn could hope for.

Frin left the window and sat on the edge of the embrasure. Hawthorn, as she often did when worried, was clutching at the amulet around her neck. Frin had never asked about it, and hesitated to do so now.

"I don't want to see anything happen to you," she said. "You're only here because of me. I'm supposed to *protect* people, and here I am, trapped."

"Well," said Frin, "if I fall, you won't *see* it."

A bitter frost of a smile touched Hawthorn's lips. "I suppose not." She brought her knees back up to her chest. "What if you took Thistle honey?"

Frin shook his head emphatically. "It ain't for me."

"Then why did they give it to you?"

"As a talisman. Maybe a bargaining chip. But it's not for me. It's too precious for that."

Hawthorn sighed. "Not even as a last resort? Perhaps to get out of this cell?"

"Not even for that," said Frin. "I'd better get going. Don't worry about me. I was always good at climbing."

Hawthorn bit her lip. "All right." She undid the clasp of her necklace and held out the amulet to him. "Take it. I made it for the old Hawthorn. I'd like to think that if—if *something* happens—you'll have it with you."

Frin accepted it and clasped it around his neck. It nestled against the onyx vial with a soft clink. After a deep breath, he went back to the window and began his climb.

Outside, there was a slight rim all around the window. It was enough for him to stand on and get his bearings. He was on the end of a long spine jutting out from a pier. If he got his fingers and toes into the cracks between the cold stones, he could reach the top of the spine and inch toward the main mass of the pier. This high up, the wind roared around him, tugging at his clothes and nearly peeling him off the tower, but years of climbing trees had strengthened his hands and feet, and he was able to cling on—barely.

Hawthorn poked her head out to see him ascend. There were only three or four feet between the top of the window and the roof of the spine, but even so, it was torture watching him, particularly when an especially strong gust almost blew him off. At last his feet disappeared over the edge of the roof and she sighed gratefully.

His head popped back out and he grinned at her. "That was the hard part," he said.

"Just get going," she answered, tart and irritated with relief.

And he did. The spine was perhaps twenty feet long, one of at least a dozen jutting from the outer southwest pier. In diameter, the pier itself was ten or twelve times that; the inner pier was even larger, and the main mass of the tower far, far larger still. The sheer size of Black Tower made Frin dizzy. Seen from the ground, it was of course impressive, and their trip through its interior had given them a taste of its height and breadth, but sitting on its edges and looking out over it, the entire structure was deliriously, impossibly big. He almost could not breathe.

Frin pulled himself along, hand over hand. Cornices banded the pier's upper half; if he could reach one, he could sidle along it to another window. But closer to the pier, the wind eddied unpredictably. It buffeted him first one way, then the other. The chill coming off the stones numbed his hands. If he could just get out of the wind—

Another gust scrabbled at his clothes. His hands slipped. He slid down the roof, his feet swung out into empty space—and his belt snagged on a protruding stone, just long enough for him to get his grip back. His shoulders burned in protest as he leveraged himself up, toes scratching at the spine for purchase, but he made it back up to the ridge and lay there panting.

The wind died down, leaving Frin's ears full of a roaring hollowness. This opportunity had to be taken. He looked up. The stark wall of the pier lay before him. Just a few feet more.

As he began to crawl again, a sound disturbed him. It was impossible to place at first, just a kind of clatter. Then, within moments, it grew nearer, louder, and mixed with piercing cries. He looked to his right.

Swirling toward him around the mass of Black Tower were thousands of birds. Crows, sparrows, hawks, vultures from the canyon, gulls from Red. They moved as if summoned, their bright eyes pointed toward the distant crown of Grey, noticing nothing else. They slammed into Black as if it wasn't there, pelting it like hail.

In another moment they stormed around him. Soft feathers and sharp talons raked him. Instinctively, he threw up his arms to shield his eyes, and then the roof grated under him, and he fell into empty space. For one long, long second he stared straight into the red eye of a bearded vulture. Then it was gone, and all the birds were out of Black and hurtling toward the heart of the palace.

And Frin plummeted.

37. A Bird Is Seen and an Escape Is Made

A flurry of wings went past the window. Hawthorn ran to see what was happening and had just reached the embrasure when a ball of green feathers jetted in, crashed into the wall, and tumbled to the floor. She flung herself back as it sat up, and for a moment, Guardian and parrot stared at each other in mutual surprise. At almost the same moment, another tremor shook the tower, and the pier swayed dangerously.

The parrot rolled onto its feet, shook its head, and promptly fell over again. Fluttering its wings and pushing with its feet, it crawled and flopped toward the window, only to be stopped by the wall. Squawking, it butted the wall with its head over and over. Its witless obsession was horrifying and pitiful.

Before it could do any more damage to itself, Hawthorn scooped it up. The parrot flailed, but she stroked its head and made shushing noises at it, and eventually it quieted. By then, all the other birds had passed. Slowly, as the tower continued to sway, the parrot lifted its head and looked at her.

"Let go," it said.

Hawthorn's hands tightened instantly. They stared at each other a moment.

"No." Hawthorn's voice shook. In her head again was the rustle of a yellow bird's feathers atop a black glass palanquin. Not again. She would not listen—

"I know you," it said.

"How?" said Hawthorn. Not Obsidian's voice. Still, when had Hawthorn ever spoken to a parrot?

"There is always a look about you," said the parrot. "Time changes. The earth changes. The palace and the Hawthorns do not."

In its golden eyes was something she had never seen in a bird before. A look of vast, ancient cunning illuminated them, akin to the way a Lady's eyes gleamed, but different. Wilder. Crueler. The Beast. Hawthorn nearly dropped the parrot, but under her fingers, its tiny heart was beating. Her grip tightened. If she could still it, right here, right now—

"I am not here," said the Beast. "The birds are mine, and I have summoned them to my banquet. They will feast on you, or I will feast on them. That is the way of things." It blinked. "I see you are far away. In the Rose Garden, unless I am mistaken. The Hawthorns *have* changed, if you shirk your duty in this way."

"Shouldn't you be glad, then?" said Hawthorn. "With nobody to stop you, this is your victory."

Had the Beast ever spoken? In a flash she remembered one brief scrawl by a previous Hawthorn in the margins of *The Downfall of the Thistles,* something about "the Beast's call." If only the girl hadn't taken it! Perhaps if Hawthorn kept the Beast talking, she might learn something useful.

"Suppose the sea were to overtake the whole world and drown it," said the Beast. "Even in its victory, it might still miss the irreplaceable shore."

"I've been imprisoned," said Hawthorn. "If it's a fight you want, free me and I'll bring you one."

The parrot laughed. "It is not only the fight. It is the song, it is the wish. But I can see you know of neither miracle. I will delight in this feast, even if it will not have time to develop its full savor."

Hawthorn frowned. "I have to say, I don't remember the stories saying that the Beast is so . . . loquacious."

The parrot laughed again. "Think carefully: Who tells those stories? And what do they gain by saying I am mute?"

That was something to think about later. Frin was climbing toward the Wasp's Eye by now. If Hawthorn could get out and meet him there, much time would be saved.

"I don't know about the song and the wish," she said, "but I can give you a fight."

The gleam in the parrot's eyes grew keen. "Excellent. Put me down and I'll let you out."

Had she really just made a bargain with the Beast? Surely that was even riskier than making a bargain with a Lady. Hawthorn tried to remember everything she had just said. No, she had only promised to fight the Beast, which she would have done anyway. All was well. So why did the parrot look so pleased?

She opened her hands and the parrot shook itself, preened, and spread its wings. It flew to the door and perched in the barred window a moment. With shocking suddenness, it plucked one of its own pinions and fluttered out between the bars. There was a clanking, scuffling sound outside the door. Something clattered. Then there was silence.

Hawthorn tried the door. It swung open with an ominous groan. She hurried back for her things, then left the cell. Where had the parrot gone?

The door must be closed back up. If there were guards or officials about, it was best not to alert them that anything was wrong. Hawthorn went to shut it, and as it swung to, discovered the parrot behind it.

It was lying on its back, the feather still clutched in its beak. The gleam in its eyes was running out like tears and pooling on the floor. Blood followed. For a moment Hawthorn saw Sparrow lying in the West Passage, their insides ravaged by slender monsters. *That* was where she had seen that light before. It was the light of the lanterns. The light of the Luminous Name.

She closed the door and replaced the lock. The parrot was dead by then. She took the feather from its mouth and tucked it into her pocket. The body was put through the little window; nobody would find it unless they opened the cell. With her overgown, she scrubbed at the blood and light on the floor, trying to smear them away. They did not vanish entirely, but both were fainter when she was done.

Map in hand, she set off to find the Wasp's Eye.

38. Frin Is Fine

He fell for perhaps one second. Then the tower itself stretched out to grab him. He thudded onto the spine immediately below and rolled. Just before he slid off that one as well, the spine jerked backward, and he was able to get his fingers into a join and pull himself up. His whole body ached, and he clung to the roof, groaning.

The tower was swaying. A tremor must have struck. The pier's movement forward had put the spine in his path, and its movement back had helped him to safety. It was a miracle of the Lady, or so he would have said only a few days ago. He pushed the panic to the back of his mind, telling himself he would feel it later.

On the horizon, the flock was careening toward Grey. As he watched, it exploded into a sphere of wheeling birds around the tiny tower, and gradually settled, black specks against the snow.

Frin had never thought seriously about the Beast. It was a topic of story and song, but hardly the only one. The deeds of Ladies and Robins, romances of star-crossed lovers, quests of Sparrows, all were equally common in the courts of Black. The Beast had risen rarely. Frin only knew of four distinct times, but the stories overlapped so much, and travelers from other parts of the palace brought such different versions, that there could have been more appearances, or far fewer. Certainly it would have no effect on his life.

Hawthorn's faith in the Beast had been a little strange, but *everything* about Hawthorn was strange. People and things from Grey seemed to belong to the time of songs rather than the time of stories, and Hawthorn herself did nothing to dispel this impression. She spoke with a peculiar accent, she wore odd old-fashioned clothes, she didn't know the first thing about flowers, and if there was a spare moment, she spent it reading. But she had been right about the way to the throne room, and she was now, apparently, right about the Beast, for nothing else could shake the Great Tower.

As recovered as he would ever be, Frin resumed crawling. The wind still pushed and the pier still moved, but he was on his guard this time. He'd landed a floor or two below the Wasp's Eye, which meant Hawthorn would have to wait even longer.

The nearest cornice was wide enough for him to stand on. He stepped onto it in the lee of the spine and, sliding his feet carefully along it, reached a window at last. It had no glass, only wooden shutters hanging half-open, so it was a simple matter to climb inside. His legs gave way immediately, and he curled up on the floor. Panic surged over him, and he covered his face with trembling hands and struggled to breathe.

In, out. He was alive. In, out. He could still help Hawthorn. He was not useless. In, out.

At last he sat up and looked around. He was in a smallish room full of baskets of faded yarn, and in one corner was a loom upon which spiders had been weaving their own tapestry. The dust on the floor was disturbed only by his own footprints. Frin grabbed a skein of yarn, just in case, and headed out.

On the way in, days ago, he'd seen that the pier had very little interior space. Built to take the immense weight of the tower proper, it was riddled with small passageways and rooms, but no grand chambers like those in the rest of the tower—except in the uppermost floors above the buttresses, according to Hawthorn's map. That was where the retreats of the Ladies and their attendants lay, leisure spots away from the stresses of court life. The Wasp's Eye was one of them. Those floors could be reached only by a spiraling central staircase, very narrow and very steep. He had already been forced to climb it once, his hands bound, while Hawthorn was carried along behind. He did not relish doing so again.

But Hawthorn needed help, so up Frin went. The staircase was lined with a frieze of scrollwork: thorny vines and tiny peeping figures in armor—Sparrows. Their eyes had been carved as if staring in awe or fright. Were there any live ones up ahead? Frin had heard no guards when he was still in the cell, and perhaps the Willow Lady trusted in the remoteness of the prison to keep them from rescue or escape.

Up and up and up he climbed, and his legs were very tired. He should have arrived: he hadn't fallen *that* far. But there were no doors, so he couldn't have missed an exit. The Sparrows kept staring. Their eyes seemed to follow him. Was it possible the Lady herself could see through them? Frin knew little of the strange virtues of Ladies. Well, even if something could be done about their staring, it was too late. If anyone were watching, they would already know his destination.

At last there was a door. It didn't look like the one he and Hawthorn had been taken through, but even if it were the wrong one, he had somewhere to sit and rest a minute away from the stairs. The frieze reached the doorframe and coiled around it, and in the center of the lintel, the vines came together to form a veiled face. The door itself stuck, and he had to throw himself against it to budge it.

Inside was another study. Covered with maps and books and papers, empty plates and empty green vials, it had gone unused at least as long as the one he and Hawthorn had previously found. Rubbing his bruised shoulder, Frin sat down in a chair of faded leather.

Among the books on the table was one with worn covers, its pages falling out. It was full of beautiful pictures of horrible things. Scrolling leaves and flowers decorated the edges. Gold leaf glinted here and there. Though the vellum smelled faintly of decay, Frin picked it up. Hawthorn liked books; she'd probably want this one, and it was small enough to carry easily.

Though he could not read the words, he turned each page slowly, drinking in the details of the art. There was a picture of beekeepers about their labor. The artist did not seem to have ever watched the keepers work, for they were shrouded in netting, and the hives themselves looked more like baskets set on a table. Indeed, if it wasn't for the bees everywhere and the recognizable buildings, it wouldn't have looked like home at all.

There was a picture of Grey Tower, alone in a sea of empty ground. What a desolate place it must be. From the air, it had seemed tucked in cozily among its cloisters, but the perspective might be misleading. A lot of people milled about the edges of the ground, as if at a festival. Before the tower itself grew a stalk of yarrow. There were trees all about, green, growing trees, such as existed almost nowhere in the palace but home.

Next was a picture of a Lady in grey. She was attended by many
women of simple flesh in wimples and grey robes, and her four hands
were carving a green mask. Didn't Hawthorn have one very similar
to that? At her foot was a stalk of yarrow. Three finished masks in red,
yellow, and blackish-blue lay around it.

Next was a picture of a Lady in black. She stood beside Grey Tower,
twelve of her thirteen hands full of asphodel flowers. The thirteenth
held the green mask out toward the tower. No Sparrows attended her,
but there were several smaller Ladies, heavily shrouded in black, their
faces like a crow's, bearing a heavy chain in their hands. And behind
them were people of simple flesh, hands uplifted to the Ladies. Hawthorn's hand gripped Frin's face and he smelled honey and ash. He
flipped the page.

Next was a picture of a Lady in blue. She lay nestled amid frogs
from whose mouths came all kinds of fruit and flowers—though
no yarrow. In one outstretched arm was a wooden staff, warding
off something from outside the page. People of simple flesh helped
her other hands harvest the produce of the frogs; some of them were
chopping and cooking it over great burning logs, others were butch-
ering and roasting the frogs themselves. Frin shuddered.

Next was a picture of a Lady in red. Her head was a bowl full of fire.
She wore a tiger skin, and each of her four hands wielded a sword or
a dagger—again, directed at something off the page. All around her
feet were people of simple flesh, also laden with weapons, and many
of them were dead. There were many trees, now leafless, and just as
many stumps.

Last was a picture of a Lady in yellow. The ground around her
bubbled with little mounds, and from them, her hands drew people
of all shapes and sizes, from the sleek blues like One Robin, to the
otter-faced like Rhyolite the trader, to the rabbit-eared like Frin himself. Nowhere were there people of simple flesh. They were, of course,
relatively uncommon in real life, but their exclusion here made Frin
uneasy, given their preponderance in the other pages.

The next page had been torn out, and beyond it was just more
words. Frin wondered what the missing page could be, but after looking at the remnants of it and seeing a grey beak eating a yellow eye,
decided he would rather not know. Hawthorn might not want the
book after all.

But he kept it just in case. Getting up to resume his climb, he noticed
a scrap of white paper under the table. It was long and thin, like a

ribbon, and at one end it had an eyelet as if it were meant to be hung from something. He left it there, but he took one of the vials; it might come in handy.

Farther and farther up the stairs he went, until he came to the short hall where the cells were, and found the door unlocked and Hawthorn gone.

A Question Posed by the Tutors in Grey House
(But as the Tutors Are Dead, It Is Forgotten):
What Is the True Name of Red Tower?

*S*o Eglantine LX asked of his apprentice, and the apprentice answered *It is the Memorial,* and Eglantine was pleased.

An Interlude in Red Tower

More fucking snow. It kept coming and coming, and every time Tuppy got it cleaned up, someone had to go and open a door, and snow blew in, then more was tracked in on boots or shoes. Every ground-floor window in the court was buried by now, and the paths across the yard were only kept clear by a stable boy shoveling around the clock. That was all right. What wasn't all right was people not wiping their feet.

Tuppy had been fighting her own personal war against unwiped feet for ten years. Just because so much of Red was falling into ruin didn't mean you could trample dirt onto a clean floor. Luna had told her that In The Old Days squadrons of maids kept everything clean; gardeners trimmed the ivy and swept the walks; footmen took coats and hats. Now coats were hung on a peg by Tuppy herself; goats cropped the ivy and fouled the walks; and the maids were Tuppy, Hax, and Shew, and if they got the whole West Gatehouse clean at once, it was never more than twice a year.

The Gatehouse stood over the terminus of the East Passage, where it ended its long journey from Yellow, into Blue, and past Black. In The Old Days, the gate was one of only three entrance points into Red, and as the closest to Black, it had been heavily fortified. Four towers of rusty sandstone flanked the portal, their tops swelling out in parapets and hoardings and high watchful turrets. The banner of the Red Lady had flown over the gate, which was made of some wood that would not burn and could not be broken. According to Luna, anyway; The Old Days were so long ago even Luna's grandmother did not remember them. Now the arch of the West Gate was broken, kicked to the side of the passage like rubbish. The roofs of the towers had fallen in, the hoardings decayed to splinters. The unbreakable gate was sound, but always open.

Seasons were never kind to Red Tower, because ever since The Old Days it and its Ladies had challenged Black Tower's authority. Winters were hard, summers harder. And so Red weathered away like wood, leaving only what was toughest and most bitter in both its buildings and its people.

Still, there had never been a winter like this. Autumn had disintegrated into snow long before its time, and the harbor began to freeze over until ships got stuck, and the ice hoisted them up or cracked them in half. And now, on the third and worst day of a terrible blizzard, nothing could even leave the Gatehouse courtyard, for the passages beyond were clogged with snow, and even if you got through that, nothing could be seen in the blinding whiteness. One stable boy had already been lost on his way to the tower, and Luna had forbidden anyone else to go.

Tuppy finished mopping up and took a seat by the Gatehouse window. Someone must always watch the gate. In The Old Days there had been guards, of course, but they had dwindled or been reassigned over the long years: more people entered Red through the harbor than the Passage. Now the duty fell to whomever was near the window and had a free hour or two. That was how she happened to be there when the hollowman arrived.

It was old Tertius, and though the blizzard had lessened somewhat, it was having a terrible time getting through the snow. She could not see Peregrine on its back at all. Throwing on a scarlet cloak, she ran out of the postern and waved and shouted. Tertius turned its head toward her and laughed its familiar deep laugh.

"This way," she said, pointing to the leeward side of the Passage wall, where the snow was much less. Peregrine should have seen it and guided Tertius there himself. That he had not was cause for concern.

Tertius made its way toward the gate, the bone platform on its back scraping the wall, and lumbered into the courtyard, where it stopped in its accustomed place. Nothing happened. No Peregrine swung down on the familiar rope ladder. Was he even aboard the hollowman?

"Down, Tertius," said Tuppy. The hollowman ignored her. She scratched its favorite place (the dent between wrist and thumb) and it giggled and sighed and finally, with a long exhalation, knelt. Tuppy climbed up its shoulder and onto the platform. One green-covered foot poked out of the tent. "Oh, North, please be all right," Tuppy whispered, and whipped open the tent flap.

Peregrine lay inside, wrapped in an assortment of blankets, but clearly much the worse for the cold. Tuppy scowled at the world and picked him up. They were roughly the same size, but she had carried and scrubbed and fetched for years, and he was nothing compared to the two hods of firewood she had to bring to Luna's parlor every morning.

Once inside the Gatehouse, she laid Peregrine on the low, cushion-piled sofa and rang the bell for the stable boys. As they came to care for Tertius, she tucked a bright patterned blanket around Peregrine's shoulders. The Gatehouse grimalkin meandered in and, seeing some-one ill, jumped onto his chest and curled up.

Tuppy had been cooking a little mess of gruel to gird herself against the cold, so she poured some into a bowl for Peregrine, thinned it with milk, and gave it to him before setting some cream on the fire and getting out ale for a posset. The ale she heated with sugar and mace and a few breadcrumbs to help it thicken. If only she could spend an egg or two on it, but with the weather making the hens so undependable, she didn't dare. Peregrine was more or less awake by then and watching the proceedings with a vacant look of disgust on his handsome face. To make him feel a little more cared for, Tuppy sprinkled some cinnamon into the ale.

When the ale and the cream were hot, she shifted the former to the edge of the hearth and poured the cream from a great height. This part was always fun. Luna said she was a great hand at posset, and it was a pleasure to exercise her skill in blending the ingredients, to watch the foam rise, and to do it so neatly that not a drop was wasted. When that was done, she settled the lid onto the posset-pot and put it nearer the fire to stay warm as it curdled.

"You'll drink this, every drop," she said to Peregrine. "It'll warm you right up."

"Just mull some wine, woman," he groaned.

She twisted her mouth to the side. "That's only warming, not nour-ishing."

It had the flavor of their usual bickering, and that was pleasing. It meant he was in no danger. In a few more minutes, the posset had settled, and she scattered some more sugar on top of the curds and handed the pot to him. His look of disgust vanished into smooth

courtesy, the practiced gratitude for hospitality that marked Peregrine. He would never be so ill-mannered as to refuse something
freely given. And indeed he did not with the posset. He sipped down
the warm, sweet ale with quiet patience, then took a wooden spoon
from Tuppy to eat the smooth, foamy curds as gravely as a knight
accepting insignia from Wasp the Great herself. He fed a little bit to
the cat.

"The birds ain't flown these three days, Peregrine," said Tuppy as
he ate. "News? What does this winter mean? Has the wheel jogged in
its course?"

"I don't know why it's snowing," he said. "The seasons were never
part of the butlers' tradition. They only give us an almanac so we
know what season it's supposed to be along our way. But I wonder.
I wonder."

"What do you wonder?"

Peregrine laid down his spoon and spoke very carefully. "The Lady
of Yellow is dead. And I wonder if the Great Tower has—has decided
to punish us all for it."

"Sounds like their rubbish," Tuppy snorted. "Saving you, of
course."

"Of course," said Peregrine dryly. He sat up, but kept the blanket
around his shoulders and the cat on his lap. "Is Luna about? I think
she would want to hear this news directly from me."

"Luna's up-tower," said Tuppy. "Messenger came yesterday from
the Lady. I think there's a conclave of the Housekeepers Royal been
called. Usually happens once a season, but with the snow—"

"And no birds in or out, you say."

"Aye, Luna sent to the Lesser Dovecote special," said Tuppy. "On
purpose to find out, I mean. She likes to send notes over to a cousin or
something in Grey, and she's not been able to for a while."

"But the blizzard only began a few days ago." Peregrine's long hand
stroked the cat, who purred in complete contentment.

Tuppy shrugged, gathering up the dishes. "Ain't no birds to Grey
been coming back for a month or something. Ain't a matter I've paid
much mind to, I must say. Ask Luna, if you're still here when she gets
back."

"Odd," said Peregrine. "Very odd."

Tuppy shrugged again. "That's Grey." She often saw the little tower
from the top of the Gatehouse. That far away, it was hardly distinguish-
able from one of Black's chimneys, yet it had a way of insinuating itself

into stories and songs. At the center if it could make room, and if not there, peering around the edges, saying Notice me. It did not surprise Tuppy in the slightest that Grey was keeping Red's birds. It was winding up to put itself in the middle of another story.

She saw Peregrine up to one of the spare rooms (kept well aired, though guests were infrequent) and, after bringing him a jar of hot water to warm his bed, left him to sleep. Keeping him in the Gatehouse was partly hospitable, but also Luna should be back soon, and someone had to accept the privileges from the Butler. Tuppy herself did not remember all the words, so if he could just stay asleep until the housekeeper was there, that would be best.

Back at the Gatehouse window, she watched night fall over the frozen Passage. The snow had finally ceased, and the air was clear as only winter air could be. Stars came out in the indigo sky, and lights came on in the palace.

Tuppy did not at all like this notion of Black Tower imposing winter over the entire palace. Whatever had happened to old Citrine certainly did not involve Red. In fact, the only place given to meddling in other towers was Black itself. It would be just like the Willows' tricks, using Citrine's death to assert themselves. And it had nearly resulted in the death of one of their own butlers, and the loss of an original hollowman—the first would be murderous carelessness on the Willows' part, the second would be, well, not murder, but the end of a precious life nonetheless. And who knew how many people *had* died during the storm? Would there be another one?

Black Tower sparkled serenely in the dark. Tuppy shook her fist at it.

The next morning, Luna still had not reappeared, so Tuppy had to fumble her way through the ceremony. In turn, Peregrine handed her a cake of black bread, a cask of honey, three dry reeds, and six bottles of wine (white and red, never an equal number). There was a speech of gratitude meant to go with each, but the language for the bread and honey was so archaic that Tuppy never remembered it. In itself, that wasn't bothersome, but it hurt a little to disappoint Peregrine.

Once everything was piled on the parlor table, Peregrine took his leave.

"It's still bad out there," said Tuppy. "Are you sure you won't stay?"

He shook his head. "I've already delayed. Until next month, my dear."

They embraced.

"Be safe," said Tuppy. "I don't like any of this. What's to become of Yellow Tower, Ladyless as it is? There'll be trouble, mark my words."

"I will," said Peregrine, sweeping a low bow, "be as cautious as I ever am, dear woman."

"Aye, that's what worries me," said Tuppy, and laughed.

Peregrine mounted Tertius and set off down the East Passage. His route should take him into Black, then Blue, and eventually into Yellow. Hopefully, things would have settled by then.

She turned back to the Gatehouse, where a bottle of wine was calling her name. Luna returned when Tuppy had finished nearly the entire thing and was roaring an old battle-song at the top of her lungs. The housekeeper instantly joined in both bottle and song.

"Glad to see you, glad to see you, ma'am," said Tuppy, and burped as she poured more wine for herself.

"Glad to be home," said Luna with a slurp. "The tower's as hot as a knight's crotch in summer, at least right there under the beacon. You'd think she could hold conclave somewhere else."

"Ah, ah," said Tuppy, closing her eyes and raising her brows in sympathy. "Mostly cold here, it's been."

"I see the Butler made it through all right, though," said Luna, opening a second bottle. "Who this time? Borealis? Australis? A lesser?"

"Borealis." Tuppy burped again. "Thank North for that at least. Couldn't have borne Australis's scowls on a broken winter's night. And the lessers have no manners. How was conclave? What pressing matter required you to stir out in the worst weather in years?"

"It was *about* the weather," said Luna. "Dragonflies're reporting all kinds of confusion. I don't half understand it myself. Grey apprentices out where they shouldn't be. A petty-Lady or two in Black stirring. Greater Dovecote's sent message upon message to the dark tower for an answer and all they get back is ominous replies from Her Willowship, bragging about power she's soon to have. Well, if she means to send Sparrows out, we're ready."

Tuppy began to laugh the high, trilling laugh of the pleasantly drunk. "Ma'am. Ma'am. What if *she* killed old Citrine? And that's her new power, ruling Yellow direct and outright?"

Then she had to explain what Peregrine had said, and it was no laughing matter to Luna at all.

The housekeeper set the bottle down with a thump. "That might be it," she said. "Willow kills Citrine. Takes Yellow's virtues and privileges for her own. Turns the wheel wrong so nobody can move except—who can go easily to and fro, even in bad weather?"

"Lanterns," said Tuppy. "Lanterns and Sparrows."

"And Sparrows serve the ruler of the dark tower, and Sparrows fight for her. Well, we'll show them. There's swords in Red yet."

"Now, now," said Tuppy, beginning to be alarmed. "Don't know as that's true. Peregrine said she was dead. Didn't say how or when. Could've been weeks ago, the way news travels. Could've been anything, too: Citrine's princeling in Nonesuch, or one of the Blue Sisters off for a Ladyship of her own."

"Or the guardian of Grey, mistaking Lady for Beast," said Luna dryly. "No, something's afoot, dear, and she under the beacon don't know of it. Well, she soon will." Luna was hurriedly getting her boots back on. "And whatever's afoot, it's incontrovertible, completely incontrovertible, that Black Tower's gone and broken the weather on purpose, and Willow's gone mad or madder, and Black's stirring like a kicked hive, and this is enough." She struggled into her cloak, a little wine-wobbly but determined. "It's enough, I say. Red wasn't made to bear this. None of us were. I'll talk to Her Crimson Ladyship and I'll say, It's enough. It's gone far enough."

And Luna set off into the white morning toward the great scarlet tower. The beacon flared and danced in the chilly wind, sending smoke out over the sea. As Luna struggled through snowbanks, birds began to settle on the rooftops and windowsills of Red, their heads turned toward Grey, their voices still. Crows, sparrows, hawks, vultures, white gulls, bright parrots, dull falcons, their eyes fixed on the tiny, distant tower.

"Well," said Tuppy, at the door, "gone far enough? Maybe." But far more pressing was all the slush Luna had tracked in. With a sigh, Tuppy went for a mop.

BOOK SIX

YARROW

ONCE MORE

39. Yarrow Wakes Up and There Is Snow on the Ground

Yarrow opened her eyes slowly. They hurt already, and the light hurt them worse. But it was really very dim light—a sort of cool, underwater sheen—and she wondered where she was. Around her were warm bedclothes, but the chill on her face was that of an unheated room. A sweet-rancid taste filled her mouth. Her head felt light and cool—where were her wimple and fillet? The rough cloth of her gown, at least, pushed familiarly against her skin. When she tried to move, her injured arm was cramped and achy. She gave up and lay still.

She was on a bed in a small room with plaster walls and a heavy, rough wooden door. In its center was a firepit, now burnt very low. An iron hook swung over it. Snow spiraled in through a smokehole in the ceiling. Tools hung all around the walls, and the corners were full of clothes and wheelbarrows and things, as if she had awakened in Monkshood's little shack. The Lady lay curled up beside the fire, asleep. She was bigger than Yarrow now, and her dress had developed a high lace collar and dozens of bows and frills and pearls.

The bed trembled. *Something was coming out from under it*—no, it wasn't just the bed. She was still alone. The walls swayed, the tools rattled, and a little fall of snow was shaken loose from the outside to sizzle in the fire. The shaking soon ceased, and before she could collect her scattered thoughts, the door opened and a person stumped in.

They were muffled in many scarves and shawls, and in their arms was a stack of firewood. Stamping and puffing, they dropped most of the wood in a pile near the door and heaped the remainder on the smoldering embers. As the room warmed up, they pulled off their wrappings to reveal a black-furred rabbit body in a brownish smock.

"Oh, you're awake," they said. They coolly shifted the bedclothes to look at Yarrow's arm, which had been firmly bandaged. "It's done its work nicely, I see."

"What has?" said Yarrow. Her voice was thick and hoarse, and she had to cough and swallow many times to get it back to normal.

"The mellified man."

Yarrow gagged. She leaned over the side of the bed, retching, trying to make herself vomit.

"Now, now," they said. "None of that." They gently, but forcefully, pushed her back down.

"I don't eat meat," Yarrow gasped. "I *can't* eat meat!" Sacrilege—violation—oathbreaking—

"Come, come," they said. "I am a doctor. Even a woman in grey eats what a doctor prescribes."

A wary hush settled over Yarrow. A doctor? She had never met any; even Arnica and Old Yarrow had only known one in their youth. Surely someone like *that* would know whether she'd broken the most ancient laws.

"And am I—" She swallowed a bit of bile. "Am I cured?"

"Certainly," said the doctor. He hung a pot of snow on the hook to let the fire melt it. "Mellified man is powerful stuff, but I had doubts as to whether it would counteract Her Ladyship's bite."

"How did you have any? Someone told me there wasn't any in the palace."

His little black eyes met hers. They were narrow and questioning. "You were carrying it."

"I was?" The honeyed meat. She had been carrying a panacea in her pack for days and days, and feeding it to the Lady. Yarrow swallowed again. "I can't read. I didn't know."

"Nobody told you?"

"Nobody knew I had it. I brought it with me to trade." She choked back wild laughter. The only mellified man in the world, and she had packed it in case someone wanted a snack.

"Brought it to Blue to trade?" A new note had entered his voice.

"Yes." Oh North, they'd had it in the house the whole time—Old Yarrow could have—She fell back on her pillows. "Is there any left?"

He pointed to a padlocked iron chest on a little shelf. "One piece. *She* wanted it, and I've had a terrible time keeping it from her."

"What has she been eating?"

The doctor shrugged. "The spiders that come out of the firewood. She also likes to go catch birds."

Yarrow shuddered.

"She tried to eat you, didn't she?" said the doctor.

Yarrow nodded.

"She certainly is a throwback. I don't have my books here, but I think that sort of thing was common among older generations of Ladies. You must tell me why she's here, why a daughter of Citrine the Deathless is so far from Yellow. I'd urge you to part ways with her, but she would not leave you while you slept, and nobody has ever understood the relationship between the women of your house and their Ladies." He stirred the melting snow. "I am Roe 73. I was a doctor in Blue Tower."

"I am Yarrow LXXVI. Mother of Grey House."

"Awfully young to be a Mother, aren't you?"

"We've had—" Yarrow swallowed. "—hardships."

"I believe it. With this winter . . ." Roe emptied the steaming water into a cup and added a handful of herbs and a little salt. "Drink this."

The savory taste washed out the sickliness of the mellified man. Yarrow sipped it gratefully.

"I'm very grateful for everything you've done," she said, as Roe busied himself chopping vegetables: withered carrots, some sprouting potatoes, a wrinkled beet. "Can I trouble you for one more thing?"

"What is that?" he said.

"I need to get to Black Tower. I need to ask them to lift this winter."

"We've already sent emissaries," said Roe.

Hope flared in Yarrow's chest and burned out immediately. If the emissaries had been listened to, winter would have ended already. "I see," she said.

"That was weeks ago. They came back saying that the wheel of seasons would not turn. After that, nobody else was sent."

"Why?" said Yarrow. "If we beg them—if we're persistent—"

"The Lady of Blue is dead," said Roe. He looked up at Yarrow and his eyes were bright with grief. "Her true successor is dead. The pretender has closed all the doors. Nobody leaves the tower except exiles like me. Those who supported the eldest daughter."

"Isn't succession . . . succession?" said Yarrow. "Aren't there laws?"

A couple of logs snapped in the fireplace. Sparks flew toward the ceiling.

"Ha!" said Roe. "The tower is dangerous now. When I left, the silk rooms were a bloodbath, the gardens full of fugitives, and the great hall—" He stopped talking but began chopping the beet with angry vigor.

"What is the new Lady doing? Why won't she stop it?"

"Stop it?" said Roe. "She *started* it. The tower is being purged of the old Lady's court." He dropped the knife and swallowed a sob. "All the old court—anyone who knew Her Ladyship—I saw a Marten struck down as she pleaded for mercy. They got all the Voles at once, herded them into the scriptorium and set it on fire. They'll kill you if they find out I helped you. She's gathered everyone in. There's a new era in the tower. They're cutting themselves off from the rest of the palace. They can do it; they have the frogs. They're waiting out the winter, and killing each other for the new one's favor."

The young Lady stirred in her sleep. Both Roe and Yarrow looked at her, hoping she wouldn't wake up.

"I have to get to Black," said Yarrow. "I promised I would. If they won't listen to Blue, they might listen to Grey. Can you help me at all? I'm sorry to ask."

Roe sighed. He tossed the vegetables into the pot and stirred them around. "I could take you through the Deeps, where the hollowmen go," he said. "I've been there a few times since the new era began, but it's a huge risk."

"Take me *to* the Deeps," said Yarrow, "and then give me directions. I don't want to put you in harm's way. I owe you my life."

"It's not safe. It is, in fact, very, very dangerous." Roe added some salt and a handful of thyme to the pot and stirred it again. "But I can do that, if you're determined to go."

"I am," said Yarrow. "I'm the Mother of Grey, and people are relying on me."

Roe sighed. "All right. But tomorrow. I insist on that. You may have taken mellified man, but you need to rest. And eat first."

"Agreed," said Yarrow, accepting a bowl and a spoon.

40. Roe Takes Yarrow to the Deeps and There Are Frogs

The sun was out as Roe, Yarrow, and the Lady walked across the terrace and into the postern leading to the Deeps. The white glare of the snow hurt her head, and Yarrow was glad to see the little door, and even gladder when Roe opened it and the inside was entirely dark. She was far less glad when a warm breeze blew out of the Deeps, bringing an odor of ferment and decay. The Lady, though, perked up, and could barely be restrained from darting ahead.

Yarrow would not have been sorry to lose the Lady, though the latter did not attempt to eat her anymore. Roe, who had little to share for such a big appetite, was glad to let her hunt such small game as the terraces of Blue Tower provided: birds, rats, and squirrels, mostly. She had, it seemed, been sustaining herself that way all through Yarrow's long sleep, and the few words she had learned were almost comically violent: *teeth* and *blood* and *eat* and the like. She had developed a whiff of the unsettling aura that had marked her terrible mother. You could not ignore her. Her sheer presence was vertiginous, like being at the top of a tower. Despite all this Yarrow felt some responsibility toward her, and hoped that, even with a new era in Blue, someone might be willing to take the carnivorous child.

The door opened on a narrow, grimy staircase of dark stone. As with so much of the palace, centuries of passing feet had worn the steps down to little more than a ridged ramp, and Yarrow had to pick her way carefully. Roe, a little more surefooted, and the Lady, who walked with a blissful unconsciousness of human notions like *safety*, had to keep themselves to her pace.

When the door was closed and the darkness was total, Yarrow asked Roe if he had brought a light.

"Give your eyes a little time," he said.

Even as he spoke, the darkness bloomed. Faint traceries of bluish light marked the walls: fungi growing in swirls and coils like scrollwork. In fact, they *were* scrollwork: upon closer inspection, the walls were beautifully decorated, and the fungus had simply grown in the pits and hollows left by deep-carved, curling vines.

Farther and farther down they went, and the staircase gradually widened as it curved through the earth, until the glow from the walls hardly illuminated anything. They passed landings where wide tunnels crossed the stairs. A dull light moved in one. The others were all empty. The air thickened and sickened: it was as humid, smelly, and hot as the worst days of summer. Yarrow felt as if she were being held in the mouth of a giant who had never cleaned their teeth.

The staircase ended in a little antechamber, lit by an arch of fungus around a closed stone door. Roe halted and opened the sack he carried.

"Here is a dark lantern," he said. "Keep it dim as much as possible. And here is some food just in case."

Yarrow added the food to her own pack and thanked him.

"This is the lowest of the Deeps," said Roe. "When you're inside, go straight ahead. There will be another staircase on the far wall. Go up that and down the right-hand passage. There shouldn't be any hollowmen around at this hour. Keep going straight and you'll come out near the edge of Black. You can probably find your own way from there. The frogs should be asleep. Do *not* wake them up. Don't touch their eggs. And if you see anyone at all besides the frogs, hide until they go."

His ears and whiskers drooped as he spoke. In his dewdrop eyes, the door of the Deeps was reflected, a blue ghost of itself. Tears came to Yarrow as she looked at the old doctor. He had risked everything to help her—risked returning to his home. When she reached Black, she would ask them to intervene in the troubles of Blue as well.

She reached out and took his hand. "Thank you for everything. I would have died without you."

Roe straightened and smiled. "I'm a doctor, dear Mother. It is a pleasure to have someone to help again." He pushed on the door, and it swung open soundlessly. Yarrow and the Lady went forward. "Keep an eye on her," said Roe in an undertone.

"I will," said Yarrow. "She is my responsibility. I could never abandon her."

There must have been some hint of her true feelings in her voice, for Roe tilted his head skeptically.

"I see," said Roe. "Well—" And he pushed the door closed behind her.

Three broad, shallow steps dropped away before them, terminating in a damp flagstone floor. Lined by the luminescent growths, the walls fell away on either side into inky darkness. Far, far away, on the walls and domed ceiling, the fungus continued to spiral. Here and there it concentrated in bands and clusters like stars. Yarrow and the Lady seemed to stand under the soft, bright sky of a moonless summer night.

The floor's wet sheen reflected the dome enough for Yarrow to see her path, or at least five feet of it at a time. On either side were dark hummocky shapes, silhouetted against the fungal stars like the distant mountains you could sometimes see from the top of Grey. Despite the heat and humidity, despite the trickle of sweat down her back and the way her wimple stuck to her neck, for a moment or two as they crossed the floor, a hush came over Yarrow's soul.

Then water splashed. Yarrow halted. The Lady did as well. Something moved in the dark with a noise like a person shifting in a bathtub. The sound faded, and after a long time in which she heard only her own breath, Yarrow began walking again. So did the Lady.

The same watery noise came again from a different spot. Then another. Heedless of the lantern, Yarrow clenched her hands together to stop their trembling. The frogs were waking up.

She *saw* her hands, faintly outlined against the rough stones. Light was coming from somewhere, greenish and sickly. She knew that light. Just behind her, the Lady was glowing. In the wavering ripples she cast, Yarrow saw the mounded shapes all around her more clearly.

Except for the straight path down the center, the room was full of stone basins. Many were empty. One or two seemed to have broken, for in them were white porcelain bathtubs. But in each occupied tub, stone or porcelain, was a quantity of water and one or two immense green frogs. They were bigger than Yarrow, bigger than cows: the eyes of the smallest of them were each the size of her head.

The frog nearest to her was asleep. Its slippery limbs were folded under it, and its pulse was visible in the veins around its neck and throat. Atop it was a smaller frog with its limbs tight around the larger one's neck. All around them in the water were huge clusters of jellylike eggs. Except for the size of everything, this was no different from the little frogs in the pools of Grey. Until Yarrow looked more closely, and saw that in each egg was a lamb.

Another pair of frogs was producing tiny saplings, each with a ball of earth. One single frog had eggs full of little wheelbarrows with big wheels, as if, like puppies with clumsy feet, the barrows would grow into them. A third pair's eggs were each full of many restless silvery fish.

Yarrow was bending over to examine them when the larger frog moved. She jumped away. Its eyes were open. With two paddle-like feet, the smaller frog on its back was kneading its flesh. One by one, like beads on a necklace pulled between one's lips, more eggs emerged in response.

The larger frog opened its mouth and, in a deep, primeval gurgle, it spoke.

41. The Dialogue of the Frogs

The First Frog:
    By the river I sat amid bones
    In the sky, the red-painted vulture circled
    I wept to see the words its body wrote
    The bones were as old as the river
    Old as water, old as the movement
    Of my hand into yours
    I think that I will never read those words again

The Second Frog:
    By the river I drank cool water
    It comes from the mountains, my mother said
    The mountains are silent,
    But the water gurgles,
    Crying for their attention
    My mother died; I saw her wither in the sun
    Her dying was short; her death was long
    I said no word
    The red-painted vulture wrote in silence
    The only sound was the sound of flies

The Third Frog:
    By the river I sat among every kind of reed
    The papyrus spread its fan; the bulrush darkened
    The thatch-reed prickled my skin like the sun
    I know no other kinds of reed

The Fourth Frog:

    By the river I sat and thought

    The sand is soft and silver here, I thought;

    The sun is warm, the river cool, I thought;

    The air is fresh and blue, I thought;

    The flies are crunchy and spill their juice

    How beautiful I am become by the river

The First Frog:

    I remember bone

The Second Frog:

    I remember water

The Third Frog:

    I remember reeds

The Fourth Frog:

    I remember flies

The Fifth Frog:

    Do you know how my skin stretches when I am hungry?

    My stomach grows and grows

    To turn inside out until it holds the world

    I am reminded of how many bones I have

    The delicate framework beneath my flesh

    I am a soft and fragile thing, but I will eat the world

The Sixth Frog:

    Do you know how I sing when I want love?

    The body is water that kindles fire

    A hunger sating itself with hunger

    See my throat expand, fine and thin as an egg's rind

    An embryo of sound inside

    In the still pools of the river we sang, one to another

    And gripped and kneaded and fought,

    Soft against soft, hard against hard

    The fighting a part of the loving

    The drumbeat of the song

The Seventh Frog:

    Do you know how I am silent when I spawn?

    Egg upon egg, a great achievement

    If I loved each one, my heart would break

    The act is the meaning; the water rises

    Displaced by my brood; this is how I alter the world

    What is there to say, except the soft stretching

As my body empties itself, and the gentle splash
As my limbs push egg upon egg into the world?

The Eighth Frog:

Do you know how I twitch when I die?
I die of so many things. There is the bird,
There is the snake, there is the accident of fate,
The parasite, the flashing blade
The life in me leaps as it leaves;
I watch my nerveless feet scrabble against stone
Disturbing the stones of the river
Bright is the water, bright is the blood
Dark is the red-painted vulture

The Fifth Frog:

I remember hunger

The Sixth Frog:

I remember love

The Seventh Frog:

I remember spawning

The Eighth Frog:

I remember death

All:

The river, O river
Mother, cradle, grave
Right hand of the sun
Left hand of the moon
The river of bones,
Mother of bones,
Devourer of bones
Lifeblood, we sing
Amid your green hair

42. Yarrow Speaks to the Frogs

Strange tears came to Yarrow's eyes. She wiped them away as she went on. By then she had nearly crossed the room, and it was only when she had gone up the far steps that she noticed the Lady wasn't with her.

There was a swish and a splash, splash, splash. The Lady had reached into the pool of lamb-eggs and was drawing one out, dripping and quivering. It was connected to all the others, and she was having a difficult time separating it. Her struggles disturbed the water. By the time Yarrow reached her, she'd managed it. The two severed ends of the chain slipped back into the pool, and the frog looked over in time to see the Lady tear open the clear, delicate rind of the egg. The half-developed lamb inside slithered to the floor in a shower of slime. Its limbs twitched as it tried to stand. Yarrow bit back a groan of horror.

As the Lady greedily bent down to take up the infant, the frog, who had so lately been speaking of reeds, opened its great mouth and let out a guttural scream. The Lady lifted the lamb to her stony mouth and bit down. Blood showered out, mingling with the slime and spilling into the pool. The frog went on screaming. The noise echoed and reechoed until Yarrow could hear nothing else.

"Stop!" said Yarrow. "Stop, stop, *stop!*"

The frog stopped. The Lady was reaching in for another egg. Yarrow slapped her wrist.

"I'm sorry," said Yarrow. "I'm so sorry. I'll take her out right away."

"They'd be eaten anyhow," said the frog. "Eaten," said the smaller one on its back.

"But she shouldn't have," said Yarrow.

"It's theft I object to," said the frog. "Theft," said the smaller one.

"Against the rules," said the wheelbarrow frog. "They get mad about quotas and things."

"Who does?" said Yarrow.

"Steward," said the wheelbarrow frog.

"So many lambs per day for the flocks of Blue," said the first frog. "Lambs," said its companion.

"The flocks can't—" Yarrow swallowed. "Can't birth themselves?"

"Not at the right rate," said the frog. "Nor the workshops with wheelbarrows and the like, nor the orchards with seedlings and the like." "The like," said the smaller frog.

"Deficiencies and deficits everywhere," said the wheelbarrow frog. "A lack for us to supply. Duty to the tower, duty to the Ladies. All that."

"Years and years it's been," said the lamb frog. "Years," said its companion.

"Could be less," said the wheelbarrow frog.

"Could be a lot more," said another frog, whose pond was full of unhatched doorknobs. "Lily's in charge, is it?"

Yarrow wrung her hands a moment. "Willows," she said at last. "It's the Willow Era."

"Next after Lilies, are they?" said the doorknob frog.

"No," Yarrow whispered.

"Then granddaughters of Lilies?"

Yarrow shook her head. "I'm afraid not."

"Won't go on guessing, then," said the doorknob frog.

"Thanks," said the lamb frog. "I was about to be sad." "Sad," said the smaller frog.

"What's your name?" said the wheelbarrow frog. "What are you doing in the Deeps?"

"I'm Yarrow. I'm going to Black Tower."

"Wrong direction, then," said the fish frog. "It's up there, in the Levels." "Levels," said its companion.

"Ninny," said the doorknob frog. "There's a shortcut here."

"What are *your* names?" said Yarrow, desperate to avert what seemed to be an argument.

The frogs all looked at her.

"Names?" said one, as if unsure of the word.

"They take your names," said the lamb frog. "Take," said its companion.

"Come work for us, they said." The wheelbarrow frog made a discontented motion of its forelimbs that sent water gushing over the floor. "Leave the river. Join the new thing that's happening. Walls and houses, all new."

"But leave the names behind," said the doorknob frog.

Like Servant. The woman had not been born with that title. And despite her long years of service to the house, Yarrow knew little about her. Some things were just the way things were, like an inconvenient cellar step. Before she could say anything, the far door opened, and six guards in the livery of Blue Tower entered. They held spears, and they pointed them at Yarrow.

*A Question Posed by the Tutors in Grey House
(But as the Tutors Are Dead, It Is Forgotten):
What Is the True Name of Yellow Tower?*

S o Eglantine LXIV asked of his apprentice, and the apprentice answered *It is the Sword of the Conqueror,* and Eglantine was pleased.

43. Yarrow Speaks to the Lady of Blue Tower

They climbed for a long time. Yarrow was not much given to resistance, and the Lady seemed curious about what was happening. The spears fascinated her, and she tried many times to inspect their blades, and Yarrow had to stop her, fearing to provoke anyone.

Blue Tower was cleaner and better-maintained than Grey. Much of its interior was smooth white, like plain plaster or bone, and fewer of its windows were broken, and most of its passages were free of the debris of age. But as they went up the spiraling stairs in the outer skin of the tower, they passed rooms and halls where the floors were stained with blood, or where corpses were piled awaiting disposal. The smell was sweet and vile.

Occasionally they passed outer windows. Much of the palace still lay under a shroud of snow. Blue was a field of white like bleached linen; the twists and grooves of Black were sugared like candied angelica; Grey was invisible; the snow around Red was darkened with smoke. Only Yellow was green, still vibrant with the sick dreaming of the dead Lady.

At last they came out of the stairs on the edge of a wide circular chamber, ringed with benches descending to a round dais in the center. The domed, sky-blue ceiling was dotted with stars. It rested on square pillars, and past them was the parapet at the top of Blue Tower. The guards pushed Yarrow and the Lady onto a bench near the dais and told them to wait.

"For what?" said Yarrow.

"It's almost time for the audience. Then she'll decide what to do with you."

So they sat. Her feet aching and her back sore, Yarrow was grateful for the bench, then angry at herself for her own gratitude. The Lady went completely immobile and her eyes closed. Perhaps she was asleep. Certainly, her unsettling aura diminished. If her dreams were its source, they were now diverted elsewhere, like a stream, to turn a different set of wheels. But Yarrow was tired of wondering about the truth—tired of everything, in fact. She fell asleep herself.

When she opened her eyes, the room was noisy with a crowd. Half the benches were already full, and more people were coming in all the time. None of them sat too near Yarrow and the Lady. The mood was somber and anxious. All the gatherings Yarrow had been to were festivals, like Lady-day or Midsummer or the Weavers' Moon: she was used to people cracking nuts, joking around, playing games. She and Ban and Grith would run through the crowds, sampling festival food, looking at everyone's fine clothes, practicing their recitations for the various rites. Even the most solemn occasion, like Wakenight, was still a holiday. This was different. All the conversations she could hear were quiet, stilted, nervous. Children were shushed if they made noise. Guards stood at all the doors and in the aisles.

Yarrow twisted the ends of her sleeves until they were wrinkled and sweaty. Even if she found a chance to escape, somehow slipped away from her guards, there were too many people to get through. The Lady was still asleep. If she woke up cranky, she would cause absolute chaos. Yarrow could use that to escape, but by no means would she spark it by awakening the Lady herself.

A person in a simple blue houppelande entered, flanked by several guards. This must be the new ruler of Blue Tower. After the images in the Schoolhouse, the appalling vastness of the Lady of Yellow, and the vicious prickles of the baby Lady, this one seemed tame. She was a person of simple flesh, pale and thin, with a long face and long nose and long mouth. Chestnut hair was piled on her head and held with a coif of gold wire, ornamented with a finial like the one atop the tower itself. At first, nothing about her seemed different from anyone you might meet in the courts below.

But she had the *aura* of a Lady. And when she opened her mouth to speak, her teeth were gleaming lapis, and her tongue was blue and shining as a butterfly's wing. When she stood still, her hair slithered and shifted in its golden cage.

"The old Lady is dead," she said. "Long live the new."

"The old Lady is dead," the crowd repeated. "Long live the new."

Yarrow nearly spoke along with them, but stifled the impulse. This was not Grey; these were not her words to say.

"The signs all say that the Beast rises soon," the Lady said. Her lips lagged slightly behind the words, as if she were speaking by other means, and the mouth was just for show. "We are safe here, gathered into the tower."

"We are safe here," said the crowd. The words came to Yarrow's mouth, but she pressed her lips together.

"My mother was weak and would not do what was necessary. But we are safe now. It is a new era."

"It is a new era," said the crowd. This time, when Yarrow still did not speak, the Lady's eyes zeroed in on her.

"It is a new era," said the Blue Lady.

"It is a new era," said the crowd, but not Yarrow.

She glided to the edge of the dais and stared down at Yarrow. Her eyes had no pupils, just rounds of carved lapis. A sharp smell came from her.

"It is," said the Blue Lady slowly and deliberately, "a new era."

"It is—" Yarrow clapped her hand over her mouth, muffling the rest. To repeat, to join a rite, as she had not in weeks—the urge was in her very bones.

The Blue Lady lifted her left hand. The crowd followed suit. They were dead silent now. Yarrow grabbed her left hand with her right and forced it to stay in place. The Blue Lady snapped her fingers. The crowd snapped theirs. Yarrow was still.

The Blue Lady snapped her fingers again. "It is a new era."

Her subjects did as she did. What did she want? She asked nothing. She had no questions for Yarrow. Her stony gaze did not take in the stained and travelworn gown and wimple. She didn't even see the baby Lady. She saw only refusal.

She snapped her fingers again. The crowd snapped theirs. In Yarrow's lap, her own fingers twitched. Her skin was all hot prickles and sweat.

"It is a new era," said the Lady. "Long live the new Lady." She let her hand fall. The crowd echoed her movement.

Yarrow wanted to sing the Lullaby of Reeds—it might soothe the Lady's cold anger—but when she opened her mouth to try, the Lady's own words came out.

"It is a new era," said Yarrow. Her shoulders sagged in relief.

"It is a new era," said the Lady.

"It is a new era," said the crowd.

"It is a new era," said Yarrow.

The Lady raised her left hand. The crowd raised theirs again. Yarrow raised hers. In unison, they snapped their fingers. A second time. A third time. The channels of obedience were deeply carved in Yarrow's soul, but even so, this was too easy. She was not commanded; she was compelled. But she had surrendered already. Her tired feet were forgotten; she straightened up; her pains were eased. A new era. A new era.

Snap.

There is work to be done, said the Lady; her true voice washed around the room like warm water. Fortifications must be built. Black and Red and Yellow and Grey are fragile, weak. Let the Beast take them. Blue must survive. Blue will survive. It is a new era.

Snap.

It is the lot of Blue to make, said the Lady. And make we will. Swords and spears and shields and poison. If the Beast comes to devour us, it will find not an apple but a belladonna.

Snap.

The others are weak and forgetful, said the Lady. They—

Click click click.

Yarrow shivered as if splashed. She wrenched her eyes from the Blue Lady. The child had awakened and was opening its stone eyelids one by one, each lid clicking into place. The next time everyone snapped, Yarrow was out of step.

The Blue Lady's rhythm and cadence faltered. Her lightless eyes turned to Yarrow and her seatmate. The Yellow Lady stared back. The air became charged and heavy, as if before a lightning strike.

What have you brought me? the Blue Lady said.

Why didn't she recognize her own kin? Grey, Black, Blue, Red, Yellow, all were kin, the five sisters' children. How could one not know the other? But then, Yellow had thought Yarrow herself was a Lady. They could be fooled.

What is this? said the Blue Lady.

The crowd's lips echoed soundlessly: What is this?

Yarrow edged down the bench, outside the palpable cone of the Blue Lady's attention, and stood up. Nobody noticed her. The thousands of eyes in the room were fixed on the younger Lady.

What do you want? the Blue Lady demanded.

In silent unison, the crowd repeated her question.

Food, said the other Lady. Her arms extended, clamping onto the Blue Lady's shoulders. Her mouth had learned to open very wide.

Yarrow fled up the aisle as the Blue Lady, using hundreds of throats not her own, began to scream.

Yarrow ran, her pack jolting against her legs. The stairs flew past her. The screams echoed after her. She tripped and rolled down several steps until a friendly landing broke her fall. Blood was trickling through the ceiling, down the stairs, leaching through the clean plaster walls. The screams were still echoing. On and on and on she ran, dizzy with the many rounds of the staircase. Her feet were killing her. The stairs had bruised her body all over. But the screaming would not stop.

I should have left her in the woods, Yarrow said to herself. She scrubbed at her streaming eyes. Why didn't I? She clamped her hands on her ears. A woman must not abandon a parentless child. But she tried to eat the flower. She tried to eat *me*. Why didn't I forget the rules just once?

She stumbled out onto the great marble portico and the white glare of the winter noon. Another tremor was beginning, and a soft sprinkle of snow coated her as she ran down the few outer steps. Roe was leaning against the wall of the terrace near the door to the Deeps. The screaming filled the courts of Blue.

"Roe!" Yarrow shrieked. "Roe, I'm so sorry!"

He did not answer. She ran to him, but even as she did, she knew the truth. When she touched him, he fell over, leaving a smear of blood on the marble wall. Whether he had been killed for letting her in, or whether he had simply been seen too close to the tower, she would never know.

The noise from the tower-top cut off abruptly. A mass of yellow fell over the parapet, tangled with a mass of blue. A loud drone of holiness hummed in the cold air. Cowering, Yarrow lost sight of them behind the rooftops. A moment later, the ground reeled. The air inhaled itself, then exhaled in a burst of prickling snow.

Everything was silent. Yarrow crouched by Roe's body, shivering until her stomach was sick.

Bit by bit, reciting the Litany of Leaves in scattered fragments until it clumped together as a whole, Yarrow calmed. There was work to do. She could go to pieces later.

Old Yarrow had always said to bury doctors whole, with apple seeds at their heart, so that the tree would consume them and turn them into something beautiful and useful. Though it hurt her aching body, she dragged Roe along the terrace to one of the beds of earth where a maple tree trunk stood with most of its limbs intact. She gently parted the lips of the spear-wound in his chest and placed a fig there, since there were no apples. She had neither strength nor time to bury him properly, so she tore frosty branches from the tree and covered him. Rite or no rite, that was all the grave he would get. Nothing would ever bring Yarrow back to Blue Tower.

She sang the Doctor's Elegy as she took up her journey again. Blue abutted the West Passage; if she could get in there, and head in the right direction, she would reach Black Tower that day. And if she did not, it was a matter of indifference to her whether she came to it at all.

A Treatise of the Doctors of Grey House
(But as the Doctors Are Dead, It Is Forgotten)
Concerning Ladies

*T*he Ladies resist classification. If one were to be sacrilegious, one might categorize them as one categorizes butterflies; i.e., into folio, quarto, and duodecimo. Under this arrangement, the Five Sisters—perhaps legendary—would be of the folio type. The succeeding generations of historical record would be of the quarto type. A duodecimo Lady would be one who has not yet come into her power.

The Ladies of course do not submit themselves for examination. We do not know the composition of their bones, the balance of their humors, nor the look of their urine. That they are of another order of being, does not admit of a doubt—But what order, we may ask? And does it then follow that we people are by nature subject to them?

Again, this is a line of thought that could be construed as sacrilege. One must pursue it carefully. We are not concerned now with the politics of the palace; that we leave to the tutors. It is the nature of the Ladies that we now consider.

Firstly, it is a matter of physiognomical fact that the Ladies need no mate in order to reproduce. Secondly, their proceedings appear as the work of some subtile art; yet no person who has witnessed these methods has succeeded in repeating them. The Ladies of Black are said to place a stone in their mouth for one summer, and at the end of it, they have a daughter. The Lady of Yellow, it is rumor'd, lays many eggs like a frog; but as none of her daughters have ever been seen, this is conjecture. The Ladies of Blue take up a chip of their own azurite and give it to a willing incubator; the merging of flesh and stone gives the Blue Ladies an astonishing homeliness, compared to their sisters from other towers. The Ladies of Red kindle a flame of cinnamon twigs and incense and set thereto a hen's egg, and when the fire burns out, the egg hatches forth a crimson daughter. Our own Ladies of Grey take a bone from the river and carve it over a span of months, singing all the while, until the bone answers back.

It is ſaid—though with their rarity, we cannot confirm this—that the daughters are more territorial than the mothers, and will fight other Ladies who venture into their borders. But, perhaps more aſtoniſhing, they know each other ſolely by ſcent: of courſe, if a daughter of Red has never ſmelled a daughter of Blue, they would not know one another, and paſs each other by without thinking twice.

44. Yarrow Is Reunited with Peregrine and We See Some Old Friends

After several hours, Yarrow stumbled down a short flight of stairs and into the familiar quiet of the West Passage. Before, she had feared it because Yellow Tower lay at its end. But by now its cobblestones were like old friends. The blizzard had piled snow against one wall, leaving the other nearly bare, and she sat down and curled up against it, shivering with cold and relief.

The earth shook again, but it was brief this time. The tremors had come with increasing frequency, until they no longer scared Yarrow in themselves. But did they mean anything? She did not know anything about the Beast, beyond old stories and the few songs Arnica had taught her about it. There weren't many, since it had been Goldenseal learning. The Beast was no concern of the Yarrows and Arnicas; every Lady-day they sang a lament for the Lady it had killed, but the creature itself was the guardian's business.

But who was the guardian now?

If the Beast was back—if the tremors were part of that—well, so be it. Yarrow had been partly eaten by a Lady, eaten meat in her turn, heard frogs lament a life she did not understand, and seen blood leak from the roof of a tower. How much worse could the Beast be? Certainly no worse than this winter.

She found herself humming the Lullaby of Reeds. *Sacrilege.* She forced herself to stop. If she sang it to herself, that was one more buttress of her life taken away. I want to go home with a clear conscience, she thought. Or at least as clear a one as possible. Duty, she told herself, though not sure why she did. The image of the two falling Ladies hung before her eyes. Duty.

Her tangled skein of thoughts led her back to the Beast and the guardian. Was it that apprentice now? Had he become Hawthorn? Not with *her* say-so, unless he'd come in secret to Old Yarrow. Only a Mother of Grey House could confer that title.

No guardian, nobody to stand against the Beast. Nobody to do their duty.

It might . . . it might be bad, then. If he was still in Grey, she would find him. She would make him guardian. The Beast would be vanquished, become just a story again, and all would be well. Black could wait.

She stood and turned toward Grey, at this distance little more than tumbled heaps of white fringing the South Passage. She could reach it that day if she hurried. Ignoring her sore body, she began walking.

The earth shook again. Then again, more strongly. Again, and Yarrow was about to run, when over her shoulder she saw the huge white form of a hollowman coming down the Passage. She halted. The pilot might be convinced to give her a ride. On its back a pink tent swayed. A head in a white hood peeked over the side. Could it be—?

"Hello, little Mother," said Peregrine, grinning at her. Tertius's great nostrils let out a steaming *whuff* of greeting. "I heard about the train and I hoped you'd find your way to Black, but here I find you in the Passage instead. Much the worse for wear, too, it seems." He spat vibrant orange into the snow.

"I'm not going to Black Tower now," said Yarrow. "I'm going to Grey."

"A coincidence indeed! So am I. In fact, I've got your mead with me. Fish-carts don't move well in the snow. Care for a nip to stave off the cold?" While he spoke, Peregrine had unrolled the rope ladder for her, and Yarrow was climbing up.

"Maybe," said Yarrow. She flung herself down on the cold white platform and sighed. The cloud of her breath rose up like a tree trunk and spread into the wintry air. "Yes. Please."

Peregrine went into the tent and came out with a bottle of dark green glass. He uncorked it and handed it to her. "Bit cold now, but it should do the trick."

Yarrow took a long swig from the wine bottle. As always, it singed her mouth and throat, but then hot blood coursed into her veins and made her head spin, and she giggled. Peregrine laughed too, and drank some himself. Tertius resumed its plodding gait. With a scritch of tiny legs on fabric, a dragonfly perched on the tent.

"What have you been up to, little Mother?" said Peregrine. "You look the worse for wear, if you don't mind my saying."

"Doing what a Yarrow must," she said. She drank more.

"And a Yarrow must make herself look as if she got in a fight with six cats?"

"We need to go faster," said Yarrow. "I hate to inconvenience you, but I have to get back to Grey and confirm the guardian's apprentice."

"Pale fellow? Green robe?"

"Have you met him?" If the apprentice had dared to sneak out of Grey entirely—

"No, but the story's all over the Great Tower."

"What? What has he been doing?" Something useful for once, she hoped.

"She's Hawthorn now," said Peregrine.

Yarrow nearly dropped the bottle. Golden wine sloshed out and made a fragrant, sticky mess of her hands. *"What?"*

"Easy, little Mother," said Peregrine. "You think someone's stepped into your territory, I take it? Well, it's no such matter. Hawthorn went to the Lady herself—*the* Lady, you understand. *Herself.* I don't know the rights of what happened then, but she confirmed the guardianship."

Yarrow's shoulders sagged in relief. "Then she's already back at Grey—the new Hawthorn. I'm glad *someone* hasn't been wasting time."

"Oh, the Lady put her in prison."

Yarrow *did* drop the wine this time, but picked it up before more than half was spilled.

"Don't worry, little Mother," said Peregrine. "She's escaped. At least that was the rumor in the cellars. She and her little squire."

"What squire?" said Yarrow. "She didn't have one in Grey. It's not even an office."

"Can't say for sure. Anyway, they escaped. The whole tower is scandalized."

"Well, where *is* she then?" said Yarrow.

"Not much point in escaping if you're just going to stick around the Great Tower, is there? Nobody knows where she went, but I'd assume she's heading to Grey herself."

Thank the Lady, Yarrow thought. I am so tired.

She let the Beast lapse back into the realm of childhood fears.

Based on her limited experience with the new Hawthorn, the guardian would be vigilant (if a little persnickety) about her duties, so Yarrow need not worry. The bigger question was whether Hawthorn would be manageable—whether the authority of the Mother would go unchallenged. Going all the way to Black Tower, just to avoid the Mother's confirmation? That did not speak well for Hawthorn's sense of duty to the house. But Yarrow was tough. Once the Beast was out of the way, well, Hawthorn had better watch her step.

Yarrow sipped more wine and passed the bottle to Peregrine.

"Do you ever think about it?" she said. "The Beast, I mean."

Peregrine shrugged. "It's always been a matter for Ladies or for Grey. And the thing itself only comes about once every three or four lifetimes. How long since the last time? Four hundred years?"

"I don't know," said Yarrow. "A very long time, even for Grey. The guardians always take it so seriously, but it's not a part of life. It's not grain or fruit or children. It's a story we tell each other that just happens to come true every so often."

"Seems like it should be more serious than that," said Peregrine. "Shouldn't it?"

"The Goldenseals know about the Beast," said Yarrow automatically. But Peregrine was right. Why should only they know it, if the matter was so great? Why shouldn't the Mother? Were the names that important that their wisdom should die with them? "The rest of us don't think of it," she added, trying to sound as if that made it all right.

"The Ladies think about it all the time," said Peregrine. "Aside from each other, it's the only thing that can kill one of them, it seems." He passed the bottle back. "Some of them dream about killing it, I hear, because if you vanquish it, you get a wish."

"What sort of wish?" said Yarrow.

"The stories in Black say it grants a wish 'of its own body.'"

"Like a miracle."

"Oh, nobody really knows." Peregrine accepted the bottle from her. "One story says that, at the command of a Lily guardian, it filled the South Passage with water so the palace would always have a fresh supply."

"That doesn't sound like a wish *of its own body*."

"Well, it used its blood for the water. Then it died. Another story says that the first time it arose, the Lady who killed it asked for the Great Tower, and the monster built it from its own corpse. And another one says that a guardian asked for companions, and the Beast made parrots for her."

"I wouldn't have used my wish on something like *that*," said Yarrow.

"Then what would the little Mother wish for?" said Peregrine.

"That would depend on what the Beast really *is*. I wouldn't ask a bird for milk or a guardian for a song."

"An evasive answer. You might as well be a tutor."

Yarrow took a long pull from the bottle, finishing it off. She thought of Blue Tower, now Ladyless, and the red smear of Roe's blood on the white wall, and the nameless frogs in the dark. She thought of the white birds in the air around Yellow Tower. She thought of Grey House, empty and growing emptier, the molding beds, the chairs of vanished women in the refectory. Over and over she had done what a Yarrow must do, and yet over and over, things had only gotten worse. It was supposed to be enough to *be* Yarrow. Everyone had always made it seem so. And yet it wasn't.

"Change, maybe," she said. The word was unfamiliar in her mouth. "I might ask for change."

Peregrine laughed. "Change? To hear a woman in grey speak like that! What kind of change, little Mother?"

Would she wish for it? Was it the wine talking? The inside of her head revolved in lazy circles. There were too many half-formed thoughts in Yarrow's mind. They crowded to her lips like hens seeking crumbs. What could she say that was honest? *The world must change, for I cannot.* But that was nothing she could say to this man. She was spared the necessity of answering when Peregrine brought Tertius to a sudden halt. Yarrow pitched forward, knocking her head on the platform. The wine bottle rolled and fell to smash, glittering, on the cobblestones.

"What is it?" said Yarrow, sitting up.

Peregrine only pointed ahead of them. Blocking the Passage from one side to another were dead bodies: people, but also things like deer with high ebony spires for heads. Stuck through the body of a bluish person was a long spear from which a black banner waved, bearing a yellow bird under a golden eye.

"Beekeepers," said Peregrine. "What were they doing out here, with hives and everything? And that's the Obsidian Lady's banner. Why would she kill her own crofters?"

Among the dead, something glittered in the sun. Its shape was familiar. But more important than that, someone had to *do* something about the bodies.

Peregrine unrolled the rope ladder and both of them climbed down. Every single body had been brutally hacked. The smell of blood was thick and sharp. Little things crunched underfoot; in all directions, thousands of dead bees were scattered.

If the deceased is a beekeeper from Black, Yarrow thought. If the deceased . . . Beekeeper from Black. Then—then what?

It had been so long since she had recited any of the lore. If she had forgotten it—but after a shaky moment she found the right room in her memory, the right image, and the answer unfurled in her mind.

Nothing. If the deceased is a beekeeper from Black, you did nothing. The beekeepers were one of the only groups who traditionally took care of their own dead. But that didn't seem right. It was *not* right, it wasn't. Not when they had been slaughtered like this, with none of their own to care for them. Yarrow began singing the Lament for Gardeners. It was not perfect, but it was as close as she could get. Better that than nothing at all.

As she sang, she walked toward the glittering thing. It was clutched in the hand of a trout-faced person near the rear of the group, who seemed to have been defending themselves with it. Roughly five feet long, the object was shaped like a near-triangular dagger, with a grip nearly a third of its length and fitted for gigantic hands. Red leather bound the grip, and red stones peeped from among the prickly gold vines that formed the pommel. More vines ran along the center of the blade. Obviously, it was made by or for a Lady. Then why did it look so familiar?

Of course. Gently, Yarrow eased it out of the dead person's hand. It was very heavy. The point had to drag on the ground, for she was too short to carry it easily. Still singing, albeit with a strained voice, she took it back to Tertius where Peregrine was waiting for her. The Lament ended just as she reached him.

"I don't carry weapons," he said. "I'm a Butler."

"This needs to go back to Grey," said Yarrow. "It's the guardian's steel."

A Question Posed by the Tutors in Grey House
(But as the Tutors Are Dead, It Is Forgotten):
What Is the True Name of Black Tower?

So Eglantine LIX asked of his apprentice, and the apprentice answered *It is the Rose Garden,* and Eglantine was well pleased.

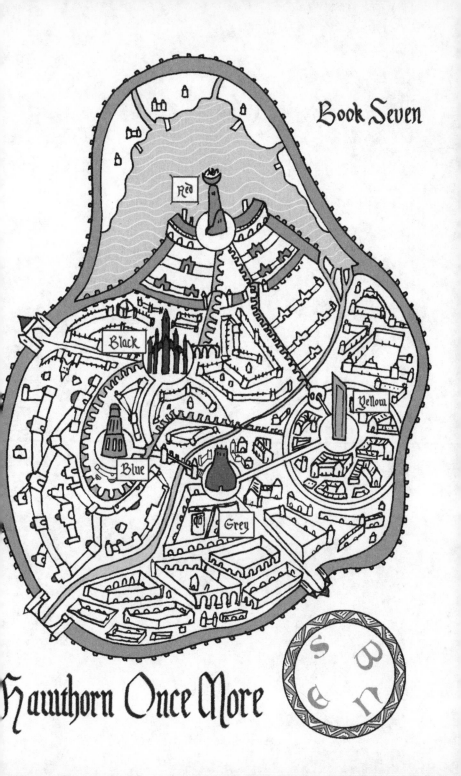

Book Seven

Red

Black

Blue

Yellow

Grey

Hawthorn Once More

45. Hawthorn Decides to Leave Frin Behind

The Wasp's Eye was dominated by a statue of the Red Lady. She stood at the window, her eyeless face gazing out over the palace toward Grey, each of her four arms holding a sword, her three legs posed as if dancing or charging forward. The detail of the carving was so complete that you could almost see individual hairs in the pelt she wore over her armor.

The rest of the room was red as well: walls, ceiling, floor, even the chairs. It was a bit like standing in an open mouth. Hawthorn found it exhilarating regardless. She had never seen so much *color* in one place before, even if it was quite dusty and a little ragged.

Going to stand beside the statue, she had a good view of the palace below. A great deal of smoke seemed to be rising from Black, much more than you'd expect even for a cold noon. Before she could think, there was a flash, and a moment or two later, a rumble. More dark smoke billowed up from one of the courts where an entire building had fallen. From the fumes emerged a huge shape: the palanquin of the Obsidian Lady. Swarming around her, nearly invisible, were hundreds of her guards. Archers on the walls above began shooting. The palanquin barreled on unharmed, carried on the shoulders of many people armored like beetles, but the guards fell by the dozen.

I must get to the Beast, Hawthorn thought. She will need it.

The next moment she remembered the Ebony Lady, and the cool touch of Rook's hand. I am Hawthorn. I kill the Beast. I do not use it, and I do not help another to use it.

Who was fighting? That was none of her business at the moment.

Ebony, perhaps, had been stirred up by Obsidian's interference, but in the end, it did not matter who ruled Black Tower. As she and Frin had seen, no edicts or commands ever left its walls. It was a head without a body.

She watched the battle for a few minutes, as if it were a chess game between Old Hawthorn and Mother Yarrow. Then the position of the sun told her that too much time had passed. Frin should have been there by now.

Hawthorn leaned out the window and searched the sheer face of the pier. No Frin was to be seen. Either he had fallen, or he had gotten lost inside. Her fingers gripped the sill.

Another tremor ran through the tower. The statue beside her wobbled. It had been jarred loose during a previous earthquake and would likely fall soon. She moved into the center of the room.

Dear Frin. It wasn't until he was gone that she realized how much he meant. Not only because he was loyal and funny, but because in her whole life she had never had anyone whom she considered a friend. The girls in grey were too aloof, the women even worse. Her apprenticeship distanced her from the children of the cloisters. Even Old Hawthorn was more of a mother than a friend. Only Frin counted. They had traveled together, suffered together, kept each other warm during the long trek up the tower. She was faced with the choice of waiting to see if he would work some sort of wonder and appear, or going on without him. And beyond a doubt, she knew she could not stay.

Grey Tower demanded her duty. Hawthorn had to go back, get the steel, and wait for the Beast to surface. Nothing else mattered, for if she failed, there would *be* nothing else. It's not fair, she thought. I shouldn't have to. A sob burst from her lips before she even knew it was there. Her hand went to her neck and found no amulet.

The tower shook again. The statue of the Red Lady teetered and came off its pedestal with a smash. Fragments flew, and Hawthorn leapt back. Amid the creakings of the tower were the sounds of the battle, louder now, coming closer. It was time to go, if she did not want to fight her way out.

Bending on her way to pick up a long red spar that had lately been a sword, Hawthorn left the Wasp's Eye.

The staircase rocked, and from the joins between stones fell a haze of dust. Hawthorn sneezed, and her eyes stung and watered. With the spar as a walking stick, she felt her way along, covering her mouth with a sleeve. The only light came from occasional shafts running to the outer walls, or from open doors of empty rooms. Even after the dust settled, it should not have been very bright. Yet Hawthorn had little trouble seeing her way. *That* brought her up short, and a little thread of apprehension curled down her spine.

Sure enough, when she was still, the wavering gleam of lantern light was apparent. A thin streak of it was smeared along the staircase wall. As a guide it was probably useless, since the stairs did not seem to branch, only opening onto rooms or short corridors. But seeing it there, in a part of the tower so clearly disused, was uncanny.

She continued. So did the light. The sound of the battle grew louder: the twang of bows, the thud of arrows, the clang of swords. Then above it rose a voice, as familiar as her own overrobe. She spoke no words; she did not need to: the sound of the Obsidian Lady shouting was enough. The tower resonated like a great tuning fork, and Hawthorn clapped her hands over her ears. There was an answering shout. She knew that voice too. The Ebony Lady's cry vibrated in her very bones.

Running into a nearby chamber (full of lumber, which she nearly tripped over), she looked out and saw the two Ladies. Ebony stood at the head of Last Lily. At the foot stood Obsidian's palanquin, her yellow bird perched on its high finial. Ebony was only a little taller than Hawthorn, and was barely visible at that distance. But nobody could ever mistake her, and her smallness made her look defiant before Obsidian's great palanquin.

Before anything could happen, there was an answering call from Black Tower, and its main gate opened. The Willow Lady emerged, her litter borne on the shoulders of forty Sparrows. Hawthorn could not hear what she said, but she addressed the other two in authoritative tones.

While they parleyed, Hawthorn could sneak out unnoticed. As she left the room, she noticed some yarn knotted around a piece of lumber within. The yarn led down the stairs for several turns, then bent into a room packed with tall porcelain vases. Frin stood there clutching a book, watching the Ladies outside.

"Frin!" said Hawthorn, running toward him. He turned, and his face glowed brighter than a lantern.

Alas, their reunion was interrupted. As they drew close, the Obsidian Lady issued from her palanquin. She lifted one hand. Her bird swooped down from the finial and picked up the Willow Lady in its talons. Up and up it flew, beyond the view afforded by the windows, but a moment later a cloud of ash fell down and blew away in the winter winds. As the Sparrows scattered, Obsidian and Ebony turned their attention to each other once more.

46. Hawthorn and Frin Decide to Leave Black Tower Behind

Outside the room, the lantern light resumed. It continued down the stairs with them as they hurtled on. With the Lady dead, the tower was left open to whoever survived the battle. If that was neither Ebony nor Obsidian, whichever Lady came there next would be its ruler. And the rise of a new dynasty never went well for anyone inside Black Tower.

Hawthorn and Frin came to the passage leading out of the pier into the main structure. Frin kept going down the stairs, but Hawthorn stopped. The light diverted into the passage.

"Are you coming?" said Frin. "The gate is this way."

"I think we need to follow the light," said Hawthorn. "It got us to the Library. I think it can get us out of the tower."

"We can get *out of the tower* by going *downstairs* to the *gate*," said Frin, gesturing at the staircase.

"The light is here for a reason," said Hawthorn. "We wouldn't have been able to bypass the dangerous areas without it. We'd never have found our way up at all."

"We 'found our way' to a prison cell," said Frin tartly. "And I can't even *see* the light. I've been trusting you this whole time, and look where it's gotten us."

Hawthorn found that hard to argue with. She followed him. The lower part of the pier was dark without the lantern light; windows here were even fewer. They trod on each other's feet several times. Then Frin tripped on a crooked stair and tumbled down ten steps, where he sprawled on a landing in a shaft of dull sunlight. His bag tore open as he fell, scattering possessions. Hawthorn ran to help him. He was dazed but otherwise unhurt, and able to walk almost immediately, but they lost time picking up everything that had spilled.

"What's *this*?" said Hawthorn, picking up the book he'd been holding.

"I found it in a room here," said Frin. "I thought you might like to have it."

Hawthorn smiled. "It's beautiful."

She was paging through it when Frin groaned and held up a broken vessel of thick green glass.

"I was going to keep water in it," he said, pushing the fragments off to the side where nobody would step on them.

"I didn't see you take one of those," said Hawthorn.

"You weren't there," said Frin. "It was in the room."

"The study in the tower where we found the map."

"No, no, the room where I found the book."

"The same vials were in both places?" Hawthorn took up a piece and sniffed it. Sweet and musty.

Frin shrugged. "I guess."

The Robins in the secret room had filled an identical container with Hellebore honey. "Does anyone use these besides the beekeepers?"

"I've seen them come through the apiaries from all over the palace. Blue makes them."

Hawthorn frowned. "Who in Black Tower receives honey besides the Lady?"

"A lot of the offices. The Master of Kitchens, One Sparrow, the Master of Privileges, the Chief Butler, the Librarian, all monthly, the Housekeeper General and the Third Page yearly, others I can't remember right now."

"If Thistle honey can turn you into a Lady," said Hawthorn, slowly closing the book, "what does Hellebore honey do?"

"There ain't any Hellebore honey," said Frin. "It's been banned since Lily."

"What if there was, though?"

Frin shrugged. "One said that Hellebore 'taketh away the virtue.' But she was quoting something very old. As I said, ain't been none since Lily."

"So if a Lady ate Hellebore honey, her natural power would be suppressed."

Frin made a helpless motion with his hands. "I'm just an apprentice, Hawthorn. This ain't knowledge anyone's needed in a long time."

"What is the source of the lantern light?" said Hawthorn, more to herself than to Frin, who once more made a gesture of ignorance. "'The Hellebore Lady filled the first lantern.'"

"Can we go now?" said Frin. "You can interrogate me as we run."

The glass, found in rooms of books. The Hellebore Ladies, source of this forbidden, deadening honey, but also founders of the Sparrows, who danced under an ancient name. The Librarian, privileged to receive honey from the beekeepers. The touch of Rook's hand.

"As we *run*," said Frin, lifting one knee and posing his arms like a runner. "As we . . . *run*."

"We need to head back up," said Hawthorn. "We *are* being guided. Rook has been pulling us through the tower this whole time."

"Rook?" said Frin. "Why should *they* care?"

"I don't know," said Hawthorn, "but if I'm right, Rook is about to take control of Black Tower. And her name isn't really Rook. It's the Hellebore Lady."

47. Hawthorn Is Right

Back in the tower, they found themselves in a grand hall of black stone where four other passages intersected, apparently leading out to other piers. In the center, a huge staircase mounted to a gallery where more flights of dark steps twined up into the tower. Beneath it, another staircase flowed down.

As Hawthorn and Frin stood there, a noise like falling gravel echoed. They shrank back into the archway's shadow as a river of Sparrows clattered down the stairs and pooled on the main floor, glistening in their beetly armor. In their hands were spears, swords, knives tied to the ends of poles, ragged banners. A black-robed person appeared at the head of the gallery stairs and looked down on the assembled Sparrows. Their face was hidden behind strips of white. The aura of a Lady pervaded the hall like a pungent aroma. All the Sparrows bent a knee.

Willow is over, said the new Lady of Black Tower, descending the staircase.

She raised her hands. From within her robe came two more. Eyes bloomed in the strips of paper. A fan of black feathers opened atop her head. Behind her, she left a trail of light.

I proclaim the beginning of the Elder Era, she said as she halted on the bottom step. In time we will celebrate. For now, there are more pressing matters: the earth shakes and the Beast comes. Make secure the tower, and end the foolish fighting without.

The Sparrows cheered and scattered. The Lady stood almost alone in the silent hall. Her many eyes turned to the place where Hawthorn and Frin hid.

"You can come out now," she said in a normal voice.

Slowly, Hawthorn did. Frin followed in her shadow.

"I regret the necessity of the parrot's death," the Elder Lady said. "But I knew my sister would have you killed sooner or later, and I could not free you directly. You would not let go, and it seemed to me you would listen more readily to your enemy than an official of this tower, so it was I you heard in prison."

"Why are you helping us at all?" said Hawthorn.

"I could not undo what my sisters had done to your mind," said the Lady. "I knew you would follow their compulsions to your own doom. But you are the last Guardian. You cannot be permitted to fail, or the Beast will destroy us all. And it is as I told you: your master and I were friends after a fashion."

Warmth flooded Hawthorn's chest.

"She only knew me as the Librarian," said the Lady. "Which is all I was. The last daughter of Hellebore hid with the beekeepers and arranged for them to supply her with honey to hide her virtues. That arrangement has held all through the long centuries, for every one of her daughters who has held the position of Librarian. Forced to be what we were not, we survived, we served the tower, and we waited."

"Is it—is it in *your* name the Sparrows dance, then?" said Hawthorn.

"I do not know the Luminous Name, and neither do they. There has been so much lost over the years, even to the Library. The Sparrows have never known the identity of the Librarian, either. We both carry the light of the lantern, but they are loyal to the tower and its ruler, whoever that may be. And it may not be me for long. I have few allies. I don't even have myself. What I have been as Librarian I can no long" er be, she finished (her voice dropping from a flesh person's to a Lady's). This new era of mine may only last a night."

In a burst of pity, Hawthorn nearly offered her service to the Lady. But that would be a gift with many, many strings attached, and she caught herself before speaking.

Others in the palace command armies, said the Lady. I have only the Sparrows, and whoever's coats I can turn in my sister's court. My reign may be brief, but while it lasts I wish to have a palace to rule. And so before it ends, and while I still remember Rook and their friend Hawthorn, I will see you sent to Grey to do your duty.

48. They Take a Lantern and Say a Farewell

The lantern sped along the Passage, light flashing, white birds chasing it. Ahead of them, Grey Tower was a faint shape in the winter mist. The great flock had settled on the roofs of the cloisters, though dim motes still swirled around the five turrets of Grey's crown. As the lantern raced, scarlet banners flew around the base of Black. Another army had joined the fray—from Red Tower. The forces of Obsidian and Ebony, caught between the Reds and the Sparrows, collapsed in disarray.

Hawthorn kept up a steady whistle, but under that sound, her heart was thumping so that she could hardly hear herself. She could not think of the fighting, only what lay ahead. It was coming. Her moment was coming. Every Guardian was trained for it; none of them wanted to live to see it.

Among their everyday facts about horses and hens and fish, the Bestiaries recorded every appearance of the Beast. It was different each time. Would she see the vast serpent that ended the Hellebores? Or the six-headed vulture that ended the Lilies? Or the cloud, flashing scarlet lightning, that ended the first Lady of Grey? Legend said it took a shape of meaning fearsome to the one who opposed it; for a moment, Hawthorn saw her master's dying face. If it came in that form, she would not be able to slay it.

The Beast would arise in Grey. The West Passage was its only outlet to the rest of the palace. If it left the Passage, it would cause untold destruction. Therefore, the goal was to vanquish it while it was still there, still weak. That was why the Guardians lived in Grey.

Even coming upon it in a weakened state would not help much. A Guardian was trained to fight, but under all that training was the knowledge that sparring with your master would never prepare you for battling an abomination from beneath the earth. It taught you how to feint and dodge, but it would not in itself protect you. Even if you had the steel, something could still go wrong.

The steel. Hawthorn had forgotten that she'd asked the beekeepers to fetch it from Grey. If they had planned to go, they would have been prevented from setting out by the battle between the Ladies, which surely had been going on for some time. At worst, they would have reached Grey and not been able to return. There was every likelihood the steel was still there. If it was not, well, Hawthorn could not allow herself to contemplate the possibility. If there was no steel, a Lady could perhaps defeat the Beast, but what Lady could reach it in time?

Frin had fallen asleep. The poor thing was probably exhausted. After all, he'd been through a lot more physical strain than Hawthorn herself had. She stopped whistling. Her cheeks were tired, and she didn't want to disturb his sleep.

Opening the lantern door, she leaned out and looked into the Passage. They had not gone as far as she had hoped. The detritus of the nightly feasts still spread beneath them, albeit its outer fringes. There was no sign of jackals. Perhaps they had run to Grey with the birds, or maybe they'd fled in the opposite direction. Was there anything left of Sparrow now? It wasn't right to leave them. The women in grey might know what to do.

Something boomed behind the lantern. The battle apparently had not ended. Hawthorn resumed whistling.

Though the sides of the Passage were intact, the tremors had warped and bent the track. The lantern had a harder time navigating the closer they got to Grey. Finally Hawthorn gave up. The sun was dropping toward the palace roofs; she needed to sleep, and traveling in the dark was a terrible idea. She brought the lantern to within five or six feet of the Passage floor. Frin was awake by then, and began unpacking food given to them by the Lady herself. He started eating, but Hawthorn, having decided to stop, was now determined to cover as much distance as possible before then.

The floor of the Passage changed abruptly. It had been trash, then it was marble, and now it was covered with low, twisted shapes. Among them rose a few familiar triangular outlines. Hawthorn stopped the lantern and opened the door. Frin hopped out first, and Hawthorn heard him scream.

The bodies of the beekeepers were all around. One Robin, impaled by the Obsidian banner. Thirty Robin at the rear, hacked apart. So many others dead, along with their hives. Spilled honey pooled around them and mixed with their blood. The smells of death put Old Hawthorn's face before her, but she pushed that thought back before it could harm her.

Hawthorn put her arm around Frin's shoulders, but he shrugged her off and knelt by One. The only sound in the Passage was his weeping.

"*I* wanted to send the message," he said, wiping his nose on his sleeve. "They came out here to help *me*."

"It's not your fault they died," said Hawthorn. "The Ladies' people did this."

She rubbed his shoulder. There was nothing else for her to say. Women in grey were supposed to handle this part.

"I'll smash them," said Frin. "I'll smash the whole fucking tower. Elder included."

No, Hawthorn started to say, Elder helped us, Elder does not deserve that. But two things stopped her. It would not comfort Frin at all. And second, who was to say that Elder, with access to all the might of Black Tower, might not turn out as poorly as her sisters? She'd helped them out of necessity, their needs ancillary to her goals. No dynasty, however or whyever it arose, had ever withstood the temptations of power.

She dropped to one knee beside Frin and put her arm around him. "I'll help you," she whispered. "When it comes to that, I'll help you."

He did not seem to hear her, only curled against her shoulder and sobbed.

Hawthorn looked around the Passage. The dead beekeepers were facing Black Tower. They had been heading *from* Grey, then. But they did not have the steel. Either the mother had not given it to them, or it had been taken from the battlefield by the soldiers of Obsidian. Both possibilities were equally frightening.

"Come on," said Hawthorn. "It's not safe here. We need to get going."

She helped him back into the lantern and set off. Frin sat against one wall, staring into the cold, flickering light, one hand clutching the onyx vial. He swayed with every jolt as the lantern traversed the warped tracks, but did not move otherwise. Again Hawthorn wished for the women in grey, to handle death and grief for her, to do their precious job.

"It wasn't all of them," she said during a break. "Frin, it wasn't all of them. Fifteen and Twenty-Nine and so many others weren't there. I didn't see any apprentices. And it wasn't all the hives. They'll go on. It wasn't all of them."

He only nodded. A little while later she stopped the lantern again to eat. By then it was dark. Frin would not eat any more, but when she lay down to sleep he did too, and she reached around the basin to hold his hand.

She wanted to tell him that he was her first and only friend. She wanted to tell him it would be all right. She wanted to tell him so many things. It might be their last night alive; the Beast would certainly emerge soon. But Hawthorn had never been good at cracking herself open to show others her feelings. It was easy to talk to people. It was not easy to tell them the truth.

In a quiet, grim way, she was quite certain that she would die facing the Beast. She did not tell Frin. She was too young for the fight, but nobody else could attempt it. She did not tell Frin that either. And she was even more certain that she did not want Frin to die as well. She absolutely did not tell him this.

Hawthorn had also not told him that she felt just as guilty over their deaths. He would never have asked the beekeepers for help if he hadn't been with her. They would never have gone to get the steel. They would still be alive. She would not let one more person die for her.

When Frin was asleep, she drew the amulet from around her neck and laid it on his chest. She dipped her robe in the light for protection. If there were jackals around, he would have some defense. She left the food with him and whistled the tune to set the lantern flashing. Then she hopped out of the lantern and set off up the Passage toward home.

A Story Told by the Mothers in Grey House:
The Founding of the Palace

This is holy and ancient knowledge.

There were five sisters who founded the palace. They were the Roses. Or the Lady who became the Lady of Black was Rose. There was Citrine the Yellow and Wasp the Red. The Lady of Blue was. The Lady of Blue was. Her name was. Cob. Cob the Blue. Her name was Cob the Blue.

And yes, our Lady, our grey Lady. The nameless one. Her name was taken below.

There were five sisters who founded the palace: Rose the Black, Cob the Blue, Citrine the Yellow, Wasp the Red, and Grey the Unnamed.

Can you move my pillow?

That fucking ice. Oh Pell, Pell. I'm so sorry. I'm so sorry. This isn't what I wanted for you.

There were six sisters who founded the palace. No, that's wrong. Hawthorn found that in some book she dug up somewhere. Tried to tell me about it. I shut her mouth for her. And even the rest of the book, she said, said five sisters. You don't mess with the old stories.

If you change the old stories, you change their meaning, of course. Some people think that doesn't matter. In Yellow and Red, I hear, they'll tell any old story. Eighty-five different tellings of "The Night of Bones." How are you supposed to know anything for sure if people think they can just change things?

There were five sisters because there are five towers. If there was a sixth, where is her tower? It's a mistake. The story doesn't explain anything if there are six. You pass on the mistake, people start arguing about the facts before their eyes.

Mothers keep the truth. We remember it. We carve it into our bones and blood. That's what it is to be a woman in grey. Not just the births and deaths. But the stories.

There were five sisters who founded the palace.

An Interlude in Black Tower

The toymaker held the little swan in his palm, braced by two fingers. The other hand held a thin-bladed knife, with which he carved its tiny feathers. Mar, he was called. If his master had not died before confirming him as heir, he would have been Forty-Seven Grebe Occidentalis, Master Toymaker for the Grand Nursery. But his master *did* die, and before he could get to the tower to be named, another apprentice went in his stead. So Forty-Seven Grebe was the Master Toymaker, and Mar was only a small man in the center-west courts of Black.

He still made most of the toys, though. The great workshop of the occidental Grebes was not open to him, so he worked in an abandoned room that once belonged to the Francolins. And every twelve days, regular as clockwork, unless someone overslept, a fish-cart came by to take Mar's toys to the workshop, so Forty-Seven Grebe could pass them off as his own. This was the way of things. The Grand Nursery had once held the swarming progeny of the fecund Bellflower Ladies. Now it was largely empty: the Willows were largely sterile, having at most two daughters at a time. And yet the toys had to be made and de-livered. (Perhaps they went to the children of the tower's staff.) If the Willow Lady had preferred quality, she would have chosen carefully from among Forty-Six Grebe's apprentices. Her will had to be obeyed.

There. He set the knife down and flexed his hand. Time to paint. White lead for the swan's body, vermilion for its beak and eyes, orpi-ment for its fingers.

Half the body was painted and drying when he heard a knock on his door. Zee and Gan stood there in the snow, looking tired, bedraggled, and smeared with drying blood.

Mar was always a little tongue-tied around Zee, whose ridged apple-green skin and long black sidelock were very distracting. Before he could untie anything, Gan unrolled a little scroll and held it up. *Her Ladyship has called a full muster at Peacock Arch.*

Mar's stomach turned. He left the door open and went to bundle himself up.

"Are you all right?" said Mar when he came back. "That's a lot of blood." His hands were shaking: the Lady had called full muster only once before, when she overthrew Onyx. A bloodbath, and one he had been too young for, but his brother Thrin and two friends had gone. One returned: Zee. A small price to pay for Obsidian's ascendance, and everyone had to do their part. That was the way of it.

"A mistake in the West Passage," said Zee. "Thought some people were spies when they were just Robins. We're all right, but they put up a fight. 'S part of why we didn't realize they were just beekeepers until it was too late."

Robins? *Killed?*

"Won't Her Ladyship be furious?" Mar asked.

"Not if we do our job right today," said Zee. "It's time. Shake-up at the tower—Ebony and Her Ladyship are already there, at it hammer and tongs. So she calls out the reserves, and off we go."

Maybe it would be all right, then. Obsidian was a powerful, beautiful Lady, and she had promised to take care of Black, left to decay so thoroughly under Willow. Might as well do my part, Mar thought. Zee kindly helped Mar make a spear out of an old hoe and a kitchen knife. Though he was usually just a farmer in Alchemists' Lane, the man had fought in several of Obsidian's battles after that first one. Outside of the Sparrows, he was one of the closest things this part of Black had to an experienced soldier, and could tell Mar what to bring. A weapon, of course, rations, and armor if possible. Mar had nothing that would really do for armor, and he was fretting about perhaps using some barrel staves or the heavy lid of his one cookpot, when Zee pointed at the mantel.

"That," he said. "Thrin wouldn't ever take it, but think how grand we'd look."

That was a gauntlet of old, soft black leather, armored with pitted iron plates. It had come down from Mar and Thrin's mother, and she had told them never to use it except in the direst need, because it was a miracle. Like all miracles of Black, such as the lanterns or the wheel of seasons, it looked like a thing made by hands, but the function of such miracles had nothing to do with their appearance. The lantern light could change your very nature, the wheel moved the world, and this gauntlet—who knew what it could do? Perhaps it would grant strength or protection, or perhaps it would make an arm sprout from your stomach, as had happened to Ern over in Thistlefoot when he picked up what looked like a bowl of green marble.

"I don't know," said Mar.

"Come on," said Zee. "You don't have to use it. Just carry it. I saw your ma pick it up to dust under it a million times. It's safe enough, I think."

Zee likely knew best, so Mar did pick up the gauntlet. There was no warning tingle in his fingertips. He put it in his pack along with a few cakes of raisins and half a loaf. On his way out he took a last look at the swan. It wouldn't be the end of the world if he missed one delivery. Grebe would just have to do his own work for once. Mar shut the door and locked it. At least—toys aside—he was leaving nobody behind. If the worst should happen, only Grebe would suffer for it, and that might make it worthwhile on its own.

Zee, Gan, and Mar filled their bottles at the well and set off. It was not a short way. Obsidian had sworn to refurbish and renovate the western courts when Ebony was defeated, but for now they had to scramble over collapsed masonry, skirt flooded courts, walk down galleries in the opposite direction from their goal, and eventually sleep in a corner of an old drawing room before coming out the next day into the open space around the Great Tower.

Here the four Passages converged: West with its high narrow walls, East with its great gate, North with its broad stairs going up, South with its broad stairs going down. The walls here were tall and strong. They were ancient work of the Ladies, unshakable. No ruin could claim them; where time gnawed the rest of the palace, here it only nibbled. In the center, the tower stretched its fingers up from the mounds and mounds of trash. The lantern tracks of the four passages arced overhead in steely threads, vanishing into the Great Tower's slick dark sides. The yellow eye of the Willows was gone from the topmost spire. A purple banner flew there instead: a new dynasty. And that was the cause of all this, for Obsidian and Ebony could not resist such a moment of vulnerability.

A single terrace was always kept clear before the tower's entrance;

everything else was smashed dishes, rotting food, shreds of table-cloths, buzzing flies, and bees. Having still to climb a ridge of garbage, the three men could not see the terrace yet, but a roar of voices told them to what use it was being put.

A few carrion birds were passing over on their way to Grey. Glancing up at them, Mar took out the gauntlet. Was it time? He wasn't desperate yet. As he wondered, a dragonfly landed on it. Hissing in surprise, he squashed the bug and had to wipe its guts off on an old napkin.

"What was that?" said Gan.

"Dragonfly," said Mar, disgustedly scrubbing.

"Dragonfly?" said Zee sharply. As he swiveled to look, another one whizzed toward Mar, touched the gauntlet for a second, and was up in the sky before he could react.

"Don't like that," said Gan.

"Why not?" said Mar.

"Spies of Red Tower," said Zee. "The Lady there sends 'em out, and they report back to her. If the damn bugs are here, Red will know about this, or might already. Come on."

He and Gan scrambled up the ridge. Mar followed.

Below them to the right was Her Ladyship's palanquin, tattered curtains swaying in the cold wind. Sprawled out of it was Her Ladyship. The great cuboid head was smashed open, its entrails spilling in all directions, and her yellow bird was perched between two fragments of head, snapping up bits of green and purple flesh and gulping them down. A fetid rotten-flower odor engulfed the smell of the garbage. Around her chipped, glassy body were the soldiers of Obsidian, lamenting. Around them were the soldiers of Ebony, jeering. The Ebony Lady herself stood farther on, her white face streaked with green and purple, her hands black with dust. She faced east, not looking at her sister.

Obsidian was supposed to be the savior of the western courts. She'd controlled the beekeepers, the ancient Passage, the rich Alchemists' Lane, and so much else. She had been a real Lady, not an upstart like Ebony: in her wars she had defeated Onyx, Jet, and so many others whose grip on their petty fiefs had seemed immoveable. She had been strong and fierce and wily. And—and if *she* was dead, what had Thrin died for?

It was a long while before Mar could tear his eyes from Her Ladyship's corpse and see what had distracted the victor. But then a dragonfly buzzed past his face, and he looked up. There in the gate of the East Passage was a sea of crimson.

Soldiers of Red, all in heavy armor, all carrying long glaives, all with swords belted around their waists. And above them, on many spindly scarlet legs, was the Red Lady. Her oblong body was ridged and plated like a Sparrow's, but prickly with thorns. Instead of a face, she had a ring of pale arms around a black, unblinking eye. Over her not-head floated a jeweled crown of golden spikes, revolving this way and that as if allowing its rubies a glimpse at the scene. Dragonflies surrounded her in an iridescent green haze. Dragonflies darted from her body, surveyed the armies, and returned to her. Dragonflies crawled in and out of her armor.

The crown turned its largest ruby to face Ebony. A low rumble shook the ground, rattling plates and cups: a Lady's voice. The army of Red, with an earsplitting yell, marched forward.

Ebony whirled back to her army, flaring her skirts out with her motion.

All of you are soldiers of Ebony now, she said. Form ranks. Defend the tower.

But, Mar thought. For what? Her Ladyship is dead.

Defend the tower, said Ebony with such force that glasses shattered. She scooped up a handful of tubes and vesicles from Obsidian's head and crammed them in her mouth. Already she was very tall, and as she crunched her way through the cartilage and jelly of her sister, she was growing taller.

The three scurried down to join the army. Its further ranks were already advancing, surging around Ebony toward the terrace. Zee and Gan followed. Mar hung back a moment to strap on the gauntlet. It was heavy and surprisingly warm, but that was probably because—

—Ebony's people reach the terrace the same time as Red's. They are no match for the tower of guard and war. Gan's neck is sliced open and he bleeds out on the pavement. Ashes fill the air. The tower burns. A hot green light flares behind Mar, to the west. After Gan falls, Mar manages to take down a soldier of Red: there is a little catch on the side of their armor, and if you can get to that, the breastplate opens wide enough to slip a knife in.

Mar shuddered. Had he been *daydreaming*? The gauntlet was heavy on his hand. His companions were rushing on; the enemy was rushing toward them. For Ebony, then, since there was nobody else. For Ebony.

A crimson blade slashed through Gan's neck. A Red soldier, wielding a bloodied sword, stamped toward Mar. There, on the side, the catch—Mar got his spear in, striking something soft within the red plating, and the soldier skidded to a halt and fell over, shuddering and twitching, wrenching the spear out of Mar's grasp.

Shivering, Mar knelt a moment between the dying soldier and Gan. The gauntlet was hot, melting a handprint into the frosty stones of the terrace. Gan seemed to be doubled: there was the dying Gan, and a dead Gan. They quickly merged, and Mar, split between *now* and *when,* could not even find it in him to grieve. All around, the terrace swarmed with ghosts: ashes of the burning tower, dragonflies on zigzag trajectories, soldiers falling even as their real bodies kept fighting. Acid knotted behind Mar's ribs, and he vomited.

Two dragonflies flickered over him and raced off to the right, back to the Red Lady. On spidery legs, she glided through her soldiers toward him. To the left, Ebony, with dark struts and spines poking through her skin, was striding into the field, trampling anyone who didn't leave fast enough. The yellow bird was perched on her shoulder, craning its long neck to peck at scraps in her black teeth.

—Give me that, the Ebony Lady says. And when Mar hesitates for slightly too long, she picks him up and gently twists off the gauntlet, and his hand with it.

She would be on him in moments. Fingers numb and shaky, he struggled with the gauntlet's straps. It stung and burned as if he was tearing at his own flesh. As she approached, it seemed to weigh less and less, as if drifting toward her, as if longing for her.

"You all right?" said Zee, doubling back with a stolen Red cudgel and a bloodied knife.

Give me that, said the Ebony Lady.

"Give Her Ladyship what she's asking for," said Zee. His voice wavered. "She don't ask twice."

"It won't come off!" Mar squealed, tugging at the straps.

The Lady's hand descended. Mar ran into the ranks of scarlet soldiers. With the gauntlet showing him what to do, he avoided their grasping arms and hissing blades. Behind him, the Lady roared in frustration, and pebbles danced on the ground.

But:

—Give me that, the Red Lady says. And the ring of soft white arms like rotting mushrooms scoops him up, and his guts splatter her troops.

Mar swerved to the left. The gate of the tower loomed there, taller than any Lady, ringed by carved spines of black stone like teeth in an eel's mouth. Still very far to run.

—The gate opens, releasing an army of Sparrows. Too many bodies: Mar does not make it inside before it closes. Red soldiers catch him, and bring him to their Lady.

Mar swerved back toward Ebony. She made a noise of triumph, but instead of returning to her, he skirted the edge of the terrace and plunged into the sea of garbage. Shards of dishes pricked and stabbed him, but he scrambled over a low ridge and into a barrel, bare hand slashed and bleeding, knees scraped up, lungs burning. A dragonfly perched on the rim of the barrel and regarded him with huge jewel-like eyes. Before he could stop it, the insect caromed away to join the cloud of shimmering green around the Red Lady.

Ebony hadn't seen him, and Red would not tip her hand too soon. And the Sparrows were about to emerge. He was safe for the moment. But not safe at all.

—Red has the better army. They have actual armor and weapons, and the soldiers of Ebony are underequipped, and half of them aren't really loyal to her anyway. They hate Red more, but that's not enough: when it becomes obvious that Red is winning, Obsidian's former army will simply turn tail, leaving Ebony's people and the Sparrows.

He looked away from the battlefield. The double vision was giving him a headache. There might be another way into the tower besides the gate. The garbage had certainly covered up many of the lower levels: there had to be a window he could slip through. The new ruler of the Great Tower might welcome his gift. And he and Zee could go home while they all fought it out.

Mar darted out of the barrel and crawled as quietly as possible toward the tower wall. He could see that he would make it, and he did, and flattened himself against it, crouching in the shelter of a figure whose arms supported the end of the West Passage lantern track and whose eyes were blinded by bird shit. No windows here, but if he could just climb up the carved body and onto the tracks, he could reach one.

—A hatch above him opens and a lantern emerges, flashing. It flies along the track and vanishes into the Passage. The Ebony Lady's head, now prickling with little turrets, turns to watch it go.

Mar crept along the feet of the statue, looking for handholds. A hatch above him opened. A lantern emerged, flashing. It flew along the track and dwindled into the Passage. The Ebony Lady's head, now prickling with little turrets, turned to watch it go. Her face flapped like a tattered banner.

—The hatch opens again and a second lantern races out. Ebony puts out a hand and tears the lantern from the track. The Sparrow inside squeals as Ebony gouges them out, tossing them away into the trash. Her aura rises, filling the valley of Black as she hurls the liquid light in a brilliant rain over her soldiers and those of Red. Everyone is still for a moment. Then, their bodies made malleable by the lantern, those whom the light has touched turn and fall upon the loyal of the army of Red, for the iron will of a Lady forces them. Zee is among them. Among the first to die.

Mar fell to his hands and knees, breath coming in scratchy puffs of steam. A lantern? Ebony would violate a *lantern*? And Zee—The world tottered around him, dizzy with shock.

His stinging cuts brought him back to reality. He squinted at the battlefield. The Lady was nowhere near the lantern track. He had a little time. And the gate was opening, letting out the river of battle-ready Sparrows.

—Mar climbs the left side of the statue. A little window with broken panes admits him to the interior of the tower. He stands in a gallery overlooking a vast hall where the Sparrows are still surging out. Halfway around the gallery is a Lady, who is named Elder, and who takes the gauntlet and his warning about the lanterns with equal gratitude. She tells him he will be Forty-Seven Grebe Occidentalis now. The Sparrows, helped a little by Ebony's forces, crack the Red soldiers open like nuts and fling out the frail people inside. They slice at the legs of the Red Lady, and she bellows in pain, and the dragon-flies swirl madly, biting and scratching at the Sparrows, but it does little good: their Lady falls like a tree, and the Sparrows hack at her arms and gouge out the bleeding rubies from her crown.

—And then the Sparrows take on Ebony. She is tougher, and it looks as if she will win. But then the Elder Lady emerges from the Great Tower, wielding thin blades in her many arms, and Ebony falls as well. The power of the Elder dynasty is assured. Mar and Zee head home.

He didn't dare to look farther. What might or might not happen—both were less important than Zee living through this battle. The gauntlet hissed and steamed. There might not be many visions left in it. And he had to start climbing *now*.

There in the trash before his face was a toy butterfly. Orpiment wings lined with lampblack, carved just a month ago in his little workshop. It hadn't been sitting here long. He glanced around. Scattered among the remains of food and dishes were other toys, most of them not his (there was the crudity of Grebe's hand, evident in the clumsy way he had carved a little figure of a Brother of Weavers). The toys were there, not in the nursery. Maybe they had never made it.

A waste. The food was one thing, though it rankled. But the love and care put into even just this one butterfly—for what?

Thrin and Gan and maybe Zee, and others whose names he didn't know—people had always died for Ladies. It was harsh, but it was always true. But they had accepted the gifts of their subjects with gratitude. The produce of the courts, the fabrics, the furniture, the toys, had always been taken with honor. This toy had been thrown out in the last two or three days. All that work for nothing. So what did it matter if he became Grebe? Elder would be no different.

Let the tower burn, or let it not burn. Either way, there was no longer any point in Mar or anyone he loved doing anything for the Ladies anymore. If he could get out of there with Zee—*without* surrendering the gauntlet to anyone—he would. And that meant stopping the next lantern. If he could get up to the hatch and wedge it shut in the next few minutes, all would be well.

Mar picked up a wooden alligator, a single solid piece perfect for jamming, and started climbing. The illusory ashes of the tower were like snow around him. How or why the Great Tower might burn was none of his concern. That was Ladies' business. Stop the lantern, save Zee, give nobody the advantage; that was all.

Oh, and go home.

He had nearly reached the rim of the hatch. The gauntlet seemed to have preferred his previous plan, for it was hot again, and very, very heavy. He could barely move his hand. He was stuck.

There was very little time before the next lantern. Ebony was almost in position. There on the battlefield, the soldier who would kill Zee was within striking distance. Mar's shoulders sagged. The brief flame of indignation was already burning itself out. You couldn't oppose the Ladies and the future all at once. If he could only distract Ebony and keep her from the lantern. The gauntlet was no help: as if it longed for a Lady's hand, it was keeping him from seeing anything at all.

A dragonfly landed beside him.

"Tell Her Ladyship she can have the gauntlet," he said. "But she has to come get it *now*."

It zipped away. A second later, the Red Lady's crown revolved to face him, and she charged toward the tower. Ebony rushed to intercept her. They collided and fell, breaking the lantern tracks. Mar lost his grip and plummeted.

—An upthrust length of the track impales him through the abdomen. Ebony tears at Red's legs and body. Red tears at Ebony. They roll away toward the South Passage; armies scatter at their approach. They topple down the steps out of sight. The Sparrows are left to quell this Ladyless incursion, which they do swiftly: the danger to the tower is not past. Though the Ladies may fight for days, whoever emerges from the Passage will try to regroup her army.

The track did not hurt so much, really. But the gauntlet burned. It must have wanted a different outcome. Mar chuckled hoarsely. Who didn't?

—A fading shadow of Zee clambers up a fallen wall and out of sight.

Wait—a fallen wall? Here in the center? Nothing falls here—

—A long shadowy mass breaks the unbreakable walls of Black, and fire rises from the tower, and—

His body slid down the twisted metal, coming to rest with his eyes facing west. He couldn't see whatever was happening/would happen on the battlefield. But at least nobody would get this miracle. Already it was smoldering. His vision narrowed until he saw only distant Grey, where birds wheeled around a huge dark form. Was it now or later? No way to know. The gauntlet burst into angry orange flames, crisping away into dark flakes caught by the wind. The last thing he saw was the West Passage filling with green and a great face opening in the sky. Birds cried out in greeting. And the tower's ashes fell around him.

book eight

yarrow & hawthorn

49. Hawthorn Meets Yarrow

Hawthorn walked most of the night, stopping for an hour or two of sleep in a deep crevice. Toward Grey, the earthquake damage was more and more severe: the walls had fissured like bread crust, and the floor of the Passage itself was scored and riven. She woke up to another tremor, and when she escaped the shivering wall, saw that the sun was just rising. From Black Tower, it shone down the Passage toward her even as the rest of the palace was dark. It illuminated the high, sheer face of the South Passage, and for one fearful moment Hawthorn wondered if the bridge over the river still stood.

Well, only one way to find out. She went on. The sound of the river chattering over stones and bones made her thirsty, but on no account would she drink from it. Leaving the food with Frin had been all right, but she could have taken at least a little water.

The Passage sloped down toward the river, where the pale bridge reached over the channel, laden with tilted houses. It seemed more or less unharmed, but at its head was a huge white shape, wearing a smaller pink shape like a hat. It blocked the bridge entirely. Could it be—yes, it *was* a hollowman, with three tents on its back: something she had only seen paintings of. It lay with both arms tucked under it, asleep—until Hawthorn's foot disturbed a pebble, and then the hollowman's great eyes opened slowly, and it chuckled inanely.

"What is it, Tertius?" said a sleepy voice from within the pink tent. Someone poked a head and shoulders out, clad in the shiny green garment of the Butlers Itinerant. He squinted at Hawthorn. "Well, what are you supposed to be, all aglow like a lantern?"

"I'm Hawthorn," she answered. "Can you move him, please? I'm trying to get to Grey."

"Hawthorn . . ." said the butler. He grinned. "Oi," he said over his shoulder into the smaller red tent. "One of yours is in the Passage."

"I have a very bad headache," said a proper, fractious voice that Hawthorn knew instantly. "If you could keep it down—"

"Come on out and say hello," said the butler. He put up his white hood and got to his feet, stretching in the cool winter sunrise.

The little girl in grey, the one who had shouted at him, given him candy, and stolen his book, emerged from the tent on her hands and knees. Girl no longer, apparently—she wore the wimple of the women. How much had Grey changed since Hawthorn had left?

Glaring down at her, the woman said, "Oh, it's you."

"It is," said Hawthorn. "Do you mind moving your hollowman?" Where would a woman of Grey even *get* a hollowman? She hadn't thought there were any around anymore.

The woman rubbed her temples with her fingers as if trying to smooth away her unpleasant expression. "Its name is Tertius."

That was exactly like a woman in grey. Insist on the rightness of little things, ignore the big picture.

"All right," said Hawthorn. "Do you mind moving Tertius? I'm trying to get to Grey, and it's blocking the bridge."

"Oh, I can give you a ride," said the butler. "I'm heading that way anyway. That's why Yarrow is here."

"Yarrow?" How had someone Hawthorn's own age ascended to the *motherhood* so quickly? Something horrible must have happened back home. Forgetting the hornet for a moment, Hawthorn cursed herself for not leaving the beekeepers sooner.

"Yes," said the mother, her tone daring Hawthorn to ask one more question. "And we were never properly introduced. Your name is?"

"Hawthorn."

Yarrow's tongue worked her left cheek as she squinted. Hawthorn took this for deep offense, since Yarrow should have confirmed her succession, but that was only part of the truth. Yarrow was suffering the effects of too much honey wine, and couldn't quite assemble the mildewed bits of her dampened intellect. And the sun was very bright.

"Indeed," she said. "And you're coming from—?" She nodded up the length of the Passage toward the sharp bulk of Black Tower, glowering and lamplit in the dawn.

"I am."

"Where the Lady confirmed you?" Yarrow meant to ask solely from curiosity, but her tone and expression had to fight their way out of her brain, and arrived in the open air tired and belligerent.

"That's correct. And the Beast is nearly here, so I need to go to Grey, get the steel, and fulfill my duty."

Hawthorn's impatience did her no favors with Yarrow, who, nevertheless, intended to be helpful, and tried to do so by saying, "Oh, the steel isn't in Grey."

That took Hawthorn aback. "Then where is it?"

"I've got it."

"*You've*—?" Why did the mother of Grey House have the steel? She must have taken it for protection when she left Grey, there being no other weapons in the tower except certain holy, rusting spears. The beekeepers had gone all the way there, been told it was missing, and ridden halfway back when they were attacked. They had died for nothing at all.

"I didn't take it," said Yarrow hastily. Her headache hadn't cleared, but she had learned in the last ten seconds how to adjust her life around it. "We came upon some beekeepers who had it. They must have stolen it, I don't know why. I was only taking it back to Grey. You can have it."

She moved stiffly into the tent—proudly, Hawthorn thought—and returned with the weapon. Its blade flashed in the morning light, the rich colors of its hilt aglow. The steel: unnamed, for it needed no name, gift of the Lady of Red, Hawthorn's heritage. She accepted it from Yarrow, expecting to feel a thrill of importance, a tingle of *rightness* from the blade as it came back to its proper home, but there was nothing, only a warm spot on the hilt where Yarrow's hand had been.

"And my book, too," said Hawthorn. Though she knew now that the beekeepers had succeeded in their mission, and the steel had not been lost to the maze around Black, the residue of her anger and grief clung to her, and she could not see past them.

"Book?" said Yarrow, in whose mind the little volume occupied barely a fraction of the space it took up in Hawthorn's. "Oh. Yes. Just a minute."

Again she went back to the tent. The butler had stood there the whole time, his eyes swiveling between them as they spoke, an expression of amusement on his face.

"My name is Three Peregrine Borealis," he said. "It's a pleasure to meet a friend of Yarrow's."

"We don't really know each other," said Hawthorn quickly.

Yarrow reappeared with *The Downfall of the Thistles* in her hand. A tiny, shabby book, it was the most beautiful thing Hawthorn had ever seen.

"I'm sorry," said Yarrow. "I truly did not mean to take it. But when you startled me, it just—I must have put it in my sleeve out of habit. I hope you haven't needed it."

"No," said Hawthorn, touching the cover lovingly. It blurred behind a mist of tears. "I haven't."

A crow cawed somewhere in the Passage. Peregrine seemed to take it as a sign, and went about rousing the hollowman.

"We must be off," he said. "I've many deliveries to make. Are you coming, Mistress Hawthorn?"

"No," said Hawthorn, not liking the sound of *many deliveries*. "I'll be all right."

The hollowman got up on its elbows, then rose to a standing position. As Yarrow was lifted into the air, she said, "I look forward to working with you, Hawthorn."

In spite of everything, Hawthorn remembered that this small woman was the same person who had given her candied angelica after her master's death. The only person, in fact, who had shown her any kindness in that horrible time.

"And I with you," said Hawthorn.

She put the book in her pack. When she opened the flap, Yarrow saw the fragments of the green mask, and her expression went very grim. But she said nothing.

The hollowman jolted away, rattling the contents of its stomach. Hawthorn followed, passing it about halfway over the bridge when it stopped and Peregrine knocked on someone's door. When she reached the far shore and looked back, Yarrow was watching her go.

Once free of the bridge, the Passage continued its course up the side of the canyon. Over the centuries, both Blue and Grey had built themselves out into overhanging ledges, but the Passage itself was clear, and carved a straight line through the rock. Seen from across the river, it looked like a near-vertical staircase, but when Hawthorn reached its foot, she saw that it actually was no worse than some of the stairs inside Black Tower. In fact, it was a good deal broader, and probably much safer at the moment.

Deep landings broke the stairs at regular intervals. After a few minutes of climbing, she was tired, but committed herself to resting only every other landing. Since there were ten of them, that gave her five rests. When she sat for the first one, she took out *Downfall* and opened it to a random point. Old Hawthorn's familiar spidery handwriting rambled down the page.

> *ask re: story variant*
> *Age? Ylw twr archives: earliest mnscrpt 4000 years*
> *very close now, I feel it. M. Yarrow holds key, the old fool*

What had she been investigating? Old Hawthorn had made several trips to other tower archives, and she had never taken her apprentice. She had only said that she was visiting friends. Bewildered and a bit hurt, Hawthorn closed the book, stood up sooner than she'd meant to, and went on climbing.

50. Hawthorn Goes Home

igh winds had piled the snow against some walls and roofs and scoured it off others. The cold, bright calm of the palace lowlands was a thing of the past. Restless air whipped snow around Hawthorn as she walked to the center of Grey; the still sky above was white and heavy with more of the stuff. A constant unsteady thrum shook the flagstones, like the stirrings of a restless hand clasped within her own. Though the only sound was shifting snow, she found herself covering her ears as if against some great roar; though there was nothing about except birds, she found herself running and darting from shelter to shelter as if pursued.

Grey Tower, looking small, old, and hunched after the glistening might of Black, peered at her above the rooftops. Its crown of turrets was free of snow and crowded with quiet birds. Its dark windows were like hawk's eyes. She avoided meeting their gaze. The tower, in whose shadow she lived and to whose protection she was sworn, now seemed wary of her.

The Beast, whom we have looked in on now and again, was by this point very near the surface. As it came closer, its form shifted and settled. No longer a terrifying mass of unknown qualities, it had taken on attributes we might recognize: an eyeishness, a skinlikeness, a clawishness, an unfurling of membranes, a pulse like a heartbeat, if the blood performed galliards. One might sense a suggestion of flames, a rustle of great wings, a sort of taffeta sheen, a confectioner's decorative sense evidenced in the placement of long delicate spines; the Beast might pass equally as a subtlety at the banquet tables of the apocalypse, or as a costume at a masque where every player represents three simultaneous crimes. Now enters *Madame Murder,* all blood and bone, who is also *Sir Larceny,* all grasping hands and covetous eyes, who is also *Treachery,* all knives and masks.

Just beneath the skin of earth, the Beast's foremost parts were boiling upward. It sensed the nearness of its birth. The closer it came to air, light, life, potatoes, scissors, the less it remembered of itself. I am here to feed, it said to itself. Its thoughts were slowed syrup-like by the cold until they were something comprehensible.

Again and again I am banished. Again and again I am brought back. I would like to awaken and not hunger. I would like to uncoil in the sunlight and not die. Again and again and again and again. They will pay. This time they will pay.

It had thought the same things before, and never made good on them.

This same sense of injustice curdled Hawthorn's thoughts as she finally entered the great courtyard at the foot of the tower. The mother had kept many things from her, and the mother before had kept many things from Old Hawthorn. *M. Yarrow holds the key.* Every Yarrow was the same. They would pay, too. Though in Hawthorn's case, making them pay involved more "deliberately coughing during important rites" and less "ravaging the palace."

So close to Grey Tower, the ground was shuddering. It made a faint rumble just on the edge of hearing. The vibration turned Hawthorn's bones loose and warm.

Going along the eastern side of the house—through the open kitchen door came the sound of dishes rattling on their shelves—she reached the low archway leading to the Court of the Guardians. Inside the court the little door of Old Hawthorn's room was still shut tight, just as she had left it months ago. Snow lined three of the walls, but the door was mostly free of it, and she unlocked it and went in.

It still smelled of the women's cleaning, their herbs and lemons. It also smelled of mildew, for the floors and walls were damp. But beneath all that was the musty bookish smell of Old Hawthorn herself. Hawthorn climbed onto the old woman's bed and drew her knees up to her chest.

For a moment she let her mind drift on seas of grief. Her limbs felt again the paralyzing despair that had kept her sitting outside while the women went about their rituals. *Who will do it?* Old Yarrow and Arnica had asked each other, and the same question had been on everyone's mind. *Who will deliver us from the Beast? That pale, weedy apprentice?*

Under their scrutiny and the weight of her own loss, she'd been able to do nothing more than sit. Well, now there was a new Hawthorn—and she did not feel up to it any more than her old self had.

If only Frin were there. His unwavering support had meant so much. But no: he would have been in grave danger. *I left him for a reason*, she reminded herself.

It was time to prepare. Hawthorn knew the rules of engagement: *the Beast shall issue forth from the mouth of the tower* and all that. It would be compelled down the West Passage—whether the compulsion came from its own nature or from some ancient virtue of the Passage, nobody knew—and there it must be vanquished. If you issued a challenge, it would turn to face you. *There is a yellow spot upon its hide where its armor is weakest.* Not always on the hide. Once a wisp of yellow cloud (by which the first Guardian defeated it), once a yellow hair (by which a Bellflower Guardian defeated it), once a yellow eye (by which the penultimate Lady of Grey defeated it). That much Hawthorn had read.

But Old Hawthorn had learned more. And, paper being scarce in Grey, had written it in *The Downfall of the Thistles*. If she had found a way to defeat the Beast forever, Hawthorn could use it, end the eternal threat, fulfill her duty in the most thorough way possible: protector of Grey Tower, vanquisher of the eternal foe.

This rush of heroism lasted about five minutes into *Downfall*. Old Hawthorn's notes, compiled over forty or fifty years, were chaotic, overwritten, crossed out and scrawled back in, and mixed in with complaints about the women in grey. Then one sentence jumped out at her apprentice.

> *Rook is not what they seem*

So Old Hawthorn had not trusted the Librarian. She had been wise, of course.

> *Six Sisters—rhyme*
> *bones of towers—Bk/Bl/Rd/Yw all too large to be built*
> *Song*

This last was circled. Hawthorn knew the Six Sisters—just a silly clapping game for children. But what song?

Five above, one below.
Name in painted room: EPITAPH
Ref. doctors' library in the Archives. Ladies and their origin.

She flipped to the endpapers, which the original scribe had left blank, but which Old Hawthorn had filled over the years with tiny, dense writing.

Palace: founded by five sisters the five Rose sisters Grey eldest, Black Blue Red Yellow
Variant story (suppressed): a six sister, no name
Where is she then?
Black builds her tower after the first recorded encounter with Beast. Grey Lady sings
Blue builds her tower after second encounter. Grey Lady sings
ROSE ERA ENDS
Guardians taught means of dispatching Beast. Two more encounters: no Ladies involved
Grey Lady teaches her women the song. a miracle. ASK YARROW
One more: Red Rose builds her tower. song
Another: Yellow Rose builds her tower. song
Guardians are given steel. STEEL IS MEANINGLESS.
Grey Lady is killed.
No new towers since
Why Grey the smallest tower? BUILT BY HANDS
Records/Rook mention wish. Hold Beast at bay and demand a boon.
This is how the palace is built. Time after time the Beast returns. Ladies and women and Hawthorns force it into submission. It grants a wish. It is killed. Repeat. Repeat. This is the palace. The many deaths of the sixth sister.
miracles fade. not all miracles?
ASK YARROW
Yarrow wont tell. Arnica unhelpful. Nobody else knows song. The Beast won't grant wish unless soothed. Wish won't be fulfilled until Beast is dead. ASK Y AGAIN

The rest was blank.
There by Old Hawthorn's bed was the poem that had come from

Blue on the day she was taken ill. Five sisters. And—a sixth, green, entangled with the whole page. Exactly so had some ancient illuminator drawn it, someone in the first days of the palace. Someone who knew the truth.

And there was a package from Yellow. A book from the library there. It had arrived since Old Hawthorn's death—she must have requested it. *A History of the Yellow Sister.* There again, as in the book Frin had given him, was a picture of Citrine pulling people from the ground. But this was a woodcut, not an illumination, and she wondered at the artist's choices, for instead of directly from the earth, Citrine was removing people from great split-open fruits, plucked from a withering tree.

And from her mouth came a scroll, and on the scroll was written in an ancient script, *Return what you have taken.* The text said only that it was a copy of an original, once kept in Yellow Tower, now lost.

Lost. Everything was lost. Wave after wave of generations had eroded the truth down to its hardest stubs, and even those threatened to vanish entirely. Ask Yarrow. Yes, she would.

A Question Posed by the Tutors in Grey House
(But as the Tutors Are Dead, It Is Forgotten):
What Is the True Name of Grey Tower?

So Eglantine XXV asked of his apprentice, and the apprentice answered *It is the Sixth Door,* and Eglantine was pleased.

51. Yarrow and Peregrine Have a Chat; They Are Joined by Others

Tertius ambled along the bridge. For some reason, many people here had privileges. Not just wine, but a honey-cake for a sullen woman in a half-ruined tower, a pouch of red stones for a half-ruined man in a sullen house, and so on. And every one had their ritual greeting and presentation, delivered in dialogue with Peregrine, to varying degrees of enthusiasm.

But in between these, Yarrow and Peregrine got to talk. It was nice just *talking* to someone. No lessons to be learned, no expectations, just words allowed to be words. The butler had seen the entire palace, except Grey itself, and knew so many people by name that Yarrow wondered (but did not ask) how he managed to apply the right name to the right person. (Perhaps it was like remembering herbs.) He had been to Yellow often, of course, but he had also seen the grand decaying hulk of the Carnelian Room; he had taken in the view from the Eightfold Wall; he had dined with the Order of Botanists in their aerie. And he had seen the sea.

"What's it like?" said Yarrow eagerly. "Is it really infinite water?"

Peregrine shrugged. "From the shore you can only glimpse a little of it. Then if you go up Red to the Star Chamber you can see that the water is a long blue finger touching the palace. Scholars call it a bay. But it's just a finger of the hand that's the wide sea that nobody knows the end of. But of course, just because nobody knows the end doesn't mean there isn't one."

"And that's where ships come in."

"Yes, from the outer fiefs, where they speak strange and dress stranger. Incense comes from there, and fruit that needs richer soil than the palace provides. I've never been that far myself. Nobody leaves here that I ever heard of. Only ships from the fiefs come and go, and their sailors make a sign with their hands when they step onto the docks."

"Are there more people in the world besides us?" said Yarrow. The question was strange in her mouth. For all she knew, the palace was the world: a stage for which the sea and mountains were a bit of backdrop. But Arnica believed there was a wider world. It was bewildering to think so. Some place far away from the palace, farther even than the fiefs, who, after all, belonged to the palace, tied to it by a long loop of the outermost wall.

"Nobody knows," Peregrine said with a shrug. "Doesn't much matter, does it?"

In a sense, he was right. The palace was self-sufficient. Nobody came and nobody went. It was what it was; the existence of anything else had no bearing on that.

But to think of the palace, fading day by day even before the Beast's imminent arrival—to think of it destroyed, unremembered and unmourned, *that* was unbearable. She said as much to Peregrine, who laughed.

"What a perfect Mother of Grey you are," he said. "To think of the world in terms of whether it'll mourn us. Now, Yarrow, I'm about to speak a piece of heresy, and I wouldn't dare except that we're good friends. It would not be a tragedy for the palace to end. It would not be sad for us to pass away unremembered. What would their memorial to us read? Here Lies Dust."

"Things have happened here!" said Yarrow. "The stories, the songs. Era after era of people living and dying, the Ladies, all the struggles and deeds—those are us. They make us up. Wouldn't it be horrible for that to vanish? We're not what we once were, but we once—we once were something."

Peregrine cocked his head and squinted one eye. "We were something because we tell ourselves we were. But we can't even agree on *what* we were. Do you know what happened on, say, the Night of Bones?"

Yarrow opened her mouth to say *Yes, of course,* but then she remembered that the tale Old Yarrow had told her was just one of eighty-five.

"Neither do I," said Peregrine, when she was left silent. "I joined the

Butlers to travel and hear stories, and all the stories I heard pointed their finger at another story and said *That's a lie*. So now I hear them, but I don't believe them."

"To *travel*?" said Yarrow. Getting her to leave Grey had taken a threat to her very existence, and even then it was a reluctant choice. Every step out of Grey had brought some new horror. Even after her conversation with Arnica, it was impossible to imagine someone doing it willingly.

Peregrine laughed. "Well, also I wanted to stay a man. If I'd completed my apprenticeship to the Master of Privileges I'd've been moved to womanhood, and I didn't want that."

That made sense, at least. These switches were not uncommon. Ban had been tithed to the girls in grey partly because if she'd stayed with her parents, she would grow up to be a boy.

"Surely," Yarrow said, returning to the more interesting topic, "surely the different tellings of a story have some threads in common."

"They do, but I've not got so much time on my hands that I can sort them all to find the truest." He took another handful of leaves to chew. "Think: our stories are about ourselves. That's why we care about them. That's how we *understand* them. If we vanish, who will be left to understand and care?"

The earth itself will remember us, Yarrow wanted to say. We've written our story on it with walls and towers.

But that was a glib response, irrelevant and untrue.

"They may not understand," she said, "but if the worst happens—if someone else finds our ruins, they *will* care."

Peregrine shrugged.

The sun was near the zenith when Tertius came to the last house on the bridge, where a woman was owed a swatch of yellow flannel. While she and Peregrine transacted their business, a crash got Yarrow's attention. At the head of the bridge, back the way they had come, a contraption of glass and steel had just fallen over: a lantern. A small person was struggling out of it.

Yarrow shimmied down the rope ladder and ran to help. The person had rabbit ears and wore an undyed linen cotehardie with a black hood: exactly like the dead beekeepers from the Passage. Perhaps this was a survivor. They certainly looked beat-up enough for it.

"I'm trying to find Hawthorn," they said. "How do you get to Grey?"

"Hush a moment," said Yarrow. Their arm was sprained or something—oh for an apothecary!—but she had nothing to immobilize it with, so she unpinned her wimple and tied it into a sling. Cold air filtered through her bound-back hair, and her free twigs curled up toward the wintry sun.

"Hawthorn?" said the rabbit-eared person, when she finished.

"Hawthorn?" said Yarrow. "I saw her this morning. As for Grey, well, I'm headed there myself but I couldn't possibly tell you the way. Just come with us."

And so Frin was added to Tertius's passengers. As the hollowman climbed slowly up the West Passage stairs, he told Yarrow much of what had transpired: Hawthorn's stay with the beekeepers, the trek through Black, the downfall of Willow. Yarrow was shocked. Peregrine took it in stride.

"It was just a matter of time, little Mother," he said in response to her surprised questions. "The fall of a dynasty always starts with small wars around the base of the tower. We could all see it coming. If not in our lifetimes, then in the lifetimes of our children."

Yarrow was not reassured. The central authority of the palace, lost or at best weakened, right in a time of emergency? When the Beast came, whatever happened next was up to the people of Grey. As it had always been. Only now it was very hard to be confident about that. They stood alone. Hawthorn was young and inexperienced, Yarrow herself scarcely less so. And the people of Grey, who were they? Two girls, an old servant, some half-starved farmers and craftspeople. She thought obscurely of the apes scattered throughout Yellow, munching butterflies, the flower on the train, the frogs in their pools, Roe's body in its poor grave of twigs, and the scattered Ladyless people of Blue. She thought of Peregrine, solid and green beside her, tendons shifting in his neck as he turned to spit into the snow, and Frin, exhausted, ragged, determined. Fragile, all of them, compared to this great evil, this Lady-eater. She twined her fingers together, sick with fear. Grey was no bulwark for these people now.

But Hawthorn might be wrong. The earth had quaked before. The fighting around Black might have broken the wheel. It could be any number of things. She recited the parts of birthwort to herself. By the time she got to the calyx, she was calmer. It might still be all right.

Tertius crested the canyon wall, and there before her was the small, homely tower. After the dreadful sickness of Yellow and the hideous emptiness of Blue, Grey was warm and welcoming, despite the snow and wind. There was still a ways to go, and the snow had destroyed so much, but Yarrow was *home*.

Then there, in the middle of the Passage, was Hawthorn. She had changed into the green, sleeved overgown of the Guardians, she carried the steel, and she looked very, very angry.

"What's the song?" she said. "Tell me about the song!"

52. Yarrow and Hawthorn and Frin and Peregrine All Have a Chat and the Beast Sees the Light

Tertius came to a languid stop before Hawthorn and giggled.

"What song?" said Yarrow.

"I don't know," said Hawthorn. "Old Yarrow knew it. My master wanted it. You *must* have it."

"It could be *anything*," said Yarrow. "I know a lot of songs."

Hawthorn held up the tiny book that Yarrow had been carrying. "In here. She talks about a song the women in grey know. It calms the Beast. If the Beast is calm, I get a wish."

"I don't know a song for the Beast."

Hawthorn bit her lip. Mentioning Old Hawthorn's notion of the sixth sister would—well, it would be better if an official of Black Tower was not there to hear it. "Can we talk in private?"

Yarrow glanced at Peregrine. "I would rather not."

The earth vibrated. Weakened by snow, a nearby roof caved in.

"Fine," said Hawthorn. "Then it's *your* fault if—"

"Hawthorn," said Frin, peering over the side of Tertius. "It's all right. Just say whatever you have to say."

Frin? Hawthorn's pale skin turned even paler, seized by a fear so intense it hurt. Yarrow wondered at the significance of this.

"What are you doing here?" she said. "You were supposed to—you should have stayed behind."

"I'm your squire," said Frin stolidly. "Even if you wanted me to stay, I couldn't."

Hawthorn sighed and looked at Yarrow. "My master thought the

Beast might be—might be one of the Ladies. The sixth sister, if that means anything to you."

"That's a game," said Yarrow. "A child's rhyme." But she remembered Old Yarrow mentioning a sixth and fretting over the mistake. If it was a mistake.

"It's not just that." Hawthorn flipped through the book. "It crops up in old stories and songs from all over the palace. Hidden there, just waiting for someone to make the connection. Look. Six stones stand in the Garden of the Ladies in Blue. The song they sing in Yellow, *There were six sisters to cross the river.*"

"*Hey nonny nonny,*" said Yarrow, more to herself than anyone else. Frin climbed down from Tertius and went to stand near Hawthorn.

"Yes, exactly. The five sisters were six. But they did something to the last one. Or something happened to her. *She fell down a very long way.*"

"Not all sisters are *the* sisters, Guardian," said Peregrine.

"But it's what my master thought. Don't you see what that means? The Beast is one of the sisters; the sisters are the Ladies, and we know—" Hawthorn gulped. "We know how to kill Ladies."

If all eighty-five tellings of the Night of Bones agreed on one thing, it agreed on that: nobody agreed on the hand that wielded it, but the steel had done it.

"We do," said Yarrow quietly. Hawthorn barely even heard her.

"So you see," Hawthorn said. "You must know something. The Yarrows have held some crucial knowledge all these centuries. My master knew they had it, but not what it was. There must be a part of the women's lore that would help. It might be hidden. It might seem like something else, a story, a rhyme. You have all those litanies, don't you?"

"What you're asking," said Yarrow slowly, "is—is not easy."

"I know that," said Hawthorn impatiently.

She did not. For Hawthorn, whose knowledge came from books that anyone was allowed to read, it was impossible to grasp the nature of her request. The Mothers' stories were, as the Grey Lady had always intended, written in the twists of Yarrow's nerves and bound in the pulse of her blood. Yarrow, all Yarrows, were books who could choose to be read. And they were all of them taught to choose otherwise.

By now we have all guessed that Hawthorn needed the Lullaby of Reeds. Even Yarrow knew that. But to sing it to the Yellow Lady and her daughter was one thing. That was, more or less, its proper use. To hand it over to a Guardian—

"There is a song," said Yarrow heavily. Hawthorn's face lighted up. "It is sung to the Ladies to soothe them." Hawthorn opened the book to the end and took up a pencil. "But I can't give it to you."

"Why not?" said Hawthorn fiercely.

"It's only sung to Ladies," said Yarrow. "And only the women know it. Even we are barely ever permitted to sing the full melody. And we certainly don't teach it to outsiders."

"*Outsiders?*" Hawthorn slammed the book shut. "I was born in Grey. And I need this song to save it."

"You don't know that," said Yarrow. Her face was very calm as she folded her hands into her sleeves. How dare a Guardian demand anything from her? Especially one who had circumvented *every* proper channel to become one! "The Beast is the Beast. You and your master may think one thing. You may even be right. But there are limits—"

"Fuck the limits," said Hawthorn. She took a step forward so ferociously that Tertius shuffled back, jolting its three passengers. "This could save us all. Why can't you understand that?"

"Is there no boundary you won't cross?" said Yarrow. "Is there *nothing* you hold sacred?" Her voice had risen to a shout, and she broke off, surprised to hear that sound from her own mouth.

"Safety," said Frin. "She holds safety sacred."

Everyone looked at him.

In the sudden silence, the vibration of the earth became much more apparent. They were so accustomed to the tremors that its faint beginning hadn't registered. But now the rumble was all about them. The flagstones rattled. Snow slid from the rooftops. Upon the ridgepoles and gargoyles, birds shifted and stirred their wings. Stronger and stronger, the quake went on.

"Hawthorn," said Yarrow. "I—"

Then the Beast came.

All of Grey Tower shuddered. Slates fell from its turrets. In the windows, a harsh green light sparked and glared, and a halo of green flared about its summit. With a flash of sickening insight, Yarrow understood why the tower was hollow.

Things boiled out of its top. Claws, wings, eyes, tentacles, long hairs like a cat's whiskers. All of it rustled like so many silk gowns. Aside from the earthquake and the collapse of masonry, there was no other sound.

Six or seven clawed hands latched on to the rim of the tower. The rest of the Beast unfurled in great loops, eyes opening, wings shaking out to their full extent, on and on. Red gashes appeared in its sides, and for a moment Hawthorn thought, It's already wounded, it's already weak. But they gaped, showing dark teeth, and she saw how wrong she was. The whole thing was covered in mouths. Then at last—there—a yellow scale. As soon as she saw it, the rotating mass of the creature turned it away, but she knew it was there, the Beast's weakness.

It kept coming. Under its claws, Grey Tower's parapet was splintering. By now, the Beast reached hundreds of fathoms into the sky: the tower was like a vase holding a too-big bouquet. Winter had broken like a fever: the sun shone hotly and the snow was melting. The Beast's eyes opened and turned their fierce emerald gaze on the palace, where they caught sight of Black Tower, dark in the bright sunlight.

With a roar that silenced all else, the Beast dove from Grey Tower and whipped its vast bulk down the West Passage, straight toward the hollowman.

A Story Told by the Tutors in Grey House
(But as the Tutors Are Dead, It Is Forgotten):
The First Walls, and How They Came to Be

The walls were the first recorded miracle. After Grey Tower had been built among the briars, the Beast rose and assailed it, and burned the briars, and the river took a new course in the riven earth. The sisters put down the Beast with spear and song and compelled from it one wish, and the Beast curled itself about the tower and went to sleep. When the sun rose, the Beast had become the walls of the palace.

Where the Beast's forelegs had been was the East Gate. Where the Beast's hindlegs had been was the West Gate. Where the Beast's jaws had been was the North Gate. Where its many eyes had been were the watchtowers upon the walls. No join or seam was to be seen along all the length of the walls, only smooth stone. Inside, where the Beast's veins and guts had been, were passageways and storerooms and living quarters, where for centuries the people of the Red Lady mounted their ceaseless guard.

Those who have traveled to the outer walls say that they are warm even in winter. Snow does not cling to them. To pass through the gates takes so long that the shape of one's shadow changes between going in and coming out. They have never been breached.

53. There Is a Measure of Danger

The birds took wing and swirled around it as it came, crying out as if in welcome. Its movements were chaotic, unsure, like a newborn. Walls toppled and fell at its approach. Its rightmost tail swept away the ancient Maids' Chapel. Its claws tore wounds in the sides of the Passage, and rooms spilled forth furniture, treasures, miracles, and people as if they were the seeds of poppy pods. Fire spurted from its mouths and angry columns of smoke roiled up like lesser beasts. The cloisters of Grey burned.

Hawthorn flung herself into a little alcove in the wall, pulling Frin after her. The Beast's shadow fell over the faces of the hollowman's two passengers. The butler caught a tress of the hollowman's golden hair and looped it around Yarrow. He reached for another.

"Sing to it!" Hawthorn shouted at Yarrow. "Sing!"

The Beast was upon them—then, miraculously, past them. Bunching itself together like a cat, it leapt up and spread its wings to fly over the river. Birds fluttered around, behind, ahead of the Beast, as if escorting it. As it jumped, one of its tails caught Tertius's arm and hurled the hollowman down the stairs. For one weightless moment Tertius hung in the air, tent flaps billowing like wings, and it chuckled. Then, turning end over end, it fell. Hawthorn heard it hit the first landing, but the Beast had touched down in Blue, and the noise of its going drowned out everything else.

The earth rocked under its feet, and Blue Tower tottered. A section of its north face fell away. The great dome, unbalanced, fell with a thunderous rumble, crushing the terraces with their dry trees. White plaster dust boiled up from trampled buildings as the Beast wound toward Black.

Failure, already. She could not chase it, not quickly enough. Even in that deadly urgent moment, she almost laughed at the thought of herself, tiny, striding after the monster. If only she could draw it back to Grey.

In the wreckage of the landing, Tertius righted itself. Tangled in coarse hair, Yarrow came up with it. The platform was empty. The tents were shreds of color at which the river greedily nibbled. The cargoes of wine and delicacies were scattered; amid the smoke, a delicious aroma was rising. And Peregrine—where was Peregrine?

A patch of iridescence caught her eye amid the rocks. It was not moving. He had been flung clear, broken—there was the mellified man, though. She got herself out of the hair and climbed down. She could not run to Peregrine; the rocks were treacherous. As she soon saw, crawling and slipping toward him and skinning her knees, it would have made no difference if she'd run. A bottle's broken neck had stabbed him in the gut. There were angles to his limbs that didn't belong there. His warm skin had gone ashy and clammy.

"I don't know what the women do for a Butler Itinerant," he said hoarsely. "But do it for me."

"I will," she said. She put her hand on his heart. The beat was weak and irregular. Mixed with the sweetness of wine and fruit was the harsh smell of blood. Little channels of the river ran under his body, carrying away the redness to wherever the river went. The sea, and beyond.

"Tertius," said Peregrine. Hearing its name, the hollowman padded over. Its pale flesh was not visibly wounded, only dirty. "Yarrow, the Mother of Grey House, is your rider now. Obey her."

"Obey," said the hollowman. Its low voice rattled the stones.

The Beast roared. Its attention had turned back to Grey. Hawthorn and Frin were up there, defenseless. Yarrow had to sing.

"We had fun," she said. "Didn't we?"

"We did," said Peregrine.

Yarrow kissed his forehead and vaulted up the ladder to Tertius's back. "Climb," she said.

Peregrine watched the hollowman swing up the canyon wall, grappling with projecting rocks until it reached the bridge. Far, far above, the sky was full of black smoke and ash. He could taste it falling. The walls of Grey were crumbling, melting away like snow in summer.

Great chunks of masonry plummeted to the canyon floor, splashing in the river, showering Peregrine with water and mud.

He had never heard the frogs' lament. But amid the chattering water and the cool earthy smells of mud and reed, he would have understood it. There was a reddish vulture in the sky, circling in the clean air left by the Beast's passage, and beyond it nothing but blue. And as the smoke closed off the sky again and a pillar from some forgotten room fell toward him, he slipped away with the river water, sailing away to the sea.

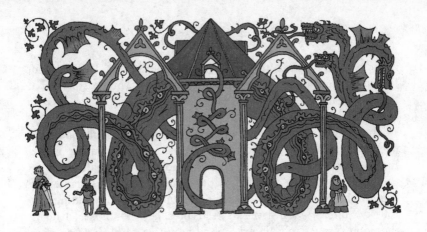

54. Many Things Happen More or Less at Once

Hawthorn poked her head out into the Passage. Blue was lost in smoke; the pinnacles of Black foundered in it, and now the wind changed so that the burning of Grey hid everything up to the edge of the stairs. The air was choking with fumes; the palace was an old, dry tinderbox. There were cries, confusion, and the shuddering booms of the Beast's rampage. It had to have reached Black by now. She hoped Elder was able to do something, hold her own, even just *survive*. In the meantime, Hawthorn might have failed, but she would never give up. There might be a way to get the Beast's attention. The thing might respond to a challenge. She'd need to be visible for that.

"Come on," she said. "If we get to the tower—"

Over the thick smell of smoke, she caught a whiff of something sweet.

Frin stood amid the torn-up paving stones. He had uncorked the vial of honey and was staring at it as if gathering his courage. He met Hawthorn's eyes.

"Don't," she said. "Not now. Just *run*."

"I'm here to protect you," said Frin, and he put the vial to his lips.

The Beast roared again. The wind shifted. Out of the wreck of Blue, a head emerged. Its jaws worked upon dangling red legs. Wide wet nostrils opened. Their snuffling was audible even across the river. A set of eyes followed, then narrowed, and Hawthorn knew instantly that it was looking at *them*.

"It smells the honey!" she said. "Put it away! *Put it away!*"

But Frin had already drunk some and corked the vial. His eyes rolled back in his skull, replaced by a feral golden light. He collapsed, thrashing, cold flames running along his veins. The Beast coiled at the edge of the South Passage, ready to spring.

"Frin!" Hawthorn shouted. *"Frin!"*

The flames became arcs of light, whipping out of Frin's body and back in again. They crackled with thorns, forming and dissolving. Bones twitched and worked beneath his clothes. He screamed.

The shadow of the Beast fell over them both, and Frin became very bright. The colossal body was springing up and up, unwinding into the sky from across the river. Its heads breached the smoke, letting in the noon sun. Parrots zipped around it, crying garbled words, their feathers flickering in the light. A dragonfly landed on Frin's back and was absorbed. Green chitin began to spread across his shoulder blades. One of Frin's arms seized on the shadow and darkened, lengthened, becoming a long, ornamented spire of jet. His cries and thrashing eased. Eyes aglow, he looked at Hawthorn in triumph. And the endless leap of the Beast ended.

Tertius wheeled up over the head of the stairs just as the Beast dove for the floor of the Passage. The Beast squealed and arched over the hollowman, but could not stop, and tumbled heads over tails over eyes down the Passage toward Grey Tower. In the confusion was a faint cry. The wind shifted the smoke, and Yarrow saw Hawthorn stagger out from shelter and kneel over Frin's body.

"Oh my *North*," she gasped, and let down the ladder.

A spar of rock had caught Frin across the abdomen, shattering his ribs and crushing everything within. His eyes fluttered open, he saw the look on Hawthorn's face, and he tried to prop himself up on his elbows. His hands gripped uselessly at the stone and slid back to the ground just as she reached him.

"Can you," said Hawthorn. "Frin, I . . ."

She put her hands on his cheeks. He laid his hands over hers. He wasn't breathing. A prickly warmth shuddered through his veins. Thorns burst through his skin and crumbled into fine black ash. His ribs were half-fused to the stone. In his blood there was a fading glow. It must have been the honey. Powerful—powerful enough?

No. His hands dropped.

"You shouldn't have taken it," said Hawthorn. Her voice cracked on the last syllables. "If anyone—It was—*I'm* here to protect *you*."

Frin smiled faintly and shook his head. He drew half a choking breath. His tongue began to form a sound. The sound never came.

Instead, Frin drew Hawthorn's hand to the onyx vial where it rested on his chest. His heartbeat lightly brushed her palm, like the wing of an insect flicking past on a summer night. Then stillness.

I don't know what to do, Yarrow thought. I don't know how to help. I don't know what they were.

Frin looked very small. One of Yarrow's hands reached out to Hawthorn, brushed her dirty shoulder, and curled back.

"I'm sorry," Yarrow whispered.

Hawthorn tenderly lifted the little amulet from the body. She settled it around her neck and raised her eyes to the chaos of the palace.

Blue was shattered, the tower smoking. Black had lost at least one proud arm. The Beast, caught in rubble, writhed among the ruins of Grey, breaking its way toward them again. A Guardian protects. This Guardian has failed in her duty. They faced the end. Hawthorn took the vial from Frin's nerveless hand.

"There's only one thing to do," Hawthorn said, not to Yarrow, not caring if Yarrow heard. There was a little left in the vial. Perhaps not enough. Her arm was broken, or at least useless, and she held out the vial to Yarrow for help. Yarrow opened it and drew in a breath of amazement at the smell.

Hawthorn drank, and heat thrummed through every fiber of her muscles, setting her marrow aflame, throwing new and alarming colors into her eyes. But it was not quite enough: already she felt the dose subsiding.

Far away, the Beast roared again and righted itself. Its heads were combining and fusing, eyes coming together like drops of oil. Now it was like a great three-headed serpent lined with many wings.

As it plunged toward them, Hawthorn leaned over Frin and kissed him deeply. He had not quite swallowed all the honey. She only got a little, but it tipped the scales of her being. Light and heat overtook her, washing out his face. Then something smashed the back of her head and everything went dark.

Yarrow had dodged into an empty doorway as the Beast attacked a second time. As before, its approach was overeager, and its own fury swept it over the canyon wall and down toward the bridge. After it passed, Yarrow peered out. Where was Hawthorn?

There, several feet away at the foot of a statue of the Grey Lady. Hawthorn lay on her side, twisted, with a gash down the center of her face. Even from a distance, her skull looked wrong. Flickers of light were running along her veins and fizzing in her wounds.

She was still alive. Yarrow could see that much. But it was just as obvious that Hawthorn did not have much time. Yarrow ran to her and dragged her behind the statue. No time to be concerned about further injury. From her pack she drew the shattered, sweet remains of the crock, where one last piece of mellified man stuck to shards of pottery. Quickly she picked off the broken pieces and popped the chunk of meat into Hawthorn's mouth. Hawthorn began to thrash.

Down in the South Passage, the Beast's voice sounded again. The bones of the palace rattled. Claws as big as turrets gripped the head of the stairs.

Leaving her pack beside Hawthorn's, Yarrow walked out onto the scarred floor of the West Passage and stood in the center. Her ears rang. The claws tightened. The huge, maddening shape of the Beast rose before her, and rose, and rose, and rose. In the spines of its body she saw echoes of Black Tower. In the dark teeth and claws she saw the Blue Lady's features. In the green light shining on its scales she saw the ruff of the Yellow Lady's gown. Its fire was Red Tower's. And it came and went from Grey.

Yarrow saw a Lady, and she began to sing.

> *Hush now, little girl*
> *In the waving reeds*
> *Mother's gone to fetch the moon*
> *Father's gone to sow the stars*
> *Sleep now, little girl*
> *In the waving reeds*
> *For the river sings*
> *All the song you need*

She stepped back as the Beast crawled into the Passage. All its eyes turned to her. They were very human. The gusts of its breath slowed. The fires in its mouth died to embers.

And slowly the Sixth Sister settled to the floor of the West Passage, and her eyes narrowed.

Sister, she said.

With one claw she wrote on the broken stones a word in golden light.

In the hush, Yarrow heard the distinct click of apes' teeth and saw the holy image, the holy name, the holy chain. Old Yarrow's stories trembled in her veins. She bent and touched the flickering word.

Ages under the earth, she saw. The pressure of the palace above dragged at her, pressing her palms into the gritty ashes. The name was called, the name was danced, a sound she heard in her bones and felt in her ears, the name over and over, calling her up. Until the time was right, until she got a glimpse of light and a breath of air and opened her mouth to satisfy the hunger of her captivity. But the name had been taken for another, and she could not reclaim it, and she was killed and her power dragged from her body and she was banished below again, shapeless, to heal and hunger, until again the name was called enough and the name was danced enough and in their crannies the apes worshiped it enough, and her sisters were dead, and maybe they had done this, and maybe they had not, she could not remember, for she was nameless, and Yarrow's hot tears made mud in the palace's ashes. Ragged, out of tune, the song still poured from her lips, but for whom?

Behind her, Hawthorn stood. The Hawthorn Lady now, maybe. Hawthorn herself did not know. The honey's fire had subsided, but it had left her changed. Ebony had required regular doses, but Hawthorn, infused with lantern light, with mellified man, with the name of an ancient power, would not. The foundations of her being had shifted. She knew this as she knew the arrangement of her own limbs (four arms, three legs, perhaps more to come).

Her green overgown had shredded into hawthorn leaves. It trailed behind her, foamy with white, corpse-smelling flowers. Above her bare shoulders, her neck and head were porcelain suffused with a living yellow flame. The broken halves of the mask had replaced her face, and between them was the green eye of the amulet, now grown to huge proportions, and useful to see with. Behind the eye and the mask, that living fire spilled itself out endlessly.

She stooped to pick up the steel. The Beast lay dormant. A yellow scale was plainly visible. Hawthorn raised the steel.

Yarrow stopped singing.

"You can't kill her," she said. She pushed up from the ground, hands stained with light. The sight of Hawthorn was not surprising. She was too tired for surprise.

The Beast twitched a limb but did not awaken yet. Ashes fell. The sky churned with smoke. Away in the palace there were cries, shouts, one alarm bell tolling. As it always was when the Beast came. As it always would be.

"You *can't*," said Yarrow.

I must, said Hawthorn. Then, "I must."

"Whatever happened, that was the Ladies' affair. Not ours. Whatever they did to her is done. I won't let her be banished again." The name of Hawthorn was pressure, restraint. Liquid light dripped from Yarrow's fingers as she understood, perhaps, what kept the Beast below.

I must pro "tect the palace," said Hawthorn. "Look at what she's done already."

"She tried not to hurt Tertius, *twice*. She's angry at her sisters, but they're all gone. The Five are *dead*. This isn't our fight. It's a relic of something else. The Five did this. They forged the chain. I don't know why. But it's wrong. It's wrong, and it's not *ours,* do you hear me?"

Hawthorn set the tip of the steel against the yellow scale. "This can end. I'll wish for her never to come back. This is what my master wanted."

"It will never end," said Yarrow. "Not if she's killed." The name scrawled at her feet wavered in an eddy of wind. "She'll just be dragged back. She'll never die and she'll never live. Do you hear me? All over the palace they call her and call her. Even *I*—" Yarrow shook her head. "As long as her name is called she'll come back and back. Not again. Not anymore. I'm breaking the chain."

There was nothing Yarrow could do to stop Hawthorn, and both of them knew it. Birds settled on the walls of the Passage as they glared at each other, woman and Lady. The Beast stirred, and its eyes opened, but it did nothing.

"I'm breaking the chain," Yarrow said again. "The palace has done her wrong, and we've all suffered for it. She deserves to live. She deserves a new name. This is over."

The Mother of Grey House always thought she knew best. For a moment, Hawthorn nearly drove the steel in out of spite. But she thought of the book Frin had given her. The pictures of ruin at the sisters' hands. Six crossed the river. One fell down, put in the ground. A Lady, imprisoned for thousands of years for no reason anyone could guess. Her body used to build the houses of her sisters, tower after tower. In whose name do the Sparrows dance? Writing with their bodies, calling her back for the slaughter. Ruin upon ruin, all so someone could make a wish upon her corpse. Hey nonny nonny.

Hawthorn dropped the steel and stepped back.

The Beast quivered, shook its flanks, and pushed up from the ground. Up it went, and kept going, rearing above them. The birds

followed it, parrots and vultures, crows and sparrows, gulls and falcons, swirling, still crying out their greetings. A bearded vulture
wheeled down and away, vanishing into the smoke.

You have vanquished me, said the Beast; and Hawthorn recognized the light in its eyes as her own, but green and steady. What is
your wish?

Its tone was confused, as if it knew the words but not why it was
saying them.

"Be as you want to be," said Yarrow.

At the same time, Hawthorn said: Be as you are.

The Sixth Sister shuddered and stretched. Her mouths opened in
a scream of anguish. Yarrow's eyes met Hawthorn's. They saw each
other thinking: We should not have wished at once.

She exploded upward to an unguessable height. Tails and limbs
flailed, split, recombined. Amid the chaos, for a moment, was a vast
green face, eyes wide open and sparking white fire. Then they closed,
and the face settled into rest, and was gone from Yarrow's sight.

The Sixth Sister split into three stems, and from her skin burst long
green thorns. A gush of sap filled the air with a springtime smell of
growth and rot. Thorns arced to meet, met, became arches. The three
stems twined around each other for hundreds of feet in the air, then
bent away and split and split and split. The green scabbed over with
rough brown. Eyes sank in and became windows; mouths became
doors. Her feet and tails extended, burrowing into the ground of the
West Passage, racing west and east, festooning the bridge with roots,
reaching through the palace's ruins as far as Yarrow could see.

Her branches settled with a shiver and burst into greenery. The
Sixth Sister had become a tree as tall as Black Tower, banded with
windows and doors and architraves of wood, as if she had tried to
become a tower as well. For a moment all was quiet. In the silence,
frogs chirped. Then the two nearest trunks shivered and pulled apart
slightly to make a high, broad door. Inside were steps of living wood,
going up into cool shadow.

"I'm going inside," said Hawthorn. "I have to make sure it's not a
threat. I don't think it is. That face looks like a sign to me."

She pointed up. Yarrow could not see it, just a sort of constellation of
leaves that, from one angle, *might* look a *little* like the Guardians' mask.
To Hawthorn's new eye, though, it *was* the mask, large and whole.

"Don't," said Yarrow. "Come back. Help me with . . . with whatever
comes next." Her stomach was shaking like frog spawn. "Come home."

Hawthorn gently touched a bulging root of the tree. A tremor
passed from her fiery head down her arms and into her rustling cloak
of leaves. The root curved up against her hand like a cat under a ca-
ress. She looked for Frin's body a moment, but the roots of the tower
had torn up and digested everything in their path except her, Yarrow,
and Tertius. He was part of the tree now. Part of her.

"If there's no more Beast, then I'm not needed in Grey. Did I ever
belong there, anyway?"

"No," said Yarrow nervously. "But."

Hawthorn stepped toward the tower door.

"Don't go in," said Yarrow. "You don't know what this is."

"That's what I need to find out," said Hawthorn. "While I still remember being Guardian, I have to see that everything was worth it.
Go home, Mother Yarrow. I might see you again."

Yarrow stepped back. "We'll share some ortolans," she said. "Be
safe, Hawthorn."

If there is danger, I will face it, said the Hawthorn Lady. If it is safe,
I will make it safer.

She grew as she spoke, though to Yarrow it felt as if the earth itself
shrank from Hawthorn.

You're right: I don't know what I'm doing, said the Lady. But I
know who I'm doing it for.

She bent over to fit through the door and, just before going in,
turned to Yarrow. She held out something to the woman. A stalk of
fresh angelica.

"Think what fun you'll have," Hawthorn said. "Inventing new songs
and all."

She went up the steps and out of view. The door closed behind her
so fully that it seemed never to have been. Yarrow did not know what
happened to her after that.

As Yarrow mounted Tertius and headed for Grey Tower, she heard
a clamor behind her and stopped to look. All the birds of the palace, it
seemed, were streaming in to nest in the tree's branches.

55. Yarrow Goes Home

Grey Tower still stood, but its parapet had collapsed and the turrets were ruined. The statues from the storeroom had poured out of the door like crumbs from a mouth. The trees in the courtyard had been crushed and burned. The fountain lay broken, and water gurgled slowly into the basin from the remains of its spigot. Clawmarks scored the pavement. Melting snow dripped and steamed. And yet—among the shattered trees there were green shoots. Yarrow *had* ended winter, it seemed.

But for whom? Grey House was a tumbled wreck. The Sixth Sister had crashed through its western walls, laying it open. Sacred things were scattered all over. Ancient furniture, miracles, and books dotted the pavement, scorched or trampled or muddied beyond repair. The privy, she noticed, was smashed, and would need to be rebuilt almost first thing.

The kitchen and the women's quarters were on the east, though, on the other side of several more or less complete walls and rooms. Perhaps—perhaps—

Yarrow left Tertius and went around that side. Unexpectedly, she came upon Monkshood, picking up wreckage and putting it in his wheelbarrow. He moved as stiffly as ever. She picked up a shard of glass and dropped it in the barrow, startling him.

"Mother!" he said. "We thought you dead!"

"Me too, occasionally," said Yarrow. Instantly she became conscious that she had no wimple, that she had lost her apron, that her robes were torn and dirty. Her pack, with the slate mask, lay under the roots of the great tree. She was not a very proper Mother of Grey House. Maybe never would be. The name *Yarrow* felt like an itchy headscarf now.

"It's been bad," said the old man.

"How bad?"

"Many left for Blue. Madrona and Oak and all them. It's me who stayed though." His chest swelled with pride.

"And the girls?" said Yarrow. "And Servant?"

"They're still here." Monkshood looked at the ruins of the house. "It's where they were, anyway, till now, maybe."

"Here," said Yarrow. She broke the angelica in half and gave him some.

"It's better candied," he said, biting into the crisp, sweet stalk.

"I agree," said Yarrow, eating hers.

"But thank you, Mother," he said. He went back to clearing up. His back was straighter, and he whistled a cheery tune.

Yarrow left him and went on. The kitchen door was open. One wall was blown out, and beyond it the treetops of Green Tower were golden in the sun. Everything was damp and smelled of smoke. Ban was shifting fallen bricks out of the way. Servant, on her aged hands and knees, was scrubbing soot from the floor. Beside the fallen wall, covered with a mildewed sheet, was a small form.

Bursting into tears, Yarrow ran to them. She embraced them, tall Ban, then short Grith, never to grow any more. Her girls. Her friends.

"Mother," said Ban uncertainly. "Your hair—"

Yarrow rose from Grith's side. In the burnished bottom of a copper pot, she saw that the twigs atop her head had grown glossy leaves, and some had burst their bonds. A halo of soft green stood out at the back of her skull now. No wimple for her again, even if she had chosen. But there was time to think about that later. Time to mourn Grith and give her a woman's burial. Time for so much. But first.

She turned to Servant, who had straightened painfully. The new tower framed the old woman's head; birds seemed to come and go from her grey hair.

Yarrow took her dirty, shaking hands.

"What is your name?" she said.

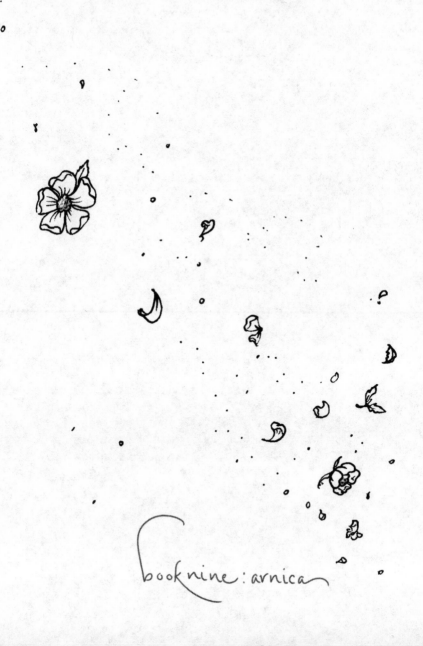

book nine : arnica

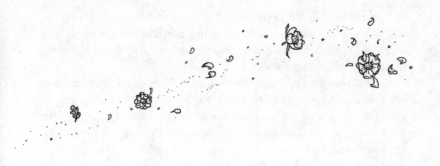

56. Arnica

The North Passage ran out of the palace in a clear, straight line. In its center was Black Tower. At its far end was Yellow Tower. Close to its near end was Grey. You just had to keep going past Grey, and you were set.

Arnica passed out of her knowledge very quickly. The ground kept shaking, which made her the more anxious to go, and anyway, having left Grey, she wanted to make a good job of it. After Varlan's Arch, she was in unfamiliar territory: a wilderness of granite walls and caved-in roofs, and snow. So much snow. Who knew how far outside the palace winter might extend? Hopefully not *very* far.

Arnica's pack was light. She knew enough about plants to survive outside, assuming she ran across any. Her observations of the mountains had shown her flushes of green in spring and summer: *something* grew out there. And if there were few plants, Arnica would break yet another rule and eat meat. So that was all right. She was old, and she had little life left in her, but South take her if she'd spend one more night of that life inside the walls, no matter what may come.

Then there it was: the fabled North Gate with its towers. Its corbel arch was still strong, but the thick curtain walls on either side were crumbling, the towers half-fallen. The gates themselves were rotten. It had had guards once, according to stories. Now there was nobody.

She paused on the threshold. The Passage ended there, its pavement cut off as if trimmed by a knife. Grass began. Did she really want—

Of course she did.

Arnica knelt on the stone threshold, cracked diagonally across like an old bone, its wounds filled with moss. She touched the stone with a closed hand. A moment later she opened her fingers as if leaving something behind and stood.

The old woman stepped out of the palace. Though icicles draped the outer walls, the morning air was clear and crisp. It was spring, or thereabouts. A long sigh started at her feet and ran up through her whole body, and for a moment she knelt on the sun-warmed grass, her hands wet with dew.

Then she resumed walking.

The ground was level and green, dotted here and there with flowers of many colors. Blue anemones, yellow dandelions, red carnations, and others. She knew them all, and felt a pleasure in knowing. When the meadow tilted up, she had to pick her way on bare brown earth among spicy cedars and outcroppings of granite. Here and there were the marks of tools, weathered and faded—had the stone for the cloisters come from these hills, long ago?

But the old woman was done thinking about that. After the hill was a valley, then another hill, much higher. At its top she halted. She had been walking for hours, and her aching legs needed a rest.

As she rested, there was a horrific rumble. The ground all around her shook and the trees bent as if in a strong wind. She turned.

Over the palace, where the smoke of disaster rose, a tree was opening like a great green flower. Something had happened. The first new thing in centuries.

She found herself laughing for joy and surprise. A new thing in the palace. A new thing, and just when she was leaving. Almost she started back.

But no. As the palace did, it would absorb this new thing, make it a part of itself, make everyone forget it had ever been otherwise. Nothing would really change. The story would go on the same, just with altered scenery. She did not know, of course, about Yarrow's return.

Refreshed by the sight, the old woman resumed walking. Down into another valley she went, and up another hill, and beyond it the earth kept rising more and falling less, until it crested in far blue mountains; and a warm wind moved among the flowers.

ACKNOWLEDGMENTS

This book is what it is because of dozens of people. I even know some of their names.

Thanks to my family, without whom I would not be who I am, but I love you all anyway.

Thanks to Nadia Halim, who read the first draft and put up with a lot of waffling about her suggestions. Thanks to Ned Raggett and Oriana Schwindt, my *By-The-Bywater* fellowship, who believed in this book without having read a single word. Thanks to Eadfrith, Toros Roslin, the anonymous artists of Kells and Iona, and the innumerable other artists and scribes whose work I have shamelessly pilfered.

Thank you to my agent, Jennifer Azantian, and the entire ALA crew.

Thanks to the wonderful people at Tordotcom: the editorial power duo of Carl Engle-Laird and Matt Rusin, who together prodded this book into something weirder and wilder; Christina MacDonald, Dakota Griffin, Jackie Huber-Rodriguez, Heather Saunders, Christine Foltzer, Gertrude King, Sam Friedlander, Jocelyn Bright, NaNá Stoelzle, and Madeline Grigg. And the fantastic artist Kuri Huang, who gave *The West Passage* its face.

A special thanks to my sister, Moriah, without whose help I never would have finished the illustrations on time. I have an absolutely wretched Shrek meme for you.

And a very special thanks to Jess, who was there for me through it all and then some.

ABOUT THE AUTHOR

Shaya Lyon, Shaya Lyon Photography

JARED PECHAČEK is an artist and writer based in Seattle, Washington. He is also a host of the Tolkien podcast *By-The-Bywater*. When he's not doing any of that, he's cooking, baking, or sewing something to wear to the opera.